'A sweeping tale of deep ... and found, *An Italian Girl in Brooklyn* spans many decades and two continents as a woman who lost everything during World War II learns to live again. Filled with the colour and warmth of northern Italy, the pain and salvation of family, and the courage and determination it takes to start life over across an ocean, the talented Santa Montefiore's latest ripples with longing, fate, and hope. The based-on-a-true-story twists will have you gasping aloud.'

KRISTIN HARMEL, *New York Times* bestselling author of *The Forest of Vanishing Stars* and *The Book of Lost Names* on *An Italian Girl in Brooklyn*

'A pleasure to read. . . . A new Montefiore novel is always a major event.'

Toronto Star on *The Temptation of Gracie*

'Nobody does epic romance like Santa Montefiore. Everything she writes, she writes from the heart.'

JOJO MOYES, bestselling author of *Me Before You*

'I couldn't put this book down.'

JULIAN FELLOWES, creator of *Downton Abbey*, on *Songs of Love and War*

'A superb storyteller of love and death in romantic places in fascinating times.'

Vogue

'Secrets abound, friendships are fractured, and life-altering decisions are made in a delicious read that leaves the reader hungry and eagerly awaiting the next course.'

Booklist (starred review) on *Songs of Love and War*

Santa Montefiore
WAIT FOR ME

Based on Simon Jacobs' true story

Published by Simon & Schuster

London   New York   Sydney   Toronto   New Delhi

First published in Great Britain by Simon & Schuster UK Ltd, 2023

Copyright © Santa Montefiore, 2023
This Canadian export edition published July 2023

The right of Santa Montefiore to be identified as author
of this work has been asserted in accordance with the
Copyright, Designs and Patents Act, 1988.

1 3 5 7 9 10 8 6 4 2

Simon & Schuster UK Ltd
1st Floor
222 Gray's Inn Road
London WC1X 8HB

Simon & Schuster Australia, Sydney
Simon & Schuster India, New Delhi

www.simonandschuster.co.uk
www.simonandschuster.com.au
www.simonandschuster.co.in

A CIP catalogue record for this book
is available from the British Library

ISBN 978-1-3985-1699-1
ISBN 978-1-3985-1397-6 (ebook)

Typeset in Bembo by M Rules

To my darling wife, Anna-Lisa,
for her patience and her love,
and to our children, Amelia, Benjamin and Hannah,
for the joy they bring us both

Simon Jacobs

★

To Sebag, Lilochka and Sasha,
who are the wind beneath my wings

Santa Montefiore

I have been here before,
But when or how I cannot tell:
I know the grass beyond the door,
The sweet keen smell,
The sighing sound, the lights around the shore.

You have been mine before,
How long ago I may not know:
But just when at that swallow's soar
Your neck turned so,
Some veil did fall, I knew it all of yore.

Has this been thus before?
And shall not thus time's eddying flight
Still with our lives our love restore
In death's despite,
And day and night yield one delight once more?

'Sudden Light' by
DANTE GABRIEL ROSSETTI,
1828–1882

PROLOGUE

South Australia, December 1995

Mary-Alice Delaware read the letter again. It was preposterous. Utterly ridiculous and, considering the circumstances, impertinent. It was so absurd, in fact, that she found herself laughing out loud. She lifted her eyes off the page and looked across the lawn. Only her mother's sunhat could be seen bobbing among the delphiniums as she bent down to pull out weeds in the flower beds and tighten the string that fastened the flowers' long stalks to the stakes. At seventy-six Florence Leveson had no intention of slowing down. She believed idleness would cause her bones to calcify, like a disused old car that is left to rust. Activity would, she maintained, keep her battery ticking over. That meant gardening, brisk walks with her basset hound Baz, baking cakes, playing the piano and, to Mary-Alice's embarrassment, yoga; to see her mother in Lycra was a sight she wished no living person to behold.

Should she or should she not give her mother the letter?

Mary-Alice decided she would sit on it for a few days. After all, there was no rush and most likely Florence would throw it in the trash. Not that her mother didn't have a good sense of humour; Florence had the best sense of humour of anyone Mary-Alice knew. A marvellous ability to heal her heart with laughter. And, considering the tragedies she had endured, this was no small feat. Mary-Alice was sure that if anyone would laugh at this preposterous epistle it was Florence. And yet, something gnawed beneath her ribcage. A doubt, warning her that perhaps this might be the one moment that Florence's infamous sense of humour failed her. Then Mary-Alice would wish she hadn't shown it to her. And once seen it would not be so easily *un*seen. No, she had to tread carefully.

The envelope was addressed to Mary-Alice Delaware but contained within it a letter to Florence Leveson. From the note that accompanied the letter the sender had made it clear that it was for Mary-Alice to decide whether or not her mother was up to reading it. In that, at least, the sender had been tactful. He wanted Mary-Alice to see it first and make the decision. He had obviously thought long and hard about it and had written the letter with care. In fact, it was a beautiful letter. She couldn't deny that. It was a very beautiful letter indeed. And that was another reason why she hesitated; the sender was clearly not a madman or a person of evil intent. He was educated and honourable. But still, the letter was highly sensitive and, well, *peculiar.*

'You want a cup of tea, Mum?' Mary-Alice shouted from the veranda. It was five o'clock in the afternoon and, having been brought up in England, Florence did like teatime. Earl Grey, egg and chive sandwiches, a slice of sponge cake or her favourite butter and Vegemite toast. Florence was not a woman concerned with her figure. She had once been slim with a small waist and long, slender legs, but now she was curvaceous. Her skin had not been damaged by the Australian sun nor, as a child, by the Indian sun. She looked much younger than her years with laughter lines in all the right places. In truth, Florence had never been vain, even when she had been a pretty young woman and much admired. She had always had thick hair and it was still glorious. Long and soft, she swept it up in a loose bun, leaving messy tendrils trailing down her neck and temples. As a girl it had been blonde, but as she got older it had darkened, so that now it was grey with a wide silver streak at the front that had inspired her grandchildren to nickname her 'Badger'. Few women would enjoy being likened to a badger, but Florence thought it funny.

'Lovely,' she replied, passing the back of her hand over her sweating brow. It was hot. She would welcome a rest in the shade. She took off her gardening gloves and scrambled out of the border. Baz, who had been sleeping beneath a pear tree, sat up expectantly. 'Do you know, I don't think the garden has ever looked so lush. Really, it's just like England,' she said with a smile that gave her face a girlish sweetness. 'You'd have thought it rained all the time. And those darling bumble bees are drunk constantly. Like Uncle Raymond they are, toddling from pub to pub. No one enjoyed a pub-crawl as much as Uncle Raymond.'

Mary-Alice laughed. Her mother loved talking about the past, and the years she spent in England seemed to have been the most dear. Mary-Alice went inside to boil the kettle. One would have thought, in this heat, that iced lemonade would be more refreshing than tea, but her mother was set in her ways so tea it was, the English way with milk. Mary-Alice popped a couple of Earl Grey teabags into the teapot and took the cake out of the fridge. When she emerged onto the veranda some minutes later, Florence was sitting on the swing chair with Baz lying beside her, his head in her lap. She was fanning herself with a magazine and humming an old tune that Mary-Alice didn't recognize. 'You know, when I was little, Uncle Raymond used to take us to the pantomime in Folkestone every Christmas,' said Florence, smiling fondly and patting the dog's head absent-mindedly. 'It was a family tradition and we looked forward to it with great excitement. It was a real thrill. My favourite was *Peter Pan*. I was fortunate enough to see Jean Forbes-Robertson play Peter. "If you believe in fairies, clap your hands!", and we all clapped heartily and Tinker Bell came back to life. It was marvellous.'

Mary-Alice poured the tea and gave her mother a slice of cake on a plate. Baz lifted his head off Florence's lap and sniffed the plate with interest. 'I wish I remembered Christmases in England,' said Mary-Alice. 'With a fire and frost. Santa Claus's sleigh looks better in the snow.'

'Yes, Christmas really isn't the same in the heat. It's meant to be crisp and cold and sparkly, like an Advent calendar. How old were you when we moved here, four?'

'Three,' Mary-Alice corrected. She shrugged. 'What you haven't had, you haven't missed. Christmas is still special in Australia.'

Florence put the plate out of Baz's reach on the low table in front of her and dropped a sugar lump into her tea. 'We used to stay with my grandparents for Christmas. I adored staying with them. As you know, Daddy died shortly after we came from India to live in England, so Mama, Winifred and I went down to Cornwall to holiday with her parents. They had a lovely big house in Gulliver's Bay called The Mariners with a private beach. I doubt very much it's a private beach now, but in those days we had it all to ourselves. There was a secret underground passageway that ran from the house to a cave where, during the Napoleonic Wars, smugglers used to take bales of wool out to fishing boats waiting in the bay and exchange them for brandy and lace. It was a magical place.'

'It sounds wonderful,' said Mary-Alice, who had heard these stories before.

'I loved Christmas. I remember the excitement of feeling the weight of the stocking on the end of my bed and hearing the sound of scrunching as I moved my feet. Grandma was extremely generous and we were very spoiled. The stockings were full of presents. Winifred and I would thrust our hands right down to the bottom where we'd find a tangerine, still wrapped in its silver paper from the greengrocer's. Nowadays no one thinks twice about tangerines, but in my day, they were a luxury, transported all the way from Tangiers by boat.' Florence chuckled and took a sip of tea, sighing afterwards – an annoying habit she'd acquired with old age. 'Christmas dinner was such a treat.' Now her cheeks flushed as memories came thick and fast. 'Dessert was my favourite part, served just before we left the men to drink their port and straight after we'd had the Christmas Stilton garnished with celery and served with Romary biscuits from Tunbridge Wells. There were always chocolates from Charbonnel et Walker in tiered boxes with silver tongs and Karlsbad plums. Oh, and those delicious *fruits glacés* and *marrons glacés* from France, my mother loved those especially.' Florence took a bite of cake and inhaled through her nose. 'Mmmm, this is heaven. No, not for you, Baz. Oh well, just a little bit.' She pulled off a piece of sponge and popped it into his mouth. 'We always had Victoria sponge for tea in Gulliver's Bay.'

'I've heard so much about Gulliver's Bay. I'd love to go there one day,' said Mary-Alice, who felt as if she'd already been.

'I'm too old to go back, sadly, otherwise I'd take you

myself,' said Florence, looking wistful suddenly. 'I don't know who owns the house now. Goodness, it might even be a hotel or a boarding house. Wouldn't that be awful? I don't suppose people want big houses nowadays with green baize doors to separate the servants' quarters from the rest of the house. People don't have servants anymore, do they? Who can afford them? But that's the way it was in those days. My grandparents were Victorian and very conventional and, I might add, a little on the grand side. We took the servants for granted, but now I look back on it all, I wonder at how hard they worked. They never got much time off and I don't imagine they got paid much either. It was a rarefied world and came to an end, of course, with the war.' She sighed and took another bite of cake, relishing the sweet taste on her tongue. Baz began to drool, but now Florence was being carried on a wave of memory and she no longer noticed him eyeing the cake. 'My father's two brothers were killed in the Great War. No one thought we'd go to war again, and so soon. What a waste it was. You'd think they'd have learned after the first one, but people never learn. That's the real tragedy.'

Mary-Alice refilled her teacup. 'Tell me more about Gulliver's Bay,' she asked. She didn't want to follow her mother down the path that led to the war. She knew where those memories would take her. Only to unhappiness.

'I was never religious, but I did enjoy going to church,' Florence continued. 'I liked the vicar, Reverend Millar. He was short and fat with a bald head and a lisp, and the most exuberant character. It didn't matter what he said, he made it all sound so exciting. I haven't met a vicar like him since. He had real charisma and vigour. If all vicars were like him the churches would be full to bursting.' She grinned roguishly.

'But I don't pretend it was solely the vicar who inspired me every Sunday morning. No, it was Aubrey Dash.'

Mary-Alice smiled over her teacup. She'd heard this story a thousand times. However, she was not about to deny her mother one of her most treasured memories. 'Even the name is romantic,' said Mary-Alice.

'I used to write it in my diary, "Aubrey Dash", over and over and then I'd write "Florence Dash" to see what my married name would look like – that's funny, isn't it, considering the way things turned out.' Florence laughed and her green eyes shone. 'But he barely noticed me.' She gave a little shrug and took another sip of tea.

'I can't imagine why not. You were really pretty, Mum.'

'I was very young, don't forget, and I like to think I was a late bloomer. I'd sit in our pew and he'd sit in his, with his family, of course, and he'd glow like a star in the corner of my vision. It was all I could do not to look at him. I'd time myself so that my glances didn't come too close together. Five minutes, six minutes, sometimes I even managed fifteen. The best was when we stood up for communion, sometimes I'd be right in front of him or behind him, and I could feel him near me as if he radiated heat. When he looked at me, which he did once or twice, I blushed all over.' She put the last piece of cake into her mouth then licked her fingers with relish. 'Sorry, Baz, all gone.' Baz sighed resignedly and rested his head on her lap again. 'He was a handsome devil, even as a boy. You see, he was tall when his contemporaries were still short and he had the most beautiful eyes: grey with long black lashes. And full lips. Full lips are rare in England, I discovered. But Aubrey had a lovely mouth.'

Mary-Alice laughed. 'Oh, Mum, you are funny.'

'Lips are important, Mary-Alice. It's not very nice kissing men with mouths like sharks.'

Both women laughed at that. 'No, I don't imagine it is,' said Mary-Alice. 'I love the way you remember the details.'

'Don't *you* remember your first love, dear?'

'I suppose I do. But not in the way you do.'

'When you get to my age, memories assault you out of nowhere. You can be digging up the elder and, puff, like a bubble rising out of your subconscious and popping, there it is, in front of you, something you haven't thought of in years. And the thinking of it brings forth the feelings that went with it and I swear, your body feels exactly as it did all those years ago, as if you're back there in the aisle, standing behind Aubrey Dash, waiting for holy communion and willing him to turn around and look at you.' Florence shook her head, astonished by her younger self. 'What little the heart knows when one is but a girl. How much it has to learn.'

Mary-Alice felt the letter in her pocket as if it were growing hot. As if it were demanding attention. She put down her cup and slipped her hand into her pocket. Just then, she noticed a cloud of dust on the track in the distance. It was getting bigger as the truck drew closer, the metal around the headlights glinting sharply in the sunshine. 'Well, that'll be David,' she said, taking her hand out of her pocket. The letter would have to wait. She stood up.

'I'd better get back to the garden,' said Florence, pushing herself off the swing chair with a groan.

'You don't think you should call it a day?'

'It's only six. The best part is yet to come. The golden light of early evening. It's my favourite time of day.' Florence sighed deeply and swept her eyes over the garden with satisfaction. 'I love the sound of birds roosting in the trees. It reminds me of Gulliver's Bay. Of course, we have different birds here, but the effect on the spirit is the same. Nothing makes me happier than the sound of birdsong.'

Mary-Alice put the cups and plates on the tray and went back to the kitchen. By the time she came out again David had parked under a eucalyptus tree and was making his way across the grass to greet her. 'Good day, darling?' she asked from the veranda, holding out a cold can of lager.

Her husband was strong and athletic for a man in his sixties. He played regular squash and tennis and, when he had time, he liked to go running and to hike. The older he got the more aware he became of his figure and worked ever harder to maintain it.

He jogged up the steps two at a time and kissed his wife. 'Just what I need,' he replied, taking the lager and dropping his bag onto the floor. He flopped into the swing chair, put his feet in their red trainers on the table and opened the can with a click and a hiss. Then he took a swig and smacked his lips. 'That's great,' he exclaimed, running a hand through his hair. He still had a fine head of curly brown hair, although the emerging grey hairs were slowly outnumbering the brown.

Mary-Alice sat on the chair she had only just vacated and listened to him tell her about his day. David co-owned a building company in the local town with his old schoolmate Bruce Dixon, and always had amusing tales to tell about his clients when he came home. Mary-Alice would normally have shared the letter with him – she usually shared everything, but she couldn't share this. It was too strange. He'd laugh and tell her to throw it away. A part of Mary-Alice wanted to do that and forget about it, yet Florence had a right to see it. Who was Mary-Alice to decide what her mother was up to reading or not?

Florence waved at David from the border. Then she resumed her toil, humming contentedly to herself. She paused a moment to watch the bees buzzing about the lavender. They were so deliciously fat, she thought with pleasure, and so busy. Then one flew away and she wondered how on earth it managed to fly with such flimsy-looking wings. Mary-Alice and David's voices were a distant drone, drowned out by the clamour of birds as they squabbled in the branches over places to roost. The sun was sinking slowly, flooding the plain with a grainy, rose-gold light. Soon the first star would glimmer in the sky and night would creep in, blanketing the garden and silencing all but the crickets and owls. Florence would stay out as long as she could. She loved being immersed in nature. Ever since she had moved out of the city to live with Mary-Alice and David on this beautiful ranch in Victoria, she had found pleasure in every single day. In the city she'd had an apartment with a wide patio that she'd filled with pots of plants and fruit trees, but her heart craved the countryside. She'd missed its tranquillity most of all. The whispering sound of the breeze rustling the leaves, nature's soft, regenerating breath – and the sense, on some deep level, of being part of it.

Baz got up and stretched. Florence knew it was time to go in. 'Come on, old boy,' she said to her dog and the two of them walked up the steps and through the fly door into the house. By now the crickets were a cacophony of chirruping. The birds had gone quiet. The peace of evening had fallen over the plain in a rich, indigo veil.

Mary-Alice was in the kitchen, cooking supper. David had gone upstairs to take a shower. Florence helped herself to a glass of wine. She took a handful of ice and dropped it into the glass. 'You want some?' she asked.

'I'd love a glass, thanks.'

Florence poured another one. 'Can I do anything to help?'

'No, you just rest up.'

'I think I'll take a bath.'

'Good idea.'

'I like a glass of wine with a bath. Very decadent. Makes me feel young again. You know, after the war, we were only allowed to run the water to the height of our ankles. It's still a luxury to draw a deep bath.'

Mary-Alice moved away from the stove. She put her hand in her pocket and pulled out the letter. 'Mum, this came for you today. I've been meaning to give it to you, but I keep forgetting.'

Florence was no fool. Since when did a person forget to pass on the mail? 'Who's it from?' she asked, narrowing her eyes. The look on her daughter's face told her that it was no ordinary letter.

'I think you had better read it,' said Mary-Alice.

Florence took the envelope and frowned as she read the handwriting. She certainly did not recognize it. 'Well, I'll take it upstairs,' she said. 'A glass of wine, a nice bath and now a mysterious letter. The day just got better.'

Mary-Alice took a breath. 'I'm not sure about that ...'

Florence turned it over to see that it was unsealed. 'Have you read it?'

'I have.'

'And?'

'It's odd. But you should read it all the same.'

'Now you've got my attention. Should I read it here with you in case I keel over and die?'

Mary-Alice chuckled. 'No, you can read it in your bath. You might need to take the bottle with you, though.'

'That bad, eh?'

'Just odd,' Mary-Alice repeated.

Florence took her daughter at her word. With the bottle in

one hand and the letter and wine glass in the other, she made her way slowly up the stairs. Once in the scented water she dried her hands on a flannel, put on her reading glasses and pulled the letter out of the envelope.

'*Dear Mrs Leveson, May I introduce myself . . .*'

CHAPTER ONE

Gulliver's Bay, Cornwall, 1937

Reverend Millar was a diminutive figure in the pulpit and yet his exuberance gave the impression that he was much bigger. His bald head was as shiny as a billiard ball, his cheeks the rosy pink of a choirboy's and his eyebrows were bushy and came to life when he spoke, like a pair of inebriated caterpillars. His lisp might have been comic had the words he articulated been less passionate and wise. Reverend Millar was a truly inspirational vicar and held captive every member of his congregation, except for one.

Florence Lightfoot sat in the middle of the pew alongside her grandparents, Joan and Henry Pinfold, her uncle Raymond, sister Winifred and mother Margaret. While her family sat with their backs straight and their attention fixed upon the vicar, Florence's attention had long since strayed across the aisle to where the Dash family was sitting with equal formality on the other side. She pretended to listen to Reverend Millar, every now and then giving a little nod, or a chuckle, to show how engrossed she was, but in truth, she heard only noise without meaning for every ounce of her focus was trained upon nineteen-year-old Aubrey.

Florence had what her sensible older sister deemed 'a crush'. Florence, who was seventeen and three quarters, knew it was more than that. A crush implied something temporary and juvenile, like a childish penchant for dolls which one quickly grows out of and deeply regrets. What Florence felt for Aubrey Dash was infinitely deeper and would, she knew, endure. She could not imagine ever falling out of love with him. For love is what it was, she was certain; she'd read enough novels to recognize love when she felt it.

Aubrey did not look at Florence. He sat rigidly, with the same serious expression as the rest of the congregation, until he smiled at something the vicar said and then his face creased around his mouth and eyes and he laughed. The sight of him smiling had an extraordinary effect on Florence. It lifted her up and caused a blissful expansion to take place in her chest, rather similar to a religious experience, which would have greatly encouraged the vicar had he noticed it. Her eyes rested on Aubrey with blatant admiration and her lips parted in a sigh. A sharp elbow in her ribs brought her attention swiftly back to her pew. She turned to her sister with a scowl. Winifred flashed her eyes and tapped her long red nails on her prayer book, instructing Florence to concentrate on the service. But Florence had never been one to follow orders or obey rules; in fact, orders and rules only challenged her to find ways of disobeying them. She trained her gaze on the vicar for a few minutes and then, when she felt her sister's attention wane, allowed it to fly back to Aubrey like a homing pigeon.

Aubrey was undeniably handsome. Even as a boy he had been good-looking. Florence had been acutely aware of him ever since she had been aware of the differences between boys and girls. The Dashes had a big house a few miles outside Gulliver's Bay with a tennis court and swimming pool and lots of land, for William Dash, Aubrey's father, was a gentleman farmer. It was a short cycle ride from Florence's grandparents' house, which, although smaller in size, boasted a stunning view of the sea and had its own private bay. As Winifred was the same age as Aubrey, and Aubrey's twin siblings, Julian and Cynthia, were the same age as Florence, the two families found themselves thrown together by default.

The Dashes were a big family with cousins of all ages who came to stay in drifts during the school holidays. Unlike Florence's mother, who had spent most of her married life in Egypt and then India and did not have many friends in England, Aubrey's parents were born and raised in Cornwall and knew everyone. They gave dinner parties and arranged picnics, boating expeditions and tennis tournaments most days during the long summer months with a flair unequalled anywhere in the county. Indeed, they were tireless and enthusiastic in the way they embraced people into their circle. Nothing was too much trouble and everyone was welcome. 'The more, the merrier' would have likely been their family motto had they had one. Margaret Lightfoot, on the other hand, was a nervous creature who descended into an unholy panic at the mere thought of having to arrange even the smallest dinner party, which she was obliged to do in repayment for the various invitations she received. For these events she relied heavily upon Winifred, who was capable, confident and unflappable like her late husband had been, and her mother, Joan, who was sweet and patient and understanding of Margaret's shortcomings. Florence was too spoiled and self-centred to be of any help to anyone.

While Margaret managed to put on a good show and host the odd lunch or dinner party for the various families in Gulliver's Bay, no family challenged her self-confidence more than the Dashes. Celia Dash was a raven-haired beauty of unrivalled style and grace; she made Margaret feel like a moorhen beside a lissom swan. William Dash was as handsome as his wife was beautiful and had the laidback charm and insouciance of a man whose greatest concerns were who he was going to rally onto the tennis court and whether Hunter, his black Labrador, had run off to the town. The weather did not worry a farmer like William Dash. His inherited wealth did not come from his crops, nor did he trouble himself with the domestic side of his life because Celia commanded a well-oiled machine made up of cooks, maids, butlers, gardeners and chauffeurs who were devoted to their employers. Celia had a gift for making each servant feel like the master or mistress of their domain, which gave them real pride in their work and a desire to prove themselves indispensable. Margaret dreaded having to repay their many kindnesses with an invitation of her own.

It was almost inconceivable that Aubrey did not feel Florence's eyes upon him in church that morning. Florence was no classic beauty but she had a mischievous esprit that most boys of her age found strangely beguiling. However, unbeknown to Florence, Aubrey's attention was taken by a stranger who had, quite by surprise, descended upon the Dashes' summer holidays from France, sent by her mother who was an old friend of Celia's, to perfect her English. Elise Dujardin was petite with the dark, wary look of a deer on foreign soil. It was her charming reserve that had caught the attention of Aubrey Dash. Seated in the row in front of him, in between his robust cousins Bertha and Jane Clairmont, Elise cut a slight and singular figure, being so very different in both looks and style from every other female in the congregation.

Florence had not noticed her. Had she even clocked the

curly-haired young woman, she would have casually dismissed her as uninteresting and certainly of no threat to her. There were, of course, various girls in Gulliver's Bay who Florence *did* consider competition – tall, elegant Natalie Carter, for example, or flame-haired Ginger Lately. Both were a year older than Florence and a great deal more sophisticated. But the curly-haired French girl had not warranted a second glance and Florence had no idea that Aubrey had even seen her.

When the service was over, the congregation gathered outside, as was customary, to socialize before heading home for Sunday lunch. The Dashes had invited the vicar to join them, as they did most Sundays, and Florence overheard Reverend Millar say to Aubrey, as Aubrey paused to thank him at the door, 'I'm looking forward to hearing your French.'

Aubrey chuckled and replied, 'I fear our new friend will find my command of the language sorely lacking.' Florence didn't have a clue what they were talking about and thought little of it as she awaited her turn to shake hands with Reverend Millar and thank him for his uplifting sermon, of which she had heard barely a word.

It was a bright sunny day in Gulliver's Bay with the usual wind that swept in off the sea. The grey stone church was built in the thirteenth century but had undergone various renovations over the years, culminating in a slate roof in the nineteenth century, upon whose spine a trio of herring gulls perched and observed the goings-on below with detachment. The tower was original, crowned with an embattled parapet with four tall corner pinnacles that had withstood centuries of hard rain and gales. Now it basked in the radiant light of early summer, tickled by the odd shadow that passed across it as every now and then a white cloud drifted in front of the sun. But what brought it to life was the movement and chatter at its feet. Being a small community, everyone knew one another and their voices, especially those of the excitable young women, filled the air like the squawking of seagulls. It had, after all, been an eventful few months leading up to that blithe summer and there was much to talk about: King George VI had been crowned, Stanley Baldwin had been succeeded as prime minister by Neville Chamberlain in a coalition government and the German chancellor Adolf Hitler had declared his decision to invade Czechoslovakia. But war could not have been further from their minds, for surely, after the last one, no one wanted to wreak such devastation upon the world again. It was only the old and wise who, like experienced hounds picking up the scent of fox, sniffed something menacing in the air.

Florence watched Aubrey cut through the crowd, nodding respectfully at those he passed, before joining a trio of young women standing chatting on the grass. Florence recognized Bertha and Jane Clairmont, but she did not recognize the dark creature who stood timidly among them. She didn't for one moment suspect that Aubrey had crossed the yard for *her*. 'That, my dear Florence, is Elise Dujardin,' said Mrs Warburton, otherwise known in the community as 'Radio Sue' – the buxom widow who could be relied upon to uncover and consequently spread the local gossip, and was not in the least contrite about it.

'Hello, Mrs Warburton,' said Florence. Usually Florence went out of her way to avoid the woman, but right now Radio Sue had something she wanted: information. 'That sounds French,' she remarked, recalling what Aubrey had said to the vicar about his command of the French language, or lack thereof.

'She is, indeed, French,' Mrs Warburton confirmed. 'Her mother and Celia met at the Sorbonne, you know. Elise has come to stay with them for the entire summer. I can't imagine having a guest in the house for that long. Guests, like fish, go off after a few days, I always think. But the Dashes seem to have a bottomless pit of endurance, don't they? The girl's not much to look at, but those French have something.' Mrs Warburton narrowed her eyes and pondered on that undefinable 'something' that gave Elise her quiet allure.

Florence was inclined to agree with the first part of that sentence, but she wasn't going to speak ill of anyone without having at least met them and made up her own mind. She certainly wasn't going to give Radio Sue copy for her transmissions. Even at the tender age of seventeen Florence was wily enough to sense a false friend in Mrs Warburton. 'How sweet of Aubrey to take such trouble with her,' she said, smiling with tenderness at the gallant way he was talking to this shy stranger in their midst. 'She must be feeling very out of place here.'

Mrs Warburton chuckled and the buttons strained on her lavender jacket – whatever she wore, it always looked a size too small. 'It's the quiet ones you want to watch,' she said, lowering her voice as if hatching a plot with a co-conspirator. 'That Aubrey Dash is quite a catch. You don't believe Madame Dujardin has sent her precious daughter across the Channel simply to practise her English, do you?'

'Aubrey is nineteen,' said Florence, affronted because how could Radio Sue suggest he was going to marry someone like Elise Dujardin when it was plainly obvious that he was going to marry *her*?

'Competition is high and it is a foolish woman who takes her eye off the ball. An eligible young man like Aubrey Dash will be snapped up before you know it and behind the match will be a focused and determined mother. Mark my words,

I know these things. I have successfully married off all four of my daughters with great success. *I* left nothing to chance.'

'Do you know, then, what sort of family the Dujardins are?'

'Rich,' said Mrs Warburton with a sniff. 'Very rich. Of course, we're no longer in the nineteenth century, but old habits die hard. A catch is a catch, and money speaks louder than words. *That* is something that will never change.'

Florence hadn't ever considered her family's wealth as either a boon or a bane in the marriage market. She had never considered it at all. Her father had been a military man. He had served in the Great War and lost two brothers. Later, in India, he had served in the 17th Punjabis, which was where Florence's memories of life truly started. Besides the grandeur of the snowy Himalayas viewed from their home in Simla, she remembered her father's sickness. His yellow-ish pallor and haggard face. He had caught the sprue, a rare tropical disease that affected the digestive system and rendered him an invalid. He had been sent back to England and retired on a meagre pension. Florence knew that her mother's parents were wealthy, because their house in Gulliver's Bay was large and had many servants, and she assumed that, since her father died, it was her grandfather, rather than provisions in her father's will, who supported them. Would that count against her, she wondered, now looking at Elise Dujardin with more interest as well as a flicker of jealousy? Were Celia Dash and Madame Dujardin hatching a plot that threatened to blow her own out of the water?

She'd ask her sister as soon as she arrived back at the house; Winifred was sure to know. However, she was detained outside the church by Mr Foyle, the local builder, and it would have been rude to cut him short. By the time Florence reached the drawing room at The Mariners, it was full of smoke and the smell of sherry. Her grandfather, Henry Pinfold, and her uncle Raymond, her mother's bachelor brother, were in the bay window smoking cigarettes, while her grandmother was on the sofa talking to Margaret and Winifred. This was how the family usually divided: the men on one side of the room, the ladies on the other. Henry had little interest in the conversation of women while Raymond was only truly fond of one: his mother.

It was going to be a while before Florence was able to get Winifred on her own. Reluctantly, she flopped onto the sofa beside her sister. They were discussing Reverend Millar's sermon in great detail. Florence sighed and looked bored for she had little patience for conversations that didn't concern *her*. 'What did you think of the sermon, Flo?' asked Winifred with a grin. She knew very well that Florence had taken in none of it.

'I got enough religion rammed down my throat at school. The last thing I need in the summer hols is more lectures from the pulpit.'

Margaret threw an anxious glance at her daughter. 'Don't say that in front of your grandfather,' she warned. 'It'll sound ungrateful.'

'I didn't say I didn't enjoy school, I only said I didn't enjoy the school services. You should have heard old Rev Minchin droning on and on every Sunday. And you know, some girls attended not one but *three* services: early communion, mid-morning matins and evensong. Dreary beyond belief. It's enough to make one convert to another religion.'

Neither Margaret nor her softly-spoken mother Joan knew how to deal with Florence. The girl was opinionated and irreverent and intent on creating drama, which was why she had been sent off to boarding school in the first place. It had, admittedly, done her some good – taught her manners and etiquette and, to a certain degree, given her some discipline. However, without a father to guide her (and restrain her), she was becoming something of a concern.

'I hear you were in the end of year play,' said Joan, smiling encouragingly at her granddaughter in the hope of steering her towards a more positive subject.

Florence's eyes lit up. 'Yes,' she replied, for when it came to theatre, Florence was full of enthusiasm. 'I was the lead in *Twelfth Night*.'

'Viola?' Joan asked.

'Yes. I gave a rousing performance,' Florence added with a smile for she had, she knew, been splendid.

Winifred, who was sipping a glass of sherry, gave a sniff. 'A little over the top, if you ask me.'

'What would *you* know? You've never acted in a play in your life!' said Florence crossly.

'I thought you were terrific,' said Margaret. 'In fact, I overheard a father in the row in front of me saying you were the best Viola he had ever seen. Better, even, than in the West End.'

'He must have been joking,' said Winifred.

'No, he was perfectly serious,' her mother asserted.

'I'm going to be an actress,' Florence reminded them.

Joan slid her eyes to her husband, who was still by the window engrossed in conversation with Raymond. 'I think you'll find there are more interesting things to do than that,' she said gently.

'Oh no, I'm certain of it. I'm going to be a *famous* actress.'

'Your father would not have liked his daughter to walk the boards,' said Margaret, looking to Winifred for support.

'It's unseemly, Flo,' Winifred agreed.

'Unseemly? Really, Winnie! Because I'm a well-bred young lady? I suppose you'd prefer me to be presented at court in a pretty white dress with a posy of flowers in my gloved hands.' Florence laughed scornfully. 'You're stuck in the dark ages. I admire women who do things with their lives, instead of sitting around waiting to get married.'

'I thought you said you were going to marry Aubrey Dash?'

Florence scowled at her sister. She lifted her chin. 'One can marry *and* have a life, Winnie!'

Noticing the maid at the door, Joan put up a hand. 'Girls, it's time for lunch.' She looked at Florence and smiled again, hoping to placate her. 'My dear, I'm sure when you eventually marry you'll have other things on your mind besides being an actress.'

Florence did not want to argue with her grandmother. She might not have had much respect for her mother and sister, but she did have an innate sense of deference for her grandparents. 'What's this I hear about acting?' said Henry, stubbing out his cigarette and fixing his formidable gaze onto his youngest granddaughter. His moustache twitched like a walrus. 'I won't hear of it. Your father would turn in his grave. Prancing about the stage, I ask you.' He walked with her into the hall, his polished brogues tapping on the wooden floorboards as they made their way towards the dining room. 'I'm not such an old fogey as to prohibit my daughter or granddaughters from working. To the contrary, I think some form of occupation is a very good thing. A woman's mind should be stimulated just like a man's.' He patted Florence's shoulder. 'Don't worry, we'll find something useful for you to do.'

'Grandpa, I want to work in the theatre. I'm not going to change my mind.'

'We've had this discussion before, my dear. A year learning

how to be a lady and then we'll revisit the subject if you think it's what you really want to do. I daresay by then you might have turned your attention elsewhere.' He chuckled as he imagined marriage and babies and other typically female concerns.

'When I was your age I wanted to be a fireman,' said Raymond from behind them.

Florence laughed. 'I don't believe you!'

'I was a bit younger, I suppose.'

'A *lot* younger, I think, would be closer to the truth, Uncle Raymond. Jumping from wanting to wield a hose to gazing upon antiques at Bonhams is quite a leap.'

'And now he has his own business,' said Henry proudly. 'You can always go and do his filing, or make him cups of tea, couldn't she, Raymond?'

'Of course. Anytime you want a job, Flo, I'll be happy to employ you.'

'I can't think of anything worse,' said Florence with a laugh. 'Not that I wouldn't love to be in your company, Uncle Raymond. Only, I think I'd find it incredibly dull looking at inanimate objects all day. It makes me sleepy just thinking about it.'

'We have our fair share of drama, I can assure you,' he replied.

They took their places at the table and stood for Grace.

'Everything's relative, I suppose,' Florence conceded, although she doubted that drama in the world of antiques could compare to the drama played out at the theatre.

It wasn't until after lunch that Florence managed to get Winifred on her own. They were in the garden and Winifred was smoking one of her mother's cigarettes. From there they had a wide view of the sea, glittering in the sunlight beneath a clear blue sky. 'It's beautiful, isn't it,' said Winifred. She sighed. 'You know, I love this time of year, when we've just arrived and have the whole summer before us.'

'Me too,' Florence agreed. 'I wish we lived here all the time. I'm not sure why we don't, really. Why does Mother have to live in Kent when her family is here?'

'It was where Daddy and she met and where they lived when they moved back from India.'

'Silly. Mama should sell up and buy a house down here.'

'I don't think she wants to.'

'She can't still be holding onto Daddy's memory? Not after all these years. One wonders, really, why she never married again.'

Winifred shook her head. 'Sometimes, Flo, your naivety astonishes me.'

Florence was put out. 'Why? It's years since Daddy died.'

'Actually, it's seven.'

'That's a long time.'

'Not for grown-ups. Besides, she probably doesn't want to marry again. She loved Daddy. He's impossible to replace.'

'Do you miss him, Winnie?'

Her sister nodded. 'All the time.' She took a drag of her cigarette, inhaling deeply, before blowing smoke out of the side of her mouth.

Florence frowned. 'I'd like to say *I* miss him all the time, but I don't. He was a distant figure even when he was home. I just remember him being sick.'

'You were very young, I suppose. My memories of him are probably more vivid.'

'Was he rich?'

Winifred looked at her in astonishment. 'What a funny question!'

'Well, was he? No one ever talks about money. Does Grandpa pay for everything or did Daddy leave Mama something in his will?'

Winifred narrowed her eyes. 'Who have you been talking to?'

Florence tossed her gaze out to sea. 'No one. I was just thinking about it in church. Are we, you and I, considered "good catches"?'

'Good catches?' Winifred laughed. 'You *have* been talking to someone.'

'Oh, all right. Radio Sue mentioned that French girl . . .'

'Elise Dujardin.'

'You know about her?'

'Of course. She's staying with the Dashes.'

'Well, apparently she's very wealthy and her mother and Mrs Dash are matchmaking Elise and Aubrey.' Florence took a breath. Her chest felt tight, suddenly.

Winifred's expression softened. 'Ah, I see where this has come from. Well, I can't tell you whether or not Elise Dujardin is in the possession of a good fortune, as Jane Austen would say. But I can tell you that Grandpa is wealthy enough to satisfy a woman like Celia Dash.'

Florence's spirits rose with a jolt. 'Is Grandpa very rich?' she asked excitedly.

'No, but Celia Dash is not a snob, nor is she particularly interested in money. She just happens to have a lot. I should imagine she'd accept a maid as her daughter-in-law if her son fell in love with one. So, my dear sister, it is neither here nor there whether or not you are a good catch, because wealth or class are not of concern to the Dashes. What you need is for Aubrey to fall in love with you.' She laughed, not unkindly. 'And that, Flo, might just be one challenge too great.'

Florence lifted her chin. If money and position were of no consequence, then it was an even playing field. 'I have all summer to work on it,' she said with confidence.

'But you don't have age on your side,' said Winifred.

Florence grinned. 'Oh, ye of little faith,' she replied. 'I might not have the answer to everything, but one thing I *do* know is that I will surely grow up. I'll be eighteen in September and nineteen *next* September. Then I'll be twenty, then thirty, then fifty, then seventy and, God willing, I might even get to eighty, and what then will two years' difference in age matter to me and Aubrey?'

CHAPTER TWO

Florence was not a particularly accomplished tennis player, but she threw herself into the Dashes' tennis tournament with gusto. If anyone could win simply by grit alone, it was Florence Lightfoot.

The Dashes' tennis tournament, which took place over two weeks at their magnificent Elizabethan home, Pedrevan Park, was one of the most anticipated events of the summer. William Dash, who had been captain of tennis in his school days, chose the pairs and arranged the seeding from the results of the year before. Florence longed to pair up with Aubrey, which wasn't an impossible desire because Aubrey was a first-class player, which meant he had to partner a third-class player, like Florence. However, luck was not on her side. Aubrey had been paired with Elise, raising Florence's suspicions that there were calculating female minds at work here. Florence was paired with John Clairmont, a Dash cousin on Celia's side and an excellent player.

Pedrevan Park did not have a view of the sea, being situated further inland in the middle of lush fields of grazing cattle and golden wheat, but it was a splendidly grand house. Built in the mid-sixteenth century in silver-grey Cornish stone, it had tall chimneys, mullioned windows with small rectangular panes, and Dutch gables. The estate was large with secret gardens hidden behind yew hedges, a vegetable garden and arboretum planted within the enclosure of a high stone wall and an ornamental lake where a neo-classical rotunda folly and a statue of the goddess Amphitrite cast an ethereal reflection upon the water. It was most certainly the grandest house in Gulliver's Bay, but the Dashes were not ostentatious or smug; they were grateful to have the means to entertain as they did, for they both loved people and made no distinction between class or creed. They simply wanted everyone to have a good time.

It was almost impossible not to have a good time at Pedrevan Park and everyone looked forward to their invitations with great excitement. The Dashes were the most generous hosts, lavishing their guests with refreshments and opening their beautiful home so that the grounds could be enjoyed. 'After all,' Celia would say in her cheerful, breezy manner, 'what on earth is the point of going to all the trouble to make them so lovely, if no one is going to see them?'

As modest and inclusive as the Dashes were, they did inspire in others, by virtue of their own effortless style and nonchalant grandeur, a desire to present themselves at their very best. The tennis tournament was, therefore, a chance for the young to show off their finest tennis whites and no one would have dared arrive at Pedrevan Park in anything less than the All England Club's standard of attire. Florence wore a pair of white tennis shorts embellished with sailor-style buttons sewn in a row down the seams of the pockets and a little cable knit sweater with short, puffed sleeves. She swept her blonde hair into clips, leaving it to fall in loose waves over her shoulders. Winifred, who was more conventional, wore a tennis dress that fell below the knee in a pleated skirt. Her dark brown hair was cut short and teased into waves, which was the only fashionable thing about her, Florence thought. The two girls cycled along the leafy narrow lanes with their tennis racquets clamped beneath their arms.

At last, puffing with exertion, they pedalled through the big iron gates and set off up the drive that snaked in seamless curves through the manicured grounds of the Park. The peaceful twittering of birds was drowned out by the sudden roar of an engine behind them. Startled, they pulled up on the grass verge to let the motor car pass. The offending vehicle was a shiny red Aston Martin. Its roof was down, revealing a plush wood and leather interior and a dark-haired young man behind the wheel wearing a pair of sunglasses. They recognized him at once: Rupert Dash, Aubrey's older brother.

'How very rude!' said Winifred as the car sped past and continued on towards the house. 'He could have slowed down.'

'And waved,' Florence added, settling onto her bicycle seat again. 'Anyway, what's the hurry?' They resumed their pedalling. 'It's not as if the tournament is going to start without him!'

'I doubt very much he'll be playing. He's not a tennis player.'

'What does he do now?'

'Besides showing off?' said Winifred. 'I think he's at The Royal Agricultural College in Cirencester. He's going to inherit this place, after all. From what I gather, he spends his winters at shooting parties and his summers in the South of France, drinking champagne.'

'Sounds like fun!' said Florence.

'I think it must be fun being a Dash.'

Florence smiled and pedalled harder. 'I fully intend to become one,' she said with a giggle and her sister rolled her eyes.

Instead of cycling up to the house, they took the familiar path that cut through an avenue of lime trees and led directly to the tennis court. The immaculately mown court lay in the partial shade of a horse chestnut tree at one end of a vast lawn, which was set up for croquet and lined with wooden benches for spectators. A long trestle table had been positioned in front of the pavilion, laid up with glasses, jugs of lemonade and plates of Victoria sponge cake and biscuits. To the right of it was an easel displaying on a big board the order of play. The place was teeming with people already, dressed in white, and two mixed pairs were knocking up. William Dash was striding around the lawn in a panama hat and linen jacket, ordering everyone about in a firm but genial manner. The younger Dash cousins, who were not included in the competition, acted as ball boys, and Julian Dash, Aubrey's younger brother, was already sitting at the top of the green wooden umpire's chair, having volunteered to officiate. Florence spotted Aubrey at once, reclining casually on a rug, smoking, while his sister Cynthia and tennis partner Elise sat demurely beside him. Florence was about to join them when she felt a hand on her shoulder.

'Hello, partner.' It was John Clairmont, Aubrey's cousin. He was looking at her keenly, holding his racquet up as if about to hit a ball.

'John,' she said with a smile. 'When are we on?'

'Not for a while. But we've got a good chance of winning our first match. Jane is hopeless and Freddie is fly-by-night. Terribly inconsistent but hits the odd winner when the wind's behind him. If you can just get the balls back, I'll put them away.'

'Brilliant,' said Florence. 'I won't let you down.'

'I know you won't, old girl. You're a real trooper.' He glanced at Aubrey, who was his greatest rival. 'I'm aiming to play Golden Boy over there in the final.'

'Do you think we'll get that far?'

'We have every chance. I'm on top form this summer. Not sure how Froggy plays,' he said, referring to Elise.

'If she's good, we're in for trouble.'

'Nothing I can't handle. Say, do you fancy a drink?'

'I'd love one.' They walked towards the pavilion. As they passed the trio on the rug, Aubrey and John bared their teeth; the smile of two lions vying for the same territory.

'Hi, Cynthia,' said Florence, trying not to look at Aubrey.

'Come and join us, Flo,' said Cynthia, patting the rug beside her. 'Elise needs encouragement. She's saying she doesn't want to play.'

Florence turned to John. 'Will you bring me some lemonade?' she asked, giving him her most charming smile so he wouldn't resent her for ditching him in favour of their greatest rivals. She sat down. 'Florence Lightfoot,' she said to Elise, putting out her hand. Elise took it shyly. Her hand was small in Florence's, like a mouse. Florence felt sorry for her, being so timid. She did not imagine she played a good game of tennis.

'Flo is my best friend,' said Cynthia to Elise. 'But she won't mind at all if I say she's rather bad at tennis.'

Florence laughed. When it came to tennis, she was not proud.

Elise looked surprised. 'I don't believe that at all,' she said in a thick French accent, for Florence certainly appeared athletic with her long legs.

'Oh, it's true,' Florence told her. 'But I run for everything.'

'Hello, Florence,' said Aubrey, settling his grey eyes on her in the polite but careless way of a man whose object of interest lies elsewhere.

'Hello, Aubrey,' Florence replied, turning back to Elise with a grin. 'You don't need to worry about partnering

Aubrey. He's the best player here, so all you have to do is stand at the net and make yourself as small as possible. Let him do all the work and you'll sail straight through to the final.'

Aubrey laughed, his face creasing into delicious folds. Florence could barely take her eyes off him. 'Elise will be very disappointed when she finds out I'm not quite as indomitable as you make me out to be, Florence.'

'Oh, but you are, Aubrey,' Florence insisted, feeling her face grow hot with an oncoming blush. 'No one plays as well as you and you know it.'

'John is not easily beaten,' he said, dragging lazily on his cigarette. 'In fact, I'd say you two have a good chance of walking away with the trophy this year.'

'Hardly,' said Florence. 'I'm sure to let him down.'

Cynthia smiled at Elise. 'You see, not everyone's a wizard on the court. The point is to have fun. It's not about winning. Even Aubrey doesn't mind losing, do you, Aubrey?'

'Certainly not mixed doubles. However, I think I'd mind if John beat me in a singles match.' He looked at Elise with kindness. 'You needn't worry. I don't mind how you play. It's just a bit of fun. Something to keep us all entertained during these long summer months. If we get knocked out in the first round, we can play croquet instead.'

'All right,' said Elise in a voice as soft as brie. 'I'll play.'

'Jolly good,' said Cynthia.

'Yes, good sport,' Florence agreed.

'Do you know croquet was invented by the French?' said Aubrey, still looking at Elise.

Elise shrugged. 'Was it?'

'Yes, it was called *jeu de mail*. The British stole it and the Scots made golf out of it.' He chuckled. 'There, a bit of irrelevant information for you.'

'I love irrelevant information,' said Florence. 'Apparently, tennis started in France too. They used to hit a ball with their hand, which led to fives.'

Aubrey was impressed. 'How do you know that, Florence?'

She shrugged. 'Oh, I pick up the odd thing here and there. Actually, Grandpa told me. He knows everything.'

John appeared with Florence's lemonade. 'Sorry,' he said, handing it to her. 'Got waylaid by your sister. I'll come and get you when we're on.' Florence watched him walk off and then turned her attention back to Aubrey, but to her disappointment he was deep in conversation with Elise and there seemed no opportunity to join them without being gauche, so she talked to her old friend Cynthia instead.

Florence was distracted then by a man wandering slowly across the lawn. He was not dressed for tennis, but was wearing a pair of pale grey, wide-legged trousers and a knitted blue polo shirt. His dark brown hair was swept off his forehead, revealing a widow's peak which looked glamorous somehow on his imperious face, like a film star. It was Rupert Dash.

Rupert was handsome and tall as all Dashes were, with a slightly aquiline, aristocratic nose and a full, petulant mouth. His brand of good looks, however, lacked the typical Dash traits of lightness and joy and had a shadiness to it, a sense of danger. Florence observed him with interest for he stuck out from the crowd of players like a wolf among sheep.

'Your brother nearly ran us over on the drive,' she told Cynthia.

Cynthia laughed. 'He's very pleased with his new car,' she said.

'It is very fine,' Florence agreed. 'Makes quite a din, though.'

'It's incredibly popular with the girls.'

'I can imagine.' Florence continued to watch him. Hands in

pockets he stood by the court and began to take an interest in the game being played. He was too late, however. The match was over and the players were shaking hands. Florence's attention was distracted by John, rushing up with an electrified look on his face. 'We're on,' he told her excitedly.

'Good luck, Flo,' said Cynthia as Florence got up. Aubrey and Elise were so engrossed in each other that they did not notice her leave.

Florence felt attractive in her shorts. She had good legs, she knew, because they had been much admired for their shapeliness. As she knocked up with Jane, who was even worse at tennis than she was, she noticed Freddie whacking balls at John, who calmly returned them as if barely trying. John really was a splendid player, she thought happily. If she could just tap the balls back, she could rely on him to win the points. She noticed Rupert, too, now smoking a cigarette as he observed them through the wire netting.

The match began. Freddie to serve. Florence gritted her teeth and watched the ball closely as it came hurtling towards her. She pulled her racquet back, knowing that, because Freddie had rudely served his best, all she needed to do was make contact with the ball and it would rebound off her racquet with the same speed with which he had served it. John watched her anxiously, willing her not to blunder, but he needn't have worried. The ball bounced off her racquet and sped over the net, straight past Jane's left ear. Freddie's mouth fell open. He had clearly expected to ace her.

Florence heard clapping from behind her. 'Bravo!' It was Rupert and he was laughing. 'That's the way you return the serve of a man who has forgotten his manners. With interest!'

'Hear, hear!' agreed William, joining his eldest son at the netting. 'Freddie Laycock I would appreciate it if you remembered your manners next time you serve to a lady.'

There were, Florence knew, unspoken rules at Pedrevan Park, and gallantry was one of them.

The match went on and Florence managed to get most balls back. However, for the majority of the game she was told to stay at the net where she had nothing to do, because even when the balls flew within her reach, she did not have the courage to hit them. John wanted her out of play as much as possible. Once or twice she caught Jane's eye, for she had obviously been given the same instructions from Freddie, and they exchanged a sympathetic smile from their positions between the tramlines. It was not a close match. Freddie lost his temper, shouted at Jane when she missed a backhand and saw his game decline. His forehand, which had appeared so formidable at the beginning, now lost its bite and most of his shots went out. 'Over-egging the pudding yet again,' said Rupert, within earshot of Florence who was now serving for the set. 'Just get it in, sweetheart, and it's game, set and match.'

Florence patted the ball. It travelled in a slow arc, dropping into Freddie's service box with a plop. Freddie, now furious, went in for the kill, but managed only to whack it with the flat of his racquet and consequently hit it out. Rupert put his cigarette between his teeth and clapped again. 'Bravo, Beauty and the Beast,' he cheered. Then he turned to his father and said, 'This is more fun than I thought it would be. I might stick around.'

'Well done, partner,' exclaimed John cheerfully as he and Florence walked to the net. 'Good game. You played well. Keep it up and we'll win the next round too.'

Florence shook hands with Freddie who scowled, and Jane who was sweet and said, 'You deserved to win, Flo. And by the way, John thinks he's the bee's knees, but I'd say *you're* his secret weapon.'

They walked off the court. Rupert was smiling at Florence. His gunmetal blue eyes trailed up and down her legs with ill-concealed appreciation. 'That was a pleasure to watch,' he said.

'Thank you,' she replied.

'You're Florence Lightfoot, aren't you? You've grown up in the last year.'

'That is what tends to happen,' she replied, tossing her hair.

He smirked. 'You did well out there.'

'Self-defence, mostly.'

'I hope you win the trophy.'

'Why?'

'Because then Aubrey won't win it.'

'Why don't *you* play, then you can beat him yourself?'

'Because I'm shockingly bad.'

'I think you'll be disappointed then. Aubrey wins every year, whoever he plays with.'

Rupert dropped his cigarette butt to the ground and crunched it beneath his shoe. 'Pity,' he said. 'But everyone's luck runs out sometime. I daresay Aubrey's will too.' He walked off and Florence was left feeling surprised by his scorn. She wondered why Rupert, who was two years older than Aubrey and heir to Pedrevan, was jealous of his brother.

She went to the pavilion for a glass of lemonade. 'Well played, Flo,' said Bertha Clairmont, sister of her tennis partner John, who was tucking into a slice of cake. 'Your return of serve wiped the smirk off Freddie's face.' She laughed, spitting crumbs into the air between them.

Celia Dash had come out to watch the fun. She was elegant in a belted, primrose yellow dress, her short hair fashionably styled into shiny black waves. The long skirt emphasized her slim figure and made her look taller. In fact, she was a picture of sophistication and glamour and Florence stopped her conversation to gaze on her.

'Mrs Dash should have been a film star,' she said to Bertha.

'She's much too classy for that,' Bertha replied, taking another bite of the cake.

'She looks like Joan Bennett.'

'Who's Joan Bennett?'

'Never mind.' Florence turned her eyes to the tennis court to see that Aubrey was walking onto the court with Elise. 'Oh, I want to watch this one,' she said. 'Are you coming?'

'Am I ever!' gushed Bertha, stuffing the rest of the cake into her mouth and following after her.

It seemed that everyone wanted to watch Aubrey's match. The croquet players stopped their game and young people appeared from every corner of the garden, like hens at feeding time. Florence was curious to see how Elise played. She didn't imagine she played very well. After all, she had nearly backed out of it altogether.

They began to knock up. Aubrey was stylish in a pair of white trousers and a terry cotton polo shirt. He hit the ball with ease and flair, smiling all the time and saying 'good shot' to his opponent, even when it wasn't a particularly good one. Elise was not as poor as Florence had expected her to be. Chic in her tennis dress with her tanned skin glowing amber in the sunshine, she looked surprisingly accomplished and hit some strong shots. Their opponents were James Clayton, who was of average ability, and Ginger Lately, who was not only beautiful but sporty too. However, even though Ginger played well, not once did Aubrey whack the ball at her, nor did he do what most men did, ignore the girls and hit only to the other boy. Elise made many blunders, apologizing each time to her partner. However, Aubrey did not patronize her. He simply said, 'Bad luck, partner,' or 'That was close,' and continued the game in his typically good-natured way. Florence, who had rather hoped that Elise played badly, now wished she played better, because Aubrey's sweetness with her grated.

It was a fun match for the spectators as there was lots of chat and laughter and fooling about. Celia clapped heartily for both couples from her pole position on one of the benches, while Rupert watched only one game before wandering off, bored. John sidled up to Florence. 'This is what we're going to be up against,' he whispered. 'Aubrey lures his opponent into making the error. Well, two can play at that game.' Florence wished he'd be a little less competitive. Aubrey's gamesmanship was so attractive.

When the match was over, Aubrey gave Elise a kiss on the cheek. Florence was stunned. It was customary for players to shake hands. 'I suppose that's what the French do,' said Bertha with a chuckle.

'Do they, do you think?' said Florence, feeling a little better about it.

'It's only right that England conquers France,' said John with a laugh.

'Oh really, John! That's vulgar,' said Bertha. However, she couldn't help but laugh as well. Florence did not laugh. She did not find it funny at all. The competition had intensified and Aubrey didn't even know there was one. Florence sighed and folded her arms. The truth was, Aubrey barely noticed her. But Florence was not a girl to give up at the first hurdle. She had the whole summer to get his attention, and get it she would, one way or another.

CHAPTER THREE

Margaret Lightfoot was in such a state of nervous anxiety that her mother had suggested she go to her room and lie down for a while. She and Winifred would see to any last-minute arrangements, she told her. The truth was that there wasn't much left to do. Dinner was being prepared by Cook in the kitchen. As there were thirteen people to seat at the dining room table, which was extremely unlucky, Rowley the butler had laid up for fourteen, setting a place for Uncle Raymond's teddy, Brownie. It was not the first time that Brownie had been invited to dinner. Fresh flowers had been placed on the hall table and in the drawing room, and the cushions had been put out on the chairs on the terrace in case it was warm enough to sit outside for pre-dinner drinks.

Florence was in her bedroom, working out what to wear. Dresses were thrown over the bed and she was standing in front of the long mirror in a green skirt and knitted sweater, biting her nails with indecision. Aubrey Dash and his family were coming to dinner; it was imperative that she looked her best. Unfortunately, Elise was coming too. In spite of Pedrevan being full of Dash and Clairmont cousins who were *not* coming for dinner, Celia had informed Margaret that Elise was included. It seemed to Florence that wherever Aubrey went, Elise went too. It was only the beginning of the holidays, Florence reassured herself. She still had plenty of time to catch Aubrey's eye.

Florence and John had managed to win their tennis matches thus far. The last two had been more challenging than the first and Florence had served a few double faults due to nerves. She didn't want to let John down, but the more competitive he became the more tense she grew, which did not help her game. 'Come on, old girl!' he'd rally before the point was played, and the way he said it, curling his fist into a hammer and scrunching up his pink face, guaranteed that she hit the ball straight into the net. It was not going well, in spite of the final score which suggested otherwise.

Tennis was not the only entertainment, however. There had been picnics on the beach, a scavenger hunt, a swimming party, a murder mystery dinner, all arranged by the families of Gulliver's Bay, each one playing their part. Margaret Lightfoot could only manage dinner for thirteen but Florence had persuaded her grandparents to allow her to host a dinner on their private beach at the end of August. It would be the final party of the holidays. They would put up a tent in case of rain, and there would be a band, candles, a big bonfire and plenty of food. Florence was as unhelpful as a person could possibly be, but for this she promised she would help. Winifred said she wanted nothing to do with it, because she was tired of always having to do all the work while Florence made herself scarce. 'It's about time you pulled your weight, Flo,' she said. 'Therefore, Mama and I will sit back and enjoy the sunshine while you take care of the arrangements.' Florence didn't imagine it would be very hard. After all, she had the servants at her disposal and there were only sixty-odd guests. How taxing could it be?

She looked out of her bedroom window. From there she had a view of the lawn that sloped into an incline of rocks and thorny shrubs and a well-trodden path that meandered down to the beach. The sea glittered and sparkled in the early evening sunshine, promising another clear day tomorrow. Far out, a little boat made its way slowly over the horizon, its white triangular sail gleaming like the wing of a gull. The thought of Aubrey coming for dinner rendered everything more beautiful. Florence's spirits soared and everywhere she looked there was a reason to be happy. Whether it was the sea, the birds frolicking in the hedges, the heaps of pink and blue hydrangeas, the grass strewn with daisies and buttercups and the fat bumble bees that toddled among them, Florence's chest swelled with joyful anticipation.

But what was she going to wear? She settled on a blue sundress imprinted with yellow flowers. It hugged her small waist and feminine hips and had a tear-shaped cut-out from the throat to the breastbone, giving a small but enticing flash of flesh. Aubrey was sure to notice it. She curled her hair, sweeping it up at the sides and fastening it with clips. She would be eighteen in September, but she looked like she was already twenty. Satisfied with her reflection, she dabbed her wrists and neck with perfume and went downstairs.

Florence found her mother on the terrace smoking a cigarette. Margaret was dressed for dinner in a teal green pencil skirt and silk blouse. She was not beautiful but she was elegant with a neat waist and a pretty, freckled face, framed by soft, curly brown hair cut fashionably short. Florence had not inherited her mother's petite frame or her freckled skin and brown hair, but she had inherited her green eyes. Margaret and Florence's eyes were the colour of Cornish rockpools, but while Margaret's were filled with anxiety, Florence's were steady and bold – the eyes of a young woman confident of her place in the world.

'You look lovely, dear,' said Margaret, taking in her daughter's luscious figure. It was bursting with womanhood like a newly ripened peach.

'You don't need to be nervous, you know,' Florence reassured her. 'The Dashes bring their own fun. All you need to do is feed them.'

Margaret took a long drag of her cigarette. She looked out to sea. 'It's hard, sometimes, being a woman on one's own, without a husband for support. Social situations make one feel terribly exposed.'

Florence had never given that aspect of her mother's widowhood a moment's thought. 'You miss Daddy very much, don't you?'

'Every day.' Margaret smiled sadly. She took a breath and rallied. 'He was such a strong and capable man. He arranged everything. It was what he was bred for. That's why the army suited him so well. I was his ADC. I'm not very good at being the leader.'

'But you have Grandpa and Uncle Raymond.'

'I know. And they're both supportive in their own ways.' She looked at her daughter with tenderness. 'You're young, Flo. You couldn't possibly understand what it is to be a widow. I hope you never do.'

'Why don't you marry again?' Florence suggested. It really was, she thought, very simple.

'I don't want to share my life with another man. I loved your father. I could never love anyone else like that.'

'Does love matter so much the second time round? Wouldn't it be nice not to be on your own?'

'It would be *very* nice. But your father is irreplaceable.'

Florence's memories of him were hazy. 'He was jolly sick at the end,' she said. She remembered the smell of the hospital most of all. It was horrid.

'I didn't mind looking after him. It gave me a role. He needed me. It's nice to be needed.'

'You're still young. Some dashingly handsome man might come and sweep you off your feet. You never know.'

Margaret chuckled cynically. 'You never know. But the way I feel right now, I can't imagine allowing anyone in. I'm not sure your father would like that.'

'He's hardly in a position to make a fuss, is he?'

Margaret looked to the far horizon. 'He's out there somewhere.'

Florence's gaze joined her mother's and she considered her words. 'Do you think he's still around?'

'Of course. The very fact that Jesus appeared to Mary Magdalene and his disciples after death was to show them that life goes on. That the body dies but the soul continues. Yes, your father's still around. I don't doubt it.'

'I've always thought the Bible was a book of fairy tales.'

Margaret was shocked. 'Florence!'

Florence scrunched up her nose. 'But those things didn't really happen. I mean, Mary wasn't really a virgin, was she? And it's impossible to turn water into wine. They're lovely stories, but they didn't happen.'

'Your father was a religious man. He would not like to hear you speaking like this.'

'Do you think there's one man out there for each of us? Do you think it's predestined?'

'I like to think so.'

'That we each have a soulmate.' Florence thought of Aubrey. 'That whatever happens in our lives, our paths will inevitably meet and we will find each other.' As far as she was concerned, she and her soulmate already had.

'Your father was my soulmate, if there is such a thing. Anyone else who happens to cross my path will only ever be second best.'

Florence pondered this for a moment. Then she tossed her hair. 'I hope I don't end up with second best. I'm sure many do, because they're afraid of being left to gather dust on the shelf, like Grandma's porcelain figurines. I think I'd rather be single than settle for second best.'

Margaret smiled. 'I'm sure your soulmate will find you. It's strange how it happens. I met your father at a dance – he was a terrible dancer. But we just liked each other, instantly. It *will* happen, Florence. Somehow, it always does.'

The Dashes were never on time. No one ever minded, because when they turned up, usually about twenty minutes late, they were so full of laughter and charm that any offence was immediately forgotten. As soon as their cars scrunched over the gravel and came to a halt in front of The Mariners, it was as if the sun had decided to change direction and shine anew. The cars themselves were things of beauty, their long bonnets polished until they gleamed and their frog's eye head-lights glinting glass and chrome. The doors opened and the family stepped out in their usual cheerful manner; the party had arrived.

Florence watched them from the upstairs window, her excitement mounting. They were somehow glossier than everyone else, as if they'd stepped straight off the silver screen. William, in black tie, opened the door for his wife. Celia was typically chic in a long, cream-coloured dress, her wasp-like waist emphasized by a thin black belt. Cynthia, elegant like her mother, was in a long, red floral dress and with her was Elise, demure and petite in a dark blue skirt and blouse. Elise was an unimpressive sight, Florence thought. Eclipsed by the blinding glare of the Dashes' glamour she could almost have been staff. Aubrey climbed out of Rupert's Aston Martin, followed by Rupert and their younger brother Julian, all in black tie. How handsome they looked, she thought, her gaze clinging to Aubrey with longing. Then Rupert lifted his eyes. On seeing her through the glass he smiled. Florence was appalled she had been spotted and leapt away from the window.

The families gathered on the terrace for drinks in the grainy golden light of the setting sun. Henry and Joan welcomed the Dashes with none of their daughter's self-consciousness. Henry asked William how the tennis tournament was progressing and Joan invited Celia to sit with her and explain this novel idea of a murder mystery dinner party that Florence had been telling her about. Celia sat beside her on the wicker sofa, tucked one elegant t-strap sandal behind the other and smoked through a black Bakelite and silver holder, her dancing eyes full of exuberance. As she explained the concept of the murder mystery dinner her dazzling light fell upon Joan, making her feel younger and more exciting than she was. Uncle Raymond mingled with the Dash boys on the lawn, a tumbler of scotch in one hand, a cigarette in the other, while Margaret, fighting a headache, joined her mother and Celia and tried to appear at ease. She was the hostess, after all, and, as Florence had so rightly told her, the Dashes brought their own fun. All she had to do was feed them.

Florence would have liked to talk to Aubrey, but Elise and Cynthia were chatting to Winifred on the lawn, and she knew it would be polite to join them.

'How are you enjoying Cornwall?' she asked Elise.

'I like it so much, I don't want to go home,' Elise replied. Since arriving ten days before, her English had certainly improved.

'You're not leaving, are you?' Florence asked, her spirits rising suddenly.

'We're not going to let her go,' said Cynthia, putting an arm around her. 'Elise is the sister I never had.' Florence couldn't understand how anyone could be enthusiastic about such an insipid creature.

'How lovely that you've been adopted by the Dashes,' said Winifred, her cigarette smoking between her manicured fingers. 'I think most would feel overwhelmed by them.' She grinned at Cynthia. 'There are so many of you, after all.'

Cynthia laughed. 'We're a tribe,' she said. 'But there's strength in numbers.'

'I'm an only child,' Elise explained. 'It's a *nouveauté* to be with a big family.'

'That's lucky. You suddenly have three brothers and a sister and heaps of cousins,' said Florence, emphasizing the word 'brother'. 'You wait until they all descend on you in France.'

'I'd love that!' Elise enthused, her soft brown eyes enlivening. There was a sweetness in her smile that Florence hadn't noticed before. 'Perhaps they better not all come at the same time.'

Florence glanced at Aubrey. As her eyes strayed to the group of men, she caught Rupert watching her through a veil of cigarette smoke. He sauntered across the grass and stopped beside her. 'What are you girls talking about over here? Your conversation looks a great deal more interesting than ours.'

'I'm sure it isn't,' said Winifred. 'But you're welcome to join us.'

His sharp blue gaze rested on Florence. Then it dropped to the cut-out in her dress and lingered there.

'When are you going to give us a spin in your new car?' said Florence, because she couldn't think of anything else to say and there was something about Rupert that made her feel uneasy.

He smiled like a wolf sizing up a hen. 'Whenever you like, Flossie. I can see you're a girl who likes speed and danger.'

Florence did not like being called Flossie and his flirtatious tone was not appropriate. 'I don't know where you've got that idea from,' she retorted crisply.

'Didn't you get into trouble at school for climbing out of your dormitory window and going out on the town?'

Florence was astonished he knew about that. But it was true, she *had* got caught. She lifted her chin. 'I broke the eleventh Commandment,' she said.

'The eleventh?' said Elise, surprised.

'*Thou shalt not get caught.* Grandpa taught me that. One of the most important Commandments, you know. It was, I daresay, foolish of me to break it.'

'I'm afraid your antics are legendary,' said Cynthia with a giggle.

'I would say more entertaining than legendary,' Rupert corrected.

'I'm glad I keep you amused,' Florence shot back.

'She doesn't keep her mother amused,' said Winifred. She dragged on her cigarette and arched a thin eyebrow at her sister.

'Poor Margaret,' said Cynthia.

'Rules are made to be broken,' Florence rallied. 'Anyway, I've left that silly place.'

'What are you going to do now?' asked Rupert, watching her lazily through the cloud of smoke Winifred had just exhaled into the air between them.

'I'm going to be an actress,' she replied tartly.

Winifred laughed. 'You have to get past your grand-father first.'

'When I'm eighteen I will do as I please.'

Rupert laughed. 'I daresay you will.' There was a twinkle of enjoyment in his eyes. 'Foolish would be the person to come between Florence Lightfoot and her dreams.'

Florence looked past him to Aubrey and wished she could wander over and talk to *him* instead of having to suffer his infuriating brother. A moment later the maid appeared to inform Margaret that dinner was ready and Florence was saved.

Florence had taken care of the placement, having found her mother dithering at the table with the little white name cards. She had put herself between Aubrey and Julian, ensuring that Rupert was at the other end of the table, between Winifred and Elise. With Rupert and Elise safely out of the way, Florence turned her attention at last to the object of her great-est desire: Aubrey Dash. He was so close, they were almost touching. She flicked her napkin onto her lap and turned to him with a smile. 'It looks like we might be meeting in the final of the tennis tournament,' she said.

He looked at her and Florence felt her stomach flip over like a pancake. His eyes were grey, the colour of sea mist just as the sun breaks through. 'We still have a match to play,' he told her. 'I can't guarantee we'll win it.'

'Of course you will.'

'You have great faith in me, Florence.'

'You've always been the best, and Elise is pretty good too, so you're sure to win the whole thing.'

He glanced at Elise. 'She's a good sport.'

'She played herself down. She's not anything like as bad as she made herself out to be.'

'I think she had a distorted view of the standard here. She thought the English were all excellent sportsmen.'

Florence laughed. 'I'm sure she's changed her opinion, especially since watching me!'

He grinned. 'She has, but not because of you. You have an abundance of enthusiasm, but not a lot of technique. If you had technique, you'd be formidable.'

'Isn't it lucky then that I don't. I might steal your crown.'

'I think you'd wear it better than me.'

They both laughed.

'How's your French?' she asked.

'As it was before Elise arrived. She insists on speaking English.'

'Which is only fair. After all, that *is* the point of her visit, isn't it? To learn English?' Florence envisaged Celia Dash and Madame Dujardin matchmaking together and hoped their plans had been foiled.

'Yes, that is *half* the point.'

'Oh? What's the other half?' Florence's heart froze.

He lowered his voice. 'To have some fun. She's an only child and her parents are divorcing.'

Florence gasped with genuine surprise. 'How dreadful.'

'Yes, she's had a difficult time.'

'I'm sure she has. How lovely of your family to take her in. There is no family in the world with such power to make a person feel good than your family. If I were in a desperate situation, I'd be drawn to Pedrevan like an ailing ship to a lighthouse.'

Aubrey looked at her steadily and frowned. 'You're sweet to think so, Florence. I do hope we've helped.'

'Pedrevan must be a welcome distraction from the horrors of home. So many young people and all that fun and games.' She glanced at Elise and saw not an insipid creature but a broken one. 'You've been incredibly sweet with her, Aubrey. You could have left her with Cynthia, but you've taken her under your wing. I'm sure she's derived great comfort from your kindness.'

'Gulliver's Bay can be overwhelming for a newcomer. Even more so for a foreigner.'

'You're right and I've been remiss. I didn't imagine what it must be like coming into a close-knit community like ours where everyone knows each other. It must be daunting. I will endeavour to take trouble with her too.'

'Thank you, Florence. She'll be so pleased. You're the life and soul of the party.'

Florence was astonished. She'd never thought of herself in that way. It was the most wonderful compliment Aubrey could give her. 'I'm an enthusiast,' she said with a grin. 'I throw myself into everything rather too much and often get into trouble.'

Aubrey laughed. 'I hear all about your antics from Cynthia. You're a bit of a legend in our family.'

'I can't believe that!'

'Oh yes, you are. Cynthia often reads out your letters.'

'She does not!' Florence was horrified. The thought of Aubrey knowing she climbed onto her boarding house roof to sunbathe topless caused her cheeks to redden.

He must have noticed her blush, for he quickly added, 'Only the highlights. Don't worry, she's quite discreet.'

'Doesn't sound like it.'

'I think you must have run rings around your teachers. I imagine they were very strict. They weren't nuns, were they?'

'No, but they rather wanted us to behave like nuns! If I hadn't left when I did, I think they would have given me the boot.'

'I don't imagine your grandfather would have been happy about that.'

'No, he'd have been very cross, although I'm not sure he thinks it necessary to educate women. He wants me to go to some sort of finishing school where I'll learn to turn down a bed and arrange flowers.'

'I think you'll make a fine actress.'

'You know . . . ?'

'Cynthia.' He grinned across at his sister, who sensed him looking at her and lifted her eyes from her plate and smiled back. 'I think one has to fight hard for what one wants to do in life. It's all too easy to allow other people to show you the path to take. Really, you should take the path of your choosing.'

'What is the path of *your* choice, then, Aubrey?'

'I'm going to Sandhurst.'

'Grandpa would approve of that.'

'Mother would prefer I went into the City.'

'She needn't worry. It's not like you're going to see any fighting.'

'No point joining the army if you're afraid of bullets.'

The thought of Aubrey being shot at was deeply distressing. 'I think you should go into the City,' she said.

CHAPTER FOUR

Florence quickly understood that the way to get Aubrey's attention was to be kind to Elise. Not that kindness was a quality Florence lacked, but sometimes she was too busy thinking of herself to notice when kindness was required. She felt genuinely sorry for Elise that her parents were divorcing. She couldn't imagine having parents who no longer wanted to be together, because hers had loved each other profoundly. She only knew what it was like to lose one of them, and even that had not impressed itself too deeply upon her because of her father's remoteness and the young age she'd been when death had taken him. Besides, every time her bottom lip had wobbled, he'd said firmly and a little impatiently, 'An officer's daughter never cries.' His words had clearly made more of an impression on Florence than they had on her sister.

Winifred had suffered terribly. Not only had she been very like Rod Lightfoot, but the two of them had shared a deep bond. Florence remembered hearing her sister sobbing in her bedroom next door and wishing that she could cry too, because by not crying she felt inadequate and excluded, and what would her father care about a soldier's daughter crying now that he was dead? She remembered her mother curled up on the sofa in the sitting room, listening to his records on the gramophone, cigarette smoke curling up from her tight little hands as her body trembled with anguish. An officer's wife cried, *a lot*.

Florence went out of her way to make Elise feel included, and Elise responded with surprise and gratitude. Florence could never have imagined that the two of them, being so very different, would become friends. But the more time Florence spent with her, the more she grew to like her. Elise was shy, admittedly, but Florence's exuberance brought her out of herself, and her English sense of humour made her laugh. Aubrey noticed Florence's kindness and the way he looked at her was now different. He *saw* her, not just as his little sister's mischievous friend, but as an accomplice, a co-conspirator and an ally. Florence basked in the warmth of his admiration, certain that out of this a shoot of attraction would grow.

As she had predicted, she and John played Elise and Aubrey in the tennis tournament final. Everyone came to watch. William Dash umpired from the top of the umpire's chair in his panama hat and white linen jacket, and the young Dash cousins acted as ball boys, scurrying around the court like a pack of unruly dogs. Rupert watched from the bench where he sat beside his mother and smoked languidly, while his eyes trailed up Florence's legs. Florence could feel his gaze and was annoyed by it.

Aubrey and John's rivalry went back years. They were first cousins and both talented sportsmen. They had attended different schools and played in all the teams, which only compounded their competitiveness as they'd faced each other time and again on opposing sides. Now they faced each other over the net at Pedrevan and Aubrey was no longer prepared to keep the ball in play. This was a serious match and he had clearly decided he was going to grab every opportunity to hit a winner.

Florence and Elise watched the balls whizz by at a speed

not yet seen in the competition. Occasionally, Elise put out her racquet from her position at the net and managed to get it back, but Florence was too scared to make a mistake and cowered between the tramlines, hoping the balls wouldn't come near her so that she didn't have to try and hit them. When it came to her serve, she was so anxious that she patted them over, which at least guaranteed they went in, but they were too easy for Aubrey, who just put them away with ease, infuriating John and inducing him to shout, 'Come on, Florence, give it more welly!' He no longer called her 'old girl', and by the tone of his voice it was apparent that he blamed *her* for their lagging behind in the score.

Florence felt a sudden upsurge of fury and gritted her teeth.

'Steady on, old chap!' shouted Rupert from the bench. 'That's no way to speak to a lady.'

'Hear, hear,' William concurred. 'May I remind you, young man, of your manners.' Aubrey gave Florence a sympathetic smile, which lifted her mood and did something surprising to her tennis. She started to play well.

From that moment on Florence ceased to care what her partner thought. Who was he to tell her how to play and where to stand? Since when had she become a person who did what she was told? In any case, what did it matter if they lost? It was meant to be fun. Everything at Pedrevan was fun.

With Aubrey's eyes upon her, Florence ran harder for the ball and she gave her shots as much 'welly' as she could muster. She managed to ace Elise, much to Rupert's amusement for he clapped loudly from the bench behind her, shouting, 'Great shot, Flossie!' John began to look quite pleased and he started to call her 'old girl' again. But Florence didn't care. It was Aubrey she was out to impress and by the look on his face she could tell she was succeeding.

Once again Florence found herself serving for the set. She was serving to Aubrey, who stood close to the service box, expecting a gentle ball and ready to whack it back. Rupert hissed at her from behind the net. 'He's going to go for your backhand, Flossie,' he said. 'Be prepared.' Florence took no notice. He was incredibly annoying making comments there behind the netting. She threw the ball into the air and hit it over the net. Having intended to ignore Rupert's advice, she found herself skipping to the left in anticipation of a return to her backhand. She was therefore ready and in position for the shot that came whizzing back. She didn't have time to think. She put out her racquet and squeezed her eyes shut. Aubrey moved calmly to the net, not expecting the ball to come back. But to his surprise, it bounced off her racquet and shot down the middle of the court. Both Elise and Aubrey leapt towards it, but Florence's ball had the advantage of being unexpected. They were both too slow. It sailed between their racquets and landed just within the base line.

'By Jove!' exclaimed Rupert, standing up and clapping gleefully. 'Bad luck, Aubrey! So close. Well done, Flossie. A perfect shot to win the match.'

Aubrey looked at Florence and smiled with astonishment. 'You've won!' he exclaimed.

'Have we?' Florence replied, amazed that the winning shot had come off *her* racquet.

'You're a dark horse, you are,' he added, scratching his head.

Florence was about to make her way to the net but John got to her first. He pulled her into a fierce embrace. He was damp with sweat and smelled rank, like rotten cabbage. Florence wriggled out of his arms. 'Well played, partner,' she said.

'No, well played *you*,' he replied. 'The winning shot was all yours.' She didn't think he'd have been so pleased with her if they'd lost.

Florence noticed Aubrey kiss Elise again. French or not, it was too intimate for her liking. She strode up to the net. Surely, in the final, he would kiss her too?

Aubrey shook his cousin's hand. 'Well played, John,' he said, shaking it vigorously. 'Good match.'

Florence kissed Elise and then smiled at Aubrey. 'We are all winners,' she said graciously. 'It's a shame only one couple can receive the trophy.'

'You deserve it, Florence. You pulled a rabbit out of the hat at the last minute. The trophy is yours.' Aubrey put out his hand. Florence looked at it and frowned. How could he kiss Elise and yet offer *her* his hand? But what could she do? Save throwing herself at him, which was beneath her dignity and would be deeply regretted later, she was left no choice but to take it.

'Thank you, Aubrey,' she said.

A few days later Florence was in town, sitting on the harbour wall eating an ice cream while Elise and Cynthia browsed in a gift shop, when Rupert roared up in his Aston Martin, drawing to a halt alongside her. The roof was down and his dark brown hair was gleaming in the sunshine. He put his elbow on the window frame and took off his sunglasses. 'Fancy a drive?' he asked.

'I don't think you want ice cream all over your seats, do you?'

'I'll wait while you finish it,' he said, turning off the engine. 'What are you doing here on your own? If you're not careful you'll get picked up by a handsome devil in a sports car.'

Florence laughed. 'I'm waiting for the girls. They're shopping.'

'Hurry up and finish that ice cream then or they'll want to come too.'

'I doubt it. Your sister couldn't be less interested in your car, and Elise will be too nervous to get in. I imagine she'd feel sick just looking at it.'

He grinned raffishly and put on his sunglasses again. 'Good. I'll take you for a whizz around the countryside then.'

Florence didn't really want to go. 'I think I should wait for the girls,' she said.

Rupert drummed his fingers on the door impatiently. 'Just pop the cone into your mouth and let's go. They'll assume you've gone home.'

Florence glanced over at the shop window. She could see the girls talking through the glass. By the looks of things, they were in no hurry to leave.

'By the way, I should congratulate you again on winning the tennis,' he said. 'It was most entertaining.'

'I imagine you're happy we beat your brother.'

'Very,' he said.

'It was a close match.'

'Much too close, if you ask me.' He watched her pop the tip of the cone into her mouth. 'Come on, in you get, Flossie.'

'Oh, all right,' she said, licking the last drip of ice cream off her fingers. 'Just a quick drive.' She walked round to the passenger door and climbed in. 'You know, my name is not Flossie.'

'It is to me. Don't you like it?' He started the engine and the car set off with a lurch.

'Not really. Most people call me Flo.'

He glanced at her and grinned again. 'I'm not most people.' His teeth were very white against his tanned skin.

The car sped down the narrow lanes, the engine roaring determinedly like a lion in pursuit of prey. Florence winced as Rupert took the corners at speed, anxious that something big might be coming in the other direction. It was impossible to see clearly for the hedges were tall and leafy and the verges thick with cow parsley and yellow rape that had seeded itself from the nearby fields. The wind whipped through her hair and every bump in the road made her bounce. She curled her fingers around the seat and prayed that it would be over soon. She didn't want to die before Aubrey had kissed her.

At last Rupert slowed down and drew the car to a halt in a layby on the top of a hill. 'Do you know this place?' he asked.

'I don't think I do,' she replied, uncurling her fingers and noticing that they'd gone white.

'It's beautiful. Come, I'll show you.' Rupert reached onto the back seat for his camera.

Florence got out, relieved to be on firm ground, and followed him to a five-bar wooden gate which led into a field of long grasses and dandelions. 'Look at the view,' he said, hanging his camera strap around his neck and then taking a photograph. 'Magnificent, isn't it?' Indeed, it was. From up there they could see the sea, spread out before them, flat and glittering beneath the big blue sky. He scaled the gate and sat on the top, then held out his hand to help her up. Florence did not take it. Had it been Aubrey's she would not have hesitated, but in truth she did not need help climbing a gate, even in a dress. She sat beside him, hooking the heels of her shoes over the bar beneath her.

'You're a pretty girl, Flossie,' he said, turning to face her. The wind lifted a chunk of his hair and the sunlight caused his indigo eyes to shine. He was handsome. Most girls would have killed to have been in her position, sitting beside him and being told how pretty she was. But Florence only wished he were his brother.

'Thank you, Rupert,' she replied. Then to deflect the

growing feeling of awkwardness, she added, 'Look, can you see those boats out there on the horizon?'

Rupert looked at the sea through his camera lens. 'Fishing boats,' he said. 'Or Papa, like the Pied Piper of Hamelin, leading the young on yet another expedition.' He lowered his camera then withdrew a silver case from his breast pocket, flicked it open and offered Florence a cigarette. She accepted. Although she didn't like smoking she did rather relish the feeling of sophistication it gave her. He cupped his hands around the lighter and they both leaned away from the wind so that he could light it. Their hands touched as they sought shelter for the flame. Florence felt the caressing of his fingertips against her skin and her heart raced. Had she realized how intimate lighting a cigarette would be, she would have declined. It took a few attempts but eventually Florence blew out a cloud of smoke and tried not to cough. She did not want him to think her childish. He lit one for himself and replaced the case and lighter in his pocket.

'Your father's a wonderful man,' she said. 'Summer wouldn't be the same without him organizing so many things for us to do.'

'They're all so bally hearty. The whole lot of them.' Rupert's tone was scathing. He drew on his cigarette. 'It's as if they're trying to prove something.'

Florence was confused. 'Like what?'

'Oh, I don't know. How fabulous they are.'

'But you're a Dash too.'

'Not a fabulous one.'

'I disagree.'

'I'm a maverick, Flossie,' he said.

'You're the eldest son, the heir. The most important child in the family.'

He laughed. 'Because I was born first, that's a great achievement, isn't it? I'm a Dash, of course, but I'm not like them. I'm very bad at tennis and I don't, on the whole, like people.'

Florence felt sorry for him then. He looked forlorn, as if he didn't enjoy being different, but resented his place in the cold, even though he was the one who had put himself there. 'I don't believe you when you say you don't like people. You have a reputation for partying. You can't party on your own.'

He sighed as if he found it all a terrible bore. 'It's for show, Flossie. Trying to fit in. Trying to be like everyone else. What else is there to do? One can't swim against the tide all the time, it gets jolly tiring. One just has to allow it to carry one along. That's what I do most of the time. Allow it to carry me along.'

Florence looked at him with different eyes. Rupert no longer appeared menacing, just lost. 'What would you rather do?' she asked softly.

'Take photographs of beautiful things,' he said, holding up his camera.

'It's a fine camera,' Florence mused.

'I'm glad you appreciate it. It's a Leica. One of my most prized possessions.' He looked through the lens and focused on the buttercups that grew in abundance among the long grasses and dandelions. 'I'd like to live a quiet life in a cottage somewhere. Preferably in the middle of a field of buttercups, and while away my days reading F. Scott Fitzgerald.'

Florence laughed. 'But you're going to inherit Pedrevan Park.'

'I know. Life's a bugger. Sorry,' he grinned. 'Shouldn't swear in front of a lady.'

'I'm hardly a lady.'

Rupert narrowed his eyes. 'You're not like others, that's true. You're fierce. Most men will find you too much of a challenge. You know that, don't you, Flossie? Most men don't want a strong woman.'

Florence wondered whether that was true. She thought of Aubrey. Would he find her too much of a challenge? There was nothing challenging about Elise. 'I'm sure you're wrong,' she said, hopefully.

'You're a confident girl, Flossie. You have a steady, bold look in your eye. Your teachers at school must have been terrified of you.'

'I did my best,' she said with a chuckle.

'And you're going to be a great actress.'

'If I ever get on the stage.'

'You don't need a stage. Life's a stage. There's plenty of drama here to dig your teeth into if you want it.'

'I still want the stage. I want to play different roles. I want an audience. I want applause.' He laughed, which encouraged her to continue. 'I want the big curtain and lights, the silence that falls over the theatre as the play begins. I want to be someone else. It's tedious being me all the time.'

He put the camera to his eye again and pointed it at her. 'I think you'll be able to have whatever you want, Flossie.' The camera clicked.

Florence turned her face to the sea. 'I need to get past Grandpa,' she said, trying not to reveal how awkward she felt having her photograph taken. 'He thinks theatre is for working girls.'

Rupert arched an eyebrow. 'You mean prostitutes?'

'Women of easy virtue would be how he'd describe them.' She laughed and he clicked the camera again.

'Beautiful,' he murmured, taking another shot. 'Your work is cut out for you then. But you have a steely nature, I can see that.'

'You're right. I won't be put off.'

'I imagine you always get what you want.'

'I do my best. I don't always pull it off, though.'

'Look how you beat Aubrey on the tennis court. That was pure force of will.'

'One good shot. John won the match, not me.'

'Yours is the only shot anyone will remember.'

'Aubrey took it well. He's a good loser,' she said with a smile. Talking about Aubrey was like turning her face to the sun.

'He doesn't often lose. It's a novelty for him,' Rupert replied tersely.

'Don't you like your brother, Rupert?'

'I love him, of course I do. Blood is thicker than water and all that. But I resent the ease with which he sails through life, when everything for me has been an uphill struggle. Nothing is a struggle for Aubrey. Everyone loves him. He can have anyone he wants, both male and female. He's got an unfair amount of charisma. People can't help being drawn to him.'

'He's got your parents' charm, that's for certain.'

Rupert looked at her with a pained expression on his face. 'Do you worship him too, Flossie?'

'I don't worship anyone,' she replied. 'No one is without fault but God.'

'Good. You're your own woman, aren't you?' He flicked ash onto the grass. 'Aubrey should be the eldest son. Pedrevan should go to him. He'd continue the Dash traditions of after-dinner parlour games and tennis tournaments. I'm afraid, when it belongs to me, the summers are going to be frightfully dull. I'll shut the gates and not allow anyone in, like Oscar Wilde's Selfish Giant.'

'Perhaps you'll marry a woman who does all the enter-taining for you,' said Florence. 'You can sit on a deckchair in one of the secret gardens and hide away with your Fitzgeralds while she arranges picnics and treasure hunts and parties.'

Rupert blew smoke out of the side of his mouth and looked at her steadily. 'Would you be that sort of woman, Flossie?'

Florence was certain that, if she were married to Aubrey, she would. 'I think I'm just as hearty as they are,' she replied, holding Aubrey's image firmly in her mind. 'I love parties and parlour games. I'd be awfully good at arranging entertainments. I'm throwing the final party of the summer on our beach. It's going to be magnificent. A big bonfire, lots of candles in jars, dancing. I've even hired a band. I hope you'll come too, Rupert. Winnie and Grandma doubt I'm up to it, but they'll eat their words when they see what a success it is.'

Rupert smiled reflectively. 'Perhaps I need a woman like you to save me.'

She laughed. Not for a moment did she believe he meant *her*. 'Yes, you need a hearty girl who loves entertaining but at the same time is tolerant of your misanthropic nature.'

'I'll be the grumpy curmudgeon in the attic, looking out over the lawn at the jolly croquet and tennis below, waiting for it all to be over so that I can have a glass of sherry with my lovely wife and watch the sunset, just the two of us.'

'I never took you for a romantic,' she said, surprised.

'What did you take me for?'

'Well, you've always been a rather dark presence, if I'm honest. Being older than me, I never gave you much thought. Your reputation is one of gallivanting around the Côte d'Azur, like a bumble bee buzzing from flower to flower, going from one house party to another. I never took you for a reclusive curmudgeon who would rather read a book than drink champagne with the wealthy European set.'

'How little you know me,' he said.

'I don't think anyone knows you, Rupert.'

He smiled and tossed his cigarette butt into the long grass. 'Not yet, Flossie,' he replied. 'But *you* will.'

* * *

The summer progressed slowly and yet it did not, even for a moment, halt its relentless tread. At the beginning of the holidays, when the months of sunshine, parties and pastimes had stretched out in front of Florence in a seemingly never-ending sequence, she had thought autumn would never come. It was inconceivable for her that so many days would ever run their course and yet, run their course they did. July merged into August and the days began to get a little shorter and the light more mellow, bouncing off the water in wistful spangles of gold.

Florence saw a good deal of Rupert. Having typically kept away from the social gatherings in Gulliver's Bay, now he seemed to be everywhere. He was at church on Sundays, at picnic lunches on the beach and at dinners and barn dances. He joined in the cricket, umpiring admittedly, but still, he involved himself, waving at Florence who watched Aubrey keenly from a rug on the grass. He even joined a scavenger hunt, driving Florence, Cynthia and Elise around the countryside in search of the long list of things they needed to acquire in order to win the game, and he drove carefully because Florence asked him to. He had confided in her that he found the whole social scene preposterous and yet he certainly looked like he was enjoying himself.

'Who'd have thought arrogant old Rupert would join in the fun,' said Winifred, lying belly down on her beach towel in her swimsuit watching Rupert, Aubrey and a few other young men building a monumental sandcastle.

Florence lay beside her, her chin resting on her hands, her eyes obscured by a pair of fashionable round sunglasses. 'I can't imagine he's enjoying building a sandcastle. It's really not his thing at all,' she mused. 'He'd much prefer to be reading a book.'

'He's always been a bit older than us,' said Winifred thoughtfully. 'Maybe now that we're more grown up, he's happier to include himself.'

'I hadn't thought of that. You might be right. Last year, when I was sixteen and he was, what, twenty, he didn't even cast me a glance. This year he's become an unlikely friend.'

'It must be annoying having such a golden younger brother.' Winifred watched Aubrey, in a pair of shorts and unbuttoned shirt, his athletic limbs tanned and lithe, pat smooth the mountain on which they were building what looked more like a palace than a castle. 'Rupert's always been a bit of a misfit.'

'I like people who are different,' said Florence, watching Rupert fondly. 'I bet he's hating larking about over that silly castle.'

'He's dark and mysterious.' Winifred sighed. 'There's something about him . . .'

Florence grinned. 'Do you fancy him, Winnie?'

'A little. He has an allure, doesn't he, and you can't say he isn't handsome. He's too dangerous for me, though. I like more wholesome men.'

'Shame, because you could marry Rupert and I could marry Aubrey and then we'll always be together.'

'Rupert and Aubrey are destined for very different lives,' said Winifred.

'Well, of course, Rupert will inherit Pedrevan and Aubrey will make his own way in the world.'

'Aubrey will go into the priesthood,' said Winifred seriously.

For a moment Florence believed her. She opened her mouth in a gasp. Then Winifred shook with laughter. 'Got you there, didn't I! Silly old thing.'

Florence sat up. 'That's so mean, Winnie! How could you? I *will* marry Aubrey. You see if I don't.'

Florence noticed Rupert looking at her across the beach and felt a little self-conscious in her bathing suit. Nonetheless, she smiled and waved and he waved back. She wished Aubrey would look at her too, then she could wave at him as well, but he was too busy with his project to even cast a glance in her direction.

At length, the palace of sand was complete. It was undeniably spectacular with towers with cone-shaped roofs and everyone crowded round to admire it. The girls began to decorate it with pebbles and seaweed. Elise appeared with a bucket full of shells. Rupert, who had barely got his hands dirty, found a stick, tied a handkerchief around it and stuck it on top to resemble a flag. He stood back proudly. 'There, now it looks very grand,' he said. 'What do you think, Flossie?'

'It looks splendid,' she enthused. 'I don't think I've ever seen such a magnificent sandcastle.'

Aubrey was delving about in Elise's bucket. The two of them were smiling and he was mumbling something that Florence failed to hear.

'Very clever of you, Elise, to find those shells,' said Florence in an attempt to include herself.

Aubrey and Elise looked up in surprise. 'That's the bit I don't have patience for,' said Aubrey with a chuckle.

'I know,' Elise replied, giving him a playful nudge. 'That's why I collected them for you.'

'And we girls like to join in, don't we?' Florence added. She hadn't had any intention of decorating the castle, but she had to do something to halt this intimate conversation going on between Elise and Aubrey. She walked over and thrust her hand inside the bucket, lifting out a fistful of shells. She unfurled her fingers to look at them. To her surprise, among the typical Cornish shells were a few smooth pieces of sea glass. 'Look! How beautiful,' she exclaimed, separating them with her finger.

Aubrey looked into her palm and gasped. 'You found a blue one, Elise. Do you know how rare blue ones are?' He picked it up and turned it around slowly until it glowed a pale turquoise-green in the sunlight. 'This is a gem. A real beauty. Where did you find it?'

'By those rocks,' Elise replied, pointing to the far end of the beach, baffled that something so simple had piqued his interest.

'Come, let's see if we can find more. This is a real discovery.' Aubrey took Elise's hand and they ran off down the sand.

Winifred sidled up to Florence. 'Let it go, Flo,' she said softly, putting an arm around her shoulder. 'You're only going to get hurt.'

Florence lifted her chin. *An officer's daughter never cries.* She nodded and blinked back tears. As she was here with a handful of shells, she might as well decorate the damn castle, she thought bitterly. With a heavy heart she proceeded to place the shells round the castle with the other girls. They seemed to be enjoying themselves, but Florence couldn't care less. The tide would come in soon and wash it all away, so what was the point? When she was done, she wiped her hands on her bathing suit and wondered what to do. For a moment she felt forlorn there while everyone around her laughed and chatted and embellished the castle.

She felt a hand on her shoulder. It was Rupert. 'Fancy an ice cream?' he asked.

Florence glanced at the small figures at the end of the beach looking for sea glass. 'I'd love one,' she said, forcing a smile. 'In fact, I've never wanted one more.'

Rupert and Florence sat on the stone wall that separated the beach from the road and licked their vanilla ice creams. A pair of plump seagulls watched them greedily from the dunes, hoping to be tossed unwanted pieces of cone. Florence glanced at Rupert and grinned. 'You didn't really enjoy building that sandcastle, did you?' she said.

Rupert arched an eyebrow. 'How could you possibly think that? I enjoy nothing more than the building of sandcastles. In fact, if I had to choose my most favourite pastime, it would be that.' The slight curl of his lips told her otherwise.

Florence laughed. 'You're doing a fine job of mucking in, you know. Really, if there was a trophy for Most Enthusiastic Newcomer, it would go to you.'

He sighed. 'You're beginning to know me, Flossie.'

'You think you've fooled everyone else?'

'Of course. They all think I'm a team player. Little do they know I can't stand teams. The very word "team" makes me shudder.' He pulled a face that made Florence laugh again.

'So why do you do it? Why not retreat to your garden like the Selfish Giant and leave us all to it?'

He looked at her and frowned. There was a long pause while he seemed to deliberate his response. Finally, he shrugged and turned his gaze back to the beach. 'There's a girl I like,' he said softly.

Florence's eyes widened. She wondered whether it was Winnie. After all, he had waved at them a lot while he was building that castle. 'Are you going to tell me who she is?' Florence asked.

'Yes, I will, but not now.'

'Spoilsport.'

He chuckled and changed the subject. 'How are you getting on with that ice cream?'

'Nearly done.'

He threw the remainder of his cone at the seagulls who pecked at it ravenously. 'Little raptors,' he said. 'I'm surprised they can still fly after the rubbish they eat.'

'If you were a bird, what would you be?' Florence asked.

'A bateleur eagle.'

'I've never heard of it.'

'It's very beautiful. Native to Africa and Arabia. It has black and grey feathers, a red beak and red legs, which are very becoming, and it mates for life.'

'Like ducks.'

'Yes, I might have chosen a duck if they weren't so easily preyed on. What would you be, Flossie?'

She put her head on one side and narrowed her eyes thoughtfully. 'Well, I wouldn't want to be eaten by a predator.'

'Not even a bateleur eagle?'

'Especially not a bateleur eagle.' She grinned. 'I'd like to be a swallow. Being so nifty, I'd have a good chance of escaping your clutches.'

'I'm pretty swift, Flossie. You'd have to be on your mettle.'

'Oh, I'd keep an eye out for the likes of you and your very becoming red legs.'

He laughed. 'If I caught you, I wouldn't eat you.'

'You promise?'

'I might keep you, though, for pleasure.'

She laughed and nudged him playfully. 'Oh, Rupert!'

'Swallows like you are rare.'

'How so? They all look the same to me.'

'Did you know there are many different types of swallow? There's the barn swallow, the tree swallow, the cliff swallow and the bank swallow to name four. But you're not one of those. No, you're a rare swallow.'

'What type am I then?'

He gazed at her fondly. 'The Sun Swallow.'

'I like that.'

'Yes, if I captured *you*, I'd most definitely keep you, so that you would shine on me at every dawn and every sunset.'

'That sounds like a fairy tale,' said Florence.

'In which case it's sure to have a happy ending. Fairy tales always do.'

'You should write it. *The Sun Swallow* . . .'

'And *The Bateleur Eagle*.' He grinned knowingly. 'I already am.'

CHAPTER FIVE

The following day it poured with rain. Winifred, who was always resourceful, took out her paint box and sat at the round table in the bay window painting a study of a flower in water-colour. Florence hadn't the will to do anything. She lay on her bed and stared at the rain clattering against the window pane. She watched the drops land and merge and trail down the glass like tears. The sky was grey and heavy, like her heart. She knew she would never love another. How was it possible that Aubrey didn't feel the same? It was clear that he had eyes only for Elise. Florence had been foolish to hope. How could she have ignored it when all along the evidence had been dis-played very obviously right in front of her nose?

Because she hadn't *wanted* to see it.

Was she too spirited, she wondered? Too outspoken? Was she too full-bodied, perhaps? Or too blonde? Elise was petite and dark, like a forest sprite. And not a pretty forest sprite, either, Florence thought resentfully. Florence knew she was not beautiful, but she was much better looking than Elise and with far more personality. The only advantage Elise had over her was her nationality. Elise was French and there was something very attractive about the way she spoke English. Florence could change many things in order to become more appealing to Aubrey, but she could not become French.

A knock on the door prised her out of the vortex of self-pity. 'May I come in?' It was Uncle Raymond.

Florence sat up and hastily wiped her eyes. Uncle Raymond didn't wait for an answer but came straight in. He took one look at his niece's tear-stained face and perched on the edge of her bed with a sympathetic smile. 'Oh dear, you're as miserable as the weather,' he said.

Florence sighed. 'The sun will come out eventually,' she replied flatly, diverting her gaze to the window. 'It always does.'

'But it'll take more than sunshine to raise *your* spirits.'

'I'm fine. I've just got a headache.'

'Heartache more like. I recognized it at once. It has a certain brooding quality.'

'What do *you* know of heartache, Uncle Raymond?'

'I've suffered unrequited love, my sweet Flo, on more than one occasion and nothing hurts quite like it.'

'How do you know I'm suffering unrequited love?' It wasn't like Winifred to be indiscreet.

Uncle Raymond tapped his nose. 'I have my sources and I'm as wily as a fox. I don't miss anything. You've had a shine for Aubrey Dash for as long as I can remember.'

Florence chuckled bitterly. 'For as long as *I* can remember,' she added.

'He's fallen for the French girl, hasn't he?'

'How do you know that?'

'It was quite obvious when they came for dinner.'

Florence was baffled. 'Was it?'

'Sometimes one only sees what one wants to see,' he said kindly.

Florence started to cry. 'I really love him, Uncle Raymond.

I know I'll never love anyone else.' She put a hand on her chest. 'It hurts so much.'

'It does and I'm not going to say it'll get better, because you won't believe me. But no experience in life is wasted. Everything has a purpose. Think of it like a bank inside you from where, in the future, you can draw wisdom when you most need it. One day that bank will be full of every sort of pleasure and pain. When things get tough, which they will because no road is always smooth, you will be able to draw things out of it that will help you cope. You'll find resilience, willpower, strength, acceptance, patience, tolerance and compassion. You can't see it now, but perhaps Aubrey isn't the man for you. You're young, you have years ahead of you to find your soulmate. One day, when you're with Mr Perfect, you'll look back and thank Elise for saving you from Aubrey, who might never have made you happy.'

'I'm going to be Mrs Dash. I can feel it. That name fits me like a lambskin glove.' She looked at him with such intensity, Uncle Raymond could do nothing but agree with her.

'All right,' he conceded with a shrug. 'Then you must be patient.'

'I will.' Florence brightened at the thought. 'He'll grow beyond Elise. After all, she'll have to go back to France and they'll be unable to keep it going. He's much too young to marry, isn't he, Uncle Raymond?'

'Oh yes. Of course he is. They're barely adults. Don't you worry, my sweet Flo. Think of the story of the hare and the tortoise.'

'I'm the tortoise,' she said eagerly. 'I'll just plod along in my own time and overtake the hare when she gets complacent.'

He patted her hand. 'That's my girl.'

Florence looked at him and frowned. 'Uncle Raymond,

why aren't *you* married? You're handsome and funny and clever. If I wasn't your niece, I'd want to marry you.'

He laughed. 'I'm not the marrying type,' he said and there was something in his expression that stopped Florence from delving further. 'I think I shall always be a bachelor.'

Florence decided she would make her party the most spectacular party of the summer. One that Aubrey would always remember. She didn't need to ask her grandfather for money in order to do it, because the ideas she had didn't cost anything. They just cost time and effort, both of which she had in abundance. Invigorated with renewed energy she spent the three days before her party out of the social whirl, scavenging the recently harvested fields for straw. Following instructions in an arts and crafts book she bought in town, she made stars in a variety of sizes and styles and embellished them with ribbon. Then she borrowed tall sticks from the Dashes' farm, which she stuck in the sand equidistant from one another and attached the string and stars like bunting. She built benches in the sand and decorated them with leaves. Uncle Raymond and Rowley the butler helped her carry trestle tables down from the house and these she adorned with vases of flowers from the garden. Then she borrowed sixty jam jars from Cook into which she put the little candles Cook used for keeping the food warm. She cut out the silver paper from cigarette packets and adorned the jars with small stars stuck onto the glass. She would light them just as it was getting dark. The effect would be stunning.

The Pinfolds' beach had one very special feature: a cave. When the tide came in it was accessible from the outside only by boat, but when the tide was out, which her grandfather had told her it would be on the night of the party, it was reachable on foot. Florence would hang little glass lanterns on sticks to mark the way and light the inside of the cave with candles, for the walls were decorated naturally by minerals that had turned the rock green, red, blue and yellow. It would be wonderfully romantic. At the very back of the cave, beyond the reach of the water, was a hidden entrance. This entrance led into a tunnel that ran all the way up to the house. Used by locals in the olden days for smuggling, and by Florence and Winifred as children for entertainment, it was a well-kept secret. 'If ever we're in trouble, we'll use that tunnel,' Henry Pinfold liked to say, but Joan would laugh and tell him that the only place one ever really used such a tunnel was in a novel.

The evening of the party, Florence came up from the beach pink in the face and panting, having supervised the last-minute details. The maids had helped bring down glasses and jugs of lemonade under Rowley's supervision. Bottles of wine were cooling in ice buckets and Oliver, Cook's son, was preparing the cocktails. Flares had been lit down the garden and alongside the path to mark the way to the beach. The sky was clear of ominous clouds and the sea was calm. It promised to be a warm, balmy night.

Winifred was sitting on the terrace, painting her nails. Their mother was flicking through a magazine, smoking a cigarette. The doors to the house were open and classical music was playing on the gramophone. 'I hope you're going to have a bath,' said Winifred, glancing at her sister in amusement.

'Of course I'm going to have a bath,' Florence replied.

'I'm curious to see what you've been doing down on the beach these past days,' said Margaret, lifting her eyes off the page.

Florence grinned. 'You must come and look, but not until just before my guests arrive. There are dozens of candles to be lit first.'

Winifred laughed. 'I hope you haven't forgotten anything

important,' she said. 'Because you're bound to have forgotten something.'

'And wouldn't you love that, so that you could feel superior?'

'I'm sure you've done a splendid job,' said Margaret. 'Why would you forget anything when you've been working so hard?'

'And I've done it all on my own,' Florence said proudly. 'Barring a little help from Uncle Raymond and Rowley when muscles were required, and the kitchen, of course. I can't claim to have cooked so much as an egg.'

'I can't wait to see it,' said Margaret.

Winifred snorted and held her fingers out to dry. She clearly did not believe that her sister had managed to arrange a party.

Florence ignored her and hurried inside to bathe and change.

As she sat at her dressing table, pinning up her hair and curling it until it shone, she thought of Aubrey. She would not let him ruin her party, she told herself firmly. He would inevitably dance with Elise, but she wouldn't mind. She wouldn't allow them to get to her. This was *her* night. She'd worked so hard to achieve it. And, contrary to what Winifred thought, she had not missed a single detail. Aubrey might not love her back but he wouldn't fail to be impressed by the beauty of the beach.

When she appeared on the terrace in a pink and white dress with puffed sleeves she found Uncle Raymond and her grandfather enjoying a glass of scotch as they watched the sunset leak streaks of copper and gold onto the water. 'Isn't it beautiful?' she said.

The men turned to look at her. 'By Jove!' exclaimed Henry, staring at her with pleasure.

'Forget the sunset, sweet Flo. *You're* beautiful,' said Uncle Raymond.

Florence was pleased. She patted her hair. 'Do you like it?'

'I most certainly do,' Uncle Raymond replied. 'Very sophisticated. You look like an American film star.'

'She needs no encouragement,' said Henry, giving his son a reproachful look.

'That's the idea,' said Florence. 'I copied it from a magazine. It took ages.' She fidgeted with excitement. 'It's the perfect night for it. Thank goodness it isn't raining.' She inhaled the smell of wood smoke coming up from the beach. 'They must have lit the fire,' she said, capturing a sense of nostalgia in that old, familiar fragrance.

'I hope you're going to bake potatoes in the embers?' said Uncle Raymond.

'Of course,' Florence replied. 'Dinner wouldn't be complete without them.' She had a flash of memory, of seasonal workers who used to come to Kent from the East End of London to pick hops. They'd make their way down the rows of vines filling their baskets and then take them to the pretty oast houses where they'd be dried on the upper floors by fires lit beneath. Once, one of the farmers had allowed Florence and Winifred to bake potatoes in the embers. It was the most delicious potato she had ever tasted. 'It's nearly the end of summer,' she said, feeling wistful suddenly. 'I thought this day would never arrive.'

'Everything comes to pass,' said Uncle Raymond wisely.

'The good and the bad,' added Florence, thinking of Elise and Aubrey.

'Indeed,' Uncle Raymond agreed. 'All things come to those who wait is another one I'm particularly fond of.' Florence noticed the knowing curl on his lips.

'I'm going to have a wonderful time tonight,' she said resolutely.

'Might I escort you to the beach?' her uncle asked.

'I want to come and see what you've done down there too,' said Henry, putting his glass on the table.

At that moment, Margaret, Winifred and Joan stepped out in their finery. 'Grandpa and I will only stay for a short while,' Joan reassured Florence. 'You don't want your old grandparents ruining the party.'

'You won't ruin it. You'll make it,' said Florence, linking her arm with her uncle's. 'Come on then. Time to reveal all.'

The beach looked spectacular. Even from the top of the hill the twinkling lights and bonfire burned brightly through the dusk. The evenings were creeping in earlier and earlier now and already a granular quality had infiltrated the light, giving it a pinky-orange glow. The path was narrow and the family had to walk in single file between bramble and elder already flaunting their berries. Once they alighted onto the sand, they gazed in wonder at Florence's ingenuity. The effect of the straw bunting was charming and the illuminated path that led to the cave looked magical.

'It's splendid,' said Winifred in surprise. 'I don't think you've forgotten a single detail.'

'It looks like the fairies have done it,' said Joan. 'Don't you think so, Margaret?'

'I'm very impressed.' Margaret frowned, for she could never have achieved such an enchanting spectacle. 'I don't know how you did it.'

'I think I should patrol the cave,' said Henry, giving Florence a warning look. 'We don't want any hanky-panky going on in there.'

Uncle Raymond laughed. 'If there's no hanky-panky, there's no fun,' he retorted.

'Oh, Raymond!' chided his sister. 'The girls don't need any encouragement.'

'In my day our chaperones watched us like hawks,' said Joan.

'In my day too,' rejoined Margaret. 'However, these young people know each other so well, I hardly think they need to be supervised.'

'Florence and Winifred need to be protected not supervised,' said Henry. 'Look at them! They're like beautiful mermaids. They need protection from the pirates of Gulliver's Bay.'

'It's all right, Papa, there will be enough adults about to fight off the pirates,' said Margaret. She smiled anxiously at Florence, and Florence knew exactly what she was thinking. That she wished her husband were here for he wouldn't have allowed his daughters to attend a party unchaperoned.

Soon the beach began to fill up with guests and the band began to play. Florence stood with her family, greeting everyone as they arrived. She was only interested in one party, however, and that was the one from Pedrevan. Everyone commented upon her pretty pink and white dress and her new hairstyle, but there was only one person she wanted to impress. By the time he arrived, with Elise, of course, who looked nondescript in a simple olive-green dress, Florence was beginning to wonder whether he was coming at all. He was accompanied by his siblings and countless cousins. 'This is the perfect way to end the summer,' he said, taking her hand and kissing her on the cheek. 'I like your new look. It suits you.'

Florence beamed. 'Thank you, Aubrey,' she said. 'I'm sad it's come to an end, but there will always be next year.'

'Let's hope,' he replied, giving her a charming smile before striding over the sand towards the growing throng.

'You're the belle of the ball,' said Rupert, bending down to kiss her cheek.

'Oh, thank you, Rupert,' she replied, tearing her eyes away from the two figures now melting into the crowd of guests. 'You look dashing in your dinner jacket.'

'Will there be dancing?'

'Of course.'

'I hope you'll save one for me.'

'Naturally.'

'I'll come and find you.' She watched him walk towards the bonfire, one hand in his trouser pocket, the other reaching for a cocktail, and knew that she should be flattered that he had chosen to come; the elusive Rupert Dash had been won over. She wondered then who the mystery girl was that he admired and felt a surprising twinge of jealousy. He'd promised her he would tell her, but she wasn't sure now, as she observed him talking to Winifred and Cynthia, that she wanted to know. She didn't like to think of him with someone else. She'd been pleased that he'd sought her company, the Bateleur Eagle, haughty, aloof and enigmatic as he was. She rather liked being his Sun Swallow.

At last Florence was able to leave her place among her family and go and join her friends. She enjoyed the compliments for the beach did look like a fairy tale, and Cook had prepared a feast. As she passed the table laid out with food, she noticed the potatoes wrapped in aluminium foil in readiness for the embers. How she would like to sit with Aubrey and talk while the potatoes baked. But Aubrey did not leave Elise's side all evening. There was no point trying to separate them; all she could do was join them and observe their closeness.

'We're leaving for Kent the day after tomorrow,' Florence told them with a sigh of regret. 'I can't believe the summer is over.'

'I'm going back to France tomorrow,' said Elise.

'Tomorrow? That's sudden.'

Elise shrugged. 'Not really. My departure date has been fixed since I arrived.' She glanced at Aubrey. 'I've had fun, though, and I've learned English.'

'You've taught me not a word of French,' Aubrey complained with a smile.

'You liar. I have taught you many words.'

'You're right, I'm not being fair. And you didn't come here to teach us your language but to learn ours. I hope I've been a good teacher.'

She nodded. 'You've been the best teacher.'

Florence felt a sickness in her belly. 'Perhaps you can come back and teach us all French,' she said, dragging her mouth into an awkward smile.

Aubrey looked pleased with her suggestion, however, which relieved some of the sickness. 'Florence is right. You'll have to come back. It's not goodbye but farewell.'

'Is there a difference?'

'Oh, yes,' he said and the way he looked at Elise was too much for Florence to bear.

'I'm sorry, I've just noticed something I need to attend to right away,' she said.

Florence hurried down the beach between the lanterns, stopping only to take off her shoes so that she could run faster in the sand. When she reached the cave, she put a hand against the damp rock and gave in to tears.

'Flossie? Are you all right?'

She turned to see Rupert's worried face in the mouth of the cave. It was no good pretending she had something in her eye. 'I'm fine, just sad the summer is ending,' she said, wiping her cheek.

He frowned. 'That's the worst explanation for tears I've ever heard.'

She smiled sheepishly as he drew nearer. 'It was the only thing I could think of.'

'You need to do better. Why not just tell the truth? We're friends, aren't we?'

'Oh, Rupert, it's not as simple as that.'

He ran his eyes around the cave. The dancing flames illuminated the walls like flickering silent movies. 'This is a splendid place.'

'It used to be a smuggler's cave.'

'Of course it did.'

'I thought it would be romantic to light it up, but what's the point?'

'It *is* romantic.' He turned to her and smiled. 'You shouldn't be crying, Flossie, not in here.' There was a tenderness in his expression that Florence hadn't seen before and she felt something stir in her stomach.

'If my grandfather found us alone together, he'd have you hanged, drawn and quartered.'

'I doubt he'll find us in here.' Rupert grinned. Like Florence, he was never worried about breaking rules. He held out his hand. 'Would you like to dance?' The music was faint, but they could hear it above the lapping of waves. The band was playing a waltz. 'Come on, a dance will cheer you up. You can't deny you need cheering up?'

She put her hand in his and let him draw her towards him with the other hand, nestled comfortably in the small of her back. They began to dance around the cave. For a while neither spoke. Rupert was a smooth dancer and a confident one too. He guided her masterfully over the sand, steadying her when her foot stumbled on uneven ground. Being so close to him did not make her feel uneasy as it had when they had sat side by side on the gate. In fact, it made her feel comforted. It was as if she now knew him so well that his touch felt reassuringly familiar. Confused suddenly by her unexpected change of heart she stepped on his shoe. They both laughed. He was right, dancing did cheer her up. 'There, now you're feeling better, aren't you?'

'I am,' she said, drawing away from him, breathless. 'I do like to dance.'

'Barring the odd clumsy step in the sand, and on my foot, you're a natural.'

'As are you, Rupert. But I expect all Dashes to dance like princes.'

'I might not be adept on the tennis court or even on the croquet lawn, but I do move lightly around the dance floor. At least I can say that for myself.' His smile was diffident.

'Who cares about tennis and croquet? It's a person's character that counts. There are so many dull people around. No one could ever say you're dull, Rupert. You're a Bateleur Eagle, after all.'

'And you're a Sun Swallow, Flossie.' His voice was full of affection. 'We have much in common, you and I. I think that's why I like you so much. I recognize a kindred spirit.'

'Because we're both naughty?'

'That's part of it, I suppose. Neither of us likes to do as we're told. But there's something else. Something I can't quite put my finger on. Something beyond naughty.' He frowned and narrowed his eyes, searching for the right word. 'I *know* you.'

Florence couldn't grasp what he meant. The way he was looking at her was now making her nervous. 'You've been kind, Rupert,' she said. 'Thank you.'

He took her hand. There was an unfamiliar glint in his

eye. A look of intent. Florence's stomach lurched with dread and yet, at the same time, excitement. He pulled her towards him, wound his hand around the back of her neck and kissed her lips. She was so stunned, she didn't know what to do. She had never been kissed before. The feeling of his lips on hers was strangely pleasurable. She did not pull away, nor did she protest. He gently parted them and his tongue found hers. Something hot and sharp shot into her belly. She caught her breath. The sensation was so sensual and so forbidden that she did not tell him to stop. She could not. Instead, she closed her eyes and gave in to it, allowing it to carry her for a moment like an ill wind to nowhere good. A wind that she knew well, having allowed it to lead her into trouble countless times before. As the kiss deepened she began to feel an ache, a voluptuous feeling of desire that she had never felt, not even in her dreams. So surprised and confused was she by the curious way her body was responding that she opened her eyes with a start.

It hadn't occurred to her that he might have found her attractive. It hadn't crossed her mind that he might want to kiss her. That she was the girl he had spoken of; the girl he liked.

She put a hand on his chest and gently pushed him away. 'No, Rupert . . .'

He laughed softly, one hand still on her waist, the other tracing her cheek. 'My darling Flossie. Didn't you realize that I love you?' She stared up at him, puzzled. 'How could you not? Why else do you think I've put up with endless social nightmares all these weeks? For the fun of watching Aubrey serve aces on the tennis court and hit sixes across the cricket pitch? For the enjoyment of building castles in the sand? No, for the pleasure of being near *you*.'

'Oh, Rupert . . .'

'You're special, Flossie. You're an original. You're not like the other girls. You have character and spirit. You have fire in you. Look at what you've created tonight. It's wonderful. No one else could have done it. Who else would think of making stars out of straw and hanging them up like bunting? Only you. Only you, Flossie. Just the sight of you makes me happy.'

'But I didn't think . . .'

'Why else would I have taken you on a drive? Why else would I have stayed in Gulliver's Bay, but for you? I want to marry you. I can see us both at Pedrevan, you hosting cricket matches and me watching you from the window, longing for them all to go home so that I can have you to myself.'

'But I'm not even eighteen . . .'

'Then I'll wait.'

'Rupert, I love another.'

He would not have looked more astonished and pained if she had punched him in the stomach. His face drained of colour and his eyes dulled suddenly, the light in them extinguished. 'Who? Whom do you love?' His expression was so full of hurt that she felt mortified to have caused it. She could not tell him the truth.

'Someone you don't know,' she mumbled. 'But he doesn't love me back. In fact, he loves someone else, so it's futile, really.'

'Now you know how *I* feel.'

'Oh Rupert, if that's true, then I've made you the most miserable man alive.'

'You have,' he replied. 'But I won't hold it against you.' He chuckled bitterly and put his hands in his trouser pockets. He shrugged. 'What a pair we are.'

'I'm sorry . . .' Florence began to cry. She felt wretched

hurting him and, for the first time that summer, uncertain of her own heart.

Rupert wrapped his arms around her and kissed her temple. 'You're young, who knows what the future holds.' He closed his eyes and inhaled the scent of her hair. 'You've given me a marvellous summer. I suppose I should be grateful for that.'

He smiled down at her sadly, taking in every detail of her face and then made for the opening of the cave.

'What will you do?' she asked, feeling something slipping away from her and not wanting it to go.

'I don't know. But I shall be far from here by this time tomorrow.'

Florence wanted to say something to prevent him from leaving, but there was nothing she could say.

'Bye, Flossie. Look after yourself now. You're a special girl. A Sun Swallow. I daresay the man you love is undeserving of you.'

'And you?'

'Oh, I deserve you. We're birds of a feather. We deserve each other. But you can't see that yet.' With one last backwards glance, he added, almost out of earshot, 'I'll wait for you.'

Florence remained a while in the cave, replaying over and over in her mind what had just happened. She traced her fingers over her lips and frowned. Her eyes lingered in the mouth of the cave, hoping that he'd come back. Water was slowly edging its way in as the tide crept up the beach, melting Rupert's footprints in the sand. When she was sure he wouldn't reappear, she climbed the bank of rock at the back of the cave, found the secret tunnel and made her way slowly up to the house, drowning in disappointment. She didn't have the heart to party anymore.

CHAPTER SIX

London, 1988

The air was thick with smoke and the loud, staccato sound of gunfire. Gripped with a fear too great to comprehend, he blinked through the cold sweat that seeped into his eyes and made them sting. Smoke caught in his throat. He struggled to breathe. He was aware of the weight of his uniform, the grip of his helmet, the gun in his hands and a sick feeling of panic cramping his stomach. The sky was filled with parachutes, like hundreds of jellyfish in a polluted sea, sinking slowly to earth. Gliders flew above them like cranes and some lay scattered on the heath, their bellies ripped apart, entrails aflame. Through the smoke he could see the tall, thin trunks of trees. He knew they sheltered him from the gunfire, but he was aware that he could not stay where he was. He had a mission to complete and although terrified to his core, the stronger part of him – courage – drove him on, lifting him above the sense of helplessness that rooted him to the ground. All around him was chaos; men running, shouting, falling, dying, and above the noise the incessant sound of gunfire.

Max sat up with a sob so violent that it made his whole body shake. He blinked into the dimness, taking in his surroundings, trying to fathom where he was. His heart was pounding against his ribs, the blood pulsating in his temples, the sensations he had felt so vividly still reverberating through him like the aftershock of an earthquake. Gradually, he began to realize that he was no longer on a battlefield but in his bed in Battersea, South London. Little by little, the grey light of dawn illuminated the pictures on the wall, the cherrywood dresser, the upholstered chair and, finally, the woman sleeping beside him. His breathing grew calmer. The sweat cooled on his brow and the sensations of fear and panic began to evaporate like mist. The black and white images receded, but the bewilderment remained, with the faint smell of cordite; he'd had this dream before, many times, as a boy. Why was he having it again now as a twenty-five-year-old man?

He climbed out of bed and went into the bathroom. He closed the door softly and switched on the light. The sudden glare chased away the last remnants of the battlefield. The floor was cold on his bare feet. It was a welcome feeling, being connected so physically to the now; what he'd just experienced was a hell to which he never wanted to return. He stood in front of the basin and looked at his reflection in the mirror. His face was pale, his eyes haunted, his brown hair sticking up in thick tufts. He ran his fingers over the few days' growth of stubble as if a moment ago he'd been someone else and now he wanted to make sure he was himself again.

Many times he'd tried to make sense of the recurring nightmare. As a teenager he'd thought perhaps it had something to do with his desire to join the army, as his father had done. But now he had left the Blues and Royals, it didn't seem relevant. Max had wondered, perhaps, whether it was a prediction of what was to come, but that didn't feel right, either. The idea of having lived before was not something he ruled out; he had

had a fascination with the esoteric since childhood and he'd read some extraordinary books on the subject. Typically, past life dreams dreamed in childhood disappeared in early adulthood, when the dominant, present life experiences took over. Max hadn't had this nightmare since he was about thirteen. Why had it come back?

He splashed his face with cold water, took some deep breaths and shook off the trauma. He looked at his watch. It was six-thirty on a grey February morning. As it was a Saturday and he was now awake, he decided he'd go for a run around the park.

Leaving his fiancée sleeping, he crept out of the bedroom and dressed in the spare room. He put on his earphones and tucked his Walkman into his tracksuit pocket. He'd recorded a good tape especially for running: Queen, David Bowie, the Rolling Stones and some tracks from *Les Misérables*. It was cold outside. A thin layer of frost covered the grass, patches of mist lingered here and there in pools of vaporous cloud, and the sun, weak and cold, tried to penetrate the flat white sky but only succeeded in sending the occasional beam of light to thaw the frozen ground. With the sound of 'Bohemian Rhapsody' in his ears Max jogged over the tarmac. There were few people in the park at this hour. The odd dog walker or cyclist wrapped in thick coats and hats, their breath foggy on the icy air. Street lamps still lit up the broad walk, and the plane trees, like petrified monsters, stood gnarled and twisted in the cold. The park looked beautiful, like a stage before the curtain rises and the footlights blaze. Max wished he'd brought his camera. By the time he returned home the light would have changed and the magic of dawn been consumed by the dreary, mundane light of morning.

After his run he found Elizabeth at the kitchen table in

her cashmere dressing gown with a cup of coffee and a bowl of cornflakes, reading the *Daily Mail*. Her wavy brown hair was tied in a ponytail and her pale English skin glowed as if lit from within. She didn't lift her eyes off the paper when he came in. Max took off his earphones and smiled, appreciating how lovely she looked first thing in the morning. 'Hi, gorgeous,' he said.

'How was your run?' she asked, turning a page.

'It's really beautiful out there. Frost, mist . . .'

'Jennifer's in Dempster again,' she interrupted. Jennifer, Elizabeth's sister, was being courted by a distant cousin of the Queen and was, almost weekly, in Nigel Dempster's gossip column.

'What's she up to this time?' he asked, taking a mug from the cupboard.

'Dancing on the tables in Tramp, apparently.'

'Sounds like Jennifer.'

Elizabeth laughed. 'It certainly does.' Elizabeth, unlike her sister, was not wild. She was conservative, sensible and acutely aware of her social status, which was, by her definition, upper class, just beneath the aristocracy. It was not a bad thing that her sister was dating an aristocrat, or even that it was publicized in the newspapers. What *was* a bad thing, however, was Jennifer's undignified behaviour that gave jealous people the opportunity to criticize. 'I hope we don't have heaps of press at our wedding,' Elizabeth added thoughtfully. 'It's incredibly tacky.'

'I don't think anyone's interested in us.'

Elizabeth looked at him with irritation. 'They're interested in Jennifer and Archie, Max, and they're coming.'

Max emptied the percolator into the bin and refilled it with ground coffee. 'I had a nightmare last night,' he told her. 'I used to have it as a child, all the time. I haven't had it for years and then, last night, I dreamed it again.'

'Discussing one's dreams is very boring, darling,' said Elizabeth, turning her attention back to the newspaper.

Max filled the base of the percolator with water and put it on the stove. 'This isn't an ordinary dream. It's a recurring dream about a battlefield.'

'Really,' she murmured with disinterest.

'It's so vivid, I can smell the cordite.' He frowned and shook his head. 'I can *still* smell the cordite.'

'I'm having lunch with Mummy today at the Caprice after my dress fitting. You have no idea how much of a perfectionist Catherine Walker is. To me it looks perfect, but every time I see her she tweaks it a little here and a little there. I'm not trying to lose weight, but it just seems to be falling off. I'm not at all nervous, but excitement can also make one lose a few pounds, apparently.'

'You haven't got any pounds to lose, Bunny.'

At the sound of her family nickname, she smiled. 'I like it when you call me Bunny.'

Max came up behind her and planted a kiss on her neck. She giggled at the scratchy feel of his bristles. '*How* much do you like it when I call you Bunny?'

'Not *that* much.' She shook him off. 'Besides, you should shower.'

'How about when I come out of the shower?' He kissed her again, his lips lingering on her skin. He inhaled deeply. 'You smell nice.'

'That's because I've showered. Really, darling, you pong, and you're very sweaty. Go and have a shower. I might have been willing had you suggested it while we were both in bed, but now I'm up, I'm up. And I don't want to shower again.'

Max was disappointed. He'd like to have spent the rest of the morning in bed, making love to her. 'All right, but you can't blame me for trying. If you weren't so ravishing, I wouldn't be interested.'

Elizabeth was ravishing in Max's eyes. She had long, chestnut-coloured hair, clear, untroubled blue eyes, warm white skin and a slim, elegant figure. He loved the sprinkle of freckles over her small nose and her cool English reserve. There was something eternally challenging about that.

'Why don't you join us for lunch?' Elizabeth suggested. 'Mummy would love to see you.'

'Isn't it a girls' lunch?'

'Not if *you* join us.'

Max hesitated. He didn't like Elizabeth's mother and he'd planned to spend the day in the dark, developing photographs he'd taken recently on holiday skiing in the Alps.

'Don't worry. You don't have to,' she added in a clipped voice.

Max knew that tone well. It warned of offence followed by a long sulk. His heart sank. 'Sure, I'd love to,' he said, trying to sound cheerful.

'Good,' she replied.

The percolator announced with a hiss that the coffee was ready. Max poured himself a cup and took it upstairs. He didn't relish the thought of having lunch with Antoinette, but if it pleased Elizabeth he'd suffer an hour or so with her mother. Elizabeth and Antoinette were extremely close and Max had to mind what he said about his future mother-in-law.

Antoinette Pemberton turned heads when she walked into the Caprice with her daughter. In her mid fifties she was good-looking, albeit a touch starched. Her red hair was blow-dried in a bouffant that was so stiff it would not have stirred even in a gale. Her long, elegant nails were varnished a rich scarlet to match her lips and her teeth were very white. A slight over-bite gave her mouth an attractive pout and her eyes, the same serene blue as her daughter's, were vivacious and acute. The maître d' knew her well and they exchanged a few cheerful words at the door. Antoinette gave her fur coat to the girl, revealing beneath it an emerald green skirt suit with sharp shoulder pads and a nipped-in waist, accentuated by a thin belt. Her heels were not too high and embellished with little gold snaffle bits. Elizabeth, in a similar suit to her mother's, glanced about the room to see if there was anyone she knew. Being a Saturday, they were mostly out-of-towners, she thought with disdain. As usual Max was late. Elizabeth sighed with exasperation; Max was *always* late.

When he arrived the two women were already at the table. Elizabeth watched him make his way between the tables and her irritation dissipated, for Max Shelbourne cut a dash and drew every female eye in the room, and a few male ones besides. He was tall and good-looking with a broad, athletic build and a confident stride. She immediately forgave his tardiness.

'Sorry I'm late,' he said, kissing Antoinette on her powdered cheek. 'Roadworks in Chelsea. The taxi had to do a detour.'

'Don't worry, Max,' said Antoinette, running her incisive gaze over his jacket and tie. She would have preferred him not to wear jeans, however. 'I'm just happy you're here. How lovely that you could join us.'

'The dress is divine,' said Elizabeth, giving him her lips. 'It has to be taken in yet again.'

Max kissed her, then sat down. 'I don't want you fading away, darling.'

'Oh, Bunny won't fade away, don't you worry,' said Antoinette, crinkling her nose at her daughter. 'It's natural to have pre-wedding nerves.'

'I'm not at all nervous, Mummy. Just excited.'

'Same thing, darling.' Antoinette smiled at Max. 'We're having peach Bellinis. What would you like?' Max glanced at her champagne flute and noticed the red lipstick ring on the glass. She also had lipstick on her teeth.

'A glass of white wine would be nice, thank you.'

Max listened with feigned interest as they told him about the dress and discussed wedding plans. Elizabeth had made a list at the General Trading Company on Sloane Street and was already receiving gifts. She was particularly excited about the Herend porcelain her godmother had given her. They ordered lunch. Antoinette requested two more Bellinis and a bottle of Sancerre. The wedding, set for May, dominated the conversation. Who had replied, who hadn't, who was lucky to have been invited, who was coming from abroad. The reception was to be held in Pavilion Road, Knightsbridge, which was suitably fashionable and conveniently close to the hotel where they were going to spend their wedding night. 'It's going to be super,' said Elizabeth, looking directly at Max. It was then that he realized that his attention had drifted off and he hadn't a clue what she was talking about.

It was only when Antoinette ordered a black coffee that she asked Max about himself. Max would rather they'd stuck to the wedding. 'How's the new job coming along?' she enquired with a smile, because her husband Michael had arranged it for him, pulling various strings and putting in the odd word.

'It's great,' Max replied, mustering up enthusiasm he didn't feel. He hated his job, working for a small stockbroking firm in the City, and he hated living in London. He hadn't intended to leave the army, but Elizabeth hadn't wanted to be an army wife, living in married quarters in Germany, and he had most definitely not wanted to go into finance. He really wanted to be a photographer, but, as Elizabeth kept reminding him, taking photographs was unlikely to make him any money, and besides, the kind of photography he wanted to do required travel, and Elizabeth had suffered enough with him being away in the army; she wanted him at home.

'You did the right thing leaving the regiment,' Antoinette continued, crinkling her nose again. 'You'll earn much more money in stockbroking and, I'm afraid to say, making money is important if you're going to marry and raise a family. It's all very well having romantic ideas of pursuing something more creative, like photography, but at the end of the day, my Bunny needs a man who can support her and,' she added, smiling affectionately at Elizabeth, 'she does have rather expensive taste. Stockbroking is a job for life, Max. Michael, as you know, has worked for the same company for over thirty years. That's security.' Max's heart sank. The thought of being tied to Smith Bellingham for the rest of his life made him want to slit his wrists.

Elizabeth put her hand on his and gave it a reassuring squeeze. 'It's always tough at the beginning, darling. Starting anything new is daunting. When I started at Annabel Jones, I was terrified. I had no idea how to use the till. I was pathetic. And having to learn what all the different stones were. I knew nothing about jewellery, only how to wear it.' She looked down at the engagement ring that had belonged to Max's great-grandmother.

'You wear it well,' he said.

Elizabeth smiled. The ring was suitably big with a sapphire sandwiched between two diamonds. 'Wasn't it brilliant that it fits? We didn't even need to alter it. That's fate for you.' She gazed at him with affection. 'It was meant to be.'

That night they made love. Max lost himself in Elizabeth's soft body and he forgot about his frustration with his job and his longing to move out of London. After three years his lust for Elizabeth had not diminished. When he was in her arms he did not want to be anywhere else. However, when they were not entwined, doubts had been creeping in for some time and taking root in the fragile bed of his happiness. The reality was that he hadn't been happy for months. It was too easy to put the leaden feeling in his chest down to his unsatisfactory circumstances, but the problem was closer to home. When he dared examine himself frankly, he realized that the reason for his discontent was Elizabeth. A coldness had sneaked into their relationship where once there had been warmth. He questioned whether she had changed, or whether, perhaps, he was only noticing now how deeply incompatible they really were. These moments of self-analysis were brief, however, because, as the wedding day approached and with it the cul-mination of all Elizabeth's aspirations, the truth was simply too uncomfortable to face.

When their lovemaking was over, Max picked up his book and Elizabeth flicked through *Tatler*. He glanced across at her. 'You know, I've been thinking about my dream.'

Elizabeth sighed. 'It's a dream, darling. Let it go.'

'I think it's more than a dream.'

She glanced at the book he was reading. *Initiation* by Elizabeth Haich. 'You read too many of those silly books. Isn't that the one about that woman who believes she was an Egyptian priestess in a past life?'

'Yes,' he replied. They'd discussed this subject before and

it hadn't gone well, but somehow Max always hoped she'd become more open to the possibility of life beyond death.

'Why is it that everyone who believes they have lived before were either Catherine the Great, Cleopatra or Henry VIII? Why isn't anyone a simple farmer or a shopkeeper?'

'They are. Most people who have past life regressions led very ordinary lives. And who's to say you weren't someone famous? Somebody has to have been.'

'It's ridiculous. The truth is we die and that's the end of it. People want to believe there's life after death or that we are reincarnated because they can't accept that there's nothing. But I wasn't aware of myself before I was born and I won't be aware of myself when I'm dead, so what does it matter? I don't need to make up stories to make me feel better about death.'

'Aren't you even open to the possibility that life goes on?'

She screwed up her pretty nose. 'Not really. I'm not particularly interested.'

'Don't you want to believe that those you love who are dead live on?'

'I haven't lost anyone I care about yet.'

'Maybe you'll change your opinion when you do.'

'If you go before me, you can haunt me. Rattle the odd doorknob or write your name in shaving foam on the bathroom mirror, then I'll believe you. Anyway, what were you saying about your dream?'

Max didn't feel like sharing it now. The post-coital glow had died in the harsh light of their differences and he felt strangely detached from her. 'Nothing.' He turned his attention back to his book.

Elizabeth put down her magazine with a sigh. 'Come on, you were going to tell me something.'

'You won't understand.'

'Try me.'

'I just did.'

'All right, don't.' That clipped tone again. She picked up the magazine and flicked through it crossly.

Max would do almost anything to avoid a sulk. 'All right, I'm thinking of finding a psychic to explore my dream. I think it could be a past life recall.'

Elizabeth rolled her eyes. 'You'll probably discover you were Henry VIII.'

'Henry VIII was not involved in an airborne battle in the Second World War.'

She smiled, more to herself than to Max. 'You're mad.'

'That's what I thought you'd say.'

'Sorry, but I can't pretend I think it's a good idea.'

'That's why I didn't want to tell you.'

'We just have to agree to disagree on that subject. I don't want our marriage to be soured by your whacky beliefs.'

Max was affronted, but he didn't want to go to sleep after a fight. 'I agree,' he said and he felt the tension in the air dissipate. But when they finally turned off the light, he was burning with such resentment he couldn't sleep. He stared at the ceiling as Elizabeth curled into a ball with her back to him. He heard her breathing slow and then the mild snoring that never normally bothered him, but now filled him with fury.

He got out of bed and dressed in the spare room. Then he crept out of the house, closing the front door quietly behind him. As he inhaled the crisp night air he felt a wave of relief. It was so profound that it took him by surprise. He thrust his hands into his coat pockets and began to walk. The streets were empty, the lights glowing orange through the mist. A light drizzle dampened the air. One or two cars came and went, but otherwise the roads were quiet. He thought of everyone asleep in their houses. The curtains and blinds were closed, the interiors dark. A stillness gave the city a surreal quality.

Max thought of his dream. He remembered every detail as if it were a recent memory. Dreams usually evaporated soon after waking, but this one remained, as if he had lived it, as if the impression of the experience was embossed upon his soul. He could feel the uniform against his skin, the boots on his feet, the helmet on his head, the gun in his hand. The sound of gunfire still echoed in his ears. If he really allowed himself to sink into it, he could taste the metallic flavour of fear in his mouth. This was no ordinary dream.

He walked faster. He thought of Elizabeth and her scorn burned. They were so very different. Of course, when they'd met, three years before at a party, their differences hadn't mattered. They'd been so strongly attracted to each other. But now, as he marched towards Albert Bridge, an increasingly familiar thought once again crept into his mind like a black shadow. What if Elizabeth was not the right woman for him?

He reached the middle of the bridge and stared down at the water. The street lamps dribbled molten copper onto the surface as a cold wind sent a ripple across it, causing the copper to quiver and spread. Max saw beauty in it and his heart ached with longing. For what, he did not know, but the longing was deep and searing. He took a breath and the shadow darkened into anxiety. He loved Elizabeth, but he did not like her intolerance, her closed mind, her obstinate materialism. She would never understand him. With such a canyon between them, could their minds ever meet? Never before had he felt so lonely. The wedding was just under three months away. He was about to tie himself to another human for life. To have and to hold, from this day forth, for ever more. The feeling of desolation was overwhelming.

If he called off the wedding he'd hurt her badly. He swore and ran a hand through his hair and closed his eyes. The thought of hurting her was unbearable. His parents would be delighted. They'd never warmed to Elizabeth. They were country people and she was too crisply urban for their sensibilities. Michael and Antoinette would be devastated and furious. They'd curse him for humiliating their daughter and for his ingratitude. Because of them he had a good job and a future – neither of which he really wanted.

No, he couldn't do it. So, Elizabeth didn't share his spiritual beliefs, but did it matter? Was it so important that she believe in life after death, reincarnation, the spirit world, the evolution of the soul? Did it matter that she was shallow? Did it matter that they didn't share the same values? He felt sick in his stomach because he knew. He felt it in his gut. It *did* matter. It mattered more than anything. As he stared into the Thames, he understood his longing. It was his soul's yearning for a more profound and meaningful connection with another. Someone who could walk beside him down this road of self-discovery. Someone who understood because she was heading in the same direction.

He put his head in his hands. What on earth was he going to do?

CHAPTER SEVEN

The following morning, Max awoke with the usual feeling of arousal. Elizabeth lay beside him. He could feel the warmth of her body and his arousal intensified. He didn't think of his midnight walk and the agony of the insight that walk had given him. In the soft light of morning all he thought about was his immediate desire and Elizabeth's likely willingness to satisfy it.

He put a hand on her waist. She stirred. He edged closer, spooning her from behind. Slowly he slipped his hand beneath her nightdress and felt the satin texture of her skin and the fullness of her hips and breasts. She murmured, a sign that she liked it. In that moment, the thought of breaking off their engagement could not have been further from his mind. His hands moved over her thighs and slipped between them where it was warm and inviting. Elizabeth let out a soft moan and parted them.

They spent the rest of the morning enjoying a long breakfast, reading the newspapers. The intimacy of their lovemaking lingered in the air between them, allaying the ill feeling of the night before. Elizabeth smiled and Max smiled back, confident suddenly that his doubts were nothing more than pre-wedding nerves. It was a relief; Elizabeth was the right woman for him, after all. How could he have doubted her? How dull it would be to spend one's life with someone who always agreed. Elizabeth was a challenge and he liked that.

They lunched at the local pub with a group of friends. Max ordered steak and chips. Elizabeth stole a chip, dipped it in ketchup and popped it into her mouth. The look she gave him made him feel warm inside, and relieved. He was getting married, not going to the gallows. He needed to calm down.

The following week Max went to work as usual. He walked across the park and over the bridge, catching the tube from Sloane Square into the City. It was a long commute, and the walk made it longer, but he needed it. The trees, bare and shivering as they were, lifted his spirits. The sight of snow-drops growing in white puddles and burgeoning green shoots of daffodils rising up from the earth made him feel happy. The birds had started to twitter, a sign that spring was on its way at last, and the mornings were brighter. When he returned home in the evening it was dark. If he didn't walk in the morning he'd miss the light altogether.

He loathed his job and it was a struggle every day to accomplish his tasks. It wasn't that he couldn't do it. The actual job was unchallenging and he was bright; he knew that if he remained there as his father-in-law-to-be had done, he would rise to the top. But at the end of each day he felt as if another chunk of his soul had been eaten away, like a mouse nibbling at cheese. He felt demoralized, dissatisfied and frustrated. He knew, deep down, that he wasn't meant to be doing this. He wasn't meant to be in an office, surrounded by concrete, gazing out of the window in search of the blue between the high-rise buildings. He was meant to be in nature, capturing the wonder of it with his Leica.

Max fought the feeling of hopelessness that usually assaulted him as he walked back through the park in the dark. He no longer saw the snowdrops and daffodils, and the tarmac, glistening in the orange glow of the street lamps, reminded him that nature was contained in this manicured urban space and was a poor substitute for rolling hills, woodland and lakes. Elizabeth worked in Beauchamp Place. She took the bus into Chelsea, then, depending on the weather, either walked or took a cab to Annabel Jones. She liked her job. The clientele was what her mother would call 'proper people'. People like *them*. Barely a day went by when she didn't see a familiar face in the shop. That made her happy. She was content with her life. She wanted nothing more than what she had and the future stretched out before her, comfortably and reassuringly familiar.

But for Max the feeling of dislocation only grew stronger. The nights were darker and, in the darkness, when material things fell away and he was left with only thoughts and the murmurings of his heart, his doubts returned with increasing power. He was getting married in three months' time. Was this it? Was this what his life was to be? Was there nothing more? And the murmurings grew louder and more succinct: *There is more, but you have to find it.* Max reached out to the higher power that he knew was with him on every step of his path and put out a simple request, one which, oddly, he had never asked before: *Help me.*

The following week he and Elizabeth went to a dinner party in Kensington. Max hadn't wanted to go, but Elizabeth had insisted; the hostess was her godmother, Valerie Alcott, and Elizabeth's parents, Antoinette and Michael, would be there. Max had tried to wriggle out of it, but Elizabeth had been deaf to his excuses, even the one that cited the possibility that he was coming down with flu. So Max found himself in Valerie's overly upholstered home, smiling politely, telling anyone who asked, how much he enjoyed his job in the City and how excited he was about the impending wedding.

Michael Pemberton was a man accustomed to being listened to. He was tall and robust with a head of thick, light-brown hair and wide-set brown eyes that took command of the room that evening as if *he* were the host and not diminutive, gushing Valerie. In a burgundy smoking jacket and matching velvet slippers embroidered in gold with the initials M.P., he dominated the gathering, one hand in his pocket, the other holding a champagne flute. The large signet ring on his left pinkie caught the light from the fire and glinted sharply as if confirming his authority. He was not interested in women. They were there to embellish a room like pretty flowers, and it was best that they did not voice opinions. He'd educated his two sons at Eton, where he himself had thrived, but his two daughters had been sent to North Foreland Lodge in Hampshire where they'd met the right sort of girls and been suitably prepared for marriage. He was surrounded by men at one end of the room, while the women sat around the fire discussing the wedding.

Max managed not to be sucked into Michael's group. They were discussing markets and investments, which bored him. He moved towards the women, but when he heard them talking excitedly about bridesmaids' dresses and pages' patent shoes, he felt a sickness in his stomach and went to the bookcase instead where he found a whole shelf dedicated to Mills & Boon romances. It was going to be a long evening.

'Hello,' came a voice. He turned to see an elderly lady looking up at him with vivacious green eyes. 'I'm Olga Groot.'

He shook her hand. She must have only just arrived, he

decided, for she hadn't been there when he had first entered the room. 'Max Shelbourne,' he replied. 'How do you do?'

'I don't imagine romantic fiction is your thing,' she said with a grin and her lively face glowed with character and charm.

He laughed. 'No, it's not.'

'What *is* your thing?' She was wearing a long purple scarf over a long purple dress and seemed quite out of place here in this conventional drawing room.

'I'm drawn to more spiritual books,' he told her, wondering why he hadn't just said Wilbur Smith.

'Me too,' she replied. 'What are you reading at the moment?'

'Elizabeth Haich.'

'*Initiation*? I loved it. Fascinating. Although there were parts of it that I had to read twenty times to even begin to grasp them.'

Max was pleasantly surprised. 'The numbers and equations bits did rather baffle me too,' he agreed, suddenly feeling wide awake and alert as if someone had slipped something into his champagne.

'Have you read Edgar Cayce?'

'Oh yes, I've read all his books.'

'Once you start searching it's wonderful how the universe conspires to help you. All at once things fall into your path.'

Max arched an eyebrow. How extraordinary that, after only two minutes of having met, they were discussing the esoteric. 'I think you've just fallen into mine,' he said, lowering his voice. 'How do you know Valerie?'

'I'm her mother,' she replied. Then in response to Max's baffled expression, because two people could not have been more different, she added, 'I'm the crazy member of the family.' She laughed. 'I'm sitting next to you at dinner.'

Max smiled with relief. 'Lucky me!'

'I think we're going to have lots to talk about,' she said.

And, indeed, they did. Engrossed in each other they barely drew breath. Max felt like a drowning man who has just been thrown a life belt. He held onto it with surprise and gratitude, and the strange feeling of the tectonic plates of destiny shifting beneath him. He looked across the table at Elizabeth and felt ever more keenly the widening chasm between them.

At the end of dinner Max had written down Olga's telephone number and made a loose plan to see her again. It transpired that Olga was psychic. 'It's no coincidence that we have met each other tonight,' she said in a quiet voice, her vivacious green eyes serious suddenly. 'I think I can help you.' And that word – *help* – which Max had sent out only the week before resonated with him on a deep and subconscious level.

'Poor you, darling, having to put up with Valerie's mother,' said Elizabeth on the way home in the cab. 'She's as mad as a March hare.'

'Actually, she was fascinating,' said Max.

Elizabeth looked at him incredulously. 'You don't have to be polite with me. I don't care what you think of Valerie's mother. Did you remember to thank Valerie for the porcelain? It's Herend, you know. Beautiful and *very* expensive. She gave us all ten dessert plates.'

'Sorry, I forgot.'

She rolled her eyes. 'Typical. Men!'

'How was your placement?'

'Jolly.'

As she told him about her conversations, Max's mind drifted to the things he had talked about with Olga. He couldn't discuss them with Elizabeth for she'd only sneer or laugh at him in that condescending way of hers, as if she pitied him for the things he believed in. It wasn't just the way she sneered, but the expression on her face as she did so that he found so perturbing. It was that expression that carried her further away from him, for in it their differences lay bare, naked and exposed.

* * *

Olga Groot lived in a small house in Barnes. Her husband had died many years ago and she lived alone with a coterie of ragdoll cats. 'I'm a cliché,' she said with a laugh when Max arrived. 'The archetypal witch with her crystals and cats.' Indeed, her home was full of both.

Max felt the energy the minute he walked into the hall. The air was warm and gentle, the lights golden. There seemed not a sharp edge in the house. Everything appeared smooth and curved and soft. Of course, there were many angular surfaces, but the crystals had imbued the place with a cosy feeling. Olga showed him into the sitting room. It had an old-fashioned feel with tasselled Victorian lampshades and potted plants. Nothing matched. There were cushions of every colour and texture on the sofa, blankets thrown over holes in the upholstery, rugs laid on the worn wooden floor-boards. Sunlight streamed in through the bay window where one of the cats dozed on the sill. Max wasn't sure it was real. It looked like a toy, until it twitched its tail as if aware of Max's thoughts and wanting to put him right. There was a television on a stand in the corner, covered in a lace shawl. The bookcases were full of esoteric books bought at Watkins bookshop in Covent Garden and photographs in frames. On the round table in the bay window were piles of notebooks, pens, paper, tarot cards and a large, round, clear quartz crystal. Max was happy that Elizabeth was not here to witness the 'witch's' paraphernalia.

'Would you like a cup of tea?' Max didn't drink tea but he said he'd love one all the same. 'You sit tight. I'll be back in a jiffy. Have a look at my bookcase. You can borrow any that take your fancy.'

Max ran his eyes over the books. There were works by Betty Shine, Edgar Cayce, Michael Hawkins and Jung. Works by authors he hadn't heard of about tarot, hypnosis, reincarnation, life after death and spirits. He pulled one out that looked interesting. Olga came back into the room with a tray of tea, including a plate of biscuits. He took it from her and after she'd swept aside some papers and books, he put it on the table by the window. The cat opened its eyes before closing them again with a sigh.

'Did you find anything?' Olga asked, pouring two cups from a chipped china teapot.

'I did. May I borrow this one?' He held it up.

'Ah, *Memories, Dreams, Reflections* by Carl Jung. Now that one's very good. A little dog-eared, but it should survive another reading.' She sat down. Max sat opposite her. 'I did feel a strong pull in your direction the other night,' she told him, dropping a cube of sugar into her tea and adding a dash of milk from the jug.

'It's funny you say that, but I think you were the answer to a prayer I put out.' He grinned bashfully. If Elizabeth heard him saying that, she'd laugh in his face; she didn't believe in prayers.

'Ah, well, that makes sense,' said Olga. 'If you ask for help, it's always given.'

Max began to talk. It was as if a cork had popped out of a bottle and all his fears and longings and dreams were bursting out in bubbles and spray. Olga sipped her tea, watching him steadily with eyes full of compassion and understanding. 'I feel I'm stagnating,' he told her, and as he spoke it was as if a great weight had settled itself on his chest. He coughed and placed a hand there.

'It's all right, dear,' said Olga. 'It's only emotion finding a way out. Take a breath.'

Max took a breath. Olga smiled. There was a sweetness in it and a certain knowing, for she knew, even before Max had told her, what was holding him back.

'I don't want to sound stupid, but I feel this longing inside me to find something deep and meaningful in my life and yet there's this block. It's as if I'm standing in a puddle of tar and can't move my feet. I'm stuck.'

Olga nodded. 'You *are* stuck. But that's okay because it's possible to get *un*stuck.'

He looked at her in discomfort. 'I have a job I hate. I live in a place that doesn't make me happy and . . .' He hesitated. He wasn't sure he could say the words.

But Olga said them for him. 'Perhaps Elizabeth is not the right girl for you.' Max took a gulp of air; those words were incendiary. 'You know, Max, we all have our paths to walk in life. They're all different. Some cross with other paths, some run parallel and some never meet. We're here to learn from one another. Elizabeth's path has run beside yours for a while because you've both had important things to learn from each other. But it doesn't mean you have to walk the same path forever. You've grown, and in so growing, you've outgrown her. Perhaps it's time your path went its own way.'

Max knew she was right, but he couldn't bear the thought of hurting Elizabeth, or the wrath of her family.

'This is just one of the many challenges you will face in your life,' Olga continued. 'You have much to give, Max, but Elizabeth is not the right partner because she will stifle you and snuff out the light you are destined to shine into the world. That is no criticism of her. She is at a different stage of her development. She has her own path to take and the lessons she will encounter along the way are not yours. Your time together has run its course. I sense there is someone else out there for you who will share the things that matter to you.'

'But I love Elizabeth.'

'Of course you do. But you also know that deep down, in your heart, the two of you are incompatible.'

Max felt the heaviness in his chest press harder against his ribs. He couldn't deny it, that feeling of longing in his heart. It was his head that told him to ignore it; to look the other way, to take the easy route. It was his head that envisaged Michael's anger, Antoinette's shock and Elizabeth's hurt. The wedding was only three months away. They'd received so many presents. The dress was already made. The feeling of tar grew stickier around his feet. The sense of being unable to move was overwhelming. He drained his teacup and watched Olga pour him another.

'Have a biscuit,' she said, pushing the plate towards him. 'Everything comes to pass, Max. The good and the bad. Life is about cycles, about change. We don't like change. We resist it, because we're afraid of the unknown. But nothing stays the same. By accepting change when change is required, we find a better world opening up to us. I feel you're at that point now. At the point of stepping into a new future. It takes courage. It's horrible making people unhappy, but perhaps that's a part of *their* karma. Perhaps unhappiness is Elizabeth's destiny at this point in her life, because unhappiness will drive her deeper. Unhappiness makes us more understanding, more compassionate, it wakes us up to our true natures and our purpose here, to become conscious of the eternal soul which is what we are.'

Max knitted his fingers and sighed. 'If I break off our engagement, it'll be the most monumental train crash.'

'That too shall pass,' said Olga. 'What do you feel in *here*?' She pressed a hand against her solar plexus.

Max dropped his shoulders. 'That Elizabeth is not the right girl for me.'

Olga narrowed her eyes. 'You have a purpose, Max, to be a light to the world. You're going to send out a powerful message, possibly through a book. You're only at the beginning of your journey. Elizabeth has been an important part of it. But now she needs to go her own way, and you need to go yours. The unhappiness you've been feeling is simply there to guide you, so you don't go in the wrong direction. You'll know you're on the right path when you start to feel happy.' Olga paused a moment, as if listening to her inner voice. Then she said, 'Max, the right people are going to pop into your life at the right time. Doors will open, things will appear in your path, people will materialize when you need them, just like I did. Keep your eyes peeled, because this is critical: there is no such thing as coincidence. Everything happens for a reason. The trick is to notice and to take action. You will be helped on your way because your purpose is important.' She smiled reassuringly. 'You will encounter cynics, of course, like Elizabeth, but you will not be hindered from your path, because what you are doing is for the higher good.'

Max ate a biscuit and Olga went to the kitchen to brew another pot of tea. He read the back of Jung's autobiography. He wondered what Elizabeth would make of it. He chuckled bitterly to himself, then felt his stomach shrink at the thought of breaking up with her. Max was a man of action; he'd parachuted out of aeroplanes, undergone rigorous training with the army, ridden his horse over four-foot hedges, skied down steep narrow couloirs and flown microlight aircraft without fear, and yet nothing terrified him quite like the idea of telling Elizabeth it was over.

When Olga came back and they were sitting once again at the table in the bay window, Max decided to tell her about his nightmare. She listened with that wise look on her face. He remembered every detail as if he had really lived it. 'I don't know if it's anything significant. I always thought it was a premonition, but now I've left the army, I'm not so sure.'

'It's not a premonition,' she said. 'It's a past life.'

He nodded. 'I thought it might be that, but . . .'

'Elizabeth told you there's no such thing.'

He grinned. 'I've always had the courage of my own convictions.'

'Have you looked into it? Done any research? Do you know what battle it was?'

'No, I've never given it too much thought. But, judging from the uniform, gliders and parachutes, it must be the Second World War.'

'You know, often we're reincarnated within our family group. Do you know whether any of your family members fought in that war?'

'It would have to be someone who had died either during the war or between the war and 1963 when I was born,' said Max thoughtfully. He felt a little spark of excitement ignite in his chest. 'I'll have to ask my parents. I don't know anyone off-hand.'

'It's worth looking into,' said Olga. 'How was the biscuit?'

'Delicious.'

'Have another.' She smiled kindly. 'You're going to need your strength.'

Max did not have time to digest what Olga had told him about his past life because the more pressing task of breaking off his engagement loomed ever larger and more ominous. Elizabeth was blissfully ignorant of what Max had in mind. If she noticed his mounting fretfulness, his midnight walks, his pallor and his reluctance to talk about what she referred to as 'the happiest day of my life', she did not let on. She was busy with arrangements. Max was busy working out how he was going to drop the bomb that was going to wreck those arrangements.

At the weekend he went microlighting at Old Sarum, near Salisbury. He'd learned to fly while he was in the army and had been such a natural that he was given his pilot's licence in double quick time. It was a relief to leave the earth behind, with all his problems and frustrations, and ascend into the blue. Up there with the world in miniature beneath him, everything seemed less important. He took in deep breaths of clean air and settled into the happy present moment. With the cold wind on his face, the sun making the sky sparkle and the rattling sound of the motor, he felt a peace he hadn't felt in a long time.

When he landed, that peace was disturbed by his troubles racing across the airfield like black shadows to harass him once again.

With under three months to go before the wedding, Max could soul-search no more. He either had to go through with the wedding, or put an end to it now. He couldn't leave it any longer.

It was with a heavy heart that he packed his bag. But

freedom shone like a light at the end of a very dark tunnel, suddenly within his reach and growing steadily. When Elizabeth returned home from work, she unwittingly made the situation easier for him by complaining that he was not engaging in the excitement. 'This is going to be the only time I get married, Max, and I want to enjoy it,' she told him without noticing the bag beside the stairs. 'I can't enjoy it if you're going around with a face like a boot.'

Max put his hands in his pockets and his shoulders stiffened, rising almost to his ears. 'I'm afraid I can't get married, Bunny,' he said, barely able to look at her.

She screwed her face into a fist. 'What? What are you talking about?'

'I can't marry you. I'm sorry.'

'Don't be ridiculous!' She laughed scornfully. 'You're being pathetic. You're just anxious before the big day. It's normal.' She walked past him into the kitchen. 'Have a glass of wine.' She opened the fridge and poured two glasses.

'I mean it,' he said, following her. 'Things haven't been right for a while now. Haven't you noticed?'

'They've been fine.' She handed him the glass. Max put it on the sideboard. 'Look, if this is about your job, quit. I don't care. Daddy will get over it.'

'I *am* quitting. I handed in my notice today. They're not going to make me work it.'

Now she looked worried. She took a gulp of wine. 'We need to talk about this, Max. Calmly.'

'There's little to say. I don't think we're right together, Elizabeth. We used to be, but we've grown apart.'

'I don't know what you're talking about.'

'We used to laugh all the time. We used to be loving. Now we rarely laugh and we disagree on everything. Perhaps it's me. Maybe I've changed. I don't know. I'm not happy. That's the truth.'

'If this is about you wanting to live in the country, Daddy can rent us a cottage somewhere, then you can have a bolthole to escape to. You can plant vegetables and do whatever it is people do in the countryside.'

'It's not about logistics, Elizabeth. It's about us.'

'Okay, what about us?' She put down her glass and folded her arms defensively.

'We have different beliefs for a start.'

'So it's because I don't subscribe to your ideas of reincarnation and life after death. God, Max, grow up. If I can tolerate you talking rubbish, then you can tolerate me not getting it.'

'It's not that. We're just different people.'

'Do you still love me?' Her eyes filled with tears.

'Yes.'

She sighed with relief. 'Then we can work it out. If we love each other, we can survive anything, even a few pre-wedding nerves.' She smiled wanly and picked up her glass of wine. 'What doesn't kill you makes you stronger. This will make us stronger, Max.'

He shook his head. 'I can't.' The weight on his chest felt more like a metal hand squeezing his heart. 'I'm sorry to hurt you.'

She drained her glass. 'Sorry?' she exclaimed, raising her voice. 'Sorry? Do you realize what you're doing? We're going to have to cancel the wedding. Send all the presents back. Tell the guests not to come. What about the hotel? The honeymoon? The dress? Do you know how much this has cost Daddy? Not to mention the humiliation. You're practically jilting me at the altar. How could you? How could you do this to me? Are you out of your bloody mind, Max?' It was rare for

Elizabeth to swear. The tears overflowed and fell in streams down her face. Then her mouth twisted with scorn. 'After all I've done for you! If it wasn't for me, you'd be wandering about the world with that silly camera of yours, taking photographs of blue tits, making no money and building nothing but an overdraft. Thanks to me you have a solid job and a future.'

'I don't want that job, Elizabeth, and I don't want that future. If you don't understand that, you don't know me at all.'

'I thought I knew you, but you're right. You've changed. You're selfish, Max. You're only thinking of yourself. Get out!'

Max did not wait for Elizabeth to throw something at him. He grabbed his bag and dashed into the street. A black cab came trundling around the corner, its orange light a beacon of hope through the mist. Max stuck out his hand. The cab pulled up against the kerb. As he climbed in and closed the door, he heard Elizabeth shouting from the upstairs window. 'When you realize you've made a horrible mistake, you'd better go grovelling to Daddy before you even think about grovelling to me!'

The cabbie raised his eyebrows. 'Where to, mate?' he asked.

'I don't know,' Max replied. 'Just drive.'

CHAPTER EIGHT

Max spent the night at Olga's house. She was deeply sympathetic. 'You've done the right thing,' she reassured him. But he swung from feeling elated with the sense of freedom, to feeling as if his heart had been wrenched in two. However, experience had made Olga wise. 'You're hurting because you've hurt *her*, not because you've hurt yourself,' she explained. Max wasn't sure. His emotions were all over the place. He couldn't tell where the pain was coming from, it seemed to flood his heart from all directions. But Olga was right, he did feel terrible for Elizabeth.

The following morning, he did what he knew he must do. He went to see Michael and Antoinette. He dreaded the meeting. He hadn't slept. He felt wretched. A small part of him wished he hadn't been so impulsive, but the greater part of him was certain he'd done the right thing and was relieved that he was now on the other side of that decision.

Michael and Antoinette lived in a large flat behind the Royal Albert Hall in South Kensington. When Max had spoken to Antoinette on the telephone earlier that morning, she had sounded sympathetic. That made him dread the meeting all the more because it suggested that she hoped he'd change his mind. He rang the bell and took the lift to the third floor.

Antoinette was standing in the doorway to the flat. She was typically formal in a pair of black trousers and a jacket with large shoulder pads and gold buttons, her red bouffant as hard as a helmet. She did not smile and stood aside to let him in.

Michael was in the sitting room, standing by the window with a cup of coffee. When he saw Max, he put down his cup. Max felt like a schoolboy in front of the headmaster. Michael looked him over, at the thick stubble on his face and his unruly hair, and his lip curled with displeasure. Max noticed his eyes linger on his jeans, but why should he have worn anything else? This wasn't a job interview, it was a resignation.

'Would you like something to drink, Max?' Antoinette asked.

'No, thank you,' he replied. He did not intend to stay long.

Michael offered him a seat, but he didn't sit down himself. He stood in front of the fireplace and put his hands on his hips. Antoinette perched on the arm of the sofa and waited for her husband to start the conversation.

'Elizabeth telephoned last night,' he said. 'She's very upset. What is this all about, Max?'

'I'm afraid I don't want to get married.'

'At all?' interjected Antoinette in a high-pitched voice.

'Elizabeth and I are not right for each other.'

'And you worked that out a couple of months before the wedding?' said Michael.

'I've felt us growing apart for some time,' Max explained, but he knew they'd never understand.

'Then why didn't you discuss it with her sooner?' Max could see that Michael was getting angry as the possibility of reconciliation faded. 'Do you have any idea how much you've hurt her?'

'Do you care?' added Antoinette.

'I *do* care. I still love Elizabeth . . .'

'Then what's the problem?' said Antoinette in a softer tone.

'If you still love each other, you can work it out. Love is the operative word here.'

'I love her, but I don't want to be married to her. We both want different things.'

Antoinette smiled, but it did not reach her eyes, which were as hard as granite. 'Could you not have discovered that a year ago? You've had plenty of time to find out what you want and what you don't want.'

'It's only come to the surface recently.' Max stood up. 'I came to apologize, not to explain myself. I don't expect anyone to understand. I'll make us both miserable if I go ahead with a marriage that isn't right. Elizabeth will thank me in the end when she's married to a man who *is* right for her.'

Michael's face was the colour of beetroot. 'I don't think Elizabeth will ever thank you. Don't console yourself with that thought, my boy. No one will *ever* thank you. Have you any idea how much this wedding has cost me? Do you have the slightest idea how you're going to make us all look? Have you no gratitude at all? You wouldn't have a job if it wasn't for me ...'

'I've handed in my notice.'

'Well, you're a bloody fool. That job was going to be the making of you. You know, when you first started walking out with our daughter, we weren't sure of you. We had serious doubts about how suitable you were. But you proved to be a loving and attentive young man who could make Elizabeth happy. I found you a good job, a job for life, and you moved into the house I'd bought. A pretty decent package, I'd say. You were given it all, Max, and now you're throwing it all away. You're ruining your life and, in the process, Elizabeth's. I don't know what you think you want, but I'm older and wiser than you and I can tell you that you won't find it. When you come to your senses, don't expect us to welcome you back with open arms. You're going to have to work very hard to win our daughter back. I doubt she'll take you, however. She'd be a fool to give you another chance. I doubt she'll ever trust you again, a dishonest man like you.'

Max made for the door. 'Breaking up with Elizabeth is the most honest thing I have ever done in my life. I'm sorry about the timing and I'm sorry that I've hurt her. She deserves better than me. I hope she finds it.'

Antoinette stared at him in horror. The vein in Michael's neck throbbed. Clearly, they had thought they'd win him over. This was not how they had planned their meeting to end. Max left as quickly as he could. When he was in the street he inhaled a lungful of air. He needed to get away. Far away. And as soon as possible.

* * *

Max watched the sun rise over the South African bush through the lens of his camera. He stood on the terrace, beneath the thatched roof, and watched the river glitter in the pale dawn light as various birds alighted on its bank. The quiet stillness of the landscape resonated with the stillness inside of him and he felt his whole being shed the trauma of the previous month and finally relax. The sky was a pale blue as the sun twinkled through the trees and danced upon the water. He'd thought it might feel strange to be alone, for every holiday he'd been on in the last three years had been with Elizabeth, but it felt wonderful. It was as if he had shed a skin in London and emerged renewed.

Among the people staying at the lodge was a young English couple from Cornwall. Daniel was an architect and his girl-friend, Robyn, was a budding writer of historical fiction. She hadn't had anything published, she told Max when they'd talked the night before at dinner, but she was working on a novel about King Charles II's mistress, Lady Castlemaine, and was hoping to find an agent willing to take her on. Daniel was a big character with a loud laugh and a penchant for telling anecdotes. He was funny and had a charm that made people instantly warm to him. Robyn was quieter and listened to Daniel's tales with an indulgent smile. She had long blonde hair and gentle grey eyes, and when she smiled she was beautiful. There was something in her smile that Max found captivating.

Earlier that morning the three of them had got up just before dawn and set off in the open-topped Land Cruiser to watch the animals. Max was in the front with Sean the ranger while Daniel and Robyn sat behind him. They had binoculars around their necks and Max had brought his camera. As they passed herds of impala grazing in the morning mists, elephants slowly moving through the bush and giraffes reaching for the highest branches of the acacia trees, they had not spoken. No one wanted to disturb the tranquillity of the natural world. Max captured it with his telephoto lens.

They returned to the lodge for breakfast and now Max was on the terrace with his camera. Just as he was about to put it down, a herd of elephants appeared round the bend of the river and began to make their way through the valley, past the lodge. Every shot felt like something one might see in *National Geographic* magazine; those elephants were mightily photogenic. He sensed someone beside him and lowered his camera. It was Robyn, watching the elephants through her binoculars. 'Isn't that wonderful?' she whispered, as if afraid they might hear her and run away.

'They're so close,' he replied. 'This is just the most amazing position up here. The variety of animals that wander up the river – really, it's such a privilege to see them.'

'I've always loved elephants,' she said, putting down her binoculars and smiling at him. 'It's so lovely to see them in the wild.'

'I agree. I'm glad I came.' They sat down in the big, comfortable chairs as the elephants stopped right in front of the terrace to graze.

'Unusual to come on your own,' she said. 'Do you always travel by yourself?'

'I've just split up with my fiancée,' he told her. 'I had to get away and be by myself for a while.'

'Oh, I'm sorry to hear that.' Robyn looked at him and her eyes had a depth and sensitivity to them, encouraging Max to confide in her. He knew he'd probably never see her again and he needed to talk.

'I broke off the engagement three months before the wedding. A pretty shoddy thing to do. I'm not proud of myself.'

Robyn gasped. 'Oh my goodness. How awful. Are you all right?'

'I'm recovering. This is the perfect place to put myself back together again.'

'And your fiancée? She must be devastated.'

'I'm afraid I've hurt her very much. That's the worst part, hurting someone you love.'

'What went wrong?'

'I realized we weren't right for one another.' He turned his gaze towards the elephants. 'I do love her, I think, but I don't want to marry her. That's a paradox, isn't it?'

Robyn thought about it a moment. 'I suppose it is, but everyone's different and there are many ways of loving. Perhaps you need more than love when it comes to choosing the person you want to spend the rest of your life with.'

'I think you're right.' He told her of the nights he'd walked through Battersea and searched for answers in the Thames. She listened as he unloaded the agony he'd been carrying, and it felt good to confide in someone who didn't know him or Elizabeth. Someone who wasn't from his world.

'Can I ask you a personal question?' she said. She was frowning now, a serious look on her face.

'Of course. You can ask me anything you like.'

'Why weren't you right for each other? If you'd been going out for three years already, how come you hadn't worked that out before? What was the catalyst?'

Max sighed and rubbed the stubble on his cheeks as he contemplated the many reasons why he had thrown in the towel. 'We just wanted different things,' he explained. 'I think at the beginning, when it was so physical, those things didn't matter. But soon after I asked her to marry me, I began to feel increasingly uneasy. I began to realize that we don't have the same values. Her father is very controlling. He took us over. He bought her a house, found me a job in the City, put me up for membership at White's, basically mapped out my life for me. A life that mirrored his. I felt stifled, as if I didn't have a say.' He hesitated. Robyn's frown deepened. 'And she's spiritually bankrupt. I know that sounds unkind. I don't mean to be,' he added quickly. 'But spirituality is important to me. She's not even open to discussing it. She shuts me down with disdain. The fact is we're on very different journeys, to use the cliché. We see the meaning of life in very different ways. Well . . .' He chuckled. 'She doesn't think there is one.'

Robyn put her head on one side. 'How do *you* see the meaning of life?'

There was something about the openness in Robyn's expression that reassured him of her understanding. 'How long have you got?' He laughed. 'I believe in reincarnation, life after death, the evolution of the soul as it makes its way towards enlightenment.'

She grinned. 'That's what I believe too.'

Max was surprised. 'Elizabeth doesn't believe in the spirit at all,' he told her, realizing suddenly that he had an ally and eager to share his thoughts with someone with a like mind. 'She believes that when we die we become nothing. She thinks I'm mad.'

'Well, if it makes you feel any better, I don't think you're mad. I've always been fascinated by the esoteric and the paranormal. You know, our lives are full of signs if we open our eyes to them. Synchronicities, strange coincidences, people who are put in our paths when we ask for help. Most people ignore them, or pass them off as chance.'

'Elizabeth thinks that people who believe in life after death are just too afraid to accept the truth.'

'But that's all right,' Robyn said with a shrug. 'She can believe what she wants. It's only a negative thing if she makes you feel bad for what *you* believe in.' She swept her eyes around the terrace, then settled them once again on Max. 'Daniel doesn't subscribe to the things I believe in, either, and, on occasions, he's laughed at me when I've woken up in the middle of the night and claimed I saw an angel or a spirit on the end of the bed. But he never makes me feel small or stupid and he never challenges me. He's intelligent enough to admit that he doesn't know it all. He doesn't share my interest, but nor do I share his interest in sailing, so, there you go.' She laughed and Max lost himself a moment in her smile. She must have noticed the way he was looking at her, for she turned her eyes to the river. 'The elephants have gone,' she said.

'Yes, they have,' he replied. Right now, with the charm of Robyn's smile fizzing inside him like champagne, he couldn't have cared less about the elephants.

'Don't worry about Elizabeth. She'll recover and most likely find someone who *is* right for her. And you'll find someone who's right for you. If you look at life from the perspective of the soul's journey of learning and becoming conscious of itself, then this is just one of those lessons you've had to endure. You'll emerge stronger, wiser and probably more informed about what you want and what you don't want in life. You'll look back in ten years and be very happy you made the decision you did. It took courage.'

He laughed. 'I hope you're right. I can tell you, though, I'm not even contemplating getting entangled in another relationship. After this one, I might spend the rest of my life on my own.'

'I doubt that,' she said with a flirtatious grin. Max noticed Daniel walking from his cabin towards the terrace. Robyn noticed too and the flirtatiousness evaporated. 'When you find the right one, you'll know,' she said seriously. 'You'll be better equipped to judge next time.' She sat up and smiled as Daniel approached. 'You've missed a herd of elephants,' she said. 'Right here in front of us.'

'Oh, that's a shame,' said Daniel, disappointed. 'Lucky old you.' He took Robyn's hand and looked out over the river. 'I'm sure they'll come again. Sean tells me that there are often elephants down there, and crocodiles. You can see their eyes light up at night if you shine the torch at them. I'm going to the pool. Want to come?'

Robyn got up. 'I'd love to,' she said. 'I'm going to make the most of the sunshine, Max. It's been lovely talking to you.'

Max watched them walk away, hand in hand. He felt a stab

of envy that Daniel had the luck to find someone like Robyn. He turned his eyes back to the river.

* * *

When Max returned to London he moved in with his sister, Liv, who had a small flat in Bayswater and was willing to put him up for a month or two. Max knew he'd have to return to Elizabeth's at some point to collect the rest of his things, as well as his great-grandmother's engagement ring. He dreaded having to face Elizabeth after what he'd done. He would also have to find a job, which wouldn't be easy because he hadn't a clue what he wanted to do. For the time being he would trust Fate and not worry about it. Things would very likely sort themselves out.

Once he was settled in he decided to do a little research on his recurring dream. If he managed to find someone in his family who had fought in the Second World War, in an airborne battle that had involved parachutes and gliders, he'd have something to go on.

On the first weekend after arriving back in the UK, Max drove his red Alfa Romeo Spider to stay with his parents in Hampshire. He relished the feeling of the wind in his hair and the sun on his face. He had remembered his mother talking about a family tree that had been drawn up by a cousin of his grandfather's who was obsessed with genealogy. At the time he hadn't been very interested. He wondered now whether it had been completed and if he could get his hands on a copy.

Max had been brought up in a manor house just outside Alresford. His parents, George and Catherine Shelbourne, had bought the Queen Anne house just before he was born. As he turned into the drive he felt the warm feeling of coming home. It was the beginning of April. The leaves on the trees and bushes were beginning to unfurl, creating the illusion of wisps of green smoke floating around the branches. Daffodils were in full flower, their heavy yellow trumpets signalling loudly the arrival of spring. Birdsong filled the air, which was now warm with sunshine and optimism; the winter was gone and nature could look forward to bright mornings and long days.

He parked outside the house and wandered into the hall. 'Hello!' he shouted. 'Anyone home?' A moment later his mother came out of the kitchen, followed by a trio of small dogs that followed her like bridesmaids.

'Darling, it's so lovely to see you.' Catherine embraced her son, who was much taller than she was. She sighed heavily and looked at him with sympathy. 'Goodness, you've had a shocking time, haven't you.'

'It hasn't been great. South Africa did me the world of good,' he replied, smiling down at her worried face.

'I hope Elizabeth is all right. I never warmed to her as you know, but I don't wish her any ill. It's horrid to be jilted so close to the wedding. But I won't ask why you didn't do it before. I really don't want you to have to live it all again. What's done is done. Come and have a cup of coffee. Your father's in the garden. I'm baking a fruit cake. I thought you might like one and I know your father will want one. Isn't it a lovely day? Just lovely.'

Max followed her and the dogs into the kitchen. He knew she was talking more than usual because she was nervous. He imagined his callous behaviour was the talk of Hampshire. He hadn't exactly covered himself in glory.

He perched on the stool at the island and told his mother about his trip while the coffee percolated. 'It sounds marvellous,' she said. 'Just what you needed.'

'I'm sorry I put you through this,' he said. 'I must have left you having to fend off all sorts of questions. I never thought how my actions would affect you and Dad.'

'Don't be silly. Much better to realize you're making a mistake *before* you walk down the aisle. I know someone who realized she'd made a terrible error at the very moment she was saying her vows. By then it was too late to stop it. Imagine that! That's far worse. You did the right thing. And that's what I've told people. It was hard for you both, but life has a funny way of righting things. It'll all work out for the best, I'm sure.'

Max smiled wryly. How often had she told him that when he was a child? 'Mum, do you remember that cousin of Grandpa's who was putting together a family tree?'

'Yes, Bertha Clairmont.'

'Did she ever complete it?'

'Absolutely. Not that I've had a good look. I'm not very interested in your father's ancestors. I'm much more interested in the people living now.'

'I'd love to see it.'

'Really? Well, I have a copy in the sitting room. Now where did I put it? In a drawer, I suspect. I'll dig it out for you if you like?'

'Thanks.' Max's attention was diverted to the door where his father was now standing, smiling.

'Max! What a nice surprise,' said George, taking off his gardening gloves and walking over to embrace his son.

'Hi, Dad. How's the garden?'

'Coming along well. Things haven't been too badly hit by the frosts. You should come and have a look at some of the trees I've planted.'

'I'd love to.'

'Good. Come on then. I need help getting rid of that old shed. I've been meaning to take it down for years so I took a sledge hammer to it yesterday. Made a terrible mess. You can help me load it onto the trailer and I'll burn it. Make a great big bonfire. Capital.'

Max followed him out. 'Dad, did any of your relations fight in the Second World War?'

'My father's brother, your great-uncle, was killed over the Channel. I think a cousin was killed in the Far East.'

'I never knew that.'

'Very sad.'

'Anyone else?'

'You'd have to ask your grandfather.'

'I will.'

George stopped in front of a sapling. 'Now, this chap here is a splendid fellow. It's going to be a great big American elm. All these trees turn gold in the autumn. You might have noticed. I've been busy planting more. I love planting a tree.'

'I know, Dad.'

'Well, nice to give something to the world that will outlive me.'

'In that case, you've given loads.'

His father chuckled. 'Right, here it is. Hope you don't mind getting dirty.'

'Of course not.'

'Good.'

After lunch Catherine went into the sitting room to find the family tree. Max and George remained at the table, talking. They hadn't discussed Elizabeth yet. The last time her name had come up, just after Christmas, they'd ended up fighting because George had made it very clear that he did not think Elizabeth was right for him. George drained his glass of wine. 'I'm glad you came to your senses,' he said carefully.

Max nodded. 'I did and just in time.'

Sensing his son was open to talking about it, he added, 'Michael Pemberton is an arrogant shit.'

'Dad!' Max wasn't used to hearing his father swear.

'I'm sorry, Max, but sometimes things just need to be said. You're well out of it. A toxic family and, don't forget, the apple doesn't fall very far from the tree.'

'I know. I'm moving on now.'

'Good. We don't need to talk about it anymore. It's a blip.' He poured more wine into his glass. 'Splendid.'

Catherine returned with a big scroll. 'Here it is,' she said brightly. She glanced at her husband's glass of wine, noticed he'd refilled it, and looked worried suddenly. 'Everything okay?' she asked.

'All's fine, Mum,' said Max with a smile.

'What's that you've got there?' George asked.

'Bertha's family tree.'

'Ah, yes. What do you want that for?'

'Curious,' said Max.

George raised his eyebrows and took a sip of wine.

Max got up from the table. 'Dad said Michael's an arrogant shit,' he said with a grin.

Catherine stared at her husband. 'George!'

'He's right,' said Max. 'Only he needn't have been so restrained with his choice of words.'

Max took the scroll to his bedroom and opened it on the bed. Inside was a family tree, written clearly and neatly in black ink. The writing was immaculate. Bertha must have got a calligrapher to copy it out for her, Max thought. His eyes honed in on the 1900s and settled very quickly on a name.

CHAPTER NINE

Eastbourne, 1937

Florence's ambitions to be an actress had been awakened when, as a child, her father had bought one of the first film projectors. She had sat cross-legged on the floor, sipping ginger beer drawn from wooden barrels in the cellar, and watching entranced as cowboys and Indians galloped silently across the big white screen, shooting madly at each other to the sound of rousing music. The adults had laughed but Florence had stared in horror, for at her tender age she did not realize that the action she was watching wasn't real. Even after it was explained to her she still chewed her fingernails with worry that one of the cowboys would get killed.

The first time she went to the theatre was to see *The White Horse Inn* in London. Due to their mother suffering a migraine Uncle Raymond had treated Winifred and Florence to an elegant lunch at the Trocadero, beneath a giant, revolving silver and glass globe that hung suspended from the ceiling and threw twinkling lights over the walls. Florence had been as enthralled by the globe as she had been by the delicious lunch of lemon sole and crispy potatoes, followed by strawberry ice cream, her favourite. Uncle Raymond enjoyed fine restaurants and they were allowed to order anything they wished. After lunch they'd made their way through Piccadilly, past the flower sellers who assembled around the statue of Eros selling bunches of violets out of big baskets, and on into the mysterious world of the theatre. Florence found the theatre enchanting. She'd sat on the edge of her velvet seat, barely daring to breathe, as the conductor raised his baton and then, after a moment's pause, lowered it with aplomb so that the music of the overture filled the auditorium. The curtain lifted and a world of charm and fantasy appeared, as if by magic.

Florence's mother did not want her to be an actress; she wanted her to be presented at court as Winifred had been, but Margaret did not have the strength of character to say no to her younger daughter. Only her father, Florence's grandfather, had the authority and the means – as Winifred had meanly put it: 'He who pays the piper calls the tune.' The tune to which Florence had to dance was a year at Miss Randall's School of Domestic Economy. She accepted on condition that when she completed it she could go to drama school. This was agreed.

Miss Randall's was based in Silverdale Road, Eastbourne, in a large white building with dark, wood-panelled rooms dominated by a wide, imposing staircase. To Florence's joy she had persuaded Cynthia Dash to enrol and the two of them attended together. The girls thought Ranny's, as they affectionately called the college, ridiculous. There they learned how to cook, plan menus, write out invitations in calligraphy, iron shirts and turn out a room. They were taught how to arrange flowers, sort the laundry and manage a household. Florence and Cynthia giggled through most of the classes and sneaked out onto the roof to smoke during breaks. At night, Florence convinced Cynthia to climb out of the window and scale down the drainpipe so that they could walk up the beach and sit on the sand beneath the stars and buy drinks at the local pub, which they could be sure that none of their toffee-nosed teachers would deign to frequent.

Florence thought of Aubrey constantly and any titbits of news that Cynthia gave her were eagerly gobbled up. Yet, as autumn advanced, it wasn't Aubrey's face that dominated her daydreams, but Rupert's. Time and again she caught herself reliving that moment in the cave when he had kissed her. The memory was so vivid that she could feel his soft lips upon hers, the wetness of his tongue, the warmth of his hand in the small of her back and the pressure of his body against her stomach. The recollection aroused feelings that she hadn't experienced before and she blushed, even though no one could read her mind and expose her fantasies.

Rupert did not have Aubrey's gentle nature, his sporting talents and carefree temperament. Rupert was dark and mysterious. He had an air of untroubled danger, was complex and unpredictable. So why was it that her body ached for him against the will of her mind, which told her that it was Aubrey she loved? It had *always* been Aubrey – hadn't it?

In the summer of 1938, at the end of the course, Miss Randall threw a dance at the Grand Hotel to celebrate the start of their independence. Brothers and boyfriends were invited. With much excitement Florence and Cynthia shopped in town for appropriate dresses. Cynthia found a demure dress in blue silk that matched the colour of her eyes, but Florence seized upon a slinky black décolleté number, which was obviously unsuitable. She spent her whole dress allowance on it. Florence's mother was horrified when she saw it and insisted Florence return it to the shop at once. Florence said that she would, but as her mother was not going to be present at the dance, she defied her instructions and hung it in her cupboard with a triumphant hoot.

A couple of weeks before the dance, Cynthia told Florence that she had arranged dates for the two of them. 'I've managed to persuade Aubrey and Rupert to come,' she said with a mischievous smile. 'Aubrey's coming down from Sandhurst and Rupert's just finished at Cirencester. You've been a terrible influence on me, Flo, and I'm breaking one of Ranny's rules. But who cares, we're leaving, aren't we? You'll have to pretend that Rupert is your boyfriend. You don't mind, do you?'

Florence didn't know what to say. Both Aubrey *and* Rupert were going to attend. It had been almost a year since she had seen either of them. 'I'm delighted,' she said, feeling the excitement swelling in her chest, to the point of bursting.

Cynthia smiled shrewdly. 'I know you have a special affection for Aubrey.'

'I'm that obvious, am I?' said Florence, drawing her thoughts away from Rupert.

'Only to me because I know you so well.'

Florence sighed. 'I behaved like a fool last summer. All the while I was hankering after him like an idiot, he was having a walkout with Elise. Do you remember?'

'Yes, I do remember. He was very keen on her.'

Florence seized on the use of the past tense. 'Was?' she asked.

'That ended long ago. Elise went back to France and that was that.'

'I'm sure they wrote to each other.'

'I don't know, but I think it was doomed from the start.'

Florence focused her thoughts on Aubrey. He was the object of her desire. The man she wished to marry. Rupert did strange things to her, like the devil, tempting her in the sins of the flesh, as Rev Minchin at school would have said. Aubrey was a gentleman, she told herself firmly. She was sure that Rupert was not.

When the evening of the dance arrived, Florence and Cynthia spent all afternoon preparing. Celia Dash always said that bathing and dressing before the party was often more fun than the party itself, but Florence was sure that this dance would not disappoint. Aubrey was coming. Elise was no longer in the picture. The dress was a stunner and Florence looked stunning in it, she knew. Her chance to win him had arrived at last.

Florence waited for all the girls to be gathered in the hall of the college before she swept down the grand staircase in her striking black dress and fashionable up-do. Aware that every eye was upon her she lifted her chin and smiled. She felt like a film star; if only Aubrey were at the bottom of the stairs to receive her. With one hand on the banister she trod carefully down each step. When she reached the last she took a deep, satisfied breath. She was the only young woman in black. The only young woman brave enough to flaunt her décolletage and all her incumbent curves.

Miss Randall stood before her with a furious look on her face. 'You cannot wear that, my girl,' she said in her clipped English voice that made her sound like royalty. 'It's highly unsuitable. What on earth are you thinking?'

Florence's mouth fell open. 'It's a beautiful dress,' she replied.

'It is certainly beautiful, but it is not appropriate for a Ranny's girl. Have you learned nothing? You'd better go and change at once.'

'But I have nothing else to wear!'

Miss Randall shrugged impatiently. 'Then you'll have to stay behind.'

Florence wanted to cry. The evening was ruined even before it had begun.

Cynthia stepped forward. 'I have a dress you can wear,' she said softly, taking Florence's hand. 'Come on, if we hurry they'll wait for us.'

Miss Randall looked at her watch. 'You have exactly five minutes and not a minute more.'

Cynthia's dress was a pretty green, cut on the bias with short sleeves and a matching belt, but it was not glamorous. 'I don't think it's very *me*,' Florence muttered despondently when she saw her reflection. 'I should stay behind as Ranny says.'

Cynthia was horrified at the thought. 'Don't be silly. You look lovely. You'd look lovely in anything. Besides, Rupert and Aubrey will be disappointed if you're not there and Rupert will be left without a date. He'll look ridiculous. You don't know what he's like when he's angry. He'll be furious with me. Please, you have to come. You can't let a dress spoil your evening. You're more than a dress, Flo.'

'All right, I'll come. But the evening is ruined,' said Florence crossly. She studied her face in the mirror, wiped away a smudge of kohl from beneath her eyes, then followed Cynthia out of the room.

'That's better,' said Miss Randall crisply when Florence presented herself at the bottom of the stairs. 'Come now, the bus is waiting.'

The humiliation of being told off in front of the girls was nothing compared with the humiliation of having to be seen in an unflattering dress by Aubrey and Rupert. Florence sat in the bus with her arms folded, staring glumly out of the window while Cynthia tried to persuade her that they wouldn't notice. That her personality was what counted, and, besides, the dress was perfectly charming.

'I didn't want to be charming, I wanted to be sophisticated and striking,' said Florence.

'But you *are*,' Cynthia told her with a sympathetic smile. 'Once you're on the dance floor you'll forget all about your dress.'

They arrived at the Grand Hotel and waited with the other girls in the foyer for their dates to arrive. One by one young men in black tie appeared to accompany their sisters and girlfriends into the ballroom. Florence felt deflated and awkward in Cynthia's dress. She no longer felt like the most glamorous girl in the room, but dowdy like a duck among a bevy of swans.

Then she saw them. Rupert and Aubrey, tall and urbane and smiling with that typical Dash confidence and charm. They strode through the big doors and Florence felt her heart race at the sight of them. One fair, one dark, but both more glamorous than any of the young men who had stepped into the Grand that evening. Florence might not have been wearing the most beautiful dress, but she knew she had the most handsome date.

Aubrey greeted her first. 'Florence,' he said, his grey eyes shining with delight as he took her hand and kissed her cheek. 'You look lovely.'

'Thank you,' she said, a grateful smile lighting up her face.

'Did you learn anything?' he asked.

'How to turn out a room and iron a shirt.'

'Very important,' he said with a grin. 'Although, I'm not sure what turning out a room means.'

Aubrey went to greet his sister. Rupert was now standing before Florence, looking down at her with a knowing smile, as if there existed between them an intimacy that the passing year had in no way diminished. 'What's the betting that you bought an unsuitable dress and have had to borrow one of my sister's?' Florence was astonished. Was it so obvious? He chuckled and put a hand on her waist. As he came to kiss her cheek, he murmured, 'Cynthia's just let the cat out of the bag.'

Florence was relieved. 'Of course she has,' she said.

Did his kiss linger slightly longer than was proper or did Florence imagine it? She was aware of his clean-shaven face against her skin and the lemony smell of his cologne. 'You know, it's the girl who wears the dress, not the dress who wears the girl,' he added. 'You'd look beautiful in a sack.'

'That's lucky because I feel like I'm wearing one.'

He offered her his arm. 'Shall we?'

She took it. 'Yes, let's. Sack or no sack, I'm not going to let it ruin my evening.'

The four of them stuck together, sipping champagne from crystal flutes. They had no desire to mingle with the other guests. They wanted to reminisce about the summer before in Gulliver's Bay. 'Your party was the highlight of the holidays,' said Aubrey to Florence. 'I doubt there will ever be another one like it.'

'That's kind of you to say. I just wanted to prove to my family that I could arrange such a thing on my own.'

'You arranged it beautifully,' said Aubrey. 'I hope they were impressed.'

'They were surprised, as I intended them to be. But I can't imagine having the energy to do that again. Proving oneself is a lot of work.'

Florence forgot about the dress and basked in Aubrey's admiration. She realized now, as she noticed the way he was looking at her, that he hadn't really seen her before. *This must be the way he had looked at Elise*, she thought, warming beneath his gaze like a spring flower.

'I shall miss our lovely long summers at Pedrevan,' said

Cynthia wistfully. 'I don't think we'll ever have long holidays like that again.'

'Certainly not if we go to war,' said Rupert.

'Trust you, Rupert, to cast a shadow over this lovely evening,' his sister reproached him. But he was not wrong. Few doubted that, after a year of broken promises and the annexation of Austria into Greater Germany back in March, war was very likely.

'It's only against shadow that we can truly see the light,' Rupert added, grinning at Florence. 'If war really is imminent, then I'm more determined than ever to enjoy myself now.'

Florence found herself seated between Rupert and Aubrey at dinner. For the first half she talked to Aubrey. He was interested to hear her plans. She told him how she was going to enrol in drama school, but hadn't decided which one yet as her grandfather thought the London Theatre School had a reputation for having lax morals. She pulled a face and Aubrey laughed. She could tell that he was enjoying her company. If only he had paid her as much attention the year before. If only he had looked at her like this when she'd been trying to catch his eye in Gulliver's Bay. However, to Florence's bewilderment, Aubrey's sudden interest in her did not have the effect she expected. It did not cause her heart to race and her face to flush. It didn't cause any reaction at all. Instead, she was acutely aware of Rupert's presence on her other side. It was as if he had a magnetic pull that kept drawing her attention, and she found herself longing for the first course to be over so that she could turn to him.

Eventually, the waiters removed their plates and the girl on Aubrey's other side drew him away. Florence smiled at Rupert. Rupert smiled back, his gunmetal blue eyes full of knowing. It was as if that kiss in the cave had given them both a sense of collusion and conspiracy. As if they were deeply aware of their secret and thrilled by it. Florence recalled his lips on hers and her face burned. She took a sip of wine to deflect her embarrassment, but if Rupert noticed, he did not let on.

'It's good to see you again, Flossie,' he said. 'I'm sorry for the way we parted.'

'So am I,' she replied. 'We should have returned to the party and danced.'

'If I recall, we did dance.' He lowered his voice. 'And you trod on my toe.'

'Did I?' Florence did not want to remember that bit. 'How gauche . . .'

'Not at all. I'd give anything for you to step on my toe again.'

She laughed. 'That's gallant of you.'

'Has your heart mended?'

Florence blushed again. 'It was never really broken. I was young and foolish.'

'Well, you're very grown up now.'

'You're teasing me,' she said, mildly annoyed.

'Not at all. I would never tease you. This year has been good for you. You've blossomed, although *I* recognized your beauty even before you flowered.'

'I've learned how to iron shirts and walk into a room.'

'I'm glad, because a young lady would soon slip into disrepute if she wasn't accomplished in those vitally important areas.'

'I've also learned how to get in and out of a car.'

'A sports car, I hope.'

'Oh yes, an Aston Martin especially. It's important, too, to know which cars to get into and which to avoid altogether.'

He chuckled. 'And how to coordinate your outfits to match. I dare say you'd look rather good in red.'

'Ranny thinks red is a highly dubious colour. She says it gives off the wrong message.'

Rupert pretended to look appalled. 'We can't have you being mistaken for a street walker. God forbid.'

'Indeed. But now I'm going to study drama in London. If Ranny knew, she'd have a fit. Actresses are synonymous with those women of easy virtue. If she thought my dress was inappropriate, she'd faint at the thought of me treading the boards.'

'I'd like to see your dress.'

Florence smiled. 'It is rather splendid.'

'Will you promise to wear it when I come and take you out for dinner after watching you in a play?'

'That's presumptuous. What makes you think I'll accept your invitation to dinner?'

'Because I *know* you.'

Florence looked at him with a serious expression. 'You've said that before.'

'Yes, but I've thought it many more times than I've said it.'

'Why?'

'Don't you feel it too?'

'That I *know* you?'

'Yes. That we know each other. Not just socially, but on a deeper level. I feel like I've known you a very long time.'

Florence didn't know what to say. She wasn't sure what he meant. 'That's strange,' she said.

'Perhaps, but it's also comfortable. I even know what you're going to do next.'

'What am I going to do next?'

'You're going to lift your glass and take a sip.'

Florence looked at her fingers on the stem of her wine glass. He was right. She was on the point of lifting it. 'How did you know that?'

'Because you do that when you're embarrassed. You avert your gaze and find something to do with your hands. It's adorable.'

She gave him a small smile. 'But I don't know what *you're* going to do next?'

'Yes, you do.'

His eyes were heavy as they rested upon her face. 'You're going to embarrass me again,' she said quietly, her gaze sliding onto her plate.

She felt him smile. 'Not here. But as soon as the music starts, I'm going to ask you to dance.'

However, when the band began to play it was Aubrey who got there first because Rupert was distracted by the girl on his left who had engaged him in conversation. Rupert watched Florence as his brother led her onto the dance floor. Florence felt his eyes follow her across the room and wished that he hadn't been so slow on the uptake. Once, she would have considered herself the luckiest girl in the world to be dancing with Aubrey. But now she wished she were in his brother's arms, being led around the dance floor like they'd done in the cave.

Rupert watched Florence and Aubrey. He was not aware of the pensive expression on his face until his sister took the empty chair beside him and said, 'They make a darling couple, don't they?'

Rupert was astonished. 'Aubrey and Florence?'

'Of course. They're a natural pair. They really should have got it together last summer, but Aubrey was sweet on Elise. Poor Flo, how she pined for him.'

Rupert stared at her as pieces of the puzzle now fell into place. 'Will you dance with me, Cynthia?' he said.

'Of course.'

Rupert moved gracefully around the dance floor. Yet his attention was not on his sister, but on Florence. Like an eagle stalking a beautiful swallow he waited for the appropriate moment to intervene.

Florence noticed Rupert dancing with Cynthia, but he was not smiling. She caught his eye for a second and saw something troubled in it. But Aubrey was speaking to her, asking her if he might invite her out when he was next in London and Florence found herself replying that she'd love him to. The music finished and Florence clapped the band. It looked as if Aubrey was going to ask her to dance another when Rupert appeared with Cynthia. 'Let's swap,' he said, not waiting for his brother to reply, but putting a hand around Florence's waist and drawing her away. Aubrey's smile faltered. He looked disappointed. Cynthia was frowning. She gave Florence a look, but Florence pretended she hadn't seen it. The band began to play a waltz.

As Rupert led her around the room, Florence felt a heaviness descend upon them. Rupert's hand was rigid on the curve of her spine and he held her hand so tightly it was almost turning white. She sensed something had been said that had upset him. Then he pulled her against him as if afraid she might bolt. 'Do you love my brother?' he whispered into her ear.

Florence was astonished. There was an intensity in the way he asked that touched her. 'No,' she replied.

'Did you?'

'I thought I did.'

His cheek rested against hers. The scent of lemon engulfed her senses. The warm, familiar smell that was his alone took her back to their kiss in the cave and she felt an overpowering longing for him to kiss her again. She closed her eyes.

'Do I have a chance, Flossie? Because if I don't, you have to tell me now. I survived a year in the hope that I'd get a second chance. I won't survive another. Tell me now if you'd rather be with Aubrey and I'll let you go.'

Florence felt strangely emotional. She squeezed his hand. 'I thought you said you knew me,' she replied softly.

'This is not the moment to tease,' he replied.

She pressed her cheek against his, desperate suddenly to reassure him. 'I want to be with *you*, Rupert, and only you.' She felt him relax. His hand softened in the small of her back, his fingers gently stroked hers. The heaviness lifted.

'And I want to be with you, Flossie,' he said.

Rupert took her by the hand and strode out of the ballroom. Florence did not care whether Miss Ranny or one of the other female teachers stalking the room as chaperones caught her leaving, because tonight was the last night of finishing school and, as far as she was concerned, she was already free.

They hurried along the path, through the ornamental garden and on down to the embankment where the vast expanse of black sea shone like oil beneath a red sickle moon. Gripped by a sense of urgency and carried on a wave of excitement, Florence took off her shoes and ran down to the beach. When she saw that it was made up of shingles, she stopped to put her shoes back on. But Rupert was impatient. He swept her into his arms and carried her into the darkness.

The lapping of waves grew louder. Gently Rupert put her down. He cupped her face, gently caressing her cheeks with his thumbs. His eyes were full of tenderness, gazing at her as if they had never contemplated anything so lovely. Neither spoke. They didn't need to. They were alone in this dark and secret place and that was all that mattered. No longer in Eastbourne, but in Gulliver's Bay, beneath Florence's straw bunting and a canopy of stars. Rupert pressed his lips to hers and Florence slipped her hands beneath his jacket and held him close, and lost herself in his kiss.

CHAPTER TEN

On 25 September 1938 the British fleet was ordered to sea. Trenches were dug into the London parks to use as air-raid shelters and sirens were installed in police stations to warn the people of attack by German bombers. Dread hung over the city like smog as Britain teetered once again on the brink of war with Germany. Hitler had vowed to invade Czechoslovakia on 1 October and it seemed inevitable that such a move would ignite conflict among the great European powers.

Two days before the deadline, Neville Chamberlain met Hitler, Mussolini and Daladier in Munich to discuss the Sudetenland crisis. Many of Florence's male friends were in the Territorials waiting to be called up, and Florence and Winifred discussed what roles they might consider to serve their country, should England go to war.

Yet, on 30 September Neville Chamberlain returned from his visit to Munich, waving the joint declaration of peace. There was a surge of relief and celebration; war had been avoided. However, in spite of the sense of jubilation, there was an undercurrent of fear. It was as if everyone knew that Chamberlain's words were fantasy. That he was simply buying them time. Florence was determined to enjoy herself as much as possible while she could. What did anything matter now that she knew where her heart lay – with Rupert's.

She enrolled in the Ginner Mawer School of Dance and Drama in Knightsbridge, lodging with Mrs Arkwright, an elderly widow who rented rooms nearby strictly for female students. She forbade male visitors and sat in an armchair near the front door from eight in the evening to midnight like a fat buzzard, ready to catch any of her lodgers who dared disobey her.

Embracing her new life with typical enthusiasm, Florence exchanged her dresses, blouses and pencil skirts for bohemian wrap-around cloaks, pyjama trousers and headbands. She adored the ballet classes with the renowned Peggy van Pragh and found a novel sense of liberation when she embodied different personalities on the stage. It was also exciting to be living in London, especially as Rupert was there as well, working for a stockbroking firm in St James's, which he made no secret of loathing.

Rupert loved bookshops. His favourite was Hatchards in Piccadilly and it was there that he took Florence at the earliest opportunity. 'I've ordered you a beautifully bound first edition of my favourite novel,' he told her. 'It's very special and I want you to have it.' Florence had been to Hatchards before, but it was quite different being taken there by Rupert. Excited to be showing it off to the girl he loved, Rupert led her by the hand around every floor as if he owned the place. He knew the booksellers by name and they, in turn, made a great fuss of him. 'I just love the smell, don't you?' he said, climbing the winding, carpeted staircase to yet another level where every wall was packed with dark wooden bookshelves and stacked with glossy hardback books. 'It smells of stories,' he told her animatedly, breathing in with relish. 'And time. You know it's been in this building since 1801. Just think how many words this place has contained. How many adventures, love stories, characters, places, plots, suspense, murder, mystery and magic? It's splendid. You can just feel the vibration of so much love poured into each work, and yet, even if we had a thousand lives, we'd never have the time to read them all.'

Florence was carried along by his enthusiasm. 'I imagine you lose yourself in here, Ru,' she laughed, gazing at him with affection. Every moment she spent with him, she loved him more deeply.

'I wander in most days,' he replied, putting an arm around her waist and pulling her close so that he could kiss her temple. 'But it's even more enjoyable coming with you.'

They went to the desk on the ground floor and the manager handed Rupert a brown paper package wrapped in string. 'This, my darling, is for you,' said Rupert.

Florence unwrapped it carefully. Inside was a beautiful hardback of F. Scott Fitzgerald's *The Great Gatsby*. 'It's stunning,' she replied, running her fingers over the indigo and gold cover. 'Thank you, Ru. I'll treasure it.'

'Have you read it?'

'No, I haven't. But I will, straight away.'

'Then you have a treat in store,' he said. 'I wish I hadn't, so I could enjoy it for the first time all over again.'

'You can relive that feeling through me when we discuss it,' she told him.

'In a field of buttercups,' he added with a grin.

Florence laughed and leaned her head against his shoulder. 'In a field of buttercups,' she repeated, remembering with nostalgia that first conversation they had had on the gate above Gulliver's Bay.

* * *

Florence's debut on the public stage took place just before Christmas. The play was *A Midsummer Night's Dream* and Florence was given the role of Helena. Her mother and Winifred came to watch, along with Rupert, who invited her for dinner and dancing afterwards at the Savoy, on the condition that she wore the dress that had sent Miss Ranny into such a state of displeasure.

Florence might not have been able to make an entrance at the Grand Hotel in Eastbourne but she made one now, in the foyer of the Savoy, to the delight of all around her. She had worn a coat over her dress when Rupert had met her at the stage door after the performance. He had tried to persuade her to take it off so that he could admire her, but she had resisted. She didn't want him to see it in the dark alley behind the theatre, and she did not want to shiver with cold, for the night, though dry, was bitter. She waited until she was in the warmth of the hotel before she allowed him to peel it off. When she turned around she was thrilled to see the glow of admiration and desire on his face. It made her feel like a film star. 'I can see why Miss Ranny disapproved,' he murmured, tracing her curves with appreciation. 'You look dangerously beautiful, Flossie.' Florence laughed. 'I'm going to have to restrain myself.' Rupert gave her his arm and escorted her into the dining room.

A long night of talking and dancing to Carroll Gibbons's famous band ensued and Florence discovered, to her joy, that she was beginning to feel that she knew Rupert too, on that deep and timeless level he had spoken about.

Florence spent Christmas in Gulliver's Bay with her mother, Winifred, her grandparents and Uncle Raymond. They were keen to hear about drama school and Florence's exciting social life in London, but they were most keen to hear about Rupert.

'What's this I hear about you and Aubrey Dash?' Henry asked when the family sat around the dining room table on Christmas Eve.

Florence glanced at Winifred, who raised her eyebrows with interest and put down her knife and fork expectantly. 'It's not Aubrey, Grandpa, it's his brother Rupert,' she replied.

'What? Not Aubrey?' Henry looked at his wife in confusion. 'I thought you said Aubrey, Joan.'

'No, Henry, I said Rupert.'

'By Jove, he might be the rebel of the family but he's going to inherit Pedrevan.'

'He's very handsome,' said Margaret, who was relieved he was suitable. It wouldn't have surprised her had Florence fallen in love with someone who wasn't.

Uncle Raymond smiled knowingly at Florence. 'Extraordinary how things turn out,' he said, arching an eyebrow.

'What does he do besides take you dancing at the Savoy?' Henry asked.

'He's a stockbroker,' Florence told him. 'But he hates it.'

Henry nodded approvingly. 'It's all good experience,' he said. 'Nothing's ever wasted.'

'Isn't Aubrey at Sandhurst?' asked Joan.

'He is,' Winifred answered. 'And I dare say he's a little disappointed that Florence has had such a sudden and unexpected change of heart.' She gave her sister a stern look.

'It wasn't as if he knew I fancied him,' Florence retaliated.

Winifred rolled her eyes. 'Of course he knew,' she said with a sigh. 'Everyone knew.'

Everyone, thought Florence, except Rupert.

* * *

On Christmas Day the families of Gulliver's Bay attended the traditional church service. Reverend Millar presided over the congregation among flickering candles, holly and the usual fir tree decorated with tinsel and glass baubles. The air was thick with the scent of melting wax and perfume, and the worshippers' good cheer, which only hushed when the vicar lifted his arms in welcome and began to speak.

Florence sat with her family and glanced across the aisle at the Dashes, who, in typical Dash style, were at their most glamorous in elegant coats, fine furs and festive hats. Celia sported a scarlet Madam Agnès hat from Paris adorned with a single jaunty feather, and Cynthia, a fashionable wool beret. As usual, they were accompanied by grandparents, uncles and aunts and cousins, and they seemed to take up most of the pews, exuding an air of dominance on account of their great number.

Florence could not concentrate on the service. Her gaze kept straying to Rupert, who every now and then glanced back, his lips curling into a barely perceptible smile. This time Winifred did not elbow her in the ribs. It would have achieved nothing; Florence behaved worse when the reins were tightened. The church filled with the uplifting sound of carols and Florence's spirits lifted with them, on the joyful crest of love.

Reverend Millar gave a typically stirring sermon, blending humour with a strong spiritual message, which was his forte, and Florence tried to keep her eyes upon him, not wanting to offend him by looking elsewhere. She could feel Rupert's eyes upon her and, after succeeding in resisting their pull for at least five minutes, she gave in and allowed her gaze to drift again. But it wasn't only Rupert who was watching her, Aubrey was as well. She sat up in surprise. Aubrey held her attention for a long moment and then let it go. Florence did not move. There was something sad about the way he had looked at her, as if it had come from a place of shadow. She had thought little of Aubrey since seeing him last summer at the Grand Hotel in Eastbourne. How strange, she thought, that someone could dominate one's mind so completely and then, from one day to the next, mean nothing. She shifted her gaze to Rupert who was watching her with a serious look on his face.

When the service was over and they congregated outside in the crisp winter sunshine, Rupert put a proprietorial arm around her waist and lowered his voice. 'Aubrey isn't happy for us,' he said.

'Why ever not?' she replied, concerned.

'Because he wants you for himself.'

Florence was astonished. 'You're imagining it. He's never been interested in me.'

'I'm afraid you're wrong, my darling.' He squeezed her gently. 'For the first time in my life I feel sorry for my brother. He's had everything he's ever wanted, but can't have *you*.'

Florence looked at him quizzically. 'The man who complained bitterly to me about his golden brother the summer before last is not the same one who is feeling compassion for him now.'

'You've changed me,' Rupert said seriously.

'How so?'

'You've taught me gratitude.'

Florence reached out and touched his face. 'Oh, Ru. That's the sweetest thing anyone has ever said to me.'

He smiled bashfully. 'It's true. Not a day goes by when I don't thank God for bringing you into my life.' He took her hand and kissed it. 'And for inspiring you to love me.'

* * *

Florence returned to the dance and drama school in January and Rupert returned to his job in St James's. London was awash with talk of war and society endeavoured to shake off its fears by partying in the usual way. Rupert accompanied Florence to a wedding reception at the majestically wood-panelled Drapers' Hall in the City where they were served dinner on solid silver and gold platters by liveried attendants in white gloves. The music and dancing helped them forget about the newspapers, which were full of Germany's escalating aggression and the formidable power of Hitler's Nazi Party, and they danced until dawn.

On 31 March Neville Chamberlain pledged to support Poland in the event of a German threat to Polish independence. Rupert and Florence decided to spend the Whitsun holiday together in Gulliver's Bay. It was unseasonably warm for April. They drove to Cornwall from London in Rupert's Aston Martin with the roof down and the wind raking through their hair, singing loudly the songs they both loved. There was a sense of intensity about their trip, as if they knew deep down that it would be their last before the threat of war became a reality. They sang with more verve, talked with more honesty and kissed as only people do when faced with inevitable separation.

Florence was a guest of the Dashes at Pedrevan Park. It wasn't full of the usual siblings and cousins, but was curiously empty with only William and Celia in residence, wandering through the big silent rooms, strangely forlorn, like remaining balloons the morning after a party. The house, customarily filled with people, music and laughter, was as quiet as a tomb, as if it too sensed a change in the air like an autumn wind at the end of summer. But the sun was hot and the blossom ablaze on the trees and in the hedgerows, and Rupert and Florence swam in the sea, walked up and down the beach and sat on the bench in the garden beneath the cherry tree and talked. The more they talked, the more they discovered they had in common. And then, inspired by the heady vibrations of nature and their own tender hearts, they reached a depth in their conversation that they hadn't reached before.

It was early evening. The sun was a burning orange ball in a pale blue sky. The sea was calm, waves lapping gently up the beach and, on the breeze, the sulphurous scent of brine. They sat together on the dunes, Florence wrapped in Rupert's coat, Rupert smoking a cigarette which he shared with Florence, and watched the mesmeric play of light upon the water. 'Look, the first star,' she said, pointing.

'That's not a star,' Rupert told her. 'That's Venus.'

'Are you sure? How funny. I've always wished upon that star.'

He chuckled. 'And what did you wish for?'

She sighed and smiled wistfully. 'You, only I didn't know that it was you I was wishing for. I was just wishing for love. I think that's what we all want, deep down, isn't it? To love and be loved?'

'I think we yearn for a more profound love than most people realize. Love is the soul's yearning for reunion with its creator. We feel it when we see a beautiful sunset, or the perfection of a flower, or listen to the singing of birds at dawn. It stirs something inside us, arouses emotions deep within us. God is love, and love expresses itself in nature. That's why we cry in the face of beauty, because beauty resonates with our soul and stirs our longing.'

'That's a lovely way of putting it, Ru. How silly it is that religions separate people from one another when we're all searching for the same thing, for love? If people understood that, there would be no prejudice, no religious persecution. We're all flowers and God is shining His light upon all of us indiscriminately. At least, that's what Uncle Raymond says.'

'I think Uncle Raymond is very wise,' said Rupert. 'Religion has an important part to play in people's spiritual lives. But as long as they look outside of themselves for God they will never find Him, because God is within each and every one of us. In any case, that's what I believe.' He grinned sheepishly. 'Do I sound mad?'

Florence shook her head. 'You don't sound mad at all, my darling. You make a lot of sense. I hated church at school and Rev Minchin was a bore. But I could listen to you talking about religion forever.'

Rupert took a long drag, then passed the cigarette to Florence. 'I've never been able to talk about these things. I've always had a burning curiosity and hundreds of questions, but I've feared I'll expose myself if I share them. My beliefs are not conventional.'

'I'm glad you feel you can confide in me.'

'I'm glad I can too. I know you understand. We share the same curiosity.' He caressed her with his eyes. 'I've never had any doubt that there's more to life than this material world. I've always known it, deep down inside.'

'I believe we go somewhere when we die,' said Florence. 'I don't know where, but I don't believe in death. At least, I don't want to. I like to think a part of us lives on.'

'Life is a training ground. We're here to learn. To grow wise, like Uncle Raymond.' He laughed.

'Do you believe you have a spiritual purpose, Ru?'

'We all do, although I have no idea what mine is. I dare say it's agreed upon before we've even been born into the world. A kind of plan, a blueprint, if you will, which sets out our tasks and the things we must experience in order to learn the lessons our soul needs in order to evolve.'

'But when we get here we don't remember what we've planned to do. Doesn't that defeat the object?'

'We have an inner guidance system,' said Rupert.

'What's that?'

'Our gut, our intuition – you know when you're doing something right because you feel happy. That's your inner guidance system. Things go terribly wrong when you don't listen to it.' He grinned impishly. 'My inner guidance system tells me you're the girl for me.'

Florence nuzzled him fondly. 'Do you think we're meant for each other?' she asked.

'I believe we have lived many lives together already.'

'So that's what you meant when you said you "knew" me.' She smiled. 'That's quite radical, Ru. Reverend Millar would be horrified to hear that.'

'Then let's keep it to ourselves.' He took the cigarette from her and put it out in the sand. 'I don't believe in coincidence. Some things are meant to happen. You and I are one of those things.' He turned and looked at her through the waning light. His eyes shone with affection. 'If there is such a thing as a soulmate, then you are mine, my darling Flossie.'

'I'm grateful to have found you,' she said. 'Otherwise I would have spent my whole life looking for you.'

Rupert laid her on the sand and stroked her face. 'Soulmates have more than a physical attraction, they have a deep, spiritual connection that comes from having known each other through many incarnations.'

Florence put her hands against his ears; they were cold now that the sun had set and the wind had picked up. 'Remind me of our physical attraction,' she said with a grin.

'In case we're in danger of becoming so heavenly as to be no earthly good.'

He smiled, lowered his head and brushed her lips with his. She closed her eyes. She felt his breath on her skin, the soft feeling of his touch, the low murmur as he savoured the moment before she parted her lips and allowed him to kiss her fully.

The day before they were due to drive back to London, Rupert took Florence to the cave where he had first kissed her. The tide was out and only oystercatchers and gulls pecked at the wet sand in search of crustaceans left behind by the retreating water. He pulled her into his arms. 'Will you dance with me?' he asked.

Florence laughed, recalling the night they had waltzed over the sand to the distant sound of the band. 'I would love to,' she replied, giving him her hand.

He put his in the small of her back and drew her against him. She felt his heart beating against her chest. His nervousness was infectious and Florence began to feel nervous too. They moved slowly around the cave and this time Florence didn't step on his foot, but glided with grace as she had been taught to do at her dance and drama school. They hadn't thought about the possibility of war, they hadn't even talked about it, but now it floated into their minds like a grey cloud across a clear sky, darkening it with dread.

Rupert stopped. He got down onto bended knee. Florence's breath caught in her throat which had constricted with the sudden surge of emotion. 'My sweet Flossie.' He took her hand. With his other hand he pulled out of his pocket a ring fashioned from seaweed. 'Until I can give you a real one.' He slipped it on her finger. 'I love you, Florence. And I want to

spend the rest of my life with you. You make me a better man.'
He took a breath and lifted his eyes. She could barely see him
for the tears that blurred her vision. 'I was lost before I met
you,' he continued. 'My inner compass had yet to find north.
But then, two summers ago, you skipped into my life in your
light and carefree way and I realized, very quickly, that you
were my north. You always have been, long before either of
us was even aware of it. Some might frown at the speed with
which I am asking you to marry me, but I don't want to waste
a moment. I know my own heart and now I know my destiny.
Whatever happens in the coming months, we'll weather it
together and hopefully grow old surrounded by children and
grandchildren, here at Pedrevan.'

Florence dropped to her knees and took his face in her
hands. 'My darling Ru, if I am your north, then you are my
guiding star. I give myself to you, body and soul, and trust
that you are the only man capable of loving me, because we
have perhaps loved each other for many lifetimes. This will
be just one more.' She pressed her lips to his, pledging their
troth with a kiss.

Rupert could not wait to ask Florence's grandfather for her
hand in marriage. They hurried straight from the cave to The
Mariners where Joan was in the garden with Henry, deciding
whether or not to pull out what appeared to be a dead hydrangea. When they saw Rupert and Florence they suspended their
discussion, picking up immediately the sense of excitement
and purpose in the young people's expressions. 'Henry,' said
Rupert cheerfully. 'May I have a minute of your time?'

Joan caught Florence's eye. Florence beamed a smile. Joan
took off her gardening gloves, her hands trembling suddenly.
'Darling, come and help me in the kitchen,' she said, making
for the house. 'I've been baking an apple and cinnamon cake

and I need you to tell me what you think.' Florence followed her grandmother towards the French doors, tossing an encouraging glance at Rupert before disappearing inside.

Once in the hall, Joan turned to Florence. 'Am I right in thinking . . . ?' she hesitated, at once uncertain and not wanting to say something out of turn.

Florence threw her arms around her grandmother. 'We're getting married!' she exclaimed.

Joan laughed, squeezing her tightly. 'Ah, I'm so pleased, darling. What wonderful news! He's a very good choice. A very good choice, indeed! Your mother will be very happy.'

Florence showed off the seaweed ring which was already falling apart on her finger. 'Until he buys me a real one,' she said, looking at it tenderly.

'Charming,' said Joan. 'What an unusual man he is.'

'Romantic,' said Florence.

'Very,' Joan agreed. 'You're lucky to have found each other. I wish you a lifetime of happiness, darling.' And Florence couldn't see any reason why that wish would not be granted.

When the two women returned to the garden Henry and Rupert were still talking beside the dead hydrangea. Henry smiled at Florence. 'So, Rupert's decided to make an honest woman of you,' he said. 'Jolly brave of him.'

'Oh, Henry!' said Joan. 'It's the most wonderful news.'

'It certainly is,' he agreed, tickling Florence's face with his moustache as he pressed it against her in a kiss. 'I thought we'd lose you to the theatre.'

'Grandpa, it *is* possible to be both a wife and an actress,' Florence pointed out.

'Of course it is,' said Rupert, slipping his hand around her waist.

Henry arched an eyebrow, unconvinced. 'You'll be busy

raising children, my dear. And one day you'll be running Pedrevan, and that's no small task. I should think your theatre days are now behind you.'

'When will you marry?' Joan interrupted, steering the conversation into calmer waters.

'In October, here in Gulliver's Bay,' Rupert replied.

'How exciting,' Joan gushed. She turned to her grand-daughter. 'Darling, would you like to telephone your mother and Winnie? They'll want to be told before word gets out, and it *will* get out, knowing this town.'

'Do you have time for a glass of champagne, Rupert?' asked Henry as the women retreated inside. 'I'd like to raise a glass in a toast. My first granddaughter getting engaged is a momentous occasion, but Flo has always been a challenge. I hand that challenge over to you, with relief. She's *your* responsibility now.'

Rupert laughed. 'I accept the responsibility gladly, but I think the challenge is all hers, Henry. In any case, we'll both rise to any challenge that presents itself.'

Henry looked at him steadily, a portentous shadow in his eyes. 'War will be a challenge, Rupert, mark my words. It's coming and it won't be pretty. Let's raise our glasses to luck. I suspect, in the coming months, we'll all be needing it.'

The Dashes celebrated Rupert and Florence's engagement in typical Dash style with a glamorous party at Pedrevan in June. Rupert had taken Florence to a jeweller in Bond Street and she had chosen an emerald and diamond ring to replace the sea-weed one he had made her on the beach. Cynthia was beside herself with excitement; Florence was not only her best friend, but soon to become her sister-in-law. Aubrey congratulated his brother with genuine goodwill and embraced Florence with affection, but Winifred noticed the way he looked at her and told Florence not to be deceived by his apparent joy. He was, in her opinion, visibly disappointed and hurt not to have won her for himself.

'He had the chance,' Florence reminded her sister when they stood on the lawn at Pedrevan in the moment before the guests were due to start arriving to celebrate her engagement. 'I was mad for him, as you know.'

'You were yet to blossom,' said Winifred. 'And he was sweet on Elise.'

'Rupert fell in love with me before I blossomed. He saw my potential.' Florence smiled wistfully. 'You know he kissed me in the cave the night of my beach party.'

Winifred was shocked. 'He didn't!'

'He did,' said Florence. 'It was the first time I'd been kissed and it was wonderful.'

'You were heartbroken over Aubrey and Elise, if I remember rightly.'

'But that kiss woke me up. From that moment I couldn't stop thinking about Rupert. He was my destiny, you see. We'd spent most of the summer together and I didn't realize that we were falling in love. I was blinded by what I *thought* I wanted.'

'Aren't you a dark horse.'

'I didn't tell you because I wasn't sure at the time how I felt about it. I was confused. I didn't expect to fall in love with Rupert. I thought I'd always love Aubrey.'

Winifred curled a lock of hair behind her sister's ear and looked at her seriously. 'Aubrey missed his moment, it's true. But that does not diminish his disappointment. I see the way he looks at you and it breaks my heart. He's always been the gifted son, but he's a sensitive soul and I do believe he's hurting. Be kind.'

'I'm always kind, Winnie. I couldn't be otherwise.'

'I know. There's nothing you can do. Rupert might never have won a trophy in all the summers we spent here in Gulliver's Bay, but he's now won the greatest trophy of all.' Winifred smiled tenderly and kissed her sister. 'You deserve each other, Flo. I know you'll be happy. Tonight is your night. Go and find Rupert and enjoy it.'

And Florence did, every moment. They dined and danced, and crystal glasses were raised in toasts to their health and happiness and future, which spread out before them like a sparkling sea of endless possibility. Florence was kind to Aubrey. She looked on him with affection and let him sweep her around the dance floor, but she saw only Rupert in her line of vision, always there, tall and dashing, catching her eye and smiling in that conspiring way of his that made her heart swell.

With the music and clamour of the party fading into the distance, Rupert and Florence walked hand in hand through the garden to the lake, where the statue of the goddess Amphitrite glowed like brushed silver in the moonlight and fireflies danced upon the water. It was quiet but for the soft rustlings of the night and the occasional screech of a barn owl. At length they came to the circular stone folly that was nestled among laurel and dogwood, guarded by a grand old oak whose knotted branches reached out in a possessive embrace. They stood on the steps and gazed over the water. It was romantic and melancholy somehow, for in its beauty was a sense of impermanence, the recognition of an unpalatable truth: that nothing lasts, that everything in this material world eventually passes away however ardently we want to hold onto it. Florence felt a stab of loss at the thought of death parting them, as it surely would one day. The inevitability of it was unbearable, even if it was seventy years from now. 'I never want to be without you,' she said, looking up at Rupert anxiously.

He frowned. 'We'll always be together, my darling.'

'But this night is so beautiful, so perfect, and yet in the morning it will be over.'

'And there will be many more beautiful, perfect nights to enjoy together.'

'I know, of course there will, but one day there won't. One day we'll die.'

He laughed and gathered her in his arms. 'My darling Flossie, we're all going to die one day. But we never leave those we love. Death is simply a new beginning, leaving one shore and arriving on another. You know that. I'll never leave you, I promise. We'll always be together.'

Rupert kissed her, cradling her neck in his hands and caressing her jaw. His kiss was long and tender and Florence felt his hands grow hot and his heart race beneath his ribs. She allowed his kiss to dispel her fears and only the longing in her heart remained, like the quivering of a violin once the bow is lifted, a subliminal dread of loss caused by the covetous nature of love.

On 1 September Hitler marched his troops across the Polish border. Florence was at Pedrevan with Rupert's family a couple of days later, listening to the wireless when Neville Chamberlain's weary voice announced that Britain was now a nation at war. There was stunned silence. Florence took Rupert's hand. In her mind's eye she saw their October wedding disappear into a fog of gunfire. Terror of losing Rupert squeezed her heart. But Fate had brought them together, she reassured herself, and it was unimaginable that it would set them apart.

CHAPTER ELEVEN

Very quickly Pedrevan filled with evacuated children who arrived by train from London with their Mickey Mouse gas-masks in cardboard boxes slung over their small shoulders, their faces pale and bewildered. Celia Dash rolled up her sleeves and threw herself into the task, suggesting they put large bowls of water in the garden for the little ones to splash about in. A genius idea, Florence thought, for they immediately forgot about their strange circumstances and being away from their families and played quite happily.

Florence went to stay with her grandparents at The Mariners. Her mother and Winifred joined them from Kent and Uncle Raymond came down from London. It was Uncle Raymond who suggested that Florence join the FANY, the First Aid Nursing Yeomanry, an all-female charity founded in 1907 to carry out nursing and intelligence work. They had achieved notoriety in the Great War, Uncle Raymond told them. Her job would be in nursing, intelligence work and transport services. Florence was excited. If she was going to contribute to the war effort, this sounded like just her thing.

Rupert joined the Royal Sussex Regiment and was immediately sent off on his officer's training course in Bedford. Florence was quickly enrolled in the FANY and embarked on an intense training programme at Camberley in Surrey. She did not want to be so far away from Rupert, but these were extraordinary times and she knew she must do her duty. Her first job was to learn how to drive an ambulance, which was no easy task for the smallest jolt could inflict terrible pain on a wounded soldier. Florence wasn't tall, which meant she was not permitted to drive the large six-wheeled vehicles. Instead, she was given a converted laundry van, which had been commandeered by the army to be used as an ambulance. She was particularly proud of her khaki uniform, tailor-made especially for her. It was modelled on the army officers' uniform but with a skirt instead of trousers. On her cap and jacket she wore the FANY insignia, a cross within a circle. Around her waist she fastened a Sam Browne belt, which had to be polished in the tradition of the Brigade of Guards: stripped down to the leather with methylated spirits then brushed with brown Kiwi boot polish and beeswax until it shone like mahogany. Being slim with long legs the uniform suited her well and she took great pleasure in wearing it.

In late September Florence was posted to Shorncliffe Barracks near Folkestone in Kent. The army had commandeered a Spanish-style mansion at Encombe for the FANY after its owners had fled to America. They had taken their furniture with them, but had left behind a shagreen bath and a collection of silver, which was looked after by the caretaker, an elderly man who took a shine to Florence and gave her a silver cocktail shaker as a gift. Conscious of the unnecessary extravagance of owning such a thing, Florence donated it to the Spitfire Fund.

For the first few weeks they had only blankets to sleep on because the army cots were yet to arrive, but Florence was so busy training and scrubbing floors and walls that it didn't matter; never in her life had she been so exhausted. With the threat of an invasion at any moment the fleet of ambulances had to be ever ready. A sergeant from the Royal Army Service Corps trained them in maintenance, shouting at them brusquely if, on leaving their vehicles, they forgot to remove the rotor arm. No one had ever spoken to Florence like that before and she was shocked. It amused her to think of what Miss Ranny would have had to say about it; she had prepared them for the management of great houses, not army vehicles.

Soon after arriving at Encombe a fresh-faced young subaltern was sent from Shorncliffe Barracks to supervise their air-raid precautions. There were no shelters on the estate and, in the event of an attack, the women had to be ready to drive the ambulances. Therefore, the young subaltern was given no choice but to allocate refuges inside the house – in the cellar, in the cupboard beneath the stairs, under the kitchen table, anywhere they could find cover. When it came to Florence's turn there was nowhere left for her to hide, for every available space had been taken. The subaltern looked harassed suddenly. He rubbed his chin, a chin too young to have even sprouted a hair, and took her outside to a cluster of overgrown rhubarb bushes. 'These will do,' he said, pointing. 'Nothing like a shrub to protect you from the enemy, eh?' He did not realize that, come winter, those leaves would have withered away and Florence would be left without any protection at all.

As the balmy autumn weather continued into winter, Florence and her fellow FANYs were transformed into a highly trained and efficient corps. One of their main jobs was to drive sick service personnel to and from hospital. They also replaced male drivers in staff cars and Florence was amused to find herself chauffeuring men she'd known in her civilian life. She enjoyed seeing the surprised looks on their faces when they saw her in her uniform, saluting and opening the car door for them. Sometimes, if she was feeling mischievous, she couldn't resist giving them a wink and a smile.

Florence's driving days were soon to come to an end, however. When the cook left without warning, her commanding officer remembered that Florence had done a domestic science course at Miss Randall's School of Domestic Economy and relegated her to the kitchen to cook meals for the entire establishment. Florence, who had never particularly enjoyed that part of her course, or given it much attention, found herself straining to remember even the basics. She rather wished, at that point, that she had concentrated during her lessons and not mucked about with Cynthia, playing Cat's Cradle with string out of sight of the teacher. The FANYs, however, when they were off duty in the house, were a cheerful regiment with little distinction between ranks. As autumn finally gave way to a cold, hard winter, the kitchen became the focal point of the house where everyone congregated around the ancient oven, which only closed if tied with string, and helped to peel vegetables and wash up to the sound of noisy chatter and songs on the gramophone.

Snow blanketed the grounds in December. Florence helped shovel paths for the ambulances and rub potato peel on the windows to stop them frosting over. She did not envy the women who had to get up in the freezing light of dawn and drive for miles along hazardous roads. She was happy in her warm kitchen and by now was good at her job.

Florence missed Rupert dreadfully. Her body ached for him at night and sometimes she gave in to tears, brought on by exhaustion as well as longing. She didn't know when they'd get the chance to marry. After having wanted a fairy tale wedding, she now simply wanted to be wed, even if it meant a short and impersonal ceremony at the Chelsea Registry Office.

She spent Christmas on leave with her family in Gulliver's Bay and was reunited with Rupert at Pedrevan, but there was little rest, for the house was teeming with evacuees and everyone was expected to help. However, the two of them managed to find time to be alone. They walked around the lake and kissed on the steps of the folly as they had done the night of their engagement party the previous summer. Now the water was frozen and the moon hidden behind snowy clouds, but its beauty touched them both with an even greater sense of transience. They knew not when they would see each other again, so Rupert, desperate to hold onto her, captured every special moment with his Leica.

In April 1940 the Germans invaded Denmark and Norway. Florence suffered her first experience of loss. Some of the Irish Guards stationed at Shorncliffe were among those who were killed at Narvik in Norway. For a young woman who had dreamed of a life of drama on and off the stage she suddenly realized the cost of such a desire. The war, which had previously appeared exciting, and glamorous even, now bared its teeth and they were sharp and bloody. For the first time since joining the FANY Florence was aware of the danger she was in, of the danger Rupert was in too. This wasn't an exercise like those she'd watched at Shorncliffe, this was real. The sight of the grieving adjutant, a pretty brunette who had been engaged to one of those brave Irishmen, affected Florence deeply. She couldn't help but think of Rupert. She prayed that they would both survive the war and enjoy their autumn years at Pedrevan surrounded by children and grandchildren, just as Rupert had dreamed they would.

A conflict of interest soon developed between the FANY

and the Auxiliary Territorial Service which was to change the course of Florence's life. She was given a few options. She could join the ATS and become a non-combatant soldier; join the Free FANY, which was a special unit for secret agents dropped into enemy territory; or leave. After much deliberation, Florence decided to leave, or, as Rupert put it, 'To give the FANY the sack!' Her initial thought was to find a position that would use her driving qualification. But when she mentioned that she'd be stationed at the East India Docks, her grandfather nearly spilled his scotch. 'By Jove!' he exclaimed, his face as red as an overripe tomato. 'There's every vice known to man in those docks. No granddaughter of mine will compromise her reputation in that den of iniquity. What on earth does Rupert have to say about it?'

Rupert was in agreement with Henry, but not for the same reason. He worried about the danger Florence would be in being based in London in the event of a German invasion. To appease both her father and her fiancé, Florence decided to train as a nurse instead.

In the weeks before Florence started her new job at the Kent and Sussex Hospital in Tunbridge Wells, she and Rupert managed to spend a blissful break together, picnicking on the Sussex Downs and gazing out over the glittering sea. They visited Glyndebourne, the five-hundred-year-old house where Captain John Christie had started the annual Opera Festival in 1934, to find the grounds closed and the theatre empty. They leapt upon the stage, re-enacting scenes from their favourite plays and singing songs to an imaginary audience, falling about with laughter and kissing with a passion that was fast becoming uncontrollable. 'I don't know how much longer I can go on without making love to you,' Rupert told her seriously, slipping his hand beneath her shirt and running his fingers over her skin. 'If we don't marry soon, I will make a *dis*honest woman of you.'

'Then let's marry, darling. Now,' said Florence. 'I don't think I can wait much longer, either. I don't need a big ceremony. I just need *you*.'

Rupert and Florence were finally married at the beginning of May in the church in Gulliver's Bay. Few family members could attend due to petrol rationing and their wartime duties. Henry and Joan were there with Margaret, Uncle Raymond and Winifred, who was engaged to a Colonel much older than herself and widowed. Henry would have had a lot to say about that if it hadn't been for the fact that he'd been at school with the man's father. On Rupert's side his parents were accompanied only by Cynthia, who had saved up her petrol vouchers to drive down from Brighton where she was serving as a VAD nurse. Aubrey, who was in intelligence, was unable to get away.

Celia had taken over the arrangements, for Margaret was too anxious to be of any use. Radio Sue had trained some of the children to sing in the choir and Celia had organized the older ones to help decorate the church with cow parsley from the hedgerows and flowers from the garden. Florence wore the wedding dress she had had made the summer before and borrowed a pair of Cynthia's satin shoes. Radio Sue was invited to play the organ, which she did with great enthusiasm, delighted that she was privy to this deeply private ceremony because she could later tell everyone all about it.

Henry took Florence down the aisle. Rupert turned to watch her stately advance, a tender smile on his face, tears shining in his eyes. As a girl, Florence had fantasized about a big, white wedding with a church bursting with people, but this was more perfect than she could have ever dreamed. There was an intimacy in the near-empty church, charm in the wobbly, high-pitched voices of the evacuated children and beauty in the simple garden flowers. She placed her hand in Rupert's and returned his smile with a shaky one of her own, blinking up at him through the mist in her eyes.

Reverend Millar married them, offering wise words to which Florence gave her fullest attention. After the service they celebrated with a lunch at Pedrevan and that afternoon Rupert and Florence drove to a small inn, nestled in the valley beside a river, not far from Gulliver's Bay. They had discovered it one afternoon three years before while on a scavenger hunt and been enchanted by it. Old and crooked, with ancient beams and a sagging roof, it looked like something out of a children's bedtime story. They were given the best room at the top of the building, beneath the eaves, with a view of the river and the mossy valley that gently cradled it. In the distance the landscape opened into rolling hills upon whose canvas the light played as if for their exclusive entertainment. The sun turned the sky pink and Venus shone for Florence to cast her wish upon; however, Florence was not gazing out of the window, but into Rupert's face as he kissed her neck and slipped her dressing gown over her shoulders. It melted into a shimmering puddle at her feet. She stood naked before him for the first time. She was not bashful or afraid. She wanted him to admire her. He ran his eyes over her fulsome body, over her breasts and hips, and smiled. 'You're a feast,' he said and she laughed.

Florence began unbuttoning his shirt, but her fingers were slow and clumsy and Rupert, keen to be rid of it, lifted it over his head and threw it to the floor. Then he was kissing her deeply and her laughter caught in her throat as the ache in her loins returned with more intensity. He stepped impatiently out of his trousers and pulled her onto the big bed. Skin against skin, heart against heart, they lost themselves in each other. As they made love beneath the eaves in this secret Cornish valley, they forgot the war and their duties and were aware only of the dizzy excitement of being man and wife at last.

At the end of their interlude Rupert returned to take command of his platoon with the 2nd Battalion Royal Sussex and Florence started work at the hospital in Tunbridge Wells. They loathed being apart, but their duties at this time of war demanded it. The war would soon be over, Florence thought hopefully, and then their married life could resume in earnest.

To Florence's dismay the hospital was filled with wounded from Dunkirk and the fraught nurses had no time to tell her what to do; she had to learn by trial and error. The first few weeks were spent in the sluice-room, washing blood-stained bandages and cleaning bedpans and urinals. There was a desperate shortage of bandages and Florence struggled to keep up with the demand. The wards were crammed with thirty to forty men and the sight and sound of suffering was horrifying to a young woman who had barely set foot in a hospital or seen the sight of blood. The most appalling part was the top floor where soldiers were treated for burns with tannic acid. Florence nearly fainted when she first saw the blackened limbs and faces, suppurating against the white sheets and pillow cases. An eerie silence pervaded that floor. It was more like a morgue than a ward, and Florence was relieved when she was able to return downstairs, although the shame of her repulsion haunted her for some time. How dare she feel revolted when those poor men were in such pain? It was during those more testing moments that Florence's heart cried out for Rupert.

After a month in Tunbridge Wells Florence was moved to a more permanent post in Canterbury, which was surrounded by the airfields Biggin Hill, Detling, Hawkinge and Manston. The battle in the skies above Britain began with the bombing of Eastchurch aerodrome on 13 August and she was able to crane her neck and watch the small silver planes high up above her, deftly weaving in and out of each other in what looked from the ground like a graceful dance. But plumes of smoke and plummeting aircraft were a reminder of the deadly war being played out in those seemingly peaceful skies, and the parachutes floating to earth were often carrying broken and burning bodies.

Occasionally, she went in the ambulance to pick up wounded airmen. She never knew whether, on those rescue missions, they'd be confronted by friend or foe. On one such occasion the ambulance drew up in the field and Florence ran across the grass to the heap of crumpled silk. A pair of brilliant blue eyes blinked up at her with gratitude. 'Have I arrived in Heaven?' the Englishman asked, his voice quivering with pain. 'Do my eyes deceive me or are you an angel?' Florence tended to each man, ally or enemy, with a heart full of compassion, for he could be Rupert. She believed that if she looked after the wounded, when Rupert's turn came to fight in Europe a kind woman on the other side of the Channel might look after him in the same way, were he to fall into enemy hands.

Florence was acutely aware of the danger she was in, but she tried not to think about it. She focused instead on a future with Rupert, envisaging them lying on a blanket on the lawn at Pedrevan, watching their children playing on the grass. She hoped that if she thought about it hard enough, it would come to pass. But danger found her, regardless. Canterbury was bombed and two colleagues at the hospital were killed. Florence was both heartbroken for those who had lost their lives and terrified for her own safety. She restrained her emotions during the day, as was appropriate, but gave in to grief at night when, pressing her face into the pillow, she howled for Rupert.

One morning she was riding her bicycle down an empty lane, enjoying the lush English countryside and the cow parsley in the hedgerows, when she noticed planes flying above her. She put on her tin hat as she had been instructed to do and continued blithely on. It never occurred to her that she might be in any peril. After all, she had cycled down this lane many times before and those planes were very far away. Her mind drifted to Rupert and lingered lovingly on his face. Suddenly, she heard the spray of machine gunfire hitting the ground behind her. The sound grew louder as the bullets came nearer. She realized, with a jolt of panic, that those bullets were aimed at her. Swiftly, she turned her bicycle into a ditch and crashed into the undergrowth. The bullets whizzed past her, missing her by a whisker. Dazed and bruised she got back on her bike and cycled shakily to the hospital, keeping her eyes on the sky and praying the plane didn't come back for another go. It wasn't until she reached the safety of the building and her peers, who gathered around her with concern, that she began to shake all over and cry inconsolably.

Rupert and Florence seized every opportunity to be together. Stationed in different parts of the country they decided that the best place to meet was in London. Florence took the train from Canterbury, sitting for hours in the blacked-out carriage, lit only by a dim blue lightbulb. She was filled with excited anticipation at the prospect of being once again in her husband's arms, only to sob with misery when she had to say goodbye and return to her post. It seemed that the journeys to and from London were longer than the time they spent together. When Florence learned that Rupert's regiment would soon be sent overseas, she was devastated. She thought of those poor wounded souls in the hospital and the fear that Rupert might get hurt, or worse die, rose from the depths of her being where she had, up until now, kept it under control, to take hold of her heart with an icy grip. She turned to prayer; only God could protect him now.

Security forbade Rupert from telling Florence where he was posted. Posters emblazoned with the phrase *Careless talk costs lives* were stuck up on billboards all over the country and taken very seriously, for everyone had a family member or a friend in the armed forces and any breach of that code of secrecy could have terrible consequences. Rupert's letters to Florence were censored. Dates were cut out and sentences obscured with ink. Florence had no idea where Rupert was, but his letters were full of clues.

> *We have had an amusing time doing PT for the ship tends to roll about. I have made up one or two queer exercises which seem to amuse the carriers; they are rapidly becoming a clique, which is a good thing as far as they are concerned but not for the rest of the people. I find that one has got to be a mother to the men . . . Last night I had to stay up for three hours watching over the men sleeping on the deck to see they did not smoke. I went up to the very front of the ship and sat and just thought – it was the first time I have been alone.*

Florence's heart went out to him for the strain he must be under. It was not in his nature to enjoy being with people;

Rupert was a solitary man. She remembered him telling her that he'd like to live in a small cottage somewhere and spend his days lying in buttercups reading F. Scott Fitzgerald. She hoped that when the war was over, they could move into a little house by the sea and lie together in the buttercups, reading out quotes from *The Great Gatsby*. She had read the treasured edition he had given her and longed to discuss it with him.

Later, in 1942, she received word from the desert:

Yesterday I went into one of the carriers tents where I found Sgt Harris 'sprogging up' – making a cup of tea – Of course it is highly illegal in a tent so in future we 'sprog up' outside. In the desert everyone sprogs up at every halt. You will be horrified when I tell you that in every lorried infantry battalion every vehicle did its own cooking each day, and very successfully we did too. To make a fire we used an old petrol tin and in it was mixed petrol and sand; yes, petrol. Roberts used to guarantee to get me a cup of tea in under ten minutes, some people were even quicker, but at the end we used to have our tea, sausages, tomatoes and bacon in about ten minutes and be ready to move off again. Someone said that if tea was taken away from the 8th Army we would lose Egypt!

Rupert never troubled her with horrors. If he felt fear or pain, he kept them from her. His letters were only ever about food and fun – and always at the end a wistful longing to be reunited with her at Pedrevan.

In June 1943 Florence learned that Rupert had joined a parachute battalion. '*Parachuting is definitely NOT dangerous,*' he wrote.

I am not pretending that I enjoy throwing myself out of a plane for I don't but it is not nearly as frightening as you might think, nor is it glamorous or tough as people make out, any more than infantry; in fact, the only difference is we land by parachute instead of lorries. Anyhow as to my feelings and what we do. We go to the aerodrome, fix on our parachutes, enter the plane and take off. The word 'Action Stations' comes and then 'GO' and out one pops like a cork, for the rushing air just whips one out. The next thing I remember is being pushed about by the wind and then a gentle tug on my shoulder and I realize my parachute has opened and I glide to the ground. I suppose to some people jumping is a drug for when a man has landed he is very virile indeed and capable of doing things that normally he can't do. People land on the ground in a very excited state, asking all sorts of mad questions!

He added, to Florence's amusement: '*Am I a criminal to have become a member of a parachute battalion?*' For many considered those brave men suicidal and without consideration for those at home who loved them. Florence, however, felt nothing but joy for him. She remembered the troubled, dissatisfied young man who had opened his heart to her sitting on the gate in Gulliver's Bay and realized that Rupert had, at last, attained a sense of purpose and fulfilment in his life. As much as she feared for his safety, she was glad that he had finally found his place in the world.

In December 1943 Rupert arrived home. Florence was now working as a nurse at Swanborough Manor in Sussex, a seven-hundred-year-old house that had been commandeered by the army as a hospital. She immediately took compassionate leave and travelled by train to Oakham in Rutland in the East Midlands where Rupert was stationed with the illustrious 10th Battalion, Parachute Regiment, known simply as the Tenth, in a secret location in the heart of the countryside. When she got off the train she spotted him immediately, her darling, inimitable Rupert, pacing the platform with his usual impatience in his greatcoat and beret. She dropped her suitcase and with tears misting her vision and overflowing down her cheeks, she flew into his arms as a light flurry of snow dusted them with glitter.

Florence had arranged to stay with some friends of her grandparents who lived in a manor house nearby, sheltered by elm trees and watched over by a family of owls who had taken up residence in a lofty hollow. Rupert had to remain at his base for he was still on active duty. But the elderly couple understood their need to be alone and assigned them a series of rooms on the top floor where they would be undisturbed. Months of separation simply gave them the wonderful pleasure of discovering each other again.

'I can't bear being apart from you, Ru,' said Florence, lying in his arms, her face nestled in the curve of his neck.

'You have to keep your focus trained on the horizon, Flossie,' Rupert told her, pressing his lips to her head. 'Imagine you're a boat, sailing towards a distant land. You can see it, shimmering on that fuzzy blue line where the sea meets the sky. That's home. That's you and me. You'll get there from your place and I'll get there from mine, and we'll be reunited. Don't take your eye off it, because that's where you're headed.'

Florence sighed. 'But it seems so far away. It's a tiny little island and the sea appears endless.'

'Everything comes to pass, my darling,' he told her wisely. 'The good times and the bad times. This war will surely end and, God willing, we'll both survive it. We have a glorious future, you know. We're going to have lots of children and they'll probably be horribly hearty, like Aubrey, Cynthia and Julian. We might even have little reprobates who refuse to play tennis and would rather lie in the shade and read a book.' He chuckled and Florence's eyes stung with tears. 'You'll be wanting to invite people for dinner and I'll be begging you not to, and we might even fight about it. But the making up will be incredibly sweet. You'll always give in in the end, because that's the sort of woman you are.' He ran a hand down her hair. 'You're kind.'

'Oh, Ru. I won't invite anyone for dinner if you don't want me to.'

He laughed. 'I might hold you to that.'

She lifted her head out of his neck and looked down at him fondly. 'You're a complicated old thing, aren't you,' she said and her expression was full of love. 'How many children do you want?'

'Five. Five little reprobates.' He rolled her onto her back and grinned, his eyes now glinting with lust. 'Let's see if we can make one now. There's no better time than the present.'

Florence reluctantly returned to her post, her heart full of sorrow once again at their parting. But it wasn't for long, for she soon discovered, to her delight, that she was carrying one of Rupert's little reprobates. Worried that the stress of her job might endanger their child, Rupert petitioned for her release from duty. He pulled every string available to him and, to her surprise and relief, Florence was given permission to leave.

A few days before she departed, Florence was in the kitchen with one of the other nurses, preparing the patients' trays and idly chatting about Rupert and her pregnancy. She was already feeling nauseous in the mornings and unusually tired at the end of the day. 'You should put your feet up, Flo,' the nurse told her. 'Or your ankles will swell and—' She was cut off by the piercing sound of a scream. Florence turned in alarm to see one of the other nurses coming at her with a bread knife. The woman's face was twisted with hatred and there was a terrifying passion in her eyes. Florence didn't have time to react but her companion lunged at the woman's arm and managed to deflect the blade, so it merely scraped Florence's stomach instead of plunging into it. With the help of another nurse the assailant was wrestled to the floor, only to curl into a ball and sob hysterically.

Florence was trembling. She looked down at her ripped uniform, afraid that the blade might have drawn blood, but it had only cut through the fabric. Overcome by a wave of sickness she stuck her face in the sink and threw up. She found out later that the woman was in despair because she'd got pregnant by a married man who had consequently jilted her. Florence's happy chatter had caused her to lose her mind.

A few days later Rupert came to whisk Florence away. As they drove over the Sussex Downs their spirits soared with jubilation. That little island quivering on the blue horizon held all their dreams and they kept their eyes firmly fixed upon it as they inched their way closer, the three of them, Rupert, Florence and their unborn child.

That night they stayed at the Metropole Hotel in Brighton before driving up to Rutland the following morning, to the Tenth's secret training camp. For a short, blissful period, Florence and Rupert settled into something closer to a normal life. They were billeted in a quaint old pub which only had two bedrooms, one for the landlord and his wife, the other for Rupert and Florence. Every morning Rupert would leave for his duties and every evening he would return, just like an ordinary husband. Florence would listen out for the rumbling sound of his jeep and rush out through the snow to meet him. It was a golden time, but it wasn't to last. The war was not yet over and the Tenth had yet to emboss their name in history.

As spring covered the hills in buttercups and swallows returned to nest beneath the eaves, Rupert and the illustrious Tenth were moved to a place near Ringway aerodrome in Cheshire. Florence returned home to Kent to be with her mother who was thrilled to spend time with her. Since her daughters had left home to help with the war effort, Margaret had been very lonely on her own. She was excited at the prospect of being a grandmother and fussed over Florence as if she were a child again, insisting that she rest and prohibiting her from helping with the household chores. Florence, as much as she enjoyed her mother's attention, had never been good at sitting still and went for solitary walks across the fields instead. Rupert would want her to exercise, she told her mother, knowing that Margaret had an unwavering respect for men and would not try to stop her.

Before the battalion departed overseas, a wealthy tycoon whose daughter was engaged to one of the officers threw a dance in their honour. It was audacious, at this stage in the war with the scarcity of resources, to throw a lavish party, but he invited the whole battalion and their partners to his sumptuous home for a sit-down dinner with dancing. Florence wore one of her mother's dresses which discreetly hid her growing belly and Rupert walked tall in his uniform. A band played during dinner, and afterwards Rupert and Florence danced only with each other. 'How is young Dash in there enjoying the music?' Rupert asked, as they moved slowly around the floor.

'He or she is going to be a wonderful dancer,' she replied. 'I'm sure I can feel the little feet tapping to the beat.'

Rupert smiled down at her and kissed her fondly. 'I do love you, my Sun Swallow. You won't ever forget that, will you, Flossie? Whatever happens, you'll always be a part of me.'

'We're a part of each other, my Bateleur Eagle,' she replied, holding him tightly. 'We've made it this far. We'll make it to the end.' Then her vision misted. 'You will take care of yourself, won't you, Rupert? I couldn't bear to lose you.'

'You're not going to lose me, my darling. I have too much to live for.'

Florence gazed into his eyes and felt a shiver ripple across her skin. When they looked at each other like this she felt the absence of time and the eternal expanse of something so much greater than the two of them to which they both belonged; the never-ending journey of the soul.

CHAPTER TWELVE

Florence put her hand against the wall of the cave and closed her eyes. Tears slid down her cheeks, dropping off her chin and onto her woollen sweater. She gasped for breath but still the sobbing came in a giant, uncontrollable wave. She had received a telegram: '*Missing. Believed Killed.*'

An officer's daughter never cries.

Her father's words surfaced, then evaporated; a captain's wife couldn't help but sob her heart out.

It was 29 September 1944. The wind whipped off the sea, salty and cold. Above, a front of cloud advanced towards Gulliver's Bay like an advancing army preparing for battle. Florence looked out of the mouth of the cave. Rain was beginning to fall, turning the sea grey. She looked down at her feet to see the water gathering. The tide was coming in.

It didn't seem that long ago since she and Rupert had danced in this cave. It had been that hot summer of 1937. She remembered the first time he had kissed her and the feelings it had aroused. She had thought she loved Aubrey, but her sister Winifred had been right. It had been a crush, like glitter, to be blown away by the tornado that was Rupert. Deep and complex, Rupert felt everything more intensely than his happy-go-lucky brother. His pain was more profound, his joy more ecstatic, his heart less easily won. Aubrey was a girl's first romance, Rupert was a woman's eternal love. When Florence had retreated into the cave to cry over Aubrey's affection for Elise, she did not know that a more meaningful connection was about to be made. That Rupert's kiss would change everything. She had entered the cave a girl and exited a woman. And now, in the face of Rupert's likely death, she was altered once again. Without Rupert, she would be forever alone. A half of a whole. The lesser half.

She did not want to be like her mother, mourning the loss of the man who had completed her.

Florence sobbed again. The glimmer of hope that shone weakly through the telegram in the word 'missing' was as small as a pin prick. The word 'killed' held more power, like the blast of a bomb; it obliterated everything.

As the water reached her ankles and edged towards the back of the cave, Florence put a hand on her belly. She carried inside her their child. The part of Rupert still living. He might never know this being they had created together and, worse, this being might never know *him*. Stunned into alertness by this shocking thought, she clutched onto the glimmer of light and the word 'missing'. Perhaps Rupert had been lucky. Maybe he wasn't dead. He might be lying wounded somewhere or in a field hospital, unconscious. He would not want her to worry. He'd want her to be strong, for their child. She dried her eyes with cold fingers and hurried through the water to the slope of rocks that led to the smuggler's tunnel. Careful not to slip and mindful of the precious cargo she was carrying, Florence made her way slowly up to the house.

When she emerged from the cellar, her grandmother was

in the morning room with Reverend Millar. They stopped talking the moment she walked in. Reverend Millar put down his teacup and stood up. Florence began to cry again at the sight of his compassionate face. He put out his hands and she took them gratefully. They were warm and spongy and reassuring. 'Don't give up hope, Florence,' he said gently. 'Let us pray that he is returned to you.'

Florence sat down and the three of them bowed their heads and closed their eyes. 'Gracious Lord, we ask you to watch over the soul of our beloved Rupert. If he is wounded, let him find aid. If he is lost, let him find refuge. If he is in torment, let him find peace. Until the time You see fit to gather him into Your eternal embrace, please comfort him and give him strength. Please comfort his family too, especially Florence. Surround her with love and light and give her courage to face the uncertainty of the coming days. In your mercy, Lord, hear our prayer.'

Joan poured Florence a cup of tea. 'My dear, until we know for sure, we must not give up hope,' she said, passing her the cup.

'Miracles happen,' Reverend Millar added. 'We must continue to hope and to pray.'

'I will not give up,' Florence told them, finding strength in their support. 'I know that Rupert would never leave me.'

The following day Florence went to Pedrevan to see her mother-in-law. The clouds had passed in the night and the rain washed the colour out of the sky. Celia was in the greenhouse, planting lettuce in trays of compost. She wore gloves and a gardening apron and still managed to look glamorous. When she saw Florence, she took off her gloves and went to embrace her. 'We must be strong,' she told her firmly. 'We're not going to break down and cry. Rupert would be appalled by all that needless emotion. He'd want us to hope and not to give up on him. He's not dead yet. He's just missing. Typical Rupert. He's always been complicated.'

Florence nodded and swallowed back her tears. 'Can I help you?'

'Do you really want to?'

'Yes, I need to take my mind off things.'

'Very well. There are gloves over there in that basket. You can plant some spinach. We have to keep those poor children strong too,' she said, referring to the evacuees.

'How are they doing? It must be difficult being away from their families,' said Florence, pulling on a pair of gloves which were much too big for her.

'They're thriving,' said Celia proudly. 'You know, some of them hadn't seen farm animals before and there were many who hadn't ever eaten anything green.' She laughed. 'It was a challenge to persuade them that it wouldn't kill them. I hope they've enjoyed being here, in spite of the obvious pain of separation and uncertainty. I've rather loved having them. When the war is over, which I hope it will be soon, they'll all go home and I'll feel bereft. I've relished the sense of purpose it's given me. I've played a small part, we all have, and I'm grateful. I can look into the eyes of my children and know that I did my bit too, while they did theirs. I wouldn't want to be sitting around doing nothing.' Her smile faltered and she patted the soil angrily. 'Bloody war. I hope Hitler burns in Hell for the misery he's caused.'

Suddenly, they heard a sing-song 'too-de-loo' wafting through the garden. Florence looked at Celia and scowled. 'That dreadful woman!' she exclaimed. A moment later Mrs Warburton – Radio Sue – appeared, carrying a basket.

'There you are,' she trilled. 'And Florence too.' Her smile

was swallowed into an exaggerated frown – a look of utmost sympathy and compassion. 'I've just heard about poor darling Rupert. I had to come over, right away. I can't bear it. It's just dreadful.'

Before Celia and Florence could respond to what was, by any account, an intrusion, Radio Sue had put down her basket and was pulling Florence into a fierce embrace. 'At times like these we must discard any formality and come together as human beings in need of comfort and support. I've brought you a cake,' she said. 'Celia,' she gushed, reaching out to grab her too. 'I'm so terribly sorry.'

Celia stepped back so that Radio Sue only managed to grasp her gardening apron. 'I'm not sure what you have heard, Sue, but Rupert is not dead.'

Radio Sue stiffened and blinked at her in surprise. 'Oh? Not dead? I thought he was missing, presumed killed.'

'Until we are informed of his death, we are not giving in to hopelessness.'

'Then I am mistaken. I do apologize. I join you in prayer.'

'Thank you, Sue,' said Celia, her voice softening. 'How kind of you to bake a cake.' Celia peered into the basket then lifted the muslin.

'Eggs from our own hens and honey from our bees,' Radio Sue told her self-importantly. 'We are so very lucky not to be hit by rationing. Besides petrol, we are our own independent power at The Grange.' She looked at her watch and gave a little sniff. 'Well, must be getting on. No rest for the wicked. I've got choir practice in twenty minutes and those children need to master their psalms for Sunday.'

Florence watched her hurry off. 'Does she always pop over without telephoning first?' she asked Celia.

'Unfortunately, she inveigled her way into teaching the

evacuees to sing. She's the self-appointed spiritual prefect of the community. Reverend Millar gave her an inch and she's taken a mile. He's lived to regret that.' She chuckled. 'Still, we've got a cake out of her. How nice. I bet it's delicious. Sue does know how to bake a good cake.'

Florence finished planting the spinach and then helped Celia dig up some potatoes. 'Easy now,' said Celia, watching Florence toiling on her hands and knees. 'You're carrying my very precious grandchild. How are you? I imagine beginning to get quite tired.'

'The baby's a feisty little thing. Keeping me awake at night with its kicking.'

'Have you got any idea about names?'

'Well, that's the trouble. We can't agree. I like the name Mary and Rupert wants Alice.'

'After his grandmother.'

'Exactly.'

'He adored his grandmother. She was the one member of the family who thought his foibles were traits of genius.'

Florence laughed. 'Not just a brooding nature?'

'Oh no. Rupert's brooding was evidence of his brilliantly creative temperament. And if it's a boy?'

'We both like Alexander.'

'I like Alexander too. Let's hope it's a boy then there'll be no fighting over names.'

Weeks passed and Florence heard no further word about Rupert. In October she gave birth to a baby girl. It was not an easy birth, but the physical pain she endured was far more bearable than the mental anguish she had been suffering. When she held her child in her arms at last, exhausted and emotional, the tears she shed were for Rupert who was not able to meet his daughter. In a moment of despair, she wondered whether he ever would.

Henry, now a proud great-grandfather, registered the birth. As Florence wasn't sure which name to choose, Henry suggested they put down both and then make up their minds when Rupert came home. That pleased Florence. It gave her something to hold onto; they'd decide on the name *when Rupert came home*. For now, she'd be called Mary-Alice.

Margaret came down by train and Henry used his precious petrol coupons to pick her up at the station. She was excited to meet her granddaughter, but at the same time desperately anxious about Rupert. She knew what it was to be widowed.

Every effort was made to find out Rupert's fate. Henry was in touch with the Red Cross, trying to discover news of prisoners-of-war, but nothing was forthcoming. Florence was up most of the nights feeding Mary-Alice and because she was too worried to sleep. One night she padded down to the kitchen where the old retainer, Rowley, who had worked his way up from a boot-boy in his youth to butler, was also finding it hard to rest. The two of them sat at the kitchen table, the big teapot steaming between them, and talked. Rowley, who was not accustomed to chatting in the kitchen with his employers' granddaughter, soon got used to it and took great pleasure from seeing Mary-Alice when Florence brought her down at six every morning. Over the weeks that followed, the two of them became unlikely friends.

Christmas was quiet and sad. All Florence wanted was news that Rupert had been found alive. Perhaps he had been captured by the Germans. Maybe he was hiding somewhere. She hoped with all her heart that he was alive and that those who were with him were treating him well. At church on Christmas Day, Reverend Millar asked the congregation to pray for those still missing and Florence cried quietly into her handkerchief, because if there was one thing that set her off, it was compassion.

On 8 May the following year, the country celebrated the end of the war in Europe. Not wanting to appear sullen, Florence went to the local pub to join in the festivities, although her heart felt like a stone. She found solace in the bottle, numbing her pain with as much alcohol as she could consume. When, by some miracle, she returned home, it was Rowley who helped her upstairs, took off her shoes, and covered her in a blanket.

'Am I a fool to hope?' she whispered, gazing up at him with shiny eyes.

He put a gentle hand on her shoulder. 'When you love, you hope. That is human nature. The heart will do anything to avoid suffering the pain of loss.' He sighed and shook his head sadly. 'But there comes a time when hope no longer sustains you, but slowly consumes you.'

'What should I do, Rowley?'

'Accept that he is gone, Mrs Dash.'

Florence squeezed her eyes shut. 'I don't think I can,' she said and pushed her head beneath the blanket.

CHAPTER THIRTEEN

Hampshire, 1988

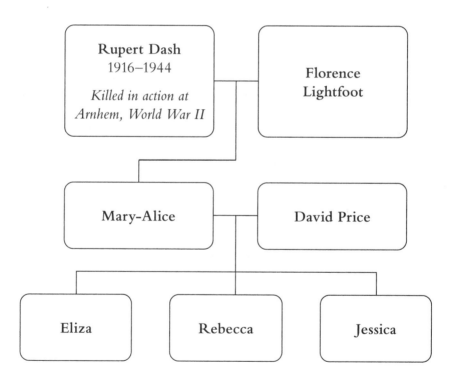

A cold current prickled over Max's skin. He stared at the name in astonishment. Arnhem had been an airborne battle with parachutes and gliders, which matched his dream exactly.

He felt a sudden jolt of excitement. A surge of energy and enthusiasm. It could, of course, be a massive coincidence, he thought, reining in his eagerness for fear of being disappointed later. If his dream really was a past life memory recall, what were the chances of him having been Rupert Dash? It seemed too easy, somehow. The dreams might be just dreams and, if reincarnation *was* a possibility, he could have been anyone. It was a million to one chance that he had been Rupert Dash. He thought of Elizabeth then and in his mind's eye he saw her roaring with laughter. He was inclined to agree with her at this point; it did seem absurd. Yet, his gut told him that there was no such thing as coincidence, that there was a reason for him having had that dream again, a reason for him meeting Olga, and a reason for him finding Rupert Dash's name on the family tree. To his surprise, Robyn's face took the place of Elizabeth's and her smile warmed him on the inside. How odd that he should think of Robyn now. She would tell him to trust his intuition and dig a little deeper. After all, what was there to lose?

Max decided to pay his grandfather a visit. He must have known Rupert Dash, being a cousin and of the same vintage. Hartley Shelbourne was Max's paternal grandfather and he lived with his wife in a quaint village in Oxfordshire, just over an hour's drive from Hampshire. Max gave them a call to warn them he was coming. He spoke to his grandmother, Diana. 'How delightful,' she said. 'Come for lunch. I'll let Gramps know. He's up a ladder, trying to find a broken roof tile.'

'He shouldn't be up a ladder at his age with his shaky hands,' said Max firmly.

'*You* tell him. He won't listen to me.'

Max knew his grandfather wouldn't listen to him, either.

* * *

When Max arrived at his grandparents' pretty stone cottage, his grandfather was still up the ladder. In fact, there were two ladders, one that took him to the edge of the roof, another, attached to the first with string and lying on old cushions placed on the tiles, which took him right up to the ridge and chimney. Max got out of the car and gazed up in horror. Hartley was in a blue boiler suit and cap, a pot of bitumen oil hanging between his teeth and a large paint brush in his shaky hand. His ladder contraption did not look very safe. 'Gramps, can I help you?' Max shouted.

'Hello, Max. Give me a minute. I think I've found the offending tile.'

'What are you doing?'

'Winning,' said Hartley with satisfaction.

The front door opened and his grandmother stepped out in a floral cooking apron. She was short in stature and full bosomed with fluffy grey hair and lively eyes, the colour of dawn. 'Max, darling, how lovely to see you.' She stood on tiptoe to give her grandson a kiss then looked him over with concern. 'I'm glad to see you're in one piece,' she said.

Max chuckled. 'It's been a bit of a rollercoaster ride.'

'I bet it has. Poor old you. Wretched.' She looked up at the roof. 'Hartley, why don't you finish that later? Come down and talk to Max. He's driven over specially to see us.'

'Nearly there. Be down in a tick.'

Diana clicked her tongue and went inside. Max followed her into the kitchen where an old yellow Labrador lay sleeping in his basket. He didn't even bother to open his eyes at Max's arrival. Max bent down to stroke him. 'He's thirteen,' said his grandmother softly. 'He's been such a good friend all these years. Now he sleeps most of the time. He can't really be bothered to even go for a walk.' The dog sighed sleepily and stirred, but he didn't wake up. 'What do you want to drink?'

'Coke, please.'

'Regardless of what we all thought of Elizabeth,' said Diana, opening the fridge, 'you've both been through a horrible time and we really do feel sorry for you, for the two of you. Is she all right?'

Max perched on a stool and shrugged. 'I don't know. I haven't spoken to her.'

'Probably better that you give her some space.'

'I still need to collect my things from her house, and the ring.'

'Those things can wait. I'm sure she won't throw them away. She's not a vindictive girl, is she?'

'I hope not.'

Diana handed her grandson the Coca-Cola can and a glass. 'What's the saying? Hell hath no fury like a woman scorned . . .'

'Exactly, that's what I'm afraid of.'

'She wasn't right for you, Max.'

'I wish I'd seen it earlier.'

'You have to kiss a few frogs before you find your princess.'

'I wish it *had* been just a kiss. I practically took my frog up the aisle.'

'But you didn't, and that's the important thing.'

The door opened and Hartley appeared, the paint pot and brush in his hands. 'Won,' he announced triumphantly, puffing out his chest.

Diana laughed. 'I'll reserve judgement until the next rainfall.'

'Hello, Max,' Hartley repeated. 'Come on your own, have you?'

'Darling, they called off the wedding, remember?' said Diana.

'That doesn't mean he's taken himself off the market.' Hartley winked at his grandson. 'A man like Max will quickly find another.'

'Not for a long time, Gramps,' said Max. 'Once bitten, twice shy.'

'Give the poor boy space to breathe. The last thing he wants to do, having jumped out of the frying pan, is to jump back in again.' Diana took off her apron. 'Shall we go and sit in the garden? It's a beautiful day.'

The terrace was surrounded by bird feeders which Hartley kept full of seeds and peanuts, even during the summer months when there was plenty in the garden for them to eat. They sat on teak benches made comfortable with cushions and looked out over the recently mown lawn and herbaceous border. 'Gramps has been very busy in the garden,' Diana told Max.

'If you don't keep busy, you die,' said Hartley simply.

'He's right, of course. Do you remember Ian Holmes? He retired, found life away from the office rather dull and whiled away the empty hours on the golf course. He died recently, on the fourth hole!'

Max did not remember Ian Holmes. 'That's a shame,' he said.

'You have to keep busy,' Hartley insisted. He turned to Max. 'How was South Africa?'

'Just what I needed.'

'Did you see wild dogs? They're my favourites.'

'I saw wild dogs and a cheetah, but no rhinos, sadly.'

'Lots of elephants, I imagine,' said Diana. 'I have a special affection for elephants. Before I was married I got a job at London zoo and fed the baby elephants with a bottle. It was marvellous.' Max thought of Robyn; she'd loved elephants too. 'I bet you took lots of photographs,' Diana added. 'You have such an eye.'

'I should have brought them to show you.'

'Next time,' said Hartley. 'Did you take any of wild dogs?'

They ate lunch in the kitchen. Diana was a good cook and she had taken the trouble to make Max a treacle tart for pudding, knowing how much he liked it. 'So, Max,' asked Hartley when Diana got up to clear the plates, 'what are you going to do now that you've left your job?'

Max sighed heavily. 'I really don't know.'

'That's a good place to start,' said Hartley.

Max laughed. 'The only way is up, I suppose,' he quipped. 'Tell me, did you know your cousins the Dashes?'

'Of course. I knew them well.'

'I've been taking a bit of an interest in our family history.'

Hartley narrowed his small eyes so that they practically disappeared. 'William Dash and my father were first cousins. He was quite flash. A brilliant rackets player and a larger-than-life character. I stayed with them on occasion at Pedrevan.'

'Sounds Cornish,' said Max.

'Yes, it's north-east Cornwall, just outside Gulliver's Bay, near Wadebridge. A big house. Beautiful. Aubrey inherited it. His elder brother was killed in the war.'

'Rupert?'

'Yes, Rupert. Very sad. He was a bit older than me and rather aloof, but he had a wonderfully dry sense of humour and used to get up to all sorts of shenanigans. My mother loved Rupert the best because he was complex and interesting. Aubrey was the golden boy, but Rupert was more enigmatic. He turned out to be brave too. He died at Arnhem. He was in a parachute regiment. I remember, after the war, the family gave a memorial service for him in Gulliver's Bay. The church was packed. Not a dry eye in the house. Aubrey was never the same after that. I think, if I'm not mistaken, that he still lives at Pedrevan. He must be rattling around in that big old place.'

Diana returned to the table with the treacle tart. 'I knew Florence Lightfoot quite well,' she said, giving Max a knife with which to slice it. 'We were at dance and drama school together in London.'

'Rupert's wife?' Max asked.

'Yes, they married during the war. We weren't close and we lost touch. I lost touch with all those girls, really. The war came and the school was closed and that was that. I never became the actress I longed to be, but I did give one performance of *A Midsummer Night's Dream*. I was Puck.' She chuckled at the recollection.

'Did you meet Rupert?' asked Max.

'Oh yes, he was very much on the London scene in those days. He and Florence. They made a very dashing couple.' She smiled at the pun.

'What was he like?'

'Tall and handsome like you,' she said with a smile. 'He was a little intimidating, actually. He didn't go about pleasing everyone. He said what he thought and it wasn't always what people wanted to hear. But those who got his point, as I did, loved him. I remember wanting to be liked by him. His affection wasn't easily won, but once won, you felt on top of the world.'

Max tucked into the tart. 'Delicious, Granny. Thank you.'

'Why this sudden interest in the Dashes?' she asked.

'Mum gave me a family tree and it's piqued my interest.'

'I see. Well, I should like to know what happened to Florence. If you find out, will you let me know? She was a mischief.'

* * *

Max would have driven straight to Gulliver's Bay had it not been for an acquaintance who telephoned him out of the blue to offer him a job. Working for a furniture manufacturer wasn't a dream occupation, but he needed to earn money and the business was based in Wiltshire, which was appealing. Max might not have known what he wanted to do, but he knew without a shadow of doubt where he did *not* want to be, and that was in London. He duly rented a cottage in Wylye, a small village just off the A303 – the road that led straight down to Cornwall.

It wasn't until July that he finally made his way to Gulliver's Bay. Caroline, the secretary in the office, had recommended a boutique hotel called The Mariners which had a nice view of the sea. She'd been there on a hen weekend, she told him, and had had a lovely time getting drunk on the beach. Max didn't care where he stayed as long as it was in Gulliver's Bay, so he made a booking, packed a weekend bag and set off.

The drive was long, but he drove with the roof down, a pair of aviator sunglasses shielding his eyes, listening to Dire Straits and The Police on the cassette player. He couldn't stop thinking about Rupert Dash. His head told him it was a long shot and not to get his hopes up, but his heart told him otherwise; something about it just felt right.

As soon as he passed Okehampton the countryside began to draw his attention more fully. The Devon landscape was wild and rugged and deeply beautiful. The roads were narrow and winding, the hedgerows woolly and overgrown with cow parsley, dandelions and campion. Green velvet pastures stretched for miles beneath a vast sky and pink heather flourished among rocks that rose out of the earth, grey and jagged, their surfaces weathered over the centuries by sea gales and rain and hot summer sunshine. Not long after crossing into

Cornwall Max saw the name Gulliver's Bay on the road sign and his spirits lifted. It was as if those words were more than white letters on a big, green board; they spoke to him. He laughed at himself. He was very likely reading too much into it; he had given his mind an idea and now it was running away with it like a dog with a ball.

Gulliver's Bay was just as he'd imagined it. A typically charming Cornish fishing town built in the embrace of a horseshoe-shaped enclave. There was a harbour packed with blue-bellied fishing boats, white houses snuggled into the hillsides and a backdrop of rocky hills and soft green slopes. He'd looked up The Mariners on a map and duly drove through the town, past the ancient church and local pub and on up the lane beneath a leafy canopy of trees. He'd also looked up Pedrevan Park too and even written to Aubrey Dash, on the pretext of researching his family history. He'd received no reply.

At last he arrived at the driveway into The Mariners and turned in. He parked in front of the house, a typical white Cornish manor with a grey tiled roof, and slipped his sunglasses into his jacket pocket. Caroline had been right about the view, it was spectacular. He lifted his bag out of the boot and pushed open the front door. It was unlocked. He walked into the hall where a round table was adorned with a big glass vase of white lilies and roses. There was no reception desk. It looked more like a private house than a hotel. He wondered, suddenly, whether he'd come to the right place.

'Hello.' He turned to see a woman striding into the hall. She was slim, in a pair of jodhpurs and white polo shirt, her blonde hair tied into a ponytail. She was unmistakable. 'Robyn?'

Robyn frowned, then she recognized him. 'Max!' She laughed and greeted him with a friendly kiss. 'What are you doing here?'

'This *is* a hotel, isn't it?'

'Yes. Did you book?'

'Of course.'

'Then you're in the right place. It's my parents' business. I'm just helping out today as they're short-staffed.' She went to a drawer and lifted out a book. She opened it and scanned down the list of names. 'Are you Mr Trent?'

'No.'

'You're not Mr and Mrs Bridge and you're not Lady Elmsworth. You must be Mr Shelbourne then.'

'That's me.'

'Let me show you to your room, Mr Shelbourne.' She grinned and Max felt happy at the sight of that infectious smile. He hadn't forgotten how good it made him feel. 'I'll upgrade you,' she said, lowering her voice. 'You're a friend of the family, after all.'

'I can't believe the coincidence,' he said, following her up the stairs.

'You know there's no such thing.'

'Of course. But it's still extraordinary.'

'Didn't I tell you I lived in Gulliver's Bay?'

'If you did, I'd forgotten.'

'What brings you here, anyway?'

'I'm doing some research.'

'I love research. What are you researching?'

'It's a complicated story. Perhaps over a drink?'

'I can't wait.' She led him down a corridor to a white pan-elled door at the end. She turned the key. 'Here you are. A grand suite just for you.'

He stepped inside. 'This is grand, indeed,' he said, putting his case on the big bed and looking around. It was flamboy-antly decorated with floral wallpaper and matching curtains.

He went to the window and looked out over the sea. 'Are you sure you're not going to get into trouble giving me this room?'

'Lady Elmsworth can have a room at the back,' she replied with a mischievous smile. 'She'll complain wherever she is, that one.'

'Well, it's a lovely room. You're very kind, Robyn. Thank you.'

'It's a pleasure. It's good to see you again.'

He'd forgotten how pretty she was. 'How's Daniel?' he asked, hoping she'd pull a face and say they'd broken up.

'Really well, thank you. I can't wait to tell him you're here. He'll be so excited. Perhaps we can all go out for dinner one night, or have a drink in the pub.'

'I'd love that. But my research is for your ears only.'

She nodded. 'Perhaps that's why we've bumped into each other, because I can help you. I've lived here all my life, you know. There's not an inch of Gulliver's Bay I'm not acquainted with.'

'You're going to be invaluable then.'

She made for the door. 'I'll leave you to it. How about a drink at six, downstairs? Then you can tell me what you're up to. I'm intrigued.'

He nodded. 'Six it is.'

She closed the door behind her. Max turned back to the view. What was the universe up to, he wondered? If it really wanted to help him out, it could start by getting rid of Daniel.

Max decided to walk into Gulliver's Bay to take a look around and soak up the scene. It was a fine day. The sun played hide and seek with the clouds, but it was warm, even when the sun went in, and there was an invigorating sea breeze. He wandered around the town, which couldn't have housed more than a thousand people, and thought that the place probably hadn't changed very much since Rupert Dash's day. The buildings were old and uneven and stacked haphazardly up the hillside. Their small windows looked out over the sea like eyes that bore witness to centuries of activity, of smugglers and fishermen and perhaps the odd shipwreck. If only they could talk, Max thought, as he made his way towards the church.

This was where the Dashes had held Rupert's memorial service, he reminded himself as he took in the ancient walls and tower and swept his eyes over the graveyard, peaceful in the summer sunshine. He wondered where Rupert was buried and found himself strolling among the gravestones, reading the inscriptions carved into the stone. Max had always had an unusual fascination with cemeteries, military cemeteries especially. Now he wondered with a shiver if he was subconsciously searching for his own grave, the grave of his _old_ self. Once again, the dream formed in his mind like a reflection on water, a memory both indelible and vivid, and he felt a strange sense of déjà vu, as if he'd already been here before. It was a vague feeling and one he didn't trust, because he knew how clever the mind was at playing tricks. And perhaps Gulliver's Bay felt familiar because it answered a deep longing, a desire he'd always had to live in a place like this, by the sea.

The door was open and Max stepped inside. This was one place he could be sure of _not_ having changed since Rupert Dash's day. Rupert would have sat here on Sundays, Max imagined, with his family, as Max had attended Sunday services as a boy with his. The place was empty. He was quite alone. He wandered down the aisle. The flagstones had been worn into smooth hollows by centuries of treading feet. The dark wooden pews seemed almost petrified with age and the vaulted ceiling and walls had been stained the colour of parchment. It had a soft, welcoming energy, the atmosphere having been honed over the years by hymns, supplications and prayer. Max sat in one of the pews and took a deep breath. It felt good to be alone.

He left the church feeling pensive. This was the first place where he'd got a real sense of Rupert. A real sense of him being a person and not just a name on a family tree. However, he was reluctant to fully commit to the idea. What if he hadn't been Rupert Dash? What if it was all a fantasy? Then any sense of déjà vu, any hint of connection between Max and his grandfather's cousin, would have been imagined. Until he had proof, he couldn't submit to his emotions, however strongly he felt them.

Max left the church and headed to a café on the waterfront for a cup of coffee and a snack. Then he wandered around the shops. He was deep in thought when he stumbled across the modest stone cenotaph, erected in the town square. As a former member of the armed forces Max always spent a moment in front of such memorials, casting his thoughts to those who had fought and died for their country; they were sobering thoughts. But this war memorial had a powerful resonance. It commemorated those who had died in the First and Second World Wars. There was no list of names, but Rupert Dash was present, in the grim vibration of sorrow that the St George's Cross gave off, and in Max's mind as he felt ever more linked to his grandfather's cousin.

When he returned to the hotel Max went to his room to bathe and change. It was teatime and the place was busier than it had been when he'd arrived. From his bedroom window he could see the terrace below where guests were sitting at tables, enjoying scones, Cornish clotted cream and jam, and a gravelled path that led down to the beach. He stood a while watching the dance of light upon the water. He'd like to go down and paddle in the sea. Perhaps Robyn would go with him. Uplifted at the thought of seeing her, he unbuttoned his shirt and went into the bathroom to shower.

CHAPTER FOURTEEN

Max pulled on a pair of jeans and a blue shirt and went downstairs to meet Robyn. As he stepped into the hall he was detained by a woman who he first assumed to be the gardener, because she was wearing denim dungarees and a white T-shirt and was picking off dead leaves from the flower display. On her feet she wore a pair of Green Flash tennis shoes and around her head her frizzy brown hair formed a halo, only marginally subdued by a silk headscarf rolled into a hairband. 'You must be Max Shelbourne,' she said with a smile. She put out her hand. Max took it. 'I'm Robyn's mother, Edwina. So lovely to meet you. Robyn's told me all about you.' She lowered her voice. 'I'm glad she gave you one of our best rooms. You're a family friend, after all.'

'It's an extraordinary coincidence,' he said.

Edwina waved her hand as if flicking away a fly. 'Nonsense. There's no such thing as coincidence. Now, she's waiting for you in the drawing room. Come, I'll show you where it is.'

'It's a lovely hotel,' said Max, following her through the house.

'It used to be a private home.'

'Yes, I can tell. It still feels like one.'

Edwina laughed. 'That's the idea. I want my guests to feel

like they're at a house party where you don't need to speak to the other guests if you don't want to.'

'That sounds ideal.'

Edwina showed him into a large, square-shaped room that looked more like a drawing room than a hotel lounge. Robyn was standing beside a card table, watching a quartet of elderly ladies playing bridge. She raised her eyes, saw Max and smiled.

'Max,' she said, striding over. She was in a white dress printed with strawberries and a pair of silver flipflops. Max felt the stirring of attraction, something he hadn't felt for a very long time, since meeting Elizabeth three years before. 'Have you had a nice afternoon?'

'I went for a wander around town.'

'It's quaint, isn't it?'

'Very, and charming,' Max replied. He took in the pink apples of Robyn's cheeks, her sparkling eyes and the gentle curve of her lips and felt the attraction deepen.

'Well, I'll leave you to it,' said Edwina. 'If there's anything you need, don't be afraid to ask. I had a guest a few weeks ago who asked for a body pillow. Have you heard of those? No, I didn't think so. Anyway, I got one. Miracle. But then, if you put out your request, they usually oblige.'

'She's a character,' Max said to Robyn as Edwina left the room.

'Oh, that's nothing. Wait until she cleanses the place with sage and brings out her tarot cards. One has to be a little careful, some of the guests find it creepy. I keep telling her to rein in her witchery.'

'She doesn't have to rein it in for me.'

'I know. I've told her. Let's sit outside,' Robyn suggested. 'What are you going to drink?'

'A Negroni?' he asked, pretty sure that a small hotel like this wouldn't even know what that was.

But Robyn nodded. 'Great, I'll have a margarita. Come on, it's lovely on the terrace.'

They sat on comfortable chairs at one end, away from the other guests who drank and smoked and grazed on glass bowls of peanuts. A waiter took their order then left them alone. A gust of wind blew Robyn's patchouli and amber scent in Max's direction. He remembered it from South Africa.

'This is the best view in Gulliver's Bay,' she said. They gazed out over the sea, tranquil in the late afternoon sunshine.

'And you have a beach down there,' said Max.

'It's technically not *our* beach, but it's hard to get to from anywhere else, so few people who aren't staying at the hotel go there. At night Mum lights it with lanterns and guests sit beneath the stars. It's romantic. We get a lot of honeymooners.'

'And hen weekenders,' said Max, thinking of Caroline from the office.

'A *lot* of hen weekenders,' Robyn laughed. 'They get pissed on the beach and then go swimming in the middle of the night. Mad.'

'I'd like to go swimming in the middle of the night.'

'Cold,' said Robyn.

'Fun,' said Max, looking at her steadily.

Robyn laughed. 'Naughty,' she added. That flirtatious smile again. Max remembered *that* from South Africa too.

'How's your book coming along?' he asked.

'Slowly,' she replied. 'She's a fabulous character, Lady Castlemaine. I'm loving the whole process. But I'm much more curious to know what *you're* researching.' The waiter returned with their drinks. 'Cheers,' said Robyn, raising her glass.

'To our serendipitous meeting,' said Max.

'I'll drink to that.' She laughed and took a sip of her margarita. 'Delicious. Malcolm makes them strong.'

Max took a sip of his Negroni. 'Better than Duke's,' he said in surprise.

Robyn shrugged. 'I don't know what Duke's is, but I'll take it as a compliment.'

'One of the best bars in London,' Max told her. 'But who needs London?'

'Come on, I'm intrigued. What's brought you to Gulliver's Bay?'

'All right,' he said, putting his glass on the table. 'You're one of the only people I can share this with.' He leaned forward and put his elbows on his knees.

Her smile broadened. 'I knew it was something unusual.'

'It's *very* unusual and I'm wary of telling even you, who has an uncommonly open mind when it comes to spiritual things. I'm researching a past life.'

Robyn's eyes lit up. 'A past life of yours? Goodness, how intriguing. Tell me from the beginning. How did you find out that you've lived before? Did you have a regression?'

'No, it started with recurring dreams . . .' Max told her the whole story. About the dreams, his meeting with Olga Groot, the family tree and finally his discovery that Rupert Dash had lived here in Gulliver's Bay.

Robyn listened with great interest, forgetting all about her drink which languished on the table getting warm. She didn't interrupt, but let Max tell his story in detail. Elizabeth had never let Max tell her anything without either interrupting or bringing it around to herself. Robyn's enthralled expression reassured him that he wasn't boring her. When he finished, she shook her head in amazement. 'That's incredible.'

Max picked up his glass. 'I don't know. I could be barking up the wrong tree. I mean, isn't it a little too easy that the first name I find on my father's family tree might be the person I was in my past life? Why not someone in my mother's family tree? Or someone totally unrelated? Maybe it's not a past life recall at all, just a dream.'

Robyn frowned at him as if she thought he was talking rubbish. 'Max, this is exciting. Of course you were Rupert Dash, why else would the wind be filling your sails, sending you to Olga Groot, to your mother for the family tree, to your grandfather for information about Gulliver's Bay, and now down here? Why do you think we met in South Africa? Nothing happens for no reason, trust me on that. At any point you could have gathered up your sails and put down your anchor, but you haven't. You've allowed yourself to be guided.'

'If that's the case, my guides have been very busy.'

'Because they want you to make this discovery.'

'Why?'

'For your own evolution. This is part of the plan. *Your* plan. Your life was mapped out for you before your feet even touched the earth. You agreed on a blueprint, so to speak, before you incarnated. Not that we do what we're meant to do when we get down here. We forget all about it, get distracted by the material world around us. Things don't always go to plan. But I suspect you're pretty much on track right now.'

'I hope you're right, Robyn. I hope I'm not a fantasist.'

She smiled at him with sympathy. 'That ex-girlfriend of yours did some damage, didn't she?'

'Elizabeth?'

'She made you doubt yourself. But that was probably part of the plan too, because it's driven you to search for proof of your beliefs. You're not going to accept anything at face value, or just because some witch tells you it's so. There was a reason Elizabeth and you spent three years together. Perhaps that was it.'

'I do need to find proof, but I don't know how to go about it.'

'The first thing I would do in your position is have a past life regression.'

Max chuckled and slid his eyes around the terrace. 'I'm glad no one else is hearing this conversation. They'd think we were mad.'

Robyn picked up her glass. 'You'd be surprised how many wouldn't. You've just been brainwashed into thinking the world is full of Elizabeths. Well, it's not. I'm a witch, my mother's a witch too – obviously not a real witch with a cat and a cauldron, but a psychic, a sensitive, someone who is able to perceive the finer vibrations that most people can't see. My point is that I meet people all the time who are fascinated by the occult – that which is hidden. Everyone wants to believe that when they die they'll live on in some shape or form. No one wants to believe we spend eternity six feet under. Often a bereavement motivates people into searching for the truth because they can't bear to think they'll never be reunited with the one they love. You and I know that this life is just a brief stay and that, when we return home to spirit having completed our earthly lives, we'll be reunited with those we knew not just in this lifetime, but in many other lifetimes too. But going back to past life regressions, they can be helpful for people who have carried trauma into this life from a past life, but also for people like you, who are just curious to know who they were.'

'I hope I don't discover I was Henry VIII.'

'That comes directly from Elizabeth,' said Robyn, draining her glass. 'I've never met her but I feel I know her. You won't discover you were Henry VIII, although someone must have been him. I imagine after the suffering he caused, his soul has had to travel through many lifetimes to learn to be kind.

You'll very likely go into your dream. That's what your guides up there want you to see. I know just the person.'

'You do?'

'I do. I've been regressed myself.'

'Who were you?'

'I was a poor housewife in Yorkshire in the early eighteenth century, married to a farmer, and a miserable wealthy woman married to a cold-hearted philanderer in nineteenth-century Spain. The interesting thing about both those lives is that I was with Dad. He was my husband in Yorkshire and my brother in Spain. You see, we travel through incarnations with the same souls, learning from those relationships. We also change sex. As you know, gender belongs only to the physical world. I had a recurring dream as a child of being a boy hunting buffalo in America. I don't know whether everyone reincarnates. I sense that most of us choose to because this is the best place to learn. We must want to learn very badly to keep coming back.'

'Have you always believed you've lived before?'

'If we hadn't, life would be very lonely meeting everyone for the first time. We connect with people because we've known them before.' She looked at him fondly. 'I think you and I have shared the odd life, Max. I don't know what our relationship was and it doesn't matter. But when we met, I felt I already knew you.'

Max drank the last drop of Negroni. 'If that's the case, then it's nice to see you again, Robyn.'

She laughed. 'Fancy another?'

'I'd love another.'

'Me too.'

The waiter brought a second round and Robyn told him that she knew Pedrevan Park. 'I don't know the Dashes,' she said, 'but I know where the house is. I've ridden past it on many occasions.'

'I wrote to Aubrey, Rupert's younger brother, introducing myself as a cousin researching the family, particularly Rupert. But I never heard back.'

'You don't want to just turn up, do you?' There was a mischievous glint in her eye.

'Perhaps after another Negroni, that will seem like a good idea,' Max replied, wondering whether a midnight swim would seem like a good idea too. 'But I think I'll change my mind in the morning. There are many reasons why he wouldn't want to talk to me and I wouldn't want to intrude. Rupert died in the war. It must have been devastating for the whole family. He probably doesn't want to unearth painful memories.'

'No, you're right, of course. It's the margarita talking.'

'When do you think this regression therapist can see me?'

'She lives in Bath. I'll give you her telephone number. Tell her you're a friend of mine and she'll bump you up the queue. She's very booked up. You're staying tomorrow night, aren't you?'

'Yes, I leave on Sunday.'

'Good. I'll show you around tomorrow. Daniel has to help his mother move house so he won't be able to join us. Do you ride?'

'Yes, I do. I grew up on horseback.'

'You can borrow boots and a hat, and tomorrow evening we'll have dinner, the three of us, at the pub. They serve delicious food.'

'That sounds like a good plan,' he said, although he'd rather dine alone with Robyn.

'You might not be able to ride into Pedrevan,' she said. 'But there's a bridleway around the estate. We can peer at the house through the trees. It's magnificent.'

That night Max lay in bed thinking about Robyn. He had found her appealing in South Africa, but then he had been getting over the trauma of hurting Elizabeth and hadn't been ready to look at another woman. He was clearly ready now; his body ached for her. She was more than appealing, she was beautiful and desirable, intelligent and wise. A perfect woman. Perfect in every way, he thought. He could still smell her perfume on his cheek from when he'd kissed her goodnight. He'd wanted to take her up to his bed, but there was no chance of that. She was like a forbidden fruit at the top of the tree, watched over by Daniel, out of reach and very much spoken for. Max sighed with frustration. The Negronis had made him rash and he had asked her if she wanted a midnight swim. She'd thought he was joking and just laughed. But he'd been serious. If she'd said yes, he would have kissed her in the sea.

The following morning Max rose early. Robyn had filled him with a burst of nervous energy; he was excited, jittery, unable to rest. The thought of seeing her again later made him even more restless. Dawn was only just breaking on the horizon in a pale, liquid light. The sea was calm, the gentle rise and fall of waves sparkling enticingly. He decided to go for a swim. He would have borrowed a surf board had there been big waves to ride. He'd surfed in North Devon in his teens and discovered a natural ability, like skiing; both required good balance. Instead, he took one of the towels from the bathroom and made his way down the path to the beach in his swimming trunks and dressing gown. It was chilly for the sun had not yet risen and there was a cool breeze blowing off the water. He tossed his towel and dressing gown onto the sand

and ran in, catching his breath as the chilly temperature bit at his legs, then he dived beneath the surface. When he came up for air, he let out a joyous cry. It felt good to be in Gulliver's Bay – with Robyn.

After breakfast Edwina produced riding boots and a hat and took Max round to the stables where two efficient young women were preparing the horses. 'I don't ride myself,' said Edwina. 'I'm terrified of the things. But my husband Gryffyn has always loved horses and so does Robyn. Gryff likes to take guests out on the hills with a picnic lunch. It's marvellous fun. Next time you come you must stay longer. You're not really getting the full Cornish experience staying only two nights.'

'I will. Now I've met you, I'll stay for a week. Where is Gryffyn?'

'He's taken guests out in his boat this morning. You'll meet him later. Ah, Robyn.' Max turned to see Robyn striding towards them, smiling broadly. She looked elegant in a pair of tight jodhpurs, leather boots and hat, her long hair tied in a plait down her back.

'Morning, Max,' she exclaimed brightly.

Max couldn't imagine her ever being anything but cheery and bursting with enthusiasm. It was infectious. 'Morning, Robyn,' he replied, his spirits rising at the sight of her.

'It's a lovely day. We're going to have fun.'

Max climbed deftly into the saddle. Edwina took a step back as his horse snorted and raised its head.

Robyn put her foot in the stirrup and swung onto her mare. 'Daniel apologizes that he can't join us. But when his mother clicks her fingers, he runs.'

Max hadn't expected Daniel to come, but knowing now that there had been a chance of him joining them, he was relieved; Daniel would have changed the subjects of their conversation dramatically and stood like an unwelcome body-guard between them. Max was grateful to have Robyn all to himself.

'We'll be back for lunch,' Robyn told her mother as she squeezed her horse's flanks.

'Lovely, Max can join us on the Private Side,' said Edwina. 'Have a good time.' She waved them off.

Robyn guided Max along a track that led into the hills. From up there they had a view of both water and land. Shadows chased the light across the meadows as the sun travelled in and out of the clouds and the wind swept through the long grasses, stirring up the aromatic scents of wild herbs that grew among them. It was beautiful. Max felt his chest expand and with it the release of tension. He inhaled deeply and savoured the sight of nature at her most magnificent. 'There aren't enough superlatives,' he said.

Robyn turned her face into the wind and closed her eyes. 'It feels good, doesn't it? When I'm up here, I have no worries.'

'You don't look like you have any worries, ever.'

She laughed. 'Everyone has worries, Max. They're all rela-tive. Even those who look like they have everything, money, success, health and friends, have worries. They might not be worries to you and me, but to them they're big dramas. Life is about problem-solving, so everyone has problems. It's just the way it is. Come, let's go to Pedrevan.'

'You're a wise old soul, aren't you,' he teased.

She grinned flirtatiously. 'Call me Wise Owl.'

They set off across the meadows until they joined a farm track. Sheep grazed in meadows of sea campion and butter-cups, and fields of barley rippled in the wind. Eventually, they reached a boundary post-and-rail fence and a high beech hedge. 'This is Pedrevan,' Robyn told him. 'If we continue along this track we'll come to a place where we can see through the trees to the house.'

Max felt his excitement mount, then reined it in. As much as Robyn believed he was Rupert Dash in a past life, he was still reluctant to surrender completely to his intuition in case he discovered that he was mistaken. He was intrigued to see the house all the same. He'd always loved old houses and his grandfather had told him that Pedrevan Park was outstanding.

They continued along the track until they reached the part of the boundary where the trees and hedge had thinned sufficiently to allow them to peer through. Max had a clear view of the side of the house. He could see Cornish stone bleached by the elements to a soft, dove-grey colour, tall thin chimneys and elaborate gables. It was a grand Elizabethan mansion, brimming with charm. He wondered whether Aubrey was in residence. He was quite tempted to ride on in and knock on the door, but he knew that would be foolish. He wasn't a close enough relation to turn up unannounced. No one liked to be visited without prior warning, especially on a weekend.

'It's lovely, isn't it?' said Robyn.

'Incredible that it's still a private house. So many of these mansions have been turned over to the National Trust or converted into hotels.'

'The Dashes must be very rich.'

'I have no idea,' said Max. 'Gramps didn't elaborate. He just said that William Dash, Rupert and Aubrey's father, was flash.'

'Maybe, when you've done more research, you can write to Aubrey again. Once you're absolutely certain of your connection to Rupert, you may find his curiosity is piqued.'

'Or he'll think I'm a fantasist, like Elizabeth does.'

'There's always that chance. I'd like to see inside the house anyway. I bet it's sumptuous.'

They returned to The Mariners for lunch. Gryffyn had come back from his boating expedition and greeted Max with a firm handshake and a crooked smile. He was tall and thin with shaggy grey hair, an unshaven face and the same gentle grey eyes as his daughter. 'Did you have a good morning?' he asked Max as they sat around the kitchen table in the family side of the hotel.

'I took Max to Pedrevan,' said Robyn. 'We spied on the house through the hedge.'

'My father is a distant cousin of the Dashes,' Max explained.

Gryffyn raised his eyebrows. 'It's a nice-looking place,' he said.

'So is this one,' Max added. Edwina looked pleased.

'It was a private house when we bought it, back in the sixties. You know what inspired me to buy it?'

'Oh yes,' Edwina gushed. 'You'll never guess!'

Max shook his head.

'It's got a secret passageway from the cellar to a cave on the beach. It was used by smugglers back in the day. Once I'd seen that, I had to have it.' Gryffyn smiled. 'How many houses can boast a secret tunnel like that, eh?'

Max's interest was aroused. 'Not many, I imagine. I'd love to see it.'

'Of course. Robyn will show you after lunch. The tide will still be out. I have a meeting at two, otherwise I'd take you myself.'

'When we get honeymooners, I light the cave with candles,' Edwina said. 'It's very romantic in there. Something about the energy. There are crystals in the rock, you see, and minerals that dye them all sorts of magical colours.'

Gryffyn didn't roll his eyes as Max expected him to do. Instead, he nodded. 'Yes, there's something special about that cave,' he agreed.

'We've had the odd pagan wedding down there, haven't we, Gryff?' said Edwina.

'We've had all sorts. But we don't put it in the brochure or we'd get every New Age traveller from miles around coming to have a look at it. The beach no longer belongs to the house so it's accessible to anyone who wants to come.' He grinned raffishly. 'We keep the beach to ourselves as well.'

After lunch, Robyn took Max to the basement of the hotel where they kept a wine cellar and store rooms. At the back, next to a stack of logs neatly piled up against the wall, was a wooden trapdoor in the floor like the ones found in old pubs. Robyn bent to lift it, but Max insisted and lifted it for her. Beneath was a stairway descending into darkness. Robyn took a torch off a hook on the wall. 'Ready?' she said, switching it on and shining it into the hole that opened like a great throat before them.

'After you,' Max replied with a bow.

'Thank you,' she laughed.

'I don't know why you're not writing a book about this place.'

'It's never occurred to me. But now you mention it, perhaps I will.'

Robyn descended carefully. Max followed. The tunnel was tall enough for Robyn to walk without stooping, but Max was a head too tall and had to bend forward. The ground was made up of steps and flat bits and seemed to go on and on, deeper into the earth. It smelt of damp soil and was quite airless. 'Nearly there,' said Robyn. 'Fun, isn't it?'

'Amazing,' Max exclaimed. 'It's like something out of a Daphne du Maurier novel.'

'She's one of my favourite authors,' said Robyn. 'But I would say that, being Cornish, wouldn't I? Right, here we are.'

They had arrived at the other end. Max stepped out into the cave and took a deep breath of clean, sea air. He jumped down onto the sand and swept his eyes over the walls in wonder. Edwina and Gryffyn were right, it had a very special energy. Streaks of colour ran down the rocks as if someone up high had poured pots of paint down them. There were nooks and crannies, sharp edges and smooth surfaces and pools of trapped water where sea urchins and shrimps awaited the return of the tide to carry them back out to sea.

'It's magical,' he said.

'I know,' Robyn agreed. She smiled wistfully. 'So romantic. If Daniel and I get married, perhaps we'll do something in here.'

Max was surprised by the ferocity of his jealousy. It blind-sided him. What right did he have to be jealous when he barely knew her? He put his hand against the clammy wall. 'Do you think you'll marry?' The thought was horrifying.

'I hope so,' she replied. 'Some men are shy of commitment, though. I think Daniel's like that. He needs to come around to the idea slowly.'

'How long have you been together?'

'Two years.'

'I suppose he's from round here, is he?'

'Yes, we were friends before we started dating.' She looked at Max bashfully. 'I'd had a crush on him for years. He didn't notice me until I practically threw myself at him.'

Max was incredulous. 'I can't imagine how any man could fail to notice *you*.'

She laughed, embarrassed. 'Perhaps I'm a late bloomer.'

Max was about to tell her what he thought of her, but he stopped himself. He didn't want to create an awkward atmosphere. Besides, she was in love with Daniel; a few compliments from him weren't going to change her heart. 'I hope he's not so shy of commitment that he loses you,' Max said, hoping the opposite.

'Oh, he won't,' Robyn replied with confidence. 'I'm very much in the bag.'

They returned to the hotel by way of the beach. Guests were sunbathing on loungers, rugs were laid out on the sand, and small children with nets searched for fish among the rocks. It was a very English scene, Max thought, as he and Robyn wandered side by side. His good mood had deflated, in spite of Robyn's charm and enthusiasm. If she hadn't been going out with Daniel he might have kissed her in the cave.

That evening the three of them dined in the local pub. Daniel was friendly. He didn't seem at all put out that his girl-friend had spent so much time with Max, taking him riding over the hills and down to the cave. The two of them were very much a couple. They finished each other's sentences, stole food from each other's plates and shared each other's drinks. They'd probably done the same in South Africa, but Max hadn't noticed back then. He noticed now, because *he* wanted to have that kind of relationship. He'd finally found a woman who was right for him and he couldn't have her.

After dinner Max climbed into his car and watched Daniel and Robyn walk off down the road, hand in hand. The sight made his gut twist with resentment. He did not like that quality in himself. Robyn had never given him any indication that he might have a chance. She'd mentioned Daniel in their conversations and any flirting had been mild. She was possibly like that with everyone. Yet Max felt a connection with her as well as a strong physical attraction. It was probably lucky that he was heading back to Wiltshire tomorrow. If he stayed any longer he'd only make himself miserable, or do something stupid after a couple of Negronis.

The following morning as he was putting his bag into the boot of his car, Robyn arrived on a bicycle. She waved then leaned her bicycle against the wall. 'You're leaving?' she asked. 'Lucky I caught you.'

'Thanks for looking after me this weekend. It's been really good hanging out with you, and it was good to see Daniel too,' he said through gritted teeth.

'Dan loved seeing you. You must come back.'

'I will.'

'And let me know how the regression goes.' She handed him an envelope. 'Here's Daphne's number and ours too, so you can call me. I hope it goes well.' She embraced him. Max held her for a moment and kissed her cheek. She smelt of patchouli. He didn't want to let her go.

'I'll keep you posted,' he replied as she pulled away.

'I hope you find out that you were, indeed, Rupert Dash, then you'll have to come back.' She laughed. 'I mean, you can come back anyway!'

Edwina appeared on the doorstep to see him off. Mother and daughter watched him turn the car around and waved as he drove out of the gate. Max glanced in his rear-view mirror, at Robyn in a pair of shorts and a T-shirt, her hair loose about her shoulders, and held onto that image all the way home. He wished he'd taken a photograph of her.

CHAPTER FIFTEEN

Max decided he would keep a journal of his research into his past life. It was beginning to get interesting and he wanted to record all the synchronicities and strange coincidences. He had a feeling it was going to read like a mystery novel.

As soon as he was back in Wiltshire he telephoned Daphne, the regression therapist Robyn had recommended. She was friendly and, as Robyn had predicted, gave him a special slot. But it wasn't until October, which was three months away. Max was busy at work. He liked the people in the office and even though the job wasn't what he saw himself doing long-term, he was grateful to be in the countryside and occupied. At weekends he went microlighting, played tennis with friends, or drove home to see his parents. He thought of Robyn often. If it wasn't for Daniel, he'd have called her.

In September he couldn't put off collecting his belongings from Battersea any longer. He telephoned Elizabeth. When she heard his voice, she went silent for a moment as if lost for words, then said brusquely, 'You know, breaking up with you was the best thing I ever did. I've met the most won-derful man.'

She'd barely said hello. 'That's great,' Max replied. 'I'm happy for you.'

'It's turned out for the best. I mean, it wasn't the greatest timing, of course, but if I was still with you, I wouldn't have met Peregrine. He works in the City. He's terribly successful. Mummy and Daddy think the world of him.'

'I'm glad.'

'And you? Have you met anyone?'

'No,' said Max. It had only been six months.

Elizabeth took a breath. Her voice lost its edge and instead acquired a patronizing tone. 'Well, I'm sure you will, Max. Although, I can't imagine you meet many girls down in Wiltshire. It's not exactly the party county, is it?' She laughed, but it had no mirth in it.

Max hadn't mentioned anything about living in Wiltshire. 'I'm happy here. It suits me. I'm busy with work and . . .'

'Oh yes, you're a tradesman now, I hear. You should never have given up your job in the City. I think you'll regret that.'

'Listen, I need to come and get the rest of my things. When would be a good time?'

'I thought that must be why you've called. I didn't imagine you were calling to find out how I am. Peregrine is taking me to Capri this weekend, so come the following Saturday, around five.'

'Great. Thanks.' There was an awkward silence that Max felt the need to fill. 'I need the ring back, too, I'm afraid.'

Elizabeth laughed. 'Oh that. Of course. It's in its box. Peregrine bought me a much bigger one. Peregrine is so like that, I mean, generous to a fault. Not that I care, it's the thought that counts, but it is the most spectacular ring.'

'Have a good time in Capri,' said Max, longing to hang up.

'Oh, I will. I always have a lovely time with Peregrine.'

Max put the phone down and felt the old feeling of unhappiness engulf him like smog; Elizabeth's sapping energy had managed to reach him all the way down the phone line. He decided to go for a walk to shake it off. The sooner he collected his belongings from her house and drew a line under that relationship, the better.

To his relief, when he went to Elizabeth's house two weeks later, he was let in by the young woman who cleaned it. Elizabeth had packed up his books, clothes and toiletries and put them in the hall, but she had made sure that she was out. He loaded the boxes into the back of the car, thanked the cleaner and set off. He didn't expect he'd hear from Elizabeth again.

In October a cold wind blew in from the north. Thick grey clouds gathered above the countryside and rain fell in a light, persistent drizzle. The grass was littered with orange and brown leaves, the ground soggy with mud. Max hadn't spoken to Robyn since he'd left Cornwall. There had been many times when he'd almost picked up the phone, only to put it down before it rang. He had no excuse to call her and he couldn't tell her the truth, that he just wanted to hear her voice. However, when the day of his appointment with Daphne arrived he knew he'd be able to call Robyn as soon as it was over. She'd even asked him to. He was filled with excitement at the thought of talking to her again.

Daphne lived in a terraced house on the edge of Bath. Max had always loved Bath – the attractive grey colour of the stone, the harmony of the architecture that gave one the sense of stepping back in time, the famous crescents, Roman baths and abbey. It was a city with a genteel and respectable air, like London must have been before the war had destroyed so much of its beauty.

He found the house, parked the car and rang the bell. Daphne opened the door wide and smiled at him warmly.

'Come on in, Max,' she said, her grey-blue eyes looking at him directly. They were the gentle, honest eyes of a wise old soul, Max thought as he followed her into a narrow corridor and on into the small sitting room. It was decorated in muted pinks and greys and had a soft energy not dissimilar to the cave in Gulliver's Bay. Max glanced around the room to see crystal spheres on the mantelpiece and a large amethyst geode in one corner. He thought of Edwina then; she would approve.

They talked about Robyn as Max took off his coat and Daphne poured him a glass of water. He began to relax. Daphne was clearly good at putting people at their ease, which was essential before embarking on a journey into the subconscious mind. 'Are you ready?' she asked after a while. 'It's time to go within. Let's see what comes up.' She led Max into a smaller room at the back of the house where the lights were dimmed, a candle lit and a portable massage table set up in the centre. Max took off his shoes and lay down on his back on the table and closed his eyes. Daphne asked him to take three deep breaths, in through the nose and out through the mouth. She then proceeded to lead him on a visualization which would take him deep into his subconscious mind where past life memories were stored.

Max allowed himself to be led through a field of meadow grass on a clear, sunny day. At the top of the slope was a stone tower. Daphne told him to approach the tower and to open the sturdy wooden door. Inside was a stairway that went underground. She asked him to descend, feeling each step upon the soles of his feet as if he were really there. As he did so, she counted down from twenty, leading him deeper and deeper into the hidden tunnels of his mind. Eventually, when he reached the bottom, he was faced with yet another door. He pushed it open.

Responding to Daphne's questions he spoke of the feeling of frustration and boredom of life in England in wartime. Countless cancelled airborne operations had left the men feeling discouraged and vexed. While they remained grounded, other divisions were seeing action. They longed to get the planes off the ground and into battle. Max told her that due to mist and fog they were delayed some four or five hours, while their impatience intensified. Then at last he was airborne and the feelings were slowly accompanied by images. What he saw was not like a film reel, viewed from a place of detachment, but a memory, and he was reliving it.

The noise of the plane was deafening. The sense of excitement and fear all-consuming. Accompanied by the men in his battalion, Max was prepared to jump. The soldiers looked at one another, their eyes full of excitement, sharing this intimate moment of camaraderie before the leap into the unknown and into the midst of battle. As much as Max felt terror, he also felt exhilaration. This was what he had trained for. He was ready and proud to serve his country.

There was no time in the open doorway of the plane to look down. One moment he was standing on the edge, the next he was falling through the sky. His parachute burst into the air, lifting him with a jolt. As he floated down he was aware of hundreds of men dangling beneath their silk canopies like him, clouding the air like a swarm of gnats. Gliders and planes flew overhead. Smoke billowed from the wreckage of planes on the ground and the sound of machine-gun fire and the barrage of artillery was all around him. They were being picked off like pheasants at a shoot; the Germans had known they were coming.

Next, he was in the thick of it, surrounded by woods and heathland, fire and smoke, in the midst of a landscape of chaos and crisis. Max ran through the trees, dodging the scything zing of bullets, seized by a blaze of blind courage and mad fury, acting on the instinct to survive. Shortly, he and another of his battalion came upon a wounded soldier lying on the ground, crying out in agony. Max knelt down and tried to give him first aid. In that moment, their eyes met and Max managed a smile. In the middle of Hell, he gave the broken man a little of his courage.

Max and his comrade discussed leaving the wounded soldier there, but they decided that they couldn't abandon him to the Germans. Instead, they lifted him off the ground and set off across the heathland to carry him to safety. Then everything went blank. Max saw nothing, just blackness. 'Where are you, Max?' Daphne asked.

'In a place of incredible peace,' he responded in a quiet, faraway voice. 'It's beautiful. Full of love . . .' Max wanted to stay there, floating in nothingness, enveloped in a feeling that was beyond the description of words, but Daphne brought him back through the door, up the steps and into the tower. Little by little he withdrew from his memory and found himself lying on the massage table, the taste of battle fading as he returned to consciousness. He took several deep breaths. There was no doubt in his mind now that he had lived another life, fighting in the Second World War, possibly at Arnhem. But it would require more research to verify. He still didn't know whether he was Rupert Dash. He hoped that the guides that Robyn spoke of would fill his sails with wind and send him in the right direction.

Daphne was excited about the regression and they spent a long time afterwards discussing it. Max was still trembling. The whole experience remained with him, like a memory reawakened, vivid and real.

After he left Daphne's, he drove into the city centre and over a cup of coffee in a café, he wrote up an account of the regression while it was still fresh in his mind. What he had seen in his memory was exactly the same as his dream, but more expansive. He knew now how he had died. If he could find out how Rupert Dash had died, he'd have a better idea of whether he was on the right track.

Later that evening, when he got home, he called Robyn. Daniel answered the telephone. 'Hi, Daniel, it's Max, Max Shelbourne.'

There was a moment as Daniel searched through his internal filing system. Max was about to mention South Africa and Gulliver's Bay to jog his memory, but then Daniel remembered. 'Max, hey mate, how are you?'

'Fine, thanks,' Max replied. 'How is everything down there?'

'Same old,' said Daniel. The two of them clearly had nothing to say to one another.

Max decided to cut to the chase. 'Is Robyn about?' he asked.

'Sure, hang on a second. I'll get her.'

Max was left hanging for a while. He heard Daniel calling Robyn's name. Eventually Robyn came onto the line. 'Sorry, Max, I was in the bath.'

Max looked at his watch. It was eight o'clock. 'No, *I'm* sorry. I shouldn't be calling you so late.' He liked to think of her in the bath. 'Shall I call you back?'

'No, it's fine. What's going on?'

'I've just been to see Daphne.'

'I'm sitting down, Max. Tell me everything, from the beginning. And don't miss out any details. You may not think they're important now, but when you start your research, every element will be important.'

Max recounted his regression to her from beginning to end. When he had finished she gasped in amazement. 'That's an incredible story.'

'I know. I'm fired up now. I need to find out about Rupert Dash.'

'How exciting. I wish I could help you with your research. I love a good mystery and I love digging.'

Max wished she could as well. 'How are you getting on with Lady Castlemaine?'

'Nearly finished the first draft,' she said brightly.

'That's great.'

'When you find out more about Rupert, will you call me? I'm dying to know.'

'You're sweet to take such an interest.'

'I'm not sweet at all. I'm genuinely fascinated. It's amazing to have had a dream and a past life regression that you might be able to prove as a past life memory. The recurring dream I had as a child is so hazy, I couldn't tell you much about it. I certainly couldn't verify whether it really happened or not. This story of yours is astonishing. I hope you get some concrete evidence. If you do, will you approach Aubrey Dash again? Then you can come back to Gulliver's Bay. Not that you need an excuse, of course. You're welcome anytime. It would be nice to see you.'

They chatted on for some time. Robyn was easy to talk to. Max could have talked to her all night. But Daniel wanted supper, so she said goodbye and hung up. Max knew he didn't have a chance with her. She was very much in a relationship and there was no indication that it wouldn't go to marriage, children and growing old together down there in Gulliver's Bay. If Daniel had been unkind or unpleasant Max might have gently tried to steer her out of it, but Daniel was a good person. There was no criticism Max could level at him, save that he held the heart of the woman Max wanted for himself.

Max returned to Wiltshire and his job. He spent Christmas with his family in Hampshire and attended a New Year's Eve party in London. To his horror Elizabeth was there with Peregrine. As soon as she saw Max, she dragged her new beau across the room to meet him. 'Max,' she shouted over the din of chatter and music, 'you must meet Peregrine, my fiancé.'

Max was surprised he hadn't heard that she was getting married. Peregrine was tall and polished with a shiny pink face and glossy brown hair. He smiled cheerfully and shook Max's hand as if he were an old friend. 'How nice to meet you,' he said, then laughed loudly. 'I should thank you. If you hadn't cancelled your wedding, I'd never have been able to propose to Bunny myself.'

'Isn't it lucky, then,' said Max, reflecting on his own luck in getting out of it.

'I'm sorry I didn't invite you to our engagement party in November,' said Elizabeth, crinkling her pretty nose. 'I just felt it wouldn't be fair.'

'I totally understand,' said Max, trying not to let her patronizing tone rattle him. 'Where are you getting married?'

'At my parents' house in Suffolk,' Peregrine answered. 'They've got the space for it.'

Elizabeth's eyes gleamed. 'We're going to have an enormous party. Five hundred guests. Big marquee. Dinner and dancing. It's going to be an all-nighter. Such fun.'

'That's great,' said Max, wondering how to extricate himself.

Elizabeth put a hand on his sleeve and crumpled her face in sympathy. 'I feel awful not including you on the guest list. I hope you understand. I just don't want any awkwardness.'

'Bunny and I have a no-ex policy,' said Peregrine, putting an arm around her.

'Yes, we do. Peregrine has one or two who will be very sorry not to be invited.' Elizabeth sighed and gave a little sniff. 'But, a policy is a policy and we must stick to it. You won't mind, will you? I feel desperately bad about it.'

'I hope it goes well,' said Max, edging away.

Peregrine guffawed. 'Better than the last one,' he said.

'I hope you find someone special,' said Elizabeth. 'You deserve the best.'

'Thanks, Elizabeth.' Max was relieved to get away. He went straight for the drinks table and helped himself to a glass of champagne. He spent the rest of the party avoiding them.

* * *

It wasn't until spring that Max set about researching the part that Rupert Dash played at Arnhem. Enjoying flying micro-lights as much as he did, Max guessed that Rupert Dash had been a glider pilot. The obvious place to start was the Army Flying Museum at Middle Wallop in Hampshire, a half hour's drive from his parents' house. It seemed obvious to Max that, if Rupert had flown gliders, he would have been in a glider regiment. Max decided to take the opportunity to stay with his parents and to drive to Middle Wallop from there. When he told them where he was going, they didn't seem in the least surprised. He was an ex-serviceman, it was natural that he should have an interest in military history.

It was a bright Monday morning when he set off. The skies were clear but for the odd fluffy cloud that bumbled lazily across it. The hedgerows were bursting with blackthorn and elder blossom and diving in and out were spirited little birds, busily building their nests. Max was feeling positive. He hadn't felt so happy in a long time. It was as if he had strayed from his path and now that he had found it again, he was filled with a sense of purpose and optimism. He had no idea what the future held. He was renting a cottage and working in a job that wasn't going to last. But right now, nothing mattered. Embarking on this adventure just felt right.

Arriving at the museum he went straight to Reception and asked the bespectacled young woman behind the desk whether someone could help him with research he was doing on a family member killed at Arnhem. The woman was eager to help and went to find someone who could assist him. A few minutes later she returned accompanied by an older man in army fatigues. Max explained what he was after. The man frowned and rubbed his chin thoughtfully. 'You won't find what you're looking for here,' he told him. 'I suggest you try the museum in Aldershot.'

Aldershot was forty-five miles away. Max returned to his car and set off. The Airborne Forces Museum was much more helpful. They were able to tell him that Rupert Dash had served in the 10th Battalion of the Parachute Regiment. He had been a captain and was buried in the cemetery in Oosterbeek in Holland. They were not, however, able to tell him where and how he had been killed. They suggested that Max contact the Imperial War Museum in London, which would have a detailed war diary of the 10th Battalion, Parachute Regiment. It would, they told him, give him a very clear narrative of their actions during the Battle of Arnhem. Max was elated. This was encouraging. He immediately returned to London, promising his parents he'd return soon.

The Imperial War Museum on Lambeth Road was suitably forbidding. With two enormous naval guns mounted in front of the stately portico and six huge pillars holding up a vast triangular pediment, it had the formal, sober air one would expect of a museum dedicated to recording the human cost of war. Originally, in the eighteenth century, it had been a lunatic asylum, but when the hospital moved to Kent the building was leased to the museum. Max realized on arrival that it might have been prudent to have telephoned first. It did not seem to be the sort of place where one could simply turn up and start rooting through files.

He was not wrong. He was, indeed, required to make an appointment. However, Max was on a mission. He was not going to allow a mere formality to deter him. He pulled out his retained military ID card, offered his most charming smile and explained what he had come here to do. Within minutes he was shown into the library and presented with the information he was after, a war diary of the Tenth. Left alone, the room receded and he sank into his research. He wasn't aware of his heart accelerating as he quickly found his first reference to Rupert Dash. He wasn't aware of anything at all except the echo of his regression as he read through the pages of the war diary.

Rupert Dash had been in the Royal Sussex Regiment when they had formed the new parachute battalion called the 10th in 1943. By September 1944 he had been promoted to captain and was the Regimental Intelligence Officer. The account of the battle was very detailed, but Max was impatient to find out exactly how Rupert had been killed. His eyes eagerly scanned the pages.

CHAPTER SIXTEEN

Operation Market Garden was the name given to the plan masterminded by Field Marshal Montgomery in September 1944 and backed by Churchill and Roosevelt, to seize a series of nine key bridges across the great rivers of Holland. The bridges, which ranged from the Dutch frontier to the Lower Rhine, would be captured initially by the First Allied Airborne Army, made up of the British 1st Airborne and the American 101st and 82nd Airborne Divisions, allowing for the land forces, led by the British XXX Corps, to then advance up a single road across German-occupied Holland. It was an ambitious plan, but if it succeeded, they would effectively cut off the German forces, outflank the Siegfried Line and break out into the open country of the North German Plain, with the very specific aim of ending the war by Christmas and, most importantly for Montgomery and Churchill, beating the Soviets to Berlin.

It was, of course, a disaster.

Max sat at the desk and scanned the pages until he reached the part relevant to his research into Rupert Dash and the 10th Battalion.

Back in England the men of the Tenth and other Divisional troops had been consumed with frustration, waiting on the airfields at Salby, Spanhoe and Cottesmore while low-hanging cloud and thick fog drifted over the country.

Max remembered how, in his regression, he had been frustrated by fog delaying their take-off. Injected with a burst of excitement, he read on. By midday the fog lifted and they were at last able to take to the skies. Having not seen action since Italy the year before, they were desperate to do their bit. A reconnaissance flight forty-eight hours prior to battle had photographed German Panzers and other armoured vehicles under camouflage nets parked up on the edge of woodland to the north of Arnhem. But due to numerous cancelled operations, and the top brass's desire to see British and US troops in Berlin by Christmas, the decision was taken to give Operation Market Garden, the largest airborne assault in history, the green light.

Rupert Dash was mentioned as having flown to Arnhem with his battalion on the second day of the battle – 18 September 1944. They had descended by parachute, under fire from German forces from both the 9th and 10th Panzer Divisions, under the command of Major Sepp Krafft. Both Divisions had only recently been withdrawn from France and were in the process of being refitted and retrained in preparation for the defence of the Reich. British intelligence had chosen to ignore photographic evidence and the lightly armed British parachute battalions found themselves up against crack SS Panzer troops. With the element of surprise lost, the British were seriously compromised.

After landing, Rupert and the men of the 10th Battalion were ordered to provide protection and cover for the medics tending to the wounded. By five in the afternoon the bulk of the injured had been evacuated and they had made their way east through the woods to an area around Hotel Buunderkamp where 4th Brigade HQ was established. After a fairly quiet night, the 10th Battalion set off at half past four in the morning, making towards a junction on the Amsterdamseweg, with orders to protect the brigade's left flank. They made steady progress with the main road providing their axis of advance, and by ten o'clock they had covered some three miles. Encouraged by the brigade commander they kept going and within three quarters of a mile came up against the German blocking line along Dreijenseweg. Fierce fighting ensued. After five hours it became clear that the Tenth advance had been halted and they were now pinned down by the better-armed Germans with their self-propelled guns, mortars and armoured cars. The order to withdraw was received around three o'clock in the afternoon and the men of the Tenth made their way back south-west towards the culvert under the railway and the village of Wolfheze. Meanwhile, the Polish gliders of the third wave were making their final approaches into the path of the withdrawing 10th Battalion, who were facing increasing pressure from the Germans.

It was during that disastrous withdrawal that Rupert lost his life.

Max read a personal account by a member of the 10th Battalion, Company Sergeant Major Hartwich.

L/C Radcliffe had been shot in the kneecap. I came across him with Capt. Dash and immediately applied the first field dressing. The poor sod was writhing in pain. It became clear that we couldn't remain there. We contemplated leaving him, but then changed our minds. It was not right to leave him to the mercy of the Germans. Capt. Dash and I carried him across the heath, towards Glider L.M. We moved slowly and had covered no more than fifty yards

when we were all three of us shot. Capt. Dash was flung
sixty feet. Radcliffe fell where he was. I was knocked ten
yards. When I discovered that I wasn't dead, I stumbled
over to Capt. Dash, who had died instantly. Radcliffe was
barely alive. I made my way to the Battalion to get help.

Max went cold. He read the paragraph again. The events
were exactly the same as the memories relived in his regression, and in his dream. He couldn't believe it. It was so
astonishing in its accuracy, giving irrefutable proof to his
theory of having lived before, that he remained frozen, mouth
agape, staring at the page until his eyes stung. It was, however,
a sobering moment as well as a triumphant one, because, as
exciting as it was to discover that he had, indeed, lived before
as Rupert Dash, he was at the same time reading an account of
his own death. It was difficult to take in and he remained for
some time, alone in the silence of the library, contemplating it.

Max couldn't wait to tell Robyn what he had discovered
and telephoned her from a phone box in the street. 'How did
you feel when you read about your own death?' she asked,
focusing immediately on the part Max had found the hardest
to digest. 'I bet that was unnerving.'

'I still can't get my head around it,' Max said, relieved to
be able to share his findings with someone who understood.
'It was the strangest thing. To see my dream and regression in print was extraordinary. I knew nothing about the
Battle of Arnhem before this, only that it was an airborne
operation. There's no other explanation I can think of than
reincarnation.'

Robyn laughed. 'Are you still doubting it, Max?'

'Not in my heart, but my head is constantly trying to find
holes in the argument.'

'You never want to listen to your head,' she said. 'Your heart will always tell you the truth.' At the mention of his heart, Max felt a swell of affection for Robyn, and with it, a wave of sorrow. She was right, his heart would always tell him the truth, but the truth of his feelings for *her* was something he could never share. Robyn understood him. They had a connection. He doubted she had a connection like that with Daniel.

'Speaking of the heart, how's Daniel?' he asked, deflated suddenly.

'He's well. I'll tell him you called.'

'He doesn't mind, does he?'

'Of course not.'

Max was a little put out that Daniel didn't consider him a threat. Not even a small one. 'That's good,' he said. 'Give him my best. Perhaps I'll come down and visit you this summer.'

'We'd love that,' Robyn exclaimed in her usual enthusiastic manner. Max bristled at her choice of pronoun. 'Mum and Dad would love to see you too.'

'Any news on your book?' he asked, hoping to keep her on the line for longer.

'I've got a publishing deal,' she replied.

'That's great! Who with?'

Robyn told him how she'd managed to find an agent who had auctioned her book to the highest bidder. 'I'm excited. Soon, I'm going to be able to say I'm an author.'

'That's fantastic,' Max said. 'When we next see each other, we can celebrate over dinner.'

'I'd love that,' she replied.

Max didn't mention Daniel. He had no intention of including him.

* * *

Max hadn't planned to share his story with his parents. Scarred by Elizabeth's constant doubting, he was reluctant to speak about it with anyone who wasn't obviously open to the esoteric, as Olga, Robyn and Daphne were. However, something urged him to confide in them. That wind in his sails again, perhaps, keeping him on course and moving him forward. He decided to stop off at their house on his way back to Wiltshire. With the revelations still fresh in his mind it seemed like the right time.

They were in the kitchen enjoying a glass of wine before dinner. His mother was cooking at the Aga, his father at the table with a large glass of Merlot. Max wasn't sure how to begin, but his father unwittingly opened the gate on the subject by asking what he had discovered at the Imperial War Museum. Max took a deep breath and told them the whole story, starting with his recurring nightmare and ending with the account of Rupert Dash's death.

Without interrupting, Catherine took off her apron and sat down. George listened, the lines deepening between his eyebrows as he tried to use logic to make sense of what he was being told. Max was encouraged by their silence and by the interest in their expressions. He knew they would not think him a fantasist or a liar, but reincarnation was a step too far for many people. 'You probably think I'm mad,' he said when he was finished. He thought of Robyn then. She'd immediately accuse him of self-doubt and blame Elizabeth. 'But reincarnation is the only explanation I can find,' he added. He knew Robyn would approve of that more confident statement.

Catherine raised her eyebrows and shook her head. 'I don't know what to make of it. It's an incredible story, Max. I don't really believe in reincarnation but I agree, there doesn't seem to be another explanation. It's certainly a remarkable coincidence to find an account of your dream in a book.'

'It's too much of a coincidence to be anything other than a past life,' said George firmly. Max was surprised. He didn't think his father subscribed to the idea of people living previous lives. George topped up his glass and then poured the remaining drops into Max's. 'The older I get the more open I become to ideas like reincarnation,' he continued. 'Frankly, I'd rather not come back. You know, quit while I'm ahead; I've had it good this time around. But I'm ready to be convinced. I certainly believe in some sort of afterlife. Reincarnation is a bit of a leap on from that, but your story, Max, is extraordinary.'

'I'd love to find a photo of Rupert,' said Max. 'I don't think I'll necessarily look like him. But I'm curious to see his face.'

'It's weird to think you might have been someone else,' said Catherine thoughtfully. 'Someone with a different mother.'

Max nodded; he understood her confusion. 'I know. It's hard to comprehend. But you have to remember Shakespeare, *"All the world's a stage, And all the men and women merely players."* While we're on the stage we're aware only of the other actors who share it with us while we're performing this play, this life. When we leave the stage, we are reunited with those we knew in other plays, on other stages, at other times. This life is simply a blink of the eye of time.'

'Shakespeare was rather enlightened, wasn't he,' said Catherine. 'If you want to see a photograph of Rupert, I suggest you contact Bertha.'

'The woman who researched the family tree?'

'Yes, that's her. I'm sure she'll have photographs. She's putting together a book about our family history. She's been doing it for years. I'm not sure who's going to bother reading it.'

'If it includes Rupert Dash, I'll read it,' said Max.

'Give her a call. She's a dotty old thing. A touch

eccentric. But she's a good egg. I'd be curious to see a photo of Rupert myself.'

'What are you going to do with all this information?' George asked.

Max shrugged. 'I don't know. I suppose it's just satisfying my curiosity.'

'At what point will it be satisfied?' he continued.

'I don't know that, either. I wrote to Aubrey Dash, Rupert's brother, but didn't get a reply.'

'That's a shame,' said Catherine. 'You're a distant cousin, I'm surprised he didn't even bother to write back.'

'What did you say in your letter?'

'That I'm researching the family history, especially Rupert . . .'

'Perhaps he's already had to deal with Bertha. She's enough to put anyone off.' Catherine chuckled. 'I'd leave him be if I were you.'

'I will, although it's a shame. I'd like to have taken a look around Pedrevan Park. I glimpsed it through the trees when I went down to Cornwall. It's a stunning house. Elizabethan.'

'Did you feel a sense of déjà vu when you were there?' Catherine asked.

'No.'

'Perhaps you should visit Arnhem,' George suggested. 'You might get a sense of déjà vu there.'

'A *nasty* sense,' Catherine added with a grimace.

Max sighed. 'I feel compelled to discover more about Rupert Dash, but I'm not sure why. Should the past have any bearing on our present lives? Whether it's our childhoods or our previous lives, does holding onto stuff do us any good? I've satisfied my curiosity. I believe I was Rupert Dash and I died at the Battle of Arnhem. That should be enough, shouldn't it? But it's not. I want to find out more. But to what end, I don't know.'

Catherine gave him a smile he recognized and he knew what was coming. 'You need to find a nice girl and settle down,' she said.

'You mean like Elizabeth and Peregrine?' said Max.

George guffawed. 'She's certainly found her equal in that hayseed. And she didn't hang around, did she? I give that marriage five years.'

'Let's not be rude about Elizabeth,' said Catherine sternly. 'I'm sure she and Peregrine will be very happy together. Now we need to find someone for *you*, Max.' He smiled to hide his desolation; he'd found someone, someone perfect, but he couldn't have her.

Max returned to work. Bertha Clairmont was pushed to the back of his mind as he was swept up in the daily requirements of his job. He thought about Robyn often and many times he picked up the telephone only to change his mind and put it down; he had nothing specific to tell her and he dreaded Daniel answering it. He suspected that Daniel's patience would run out if he called too often. There was only so much a man could take of his girlfriend speaking to another man before he got jealous. Then one day in June Robyn called *him*.

Max was delighted by the surprise, but his delight swiftly turned to despair when she told him she was engaged. 'I wanted to tell you myself,' she explained. 'Rather than you reading it in the newspaper.'

'That's great news,' said Max in a thin voice. He felt as if an invisible hand was choking him.

'We're getting married the last weekend in August. The Bank Holiday weekend. I hope you can come.'

'I'm sure I can,' said Max. He wished he had a valid reason for saying that he couldn't.

'We're marrying in the church in Gulliver's Bay and having a party on the beach.'

Max thought of the cave and something snagged inside his heart. 'Wow, that sounds great,' he said lamely. He was aware that his voice was flat and wondered whether she noticed. Whether she cared.

'You will put it in your diary now, won't you? I won't accept a refusal.' Robyn laughed as if she didn't have a care in the world. That laugh, usually so infectious, now gave him pain.

'Send my best to Daniel,' he said.

'I will. I can't believe he finally got off the pot. Truly, I thought we'd just drift on and on like this forever.'

'Some men are like that.'

'Are you like that, Max?'

'No. If I found the right woman, I'd ask her to marry me immediately.'

She laughed again, this time softly. 'She'll be a lucky girl, whoever she is.'

When Max put down the phone, he hung his head in his hands.

After his conversation with Robyn, Max felt a terrible sense of emptiness – and aimlessness. He was drifting through life as if on autopilot, doing a job that didn't excite him, living in a rented cottage that was only temporary, and loving a woman who was engaged to be married to someone else. The only thing driving him on was that persistent wind in his sails that seemed never to give up, however deflated his heart was. There was nothing else giving his life meaning right now, not even his photography, so he gave in to that wind and allowed it to blow him onto Bertha Clairmont's doorstep.

Bertha was seventy-three years old and lived in a small flat in Fulham with her Norfolk terrier Toby. The place was messy, with papers and magazines strewn over every surface along with a thick layer of dust and dog hair. She clearly had no interest in decor or hygiene, Max decided. Everything about her was grey. She looked like a white dishcloth that had been put in the washing machine with a black sock and come out grey. Her hair was grey and wiry, her skin was grey and lined, her eyes were grey and bloodshot and her hands were grey and covered in liver spots. The only thing that was not grey were her fingers, which were yellow from where she permanently held a smouldering cigarette. The air of the flat was foggy with the smoke that she inhaled with every breath. Max wanted to leave as soon as he arrived.

'Come on in, Max,' she said in a gravelly voice. 'I'd offer you a cup of tea, but I'm out of teabags. Fancy a vodka? Or gin? I'm sure I can find some tonic water somewhere.'

'No, I'm fine, thanks,' he said, sweeping aside an old coat and a newspaper and sitting down on the sofa. Toby sniffed his shoes and then scratched his trousers in the hope of being lifted onto his knee.

'Ignore Toby,' said Bertha. 'If you let him up he'll just be annoying. Down, Toby. Good boy.' She chuckled. 'Don't catch his eye or he'll roger your leg. There, now he's lying down. Good.'

Bertha sank stiffly into an armchair. She was short and plump, in a grey tent-shaped dress that reached her ankles. 'How is your mother?' she asked.

'She's well, thank you.'

'Is your father still planting trees?' Bertha smiled, revealing a set of crooked yellow teeth. 'I remember going to visit them in Hampshire a few years ago and he was planting an avenue of lime trees.'

'Yes, he loves his trees.' Max's eyes were beginning to sting from the smoke. He wondered how the poor dog endured it. 'Do you mind if I open a window?' he asked.

'Not at all. I like fresh air.' She chortled and then coughed wheezily. 'I haven't been out for days. Been working frantically on my book.'

Max got up and unlatched a window. He inhaled the London air greedily. 'Your family history?'

'That's the one. Your family too, Max.'

'I suppose it is, yes.'

She looked at him with hooded eyes. 'You said you're interested in Rupert Dash.'

'Yes, I am ...'

Bertha blew smoke out of the side of her mouth. 'I knew Rupert. Handsome devil he was. Died in the war. Tragedy. His family never got over it. They were golden, they were, the Dashes. The golden side of the family. None of us could compete. We all looked dreadfully dull by comparison. Aubrey Dash, his younger brother, was a real charmer. He went on to marry Ellen Chadwick. It wasn't a happy marriage. They had three children, divorced and then he married again. A mouse of a woman called Minnie – that's a joke, isn't it.' She laughed throatily. 'I lost touch. Life does that, doesn't it? He still lives at Pedrevan. We used to spend summers there when we were young. It was fabulous. Lots going on. It's rather sad now. Have you been there?'

'No, I haven't.'

'Better not see it as it is now. It's not the same. I wrote to Aubrey, requesting a visit. I wanted to find a few missing pieces of the family puzzle. He wrote back very curtly. He said he's not interested in the family history. Sounded very bitter if you ask me. That's unhappiness for you. Strange, he used to be such a carefree boy.'

'Might you have a photograph of Rupert?'

'Yes, I do. See that box over there?' Bertha pointed a crooked finger at a table pushed against the wall. 'Bring it over and I'll find one for you. I keep all the family photos in there. I've been collecting them for the book.'

When Max got up, the dog got up too and watched him suspiciously. Max brought the box over and placed it on Bertha's lap. She perched her cigarette in the ashtray and put on a pair of spectacles which were attached to a beaded chain hanging over her bosom. She began shuffling through the photographs. Max sat down again and caught the dog's eye. 'I told you not to do that,' said Bertha as Toby jumped up and grabbed him round the shin. 'Get down, Toby!' Bertha growled. Max tentatively shook his leg, then pushed the dog off with a hand. 'Lie down, Toby. There's a good boy.' Toby put his head on his paws and sighed. 'Ah, this is Aubrey,' said Bertha, taking out a photograph. She handed it to Max. 'He was handsome, wasn't he?'

Max took a good look at the black and white photograph, impatient to see the characters of his research come to life in pictures. 'And this is their mother Celia, now *she* was a beauty.' Celia was, indeed, beautiful, with short black hair, slanting cat's eyes and a beguiling smile. It was a formal photograph of her in an evening dress, presumably taken by a professional, perhaps marking an anniversary or some such significant date. 'Here's Rupert.' Bertha looked at Max. 'Funny, he looks rather like you.'

Max's heart missed a beat. He took the photograph with

nervous anticipation. It was a profile picture in black and white of Rupert in uniform. He wore a beret and a big smile, and Bertha was right, there was something about the position of the eyes and brow that they both shared. It wasn't like looking at himself, more like looking at a brother or a close cousin.

'And this is Florence.' Bertha passed over another photograph. Max took it. Florence had a winsome face and a gentle, dreamy expression, probably enhanced by the old-fashioned, softly lit quality of the photograph. Her hair was long and wavy, pulled off her face and secured in clips, as was the fashion in the thirties. There was something about her smile that drew his attention; it had mischief in it.

Bertha took a long drag on her cigarette. 'After Rupert was killed, Florence emigrated to Australia with their daughter Mary-Alice. I never found out why she left. Bearing in mind that Rupert's family and her family both lived in Gulliver's Bay, you would have thought she'd have wanted to be near them for support. But no, she travelled all the way to the other side of the world. Very odd.'

'Did you say Florence's family lived in Gulliver's Bay?' Max asked.

'Yes, her grandparents, the Pinfolds. They had a lovely house with a secret tunnel leading down to the beach. A smuggler's tunnel. Rather romantic.'

Max froze. He stared at her in astonishment. Bertha looked at him and narrowed those hooded eyes. 'Do you know it?'

'Yes, I stayed there when I went to Cornwall. The Mariners.'

'Yes, that was the name. The Mariners. It's coming back to me now. Florence threw a wonderful party on the beach. That was the last year we all went down there. Then the war came and things were never the same again after that. I remember that party. She made bunting out of straw. Very unusual and quite effective. She was a character, Florence. Naughty too. I wonder what happened to her?'

Max was once again filled with a sudden burst of energy and enthusiasm. He knew he had to get down to Gulliver's Bay. Not only to show Robyn the photograph of Rupert, which Bertha had lent him, and to tell her that Florence had lived in The Mariners, but to stop her getting married. Why hadn't he thought of that before?

CHAPTER SEVENTEEN

Max found himself once again at The Mariners. This time he looked at it with different eyes. From his bedroom window he gazed out over the garden and on to the sea. This was the view that Florence would have seen, perhaps Rupert too. Maybe they had stood at this very window and stared out over the water as he was doing now. He felt that strange shiver cover his skin with goose bumps again and folded his arms. How he longed to share this view with Robyn.

Max had arranged to come down to Cornwall and see her, telling her he had something exciting to show her but giving no hint as to what it was. He felt nervous. Robyn was engaged to Daniel. Their wedding was planned for the end of August. It was now early July. Max had ruined one wedding already and now he was planning to ruin another. The consequences could be terrible. And Robyn had given him no indication that she liked him any more than as a friend. There had been a mild flirtation, for sure, but she was the sort of girl who couldn't help but flirt. She was lively and full of joy, making each person she met feel special. She made Max feel special, but no more, perhaps, than the postman, the butcher and the man behind the checkout in the supermarket. Max couldn't be sure he was really special to her at all.

Yet he had to try. If Robyn married Daniel, Max wanted to be certain that he had given himself a chance. He didn't want to spend the rest of his life wondering what might have been. It was a gamble, but one he was willing to take. He was aware that it was an all or nothing kind of gamble. In declaring himself to Robyn he risked losing her if his feelings weren't reciprocated. Of course, if she felt the same, then he would win everything.

Robyn arrived at The Mariners at six for a drink that evening. She'd arranged for them to have dinner afterwards with Daniel and her parents on the Private Side. The dinner Max had promised just the two of them in celebration of her publishing deal was not going to happen now. The following day they were going to sail in Gryffyn's boat and have a picnic on a beach somewhere. Robyn wanted Max to see where she and Daniel lived and had invited him there for supper on Saturday night. He'd leave on Sunday morning like he had the last time. Max was aware that this evening would be the only opportunity he'd have to get her on her own. It wasn't ideal, having only just arrived, but it was all the time he had.

Robyn appeared on the terrace in a pair of white jeans and a pink shirt. Her hair was loose over her shoulders, her skin tanned and she was glowing with good health and happiness. Max was elated to see her. They embraced. 'You look radiant,' he said, taking her in; the shining eyes, the compelling smile, her sweet nature expressed in every contour of her lovely face.

'I'm happy,' she replied. 'You look good too. Life must be treating you well also.'

They sat down and Max ordered a Negroni and a margarita. She noticed he'd brought his camera. 'That's a Leica,' she said with admiration. 'A beautiful camera.'

'It's very special,' he replied, looking at it fondly. 'My grandmother gave me money on my eighteenth birthday and

I bought it with that. I'd always wanted a proper camera but had never been able to afford one. I hadn't planned on getting a Leica. But when I saw it in the shop I had to have it. It's been a trusty friend over the years.'

'What are you going to photograph?'

He grinned. 'You.' He was sure she blushed.

'I'm not very photogenic,' she laughed.

'The camera never lies, so you'll come out beautifully.'

She averted her eyes. 'I'm sure you say that to all the girls.'

'No, only you.'

The waiter brought their drinks and they clinked glasses. 'To us and our friendship,' she said.

Max was encouraged. 'To our *special* friendship,' he said with emphasis and took a sip.

'So, what is it you want to tell me?' she asked. 'I'm dying to know.'

Max put his hand in his jacket pocket and pulled out an envelope. He handed it to her. She frowned. 'Open it.'

'All right.' She slipped out the photograph. Her expression changed to wonder. 'Oh my God!' she exclaimed, staring at it. 'This is Rupert Dash, isn't it? He looks just like you.'

'There is a similarity, I agree. We are cousins. Distant, but still.'

'Where did you get it?'

Max told her about Bertha Clairmont. 'She also told me something else.'

'Go on.'

'Florence, Rupert's wife, grew up here.'

'In Gulliver's Bay?'

'Here. In this very house.'

'Really?'

'Her grandparents lived here and she presumably stayed a lot.'

'That's freaky.'

'Isn't it. Another coincidence. Although, as you rightly say, there are no such things.'

Robyn looked at him intensely. 'Max, this has to be a book.'

'Do you think?'

'Yes, it's the most extraordinary story.'

'But I can't write to save my life. I can barely write a thank you letter.'

'*I'll* write it. We could do it together.'

'Is there enough for a book?'

'Of course. You wrap a work of fiction around the truth. How many novels about reincarnation have you read?'

'Novels? None. Non-fiction, lots.'

'Exactly. It would be unusual and we'd reach a wider audience. Think about it.'

'All right, I will.' Max began to feel more confident. Robyn wanted to write a book with him. That must surely be a good sign.

'Do you think Florence is still alive?' Robyn asked, handing back the photograph.

'I don't know. Bertha didn't know, either.'

'You have to find out somehow. I mean, how strange would that be if your wife from a past life was still alive? You could meet her.'

'That would be weird.'

'Not really. The only weird part is that you know about it. We must be surrounded by people we shared past lives with.' She laughed. 'Dan might have been my father in a past life, or my daughter. I'm glad I don't know about that!'

'Now I realize why it's better that we don't know,' said Max, his spirits sinking at the mention of Daniel.

'So why are you finding out about your past life? Because

you're meant to. Why? To write a book about it so that people realize that life goes on. That there is no death. That existence is an endless series of cycles. We live, we move into spirit and then we come back. Again and again until we have learned all the lessons our soul needs to know in order to move on to the next stage, whatever that might be. We think heaven is the destination, but I bet it's just another stage in our journey and there are perhaps many heavens on from that. Who knows?'

Max drained his glass. 'Will you walk with me on the beach?'

'Sure,' she said, getting up from her chair. 'It's a beautiful evening.'

Max took in the expanse of sea and the orange sun sinking slowly towards it. 'It's strange to think that Florence and Rupert probably looked out over this view together.'

'I'm sure they did.' Robyn stood beside him, soaking up the splendour of it. 'You have to find out what happened to Florence,' she repeated.

'I know. Bertha said she emigrated to Australia with their daughter a few years after Rupert died. It's odd when you think about it. Florence's family were here, Rupert's were here too. You'd have thought she'd want to stay and bring her child up surrounded by cousins.'

'Something must have gone wrong.'

'Yes, I suppose so.'

She grinned at him. 'More fodder for the book.'

They made their way to the beach. Max couldn't help but picture Rupert and Florence walking down the same path, their feet treading the same ground, their vision taking in the same view. He didn't imagine it had changed very much since the thirties. And here he was with Robyn, about to confess that he loved her. He was filled with anxiety but also hope.

The sun was low in the sky, turning it a dusty pink. The tide was out, leaving the damp sand teeming with small crustaceans for the birds to find and squabble over. Far out, waves lapped the beach in their lazy rhythm. A light, salty breeze caressed their faces as they strolled up the sand. It was as romantic as it was beautiful and Max felt his chest flood with longing. He knew Robyn was the right woman for him. He knew he could make her happy. He had to stop her marrying Daniel, somehow. He was sure, as he gazed out over the horizon, that if she married Daniel, it would not end well.

He took some photographs. He took them of the sea, the birds, the sunset, but only so that he could capture Robyn while not looking too obvious about it. She laughed bashfully, curled her hair behind her ear and smiled. He knew it would embarrass her to take more than a couple. He hoped he'd managed to hold the camera steady.

They walked on, talking in the relaxed, fluid manner of two people who had known each other a long time. Yet beneath the affable surface of their friendship simmered an undeniable attraction. Max felt it. He was sure Robyn felt it too. How could she not? Their conversation seemed farcical, somehow, as if they were both making an effort to avoid what was abundantly clear but unmentionable.

Intensified perhaps by the tender pink light of sunset, the melancholy cry of gulls and the awareness that he teetered on the brink of losing her, Max felt his heart grow heavy with an unbearable yearning. They found themselves at the mouth of the cave. That place of enchantment where the resonance of romantic trysts from bygone years still remained, trapped in the atmosphere like whispering ghosts. Max went inside, Robyn followed. He felt as if he were stepping into his destiny, that it was unavoidable, and that Robyn knew it too. Why else would she follow him? Why else would she allow herself to be drawn into this intimate, deeply romantic place, just the two of them?

'Robyn, I need to tell you something,' he said, turning to face her.

She looked at him with an uncertain expression in her eyes. 'That sounds ominous,' she said with a laugh, but her laughter caught in her throat.

He stepped closer, unsure suddenly how to put his feelings into words. Having thought about what he was going to say all the way down in the car, those words now eluded him. Robyn did not move away as he slipped his hand around the back of her neck, beneath her hair. She gazed up at him, unblinking, her face serious, pensive, anxious. Still, she did not step back or attempt to remove it. She did not tell him to stop.

Max kissed her then. He kissed her fully, pulling her against him, wrapping his arms around her and holding her tightly. She responded, parting her lips and kissing him back. A deep moan escaped her throat and he felt her soften. She put a hand against his cheek, closed her eyes, surrendered to the moment.

It was quiet in the cave. The roar of the sea was far away, the wind a distant murmur. Only the soft sound of their breathing interrupted the silence and merged with the trapped energy of thousands of kisses given long ago. Max kissed her deeply. It felt right, as if every kiss that had gone before was but a blind attempt to find the real thing. And now he had found it. He knew he never wanted to kiss anyone else ever again.

Then Robyn pulled away.

She put her forehead against his shoulder and sighed. 'Oh, Max . . .'

'I love you, Robyn. I've loved you since the first moment I saw you. I think I've loved you my whole life, only I never knew it.'

She looked up at him sadly. 'This is wrong,' she said. 'I'm engaged to Dan.'

He took her face in his hands and held her eyes with his. 'You can break it off. You can end it, Robyn.'

'I love Dan and I'm going to marry him.'

'But you kissed me back,' he said, searching her expression for a sign of encouragement. 'If you truly loved Dan you wouldn't have kissed me back.'

Robyn took his hands off her face and shook her head, clearly confused. 'I can't say I'm not attracted to you, Max. I am. And I *did* kiss you back. I don't know why. I shouldn't have.' She chuckled mirthlessly. 'Perhaps it's the beauty of the evening, the enchantment in this cave, the margarita. I don't know. I'm attracted to you, but I *love* Dan.'

'You barely know me, Robyn. Give me a chance. Ours isn't a chemistry you can ignore.'

'I *have* to ignore it, Max. I'm sorry.' She let go of his hands and stepped away. 'We should get back.'

Max felt the ground spin away from him, taking Robyn with it. He pushed his hair off his forehead and sighed loudly. 'It's going to be awkward now, isn't it?'

Robyn smiled affectionately and embraced him. She rested her head against his shoulder. Max felt like crying; he was a twenty-six-year-old man and he felt like crying. He closed his eyes.

'It'll only be awkward if we allow it to be,' she said. 'Our friendship is too precious to lose simply because you've told me you love me. I'm lucky to have your love, Max. I'm not going to toss it away. I'll treasure it.' She released him and her eyes were full of compassion.

'You're one in a million, Robyn,' he said, caressing her face with his thumb. 'You're wise and kind. I'm sure I'm not the only man who's going to feel sad at your wedding. I hope Daniel knows how unique you are.'

'I think he does. He's a good man, Max.'

She slipped her hand through his arm and they walked out of the cave. The roar of the sea grew loud suddenly, the wind blew cold off the water, reality invaded with the first drops of rain. 'Let's talk about our book,' she said, changing the subject. But Max knew, deep down, that he had lost her.

He left Gulliver's Bay early the following morning. He made up an excuse which satisfied Edwina and Gryffyn, but he knew Robyn saw through his lie. However, he couldn't spend the weekend with Daniel, not after he had confessed his feelings for Robyn and been rebuffed. He just couldn't stomach it.

As soon as he got back to the cottage he developed his roll of film. The photograph of Robyn was perfect. He had captured her gentle nature, her wisdom and her beauty; the way he saw her every time he closed his eyes.

* * *

Max did not want to attend Robyn's wedding. He thought of many excuses he could use: illness, a parent's illness, a funeral, a business trip, a flat tyre, but in the end he packed his morning coat and drove down to Cornwall. Robyn would know it was a lie and Max did not want to let her down on such an important day, even though it would be unbearable for him. He would simply have to bite the bullet and go through with it.

As The Mariners was full of Daniel and Robyn's families, Max booked into another hotel on the other side of Gulliver's Bay. His room did not have a view of the sea, but he didn't care. He just wanted to get the weekend over as quickly as possible.

The weather was fine. Blue skies, white clouds, a light

breeze. Max saw nothing beautiful in it for his heart was heavy with regret and sorrow. A deep, bewildering sorrow. How come Robyn was marrying Daniel? The universe had got it wrong. This was *not* meant to be happening.

Staying in the same hotel was a girl he had known in his childhood. Mandy Franklin. She had always been wild, the sort of party girl Max had taken out in his army days. The sort of girl his mother described as having 'been around the block a few times'. They met at breakfast on the day of the wedding and shared a table. It transpired that Mandy was an old friend of Daniel's. They'd been at university together. Bumping into Mandy turned out to be a lucky twist in what promised to be a miserable weekend. She drove a white Golf Cabriolet and offered to chauffeur Max around. It seemed silly for both of them to take separate cars when they were coming and going from the same place. Mandy wasn't unattractive, either. With thick brown curls, vivacious hazel eyes and the dirtiest laugh Max had ever heard, she was certainly fun. Max was grateful to have a friend for, besides Mandy, it transpired that he didn't know a single person at the wedding.

He arrived at the church where Rupert Dash's memorial service had taken place over forty years before. Mandy sat beside him in the pew, waving at friends and turning around to speak to the people behind them. Max didn't want to speak to anyone. He wanted to take in the building and imagine what it must have been like before the war when Rupert and Florence had sat there. However, his desire for peace was thwarted by Mandy's keenness to talk to him and to introduce him to her friends. 'Cheer up!' she hissed through her smile. 'Anyone would have thought you were attending a funeral, not a wedding.'

Max apologized. 'I've just been to a funeral,' he lied. 'Sitting here in church is bringing it all back.'

Mandy put a hand on his knee and squeezed it. 'I'm so sorry, darling. How dreadful. We'll soon be out and partying and then you can forget all about it.'

The sound of the choir silenced her and the congregation got to its feet and turned to face the door expectantly. There was movement in the archway. Max peered past the people standing behind him and saw Gryffyn, barely recognizable in a morning suit, clean-shaven with his shaggy hair brushed off his face. Beside him stood the bride. She looked beautiful in her white dress, Max thought with a twist of his gut. Her hair had been pinned up and her veil, which misted her face, was embroidered with tiny sequins, making it sparkle. They proceeded to walk slowly down the aisle. Max couldn't take his eyes off her and yet, at the same time, he wanted to look away; the sight was too painful. Robyn should have been walking towards *him*, not towards Daniel who stood in the nave, smiling proudly at his radiant bride-to-be. It was like a nightmare. Max wished with all his heart that he would wake up and find that this wasn't happening, that Robyn was, in fact, engaged to him and this had all been a bad dream.

The service continued regardless of the turmoil in Max's heart. Then the vicar asked, 'If anyone should show just cause why this couple cannot lawfully be joined together in matrimony, let them speak now or forever hold their peace.' Max wanted to jump up and yell: 'Me!' If it were a movie he would have stopped the ceremony, told Robyn again that he loved her and she would have thrown off her veil, taken his hand and fled up the aisle and out of that big door into the happily ever after. But this was not a movie. This was life and Max had gambled and lost. The ceremony continued and the vicar pronounced them man and wife. Max wanted to be sick.

At the reception in the hotel he managed to hold it together in order to congratulate the bride and groom, then helped himself to a glass of champagne and downed it in one. He helped himself to another. Soon after, Daniel's best friend gave a speech. Max stood at the back of the room and listened with half an ear. He wished the evening were over so he could go to bed but he still had a party to get through. This was turning out to be the longest day of his life.

As people started leaving the reception for a brief respite before returning for the dinner-dance, Mandy appeared. 'Shall we head back to the hotel?' she asked. Max was only too happy to leave.

In his hotel room at last, he showered, switched on the television and lay on the bed in his dressing gown, wondering how to get out of the evening event. Perhaps there wasn't a seating plan and no one, besides Mandy and Robyn, would notice that he had failed to attend. As he sobered up, the misery intensified. Robyn had said that his declaration wouldn't change their friendship. That might be so, he thought, but he now knew that his unhappiness *would*; if it was going to hurt this much every time he saw her, how on earth could they still have a relationship?

Max had been lying on the bed for some time when there came a knock on the door. It was Mandy. She was in the white hotel dressing gown. 'Darling, there's something wrong with my bath. Can I borrow yours?' Without waiting for him to reply, she walked straight in. 'You've got a much bigger room than mine. What makes you so special?' She laughed and went over to the window. 'No view of the sea, though.' She smiled and bit her lip. 'It's nice bumping into you, Max. You've improved with age.'

He couldn't help but smile back. 'Thanks.'

'I'll go and have my bath then. Don't feel you can't come in if you need something. I'll fill the bath with bubbles.' She gave a throaty laugh and flounced into the bathroom, leaving the door wide open. A short while later Max heard her turn off the taps and step in. To his surprise he began to feel aroused. Here he was in the depths of despair feeling aroused at the thought of Mandy Franklin naked in the bath. His heart and his body were clearly not in synch.

It wasn't long before Mandy appeared in a towel, her skin damp and glittering with foam. Her hair was pinned up but the tendrils that hung loosely at her neck were wet. Max felt his arousal build. He grinned. 'Do you want to watch TV with me?' he asked, patting the space beside him.

She grinned back. 'What are you watching?'

'You.'

'Hmm, and how do I look?'

'Pretty good, actually,' he replied, taking her in. 'You'd look better without the towel.'

Mandy needed no encouragement. She let it drop to the floor. 'Better now?' she asked, standing naked before him.

'Much better.'

She climbed onto the bed like a panther and sat astride him. 'Max Shelbourne, who'd have thought you'd grow to be so handsome?' She ran a tongue across his lips. 'Or so tasty.' Then Max forgot all about Robyn with the only thing powerful enough to distract him.

Later, when Max arrived at the party with Mandy, he was feeling a little less sorry for himself. He decided that there was no point moping about. He had to make the best of things. Robyn wasn't the only beautiful woman in the world. There were many, and one of them was destined for him. He took a glass of wine off the tray and strode into the throng of guests.

The wedding feast was held in a big white tent on the lawn. Guests sat at round tables decorated with tall flower displays and candles, and afterwards they made their way down the illuminated path to the beach to dance on the sand beneath the moon. Max was suitably drunk by this point. Mandy helped him out of his jacket then led him by the hand onto the dance floor. A band played on a stage set up at the back of the beach and all around were fairy lights and flares. Max's vision was blurred with intoxication. All he could see were jiving bodies and twinkling lights. He was grateful for the darkness because he couldn't make out faces, not even Mandy's, so he couldn't see Robyn; the last thing he wanted to witness was Robyn cheek to cheek with Daniel.

Max danced to forget his sorrow. He danced wildly until the slow songs started and then he pulled Mandy into his arms and kissed her with all the passion he could muster. She tasted of chewing gum and cigarettes. With his heart brimming with longing he held her close simply to have someone to hold.

Dawn was a blush on the horizon when Max led Mandy to the end of the beach and into the cave. Robyn had lit it with a hundred candles which were now burned down to the ends of their wicks. Some had gone out, but the effect was still magical. They were alone, ankle-deep in water. The dizzying effects of the alcohol were wearing off. Max took in the beauty of the place that still vibrated with the memory of that kiss and felt the familiar ache in his chest once again. Robyn was married; Robyn was lost to him; he might never see her again.

Mandy was dancing drunkenly, singing tunelessly, her voice echoing eerily against the rock. Max suppressed a sob. He felt the quivering of something deep within him, the resonance of an old memory, buried long ago. He put his hand against the wall and closed his eyes.

CHAPTER EIGHTEEN

Gulliver's Bay, 1945

Florence put her hand against the wall of the cave and closed her eyes. Finally, after months of doubt, she had discovered from Company Sergeant Major Greene of the Tenth that Rupert had been mortally wounded on the battlefield while trying to carry an injured soldier to safety. Neither she nor her family had ever been officially informed of his death. In spite of this new information, Florence still clung onto the tiny shred of hope. While there was no formal notification, there remained a sliver of a chance that by some miracle Rupert might have survived.

For a year she remained at The Mariners with her mother and grandparents. Winifred came down with the Colonel she had married in London during the war. He was fifteen years older than her with a thick red moustache and thinning hair and a penchant for smoking cigars and drinking port. He might easily have been sixty, Florence thought, wondering what her sister saw in him. But Winifred seemed happy enough. She smoked, played bridge and occasionally allowed Mary-Alice to hold her little finger. Winifred wasn't very interested in children. 'I'll do my duty if Gerald wants them,' she told Florence. 'But I'd rather not. There's something very binding about children.'

Uncle Raymond appeared, looking older but still his usual jovial self. He had spent the war doing his bit for Home Defence. While Winifred had barely mentioned Rupert, save to say how sorry she was, Uncle Raymond took Florence by the hand and led her down to the beach where they sat on the dunes and talked. 'I know how much you loved him, Flo,' he said. And with that small, heartfelt sentence, she cried in his arms.

The war might have ended but the country was blighted by shortages. There was an edict instructing people to fill their baths ankle-deep, meat was bought on a points basis and one was only allowed to buy two ounces of butter or margarine and cheese a week. Mary-Alice, along with all the other babies, was permitted an extra half-pint of milk a day and was given a free bottle of rosehip or orange juice a month. When Winifred was staying, that precious bottle mysteriously found its way into her gin.

William and Celia Dash did not hold onto hope like Florence did. They accepted Rupert's death with stoicism and dignity. Aubrey returned home from Greece where he'd had an intelligence posting, Julian from Italy and Cynthia from Brighton. It was not the jubilant homecoming they had all hoped for. Devastated by the loss of their brother, they were desperate to meet eight-month-old Mary-Alice, the only remaining part of Rupert they could hold onto.

Florence was anxious about being reunited with Rupert's siblings. She had remained close to William and Celia, but it had been years since she'd seen Aubrey and Julian, and the last time she'd seen Cynthia had been at their wedding. This would be a sorrowful meeting. She wasn't sure she'd be able to handle it.

Nervous about going alone she asked Uncle Raymond to accompany her, driving her and Mary-Alice to Pedrevan in his Rover. The family was on the terrace when they arrived. They stopped talking the minute Florence appeared, carrying Mary-Alice in her arms. Emotion stole their voices. One by one Rupert's brothers and sister came to find him in his daughter.

Cynthia stifled a sob. 'She's every bit her father's girl,' she said, reaching over to kiss her friend. 'Darling Flo. I'm so terribly sorry.'

Julian took in the child's dark hair and gunmetal blue eyes and nodded. 'She's beautiful, Flo. Rupert would be proud.'

Aubrey looked at Florence. He was no longer the insouciant boy of their youth, but a man honed by the experience of war. He put a hand on her arm and kissed her cheek. 'I'm sorry, Florence.'

After that, they sat around, reminiscing about the good old days, while Mary-Alice charmed everyone with her playfulness.

At the end of June, William arranged a memorial service for Rupert. Celia filled the church with flowers and printed a photograph of him in his uniform on the cover of the order of service. The numbers were so great they couldn't fit everyone in and had to put up a tent outside to accommodate the overspill. Florence sat in the front with the Dashes. She'd always wanted to be a Dash, she mused as she remembered those services that summer before the war when she and Rupert were carefree and optimistic about their future. She could never have predicted this. That she'd be sitting in the same church, mourning his death – yet still hoping that there was some mistake.

The evening after the memorial service Margaret came into

Florence's bedroom. Mary-Alice had been put to bed down the corridor and the two women were alone. 'I'm glad today is over,' said Florence, her face pale and thin in the reflection of her dressing table mirror where she sat brushing her hair. 'I can't accept that he's gone. It seems farcical somehow, to celebrate his life when we haven't even buried his body.'

Margaret sat on the bed and put her hands in her lap. 'Darling, you have to accept that Rupert is gone,' she said.

Florence stopped brushing and turned around. 'I will never give up hoping he's alive.'

'Hoping won't bring him back, darling.'

'What will I tell our daughter?' Florence asked. 'What will I tell Rupert, when he comes back and I've given him up for dead? Where's the loyalty in that?'

Margaret sighed. She looked at her daughter fearfully, as if she'd gone a little mad. 'Didn't the Sergeant Major tell you that he'd been "mortally" wounded? That means that he died, Florence.'

Florence's jaw stiffened. 'Until I see his body, I will not let him go. I will not give up on him. I'm his wife until death do us part, and death has not parted us yet.'

'I think you need to start considering your daughter. You need to have a place of your own, a home for Mary-Alice, and a job. You cannot waste your life in waiting. For your sanity, Florence.'

'You don't understand . . .' said Florence hotly.

Now it was Margaret's turn to stiffen her jaw. 'I lost my husband when I was thirty-seven years old. I loved him as much as you love Rupert. I had two young girls to bring up on my own. I would have liked to put my head in the sand and fool myself into believing that he was going to come back. But I knew, for your sake and Winifred's, that I had to put my life back together. I never wanted to marry again. No one could begin to compare to your father. But I needed to give you both a good home and I needed to be there for you. Not in the clouds, dreaming impossible dreams. You won't get Rupert back, Florence. I'm sorry, but he died on that battlefield. He's gone. You have to let him go.'

Florence began brushing her hair again. She stared unblinking at the stubborn girl staring back at her. Margaret knew she had spoken hurtful truths and decided to leave the room to allow Florence to digest them. 'We're here for you, darling,' she said gently as she turned the doorknob. 'To support you any way that we can. But someone has to tell you the truth.'

As soon as she was gone, Florence put down her brush. She dropped her head in her hands and wept.

Florence did not heed her mother's advice. She continued to stay with her grandparents, helping Joan around the house and keeping her company after Margaret returned to Kent. The summer months gave way to autumn and rain. On 2 September Japan surrendered and the war was finally over. Another Christmas came and went. For Florence the days blurred into one long limbo. She felt like she was hanging suspended in time, waiting. She knew she wasn't much fun. She hadn't kept in touch with her friends from drama school and the various jobs she had undertaken during the war, and Cynthia now lived in London. Florence kept to herself at The Mariners, remembering Rupert; taking long walks up and down the beach, sitting in the cave or gazing out to sea as if hoping she'd spot a ship on the horizon, bringing him home to her.

Then Aubrey turned up at the house. It was a rare sunny morning in February. Gulls squawked noisily, a strong wind buffeted the coast and the sun fought valiantly to warm the frosted ground. Rowley showed Aubrey into one of the smaller sitting rooms that had been converted into a nursery for Mary-Alice. Florence was on the floor, playing with the wooden farm animals Joan had given Mary-Alice for Christmas. When she saw Aubrey, she stood up in surprise to greet him. 'I've got news,' he said. They sat together on the sofa. Hope flared in Florence's heart only to fade as quickly. 'Rupert is buried in Oosterbeek in Holland,' he told her. Florence blanched. Aubrey took her hand and sandwiched it between his. 'I want to go and pay my respects and I want you to come with me.' He smiled sadly. 'I think it's time we said goodbye.'

CHAPTER NINETEEN

Florence's hope died with those words of Aubrey's. Rupert's grave was in Holland. Rupert was dead.

At last she had to accept the truth. It was, indeed, time to say goodbye.

She left Mary-Alice, who was now nineteen months old, with her grandparents and the young nanny she had recently taken on and departed with Aubrey on a foggy spring morning, arriving in France to clear blue skies and sunshine. From there they took the train to Paris. William was concerned about Jewish friends of his who had been forced into hiding for the duration of the war and had asked Aubrey to check up on them. Aubrey hadn't been to Paris since before the war and was excited to see it again. But Florence did not share his excitement. In losing Rupert, she had lost a part of herself. She wondered whether the part that remained would ever feel joy again.

The city was still reeling in the aftershock of German occupation. The Parisians continued to suffer terrible deprivations. The little food there was was rationed and there were no cigarettes, fuel or soap – Florence would discover to her distaste that most of the coffee on offer was made out of acorns. However, black market restaurants had sprung up like mushrooms in dark corners. Aubrey took Florence to dinner in one of these clandestine places. The waiters told them how delighted they were to serve an Allied officer because none of the lower ranks could afford the inflated prices, and they loathed the Boches.

'I'm sorry I'm not very good company,' said Florence as Aubrey lit a cigarette from the packet he'd brought with him from London.

'I understand,' he replied. 'Perhaps once you've said good-bye at his grave, you'll be able to move on.'

Florence had no intention of moving on. Move on to where? What was there in her future besides a great big black hole where Rupert used to be? 'You're kind to invite me,' she replied.

'It's important to pay one's respects,' he said. 'I hope Mama and Papa and the twins are able to make it to Arnhem one day. It's impossible to get one's head around death unless one faces it at the grave.'

'I'm nervous about it,' Florence confessed.

'You're not alone. I'll look after you.' Aubrey took her hand across the table. 'You know, Florence, you've always been dear to me. We go back a long way and, when one's survived a war, one cleaves to old friends. So many are gone, I want to hold the ones who remain ever closer.'

Florence smiled gratefully, although her hand felt awkward in his. 'I know what you mean,' she replied. 'I, too, want to be cocooned in familiarity. I suppose it's going to take some time before the world learns to live again.'

'We are all going to have to learn to live again. To let go of our losses and start over. I'm not only your brother-in-law, I'm your friend. Rupert would want me to look after you, but *I* want to look after you. What I'm trying to say, clumsily, is that I'm here for you, Florence, always.'

Florence wanted to remove her hand but felt, after his sweet words, that it would be rude. So she left it there, lying limply in his. 'Thank you, Aubrey. You're very special. I'm lucky to have married into your family. I know Mary-Alice and I will always be welcome at Pedrevan.' At that moment an image flashed into her mind. She was on the croquet lawn. Rupert was at the window of the house, gazing at her with a proud smile on his face. *I'll be the grumpy curmudgeon in the attic, looking out over the lawn at the jolly croquet and tennis below, waiting for it all to be over so that I can have a glass of sherry with my lovely wife and watch the sunset, just the two of us.* Florence's eyes stung with tears. She stiffened her jaw to hold them back. Rupert would never be the curmudgeon in the attic and they'd never watch another sunset together. He was gone and he'd taken their dreams with him.

Aubrey had arranged for them to stay the night in a small pension. They walked through the cobbled streets of Paris and, even though the city still resonated with the tremors of war, there was beauty in Haussmann's elegant buildings and in the street lamps that threw their golden light onto the leafy avenues and squares. They reminisced about the days before the war. Those long, languid summers when, without a care, they had partied, picnicked and played all sorts of games in the grounds of Pedrevan. 'You were in love with Elise, I remember,' said Florence, feeling lighter in spirit now that they were outside in the cool night air.

Aubrey laughed. 'I was mad about her. Silly, really.'

'Not silly. She was sweet. There was more to her than met the eye.'

'She had something. I liked her French accent.'

'I thought you'd marry her.'

He looked at Florence incredulously. 'That was never going to happen.'

'I suppose you were a little too young, on reflection.'

'It was a crush, nothing more.'

'We all had those,' said Florence with emphasis.

Aubrey chuckled bitterly. 'It blinded me to the person I should have noticed who was right beneath my nose. Then it was too late. She'd fallen in love with someone else.' Florence felt nervous, suddenly. She folded her arms. 'Are you cold?' he asked.

'A little,' she lied. He took off his jacket and put it around her shoulders. 'What happened to Elise?' she asked.

'I have no idea. She returned to Paris. I lost touch. I hope she and her family survived the war. I should try to find out, shouldn't I?'

'You never know. Elise might not be married . . .'

Aubrey shook his head. 'The embers of that romance died long ago.' He gazed down at her then with a strange look on his face. Florence sensed he was about to tell her something. She averted her eyes, willing him to hold his tongue. A long moment passed, which seemed to Florence like an eternity, before he straightened his shoulders and sighed. 'It's nice, walking through Paris with you,' he said finally. 'I only wish the circumstances of our visit were different.'

The following morning, they found their way to a narrow alley in Montmartre where William's friends the Chabats lived. They rang the bell. An elderly woman answered in a pair of wooden-soled shoes and shabby clothes. In spite of her well-worn attire she looked elegant, as Parisians always do. Her grey hair was brushed off her face and tied in a chignon, her deep-set hazel eyes warm and inquisitive. Aubrey explained who they were and the elderly woman's face immediately opened into a beautiful smile. She embraced him enthusiastically and then, assuming that Florence was his wife, embraced her too. Florence's French was not good enough to correct her mistake.

The woman's name was Sylvia. She welcomed them into her house where she lived with her daughter, Esther, and grand-daughter, Nicole. Esther was as graceful as her mother with long black hair and large, bewitching eyes. Nicole was about ten years old and Florence wondered at what the poor child had seen, for her gaze was wary and she never spoke a word.

They had nothing, but they managed to produce a meal of small, crab-like shellfish in a delicious sauce, washed down with vintage wine brought up from the cellar in celebration of this happy meeting. The bottle was still covered in dust. Sylvia explained that they had spent the war hiding in an attic in Normandy. The men in their family had perished, but Sylvia, Esther and Nicole had miraculously survived. In spite of the trauma of their experience and their unspeakable loss, they were full of positivity and grateful to be alive. Florence wondered at their ability to laugh and realized then that it was perhaps possible to find joy in the wake of sorrow, if one allowed oneself to feel it. Sylvia and Esther were shining examples of the strength of the human spirit and of life's long-ing to express itself. Like little green shoots emerging out of charred ground, life's power to regenerate was unstoppable in these two women who were determined not to dwell on the past but to find light in the present moment.

When they said goodbye, Sylvia held Florence by the hands and in stilted English said, 'I am so happy to meet you. You are fortunate to have your husband. Look after him.' Sylvia was gazing at her with such tenderness that Florence didn't have the heart to tell her they were unmarried and on their way to visit her real husband's grave. She simply thanked her for her kindness.

Aubrey and Florence left Paris and travelled by train to Arnhem via Brussels, then they took a taxi to Oosterbeek, a small village a couple of miles outside Arnhem where much of the fighting had taken place. Florence bought a small posy of lily of the valley at a grocery shop. She did not want to arrive empty handed.

Their conversation died as the landscape bore witness to the battle which had claimed so many lives only a year and a half before. Buildings still stood in tatters, craters pock-marked the ground, simple crosses marked the places where soldiers had fallen. From the comfort of the taxi it was hard to imagine what had taken place there. Florence tried to picture what Rupert had seen. She tried to imagine a sky full of planes and parachutes, the woods and meadows echoing with the sound of gunfire. But all she saw was Rupert, running through fog.

The full force of his death hit Florence when she first laid eyes on the cemetery. It took her breath away and she stood a moment, paralysed with shock. A field of nearly two thousand small metal crosses spread out before her like a grim crop frozen in an eternal memorial to the dead. A shroud of silence hung over the place. Trees surrounded the field like contemplative guards watching over the bodies of soldiers who had given their lives in a battle both ferocious and futile. As Florence and Aubrey wandered down the rows, looking for Rupert's name, Florence felt overwhelmed by the senseless-ness of war and the incomprehensible scale of loss. Some of the crosses bore photographs of the men killed, many of them mere boys. Some had flowers or cairns of stones placed upon them. Florence's throat grew tight. Each one of these men had someone who loved them, who now had to live without them. Each one was an unbearable personal tragedy.

Then they came across the most unbearable tragedy of them all.

Rupert's grave was like all the others. A metal cross that bore his name, his regiment and the date of his death. Aubrey took Florence's hand. 'It shouldn't have ended like this,' he said and his voice cracked.

Florence was too moved to speak. Too filled with sorrow and emptiness to find words to fill the void. She felt as if she'd come up against a brick wall of loneliness and all she could do was look back and regret what she had lost. The little island of hope sank slowly below the horizon and into the sea. What a waste of a life, she thought. One of many. Why would God give them such happiness only to snatch it away? What was the purpose of it? She knew Rupert would have an answer. He seemed to know a lot about these things. If he could speak to her now he'd tell her that he'd completed his life and that through his death Florence and those who loved him would grow. But Florence didn't want to grow, if this is the price she had to pay for it. It wasn't worth the pain. She raised her eyes to the sky and knew that Rupert wasn't in the ground at her feet, in this unfamiliar country, but in a place of love and light. She closed her eyes and asked him to draw near. *If you are spirit, darling Rupert, send me a sign. Anything. Something to reassure me that you live on. In this moment of doubt, give me certainty that we will meet again.*

Then she placed the flowers at the foot of the cross.

When Florence returned to Gulliver's Bay, William offered her the use of one of his farm cottages that had just been vacated by an elderly lady who'd gone into a nursing home.

It was a pretty white house with a thatched roof and a garden where Florence could grow her own vegetables and flowers. She put a notice in the town hall advertising for a handyman to help her. She was surprised when a young ex-RAF pilot responded. Joe Brown had just set up his own gardening company and wanted part-time work. Happily, Florence took him on. With his encouragement she began a small business of her own, drawing on the flower-arranging classes at Miss Ranny's at which she and Cynthia had so rudely scoffed. Now she appreciated what she'd been taught and arranged flowers for country clubs, hotels and inns. It kept her busy. It kept her mind on the present and it kept her sane.

Vases and cachepots were scarce, for as soon as something was manufactured it was exported straight to America in exchange for the precious dollar. Joe suggested she use trugs. These were baskets made out of willow, used for carrying vegetables. Every household had one, and if they didn't, they were cheap and easy to come by. Delighted by the idea, Florence lined them with zinc so the water wouldn't seep through and went for a simple country look. They were very popular and little by little her cottage industry grew.

When local flowers would not suffice Florence had to go to the flower market in Wadebridge. She'd awaken at dawn and drive down the sleepy lanes, finding pleasure in the hedgerows bursting with white blossom and in the small birds that fluttered blithely about them. She was beginning to feel more positive. Visiting Rupert's grave had been hard, but it had helped her move beyond his death to a more tranquil place the other side of it. Not a moment of the day passed without her thinking of him, and yet she was slowly beginning to find cracks in the darkness that let in slivers of light. Whether it was her daughter's beautiful smile, the splendour of the flowers or the uplifting twittering of birds, her heart was starting to thaw. She could not claim to feel joy, but she was slowly remembering what joy felt like.

It was on one of these early morning drives into Wadebridge that she felt a strange tug beneath her ribs. It was a feeling of compulsion, of having to do something, but what that something was, she didn't know. She just felt a sense of urgency and purpose and a nervousness building in her stomach. She wondered whether it was a premonition. Perhaps something bad was going to happen and her intuition was trying to warn her. Yet, she did not feel compelled to turn around and drive home, rather an urgency to continue in the direction she was going.

With this sensation intensifying in her belly, she drove into Wadebridge and parked the car outside the flower market. As usual she wandered among the stalls, buying what she needed for the contracts she was committed to fulfil. The sight of so much colour was heartening and like a bee she buzzed about the flowers, smelling their gentle perfume and taking pleasure from their intricate patterns, created, she knew, by an ingenious god.

She came upon a stall she hadn't noticed before. It was around a corner, a little hidden away, and full of second-hand bric-a-brac. Among the lilies and carnations were Christmas baubles (in July!), old watering cans, gardening equipment and books. Florence did not need anything from that stall and yet she found herself drawn to it, as if there was something among the junk that she had to find.

The man tending the place looked up from his newspaper and smiled. He wore a black eye patch and had thick, curly brown hair. 'Good morning,' he said, standing up.

'Good morning,' Florence replied politely. 'I haven't seen your stall before.'

He smiled. 'I've been here for a year now. I'm a bit off the beaten track, being tucked around this corner. I don't fit in with the flower stalls, but you'd be surprised how much people want my bits and pieces.'

'We're in no position to turn up our noses at second-hand goods, are we?' said Florence, picking up a trowel.

'One person's trash is another person's treasure,' he said.

'Where do you get it from?'

'Word gets around and people bring me things. If you have anything you want to sell, especially gardening things, I'm sure I can give you a good price for it. I sell all over the country.'

She put down the trowel. 'Where are you from?'

'Norfolk originally. After the war I settled down here. My wife's from around here, you see.'

Florence felt that nervousness in her stomach again. She didn't know why she was engaging in conversation with this man, but she knew instinctively that there was something interesting about him. 'Where did you serve in the war, if you don't mind me asking?'

'I was a co-pilot in a glider regiment.'

Florence stared at him in amazement. 'My husband was killed at Arnhem,' she whispered.

'I'm sorry to hear that,' he said. 'What regiment was he in?'

'The Tenth.'

The man nodded in recognition. 'Brave men, the Tenth.'

'Did you fight at Arnhem too?'

'I did, indeed.'

'Then you must have been brave too.'

He put his fingers on his eye patch. 'Shot in the eye. But I'm still here.' He grinned. 'What was your husband called?'

'Rupert Dash.'

He shook his head. 'I didn't know him. But those men of the Tenth were heroic.'

'They were,' said Florence. She looked around, keen suddenly to buy something from him. Her eyes dropped to a basket of tatty books. Bending down, she started to go through them. There was nothing that she really wanted to read. Then a dog-eared paperback caught her eye. The cover was a picture of a lighthouse and the author's name was Rupert Clinch. She turned it over to read the back when she noticed a piece of paper tucked between the pages. She pulled it out and unfolded it. It was a poem. As she read it, her heart began to beat faster. The nervous feeling grew into excitement. A voice from beyond the grave spoke to her through the words:

> *Wait for me – I will come back.*
> *Only wait . . . and wait.*
> *Wait though rainclouds louring black*
> *Make you desolate;*
> *Wait though winter snowstorms whirl,*
> *Wait though summer's hot;*
> *Wait though no one else will wait*
> *And the past forgot;*
> *Wait though from the distant front*
> *Not one letter comes;*
> *Wait though everyone who waits*
> *Sick of it becomes.*
>
> *Wait for me – I will come back*
> *Pay no heed to those*
> *Who'll so glibly tell you that*
> *It is vain to wait.*

Though my mother and my son
Think that I am gone,
Though my friends abandon hope
And back there at home
Rise and toast my memory,
Wrapped in silence pained,
Wait. And when they drink their toast
Leave your glass undrained.

Wait for me — I will come back
Though from Death's own jaws.
Let the friends who did not wait
Think it chance, no more;
They will never understand
Those who did not wait
How it was YOUR WAITING that
Saved me in the war.
And the reason I've come through
We shall know, we two;
Simply this: you waited as
No one else could do.

KONSTANTIN SIMONOV

CHAPTER TWENTY

England, 1993

Four years passed and Max heard nothing from Robyn. As
much as it troubled him, it did not really surprise him; he
had declared himself to her and she had rebuffed him. It was
almost impossible to maintain their friendship after that. It
saddened him deeply. During those years, Max moved into a
rented house in Somerset and changed jobs yet again, becoming a buying agent for an old army friend who had set up a
business helping clients find what Max's mother would call
'proper' houses: big, old mansions. Typically, Queen Anne
and Georgian. That's what anyone with real wealth wanted,
apparently. Max had always been fascinated by architecture –
castles and stately homes especially. When he was a boy he'd
loved 'castle creeping' with his father. They'd gone to Ireland
once, just the two of them, and visited the ruins of famous
great houses in County Cork which had been burned down
during the Irish Civil War. Max had been inspired by the
sense of history in those relics, and in the air of transience
and mortality that wafted about the crumbling, neglected
walls like ghosts. He'd imagined the people who had once
lived there. Their lives had been as vital as his and yet they

were gone. That had probably been the first time he'd thought about death and what it meant. Nothing material lasted, stone walls and bones perished eventually, but Max had known, even then, that there was a part of him that did not belong to the material world, but would live on in a different way. A part that came from somewhere else and was only destined to remain here for a short while. Why that eternal part needed to go through a life at all, a life which was unavoidably full of suffering as well as joy, was baffling. But Max was only a boy and his heart was not aware of love because he had not yet suffered loss; it is only through losing that one really appreciates, or even notices, what one has.

This new job was the perfect excuse to look around beautiful properties and he discovered, to his surprise and delight, that he was very good at negotiating for his wealthy clients. He enjoyed meeting people and his old friend was easy-going and fun to work with. Max was filled with enthusiasm, and with this new enthusiasm he began to shed his sense of aimlessness and feel a renewed sense of purpose. Busy with his new job he had no time to look into his past life. Somerset had a lively social scene and a relationship with a local girl soon blossomed. Max dropped the threads of the various leads he'd been following and focused his attention on the present. Until a telephone call encouraged him to turn his mind once again to the past.

It was Daphne. She was writing a book about her most interesting clients and their past lives and was ringing to ask permission to include Max's story. Max remembered Olga telling him that one day he would write a book that would be important and wondered whether this was it. The book Robyn had wanted to write with him was sadly never going to happen now. So he gave his permission on the condition that he could read it before publication, and filled her in with his discoveries. She suggested that he try to contact some of the men who had served with Rupert in the Tenth; it would be interesting to hear what they had to say.

Max was injected with renewed excitement. The wind that had gone quiet over the last few years now picked up and filled his sails once again.

His research had inspired him to buy a book by Martin Middlebrook called *Arnhem 1944: The Airborne Battle*. He decided to write to Nick Hanmer, mentioned in the book, who had been the adjutant of the Tenth and a friend of Rupert's. The Airborne Museum in Aldershot put Max in contact with the secretary of the Old Comrades Association. However, the secretary had no record of Hanmer's address. He *was* able, however, to give Max the names and addresses of two other men who Max might find helpful. They had been in the Intelligence Section under Rupert Dash, who had been the Regimental Intelligence Officer. Charlie Shaw lived in Kent, and the other was Oliver Giles, who lived in the Isle of Man. Both men were mentioned in Middlebrook's book. Max knew they were still alive. He just hoped that they had all their faculties and were willing to talk.

Max wrote to both of them explaining that he was a cousin of Rupert Dash and was interested in learning how Rupert had died at Arnhem. He was surprised when they wrote back almost immediately.

Isle of Man 03/06/93

Dear Captain Shelbourne,
Thank you for your letter enquiring into the death of your cousin Rupert Dash, who was my superior officer.

*I didn't witness his death but as I was part of his
section I made many enquiries after the battle and whilst in
hospital as a POW.*

*Regarding the War Diary. I kept the original one which I
buried to avoid it falling into German hands.*

*The one to which you refer was 'cobbled' together after
the war. What I consider to be the correct sequence of events
is contained in 'The Tenth', published in 1965 by R.
Brammall. In which is related by Major Hartwich who stated
that Captain Dash was with Hartwich when they came across
L/C Radcliffe who had been shot in the knee. They carried
him across the heath but hadn't gone more than fifty yards
before all three of them were shot. Captain Dash would have
been buried by the Germans where he was found.*

*I am sorry I am unable to give further details but hope this
letter will be of some comfort to you.*

*I got on well with Rupert Dash. He was a well-liked and
able officer. He wasn't pedantic and had that rare ability to
know when to 'back off'.*

Sincerely yours,
Oliver Giles

Corporal Giles had included a photocopy of the landing
zone and woods taken from the air in September 1944. He
gave an estimated position of Rupert Dash's field burial north
of Johannahoeve Farm. This, he said, would be between the
wood, which they were leaving, and the farm, which was
occupied by the Regimental HQ of the 6th Battalion King's
Own Scottish Borderers. This would have been the obvious
place to seek help for the wounded Corporal Radcliffe. It was
customary during the war for soldiers to bury the enemy's
dead by marking the shallow grave with the rifle, helmet and

ID tags so that, at the end of the war, their bodies could be found and identified and given a proper burial.

A week later, the letter from Charlie Shaw arrived:

Kent 10/06/93

Dear Captain Shelbourne,

I am sorry I could not reply earlier to your letter dated 22 May but I am glad to do so if anything I say will help you.

In regard to the circumstances of his death I can say nothing since I was wounded and removed to a first aid post the day after we landed. However, Rupert was the last comrade to whom I remember speaking. In fact, he passed me his flask of brandy a few minutes before I passed out on a stretcher.

I cannot now remember when he joined 10 Bn nor precisely when he took over the Intelligence Section but we certainly had a good deal to do with each other especially in the last 48 hours before the battle when we knocked up a sand table model of the dropping zone. I liked him.

Finally, I recalled that I have a photograph of Rupert taken with Peter Kildare during a training flight – I was further back. You may like to see it and perhaps copy before returning.

Yours sincerely,
Charlie Shaw

Max's first impulse was to telephone Robyn to tell her about the letters and the photograph. He knew she'd be thrilled to hear about it. But as he lifted the receiver his enthusiasm died. She was married now and he didn't imagine that Daniel would be too pleased to hear from him. A familiar heaviness filled his chest. He was used to it now, that feeling of longing, grief and sorrow. He wondered whether he'd ever get over Robyn, or whether he'd spend his entire life regretting the distance that had grown between them. He knew, however, that he'd never regret that kiss.

He decided to call Charlie Shaw instead.

Charlie Shaw sounded delighted to hear from him and suggested they meet at his house near Sevenoaks in Kent to discuss Max's letter face to face. When Max turned up in his car, Charlie came out to greet him, leaning heavily on a walking stick. A big smile lit up his seasoned face. Charlie was now seventy-nine. His hair and moustache were white and his body frail and stooped, but his eyes were lucid, like those of an old eagle who was still capable of spotting the most minute prey in the grass. 'Hello, dear boy,' he said and Max was immediately struck by how familiar he seemed. It was as if Max was meeting an old friend; it was as if they had met before.

Max remembered Robyn's words about reincarnation: *Life would be very lonely meeting everyone for the first time,* and wondered whether he was remembering Charlie on a deep, subconscious level. On the level of his soul. The very fact that he had to question it made him think once again of Robyn, and he smiled to himself. She would blame Elizabeth for sewing those seeds of doubt and would encourage him to trust his instincts and the proof, which was being confirmed and reconfirmed at every stage of his investigation.

Max and Charlie shook hands. Charlie's hand was rough like sandpaper, and bony. 'How good to meet you,' he said, studying Max's face with interest. 'Gosh, you're very like your cousin,' he added. 'You're taking me right back.' Max followed him inside and closed the door behind him. An elderly woman came out of the kitchen. 'This is Willa, my wife,' said Charlie.

'I'm delighted to meet you,' she said. 'Charlie's told me all about you.'

Max followed them through the house to the garden where they sat at a round table in the sunshine. Charlie was frail. Willa helped him into the chair and leaned his walking stick against the table. 'What would you like to drink, Max? Cordial? I make my own elderflower cordial and I bought some nibbles.'

'That would be lovely, thank you,' said Max.

She put a hand on her husband's shoulder. 'It's nice for Charlie to talk about the past. So many of his old friends have gone. It's good of you to come.'

Max looked at Charlie. His face was alert with expectation and Max realized that he was longing to reminisce. 'Arnhem was a bloody cock-up,' he said. 'Chaotic and confused. The Germans knew we were coming. But I was a young corporal and knew nothing about what went on in the officers' mess.' He looked at Max. 'You have something of Rupert Dash,' he said. 'Around the brow and eyes. A cousin of your grandfather, I think you said.'

'Yes, he was my grandfather's second cousin.'

Charlie nodded. 'That's quite distant. Still, you have a look of him. He was relaxed and nonchalant; that's not to say he didn't do his duty and do it well. He did. He just let us get on with it, and by doing that he got the best out of everyone who worked with him. You know, when we were stationed at Somerby Hall, 1944 it was, we'd just returned from Italy, some of the boys raided the wine cellar by getting the fire brigade to knock down a wall. We all got as drunk as skunks, Rupert included. I remember because he sang the loudest.'

'Was there trouble?'

'It was hushed up and no one was charged.' Charlie grinned

wickedly. 'We should have had terrible hangovers in the morning, but we didn't. The wine was of a very high quality. I still feel a bit bad about that.'

They discussed Arnhem and Charlie's eyes lit up as he relived the drama. As terrible as that battle had been, he was clearly proud of the part he had played in it. At length Willa returned with the cordial and snacks; she had obviously lingered in the kitchen to give the two men time to talk.

'Charlie tells me your cousin fought with him at Arnhem,' she said, sitting down.

There was something about the gentleness of her expression and the interest in Charlie's that encouraged Max to tell them the truth. 'This might seem odd, but there's more to my desire to learn about my grandfather's cousin's life,' he began. 'I believe I have lived before. I believe I might have been Rupert Dash.'

Max was grateful to them for not laughing at him or looking incredulous. Both took in his words with open minds and asked him to elaborate. So Max shared his story with them. Rather like his parents, they didn't interrupt or argue, and at the end they agreed that reincarnation was the only explanation. Max began to wonder whether Robyn was right. He had thought the world was full of Elizabeths, but he was starting to realize that there was more curiosity and acceptance around than he had previously imagined.

As they sipped their drinks and grazed on bowls of peanuts and raisins, Charlie told Max about life in Rutland and Leicestershire, leading up to September 1944. He was unable to tell him anything about Florence, or indeed anything about Rupert that Max didn't already know. Then he remembered a small but touching story about Rupert and a flask.

'You know, dear boy, Rupert treasured this silver hip flask. It was curved to fit against his body and engraved with his initials, R.J.D. He'd fill it with brandy and pass it around. I'll never forget the moment he gave me a slug, seconds before I passed out. Gave me comfort, it did. It's a memory that's stayed with me.'

'That's a nice memory,' said Max.

Charlie nodded. 'It was typical of Rupert. That flask went everywhere with him and he shared it whenever he felt anyone needed fortification. He was kind like that, thoughtful.'

'I suppose it was buried with him.'

'Funny you should say that, because I wondered about that. It was a treasure, you see, and should have been given to his wife, but I suspect it was stolen. Anything of value generally was.' He smiled. 'Your story is encouraging, Max. Thank you for telling us about it.'

'I have doubted myself so many times. Reincarnation seems incomprehensible.'

Willa smiled. 'I don't think it's so incomprehensible.' She bent down and plucked a blade of grass. 'If you were to try and explain to an ant sitting on this piece of grass that there is a big world out there, full of cities, villages, mountains and lakes, do you think it would understand? Of course not. So what is the difference in telling us that there is a greater reality beyond the one we're experiencing now?'

'When you put it like that, it doesn't seem so odd, does it?' said Max.

'We are only given the information we need to live this life,' she continued. 'If we were aware of all our past lives we'd never concentrate on the one we're living now.'

'It does give one hope, though, when you get to our great age, that it doesn't all end,' said Charlie thoughtfully. He looked at his wife with affection and patted her hand. 'We might meet again in another incarnation.'

Willa laughed. 'We might have already lived lives together before.'

'That's a nice thought,' said Charlie. 'Perhaps you've always been my girl.'

Before Max left, Charlie opened out a map on the table and explained the battle to him. 'The Tenth made their way between the Amsterdamseweg and the railway line here. But they came up against a German line of defence here. The Germans had tanks, armoured cars and artillery, whereas the Brits had only rifles, automatic pistols and hand grenades. It was a trap. They didn't stand a chance. It was broad daylight and they were trying to cross open heathland. They had nowhere to hide. They were immediately given orders to withdraw, which was suicide, really. As they withdrew, the Poles were landing in their gliders to give support. They were part of the third wave that was due in that afternoon. But in the chaos, they didn't know who were Allies and who were Germans, and shot at both. It was bedlam. Gliders on fire, smoke everywhere, gunfire. Just like in your dream.' Then he tapped his forefinger on the paper. 'This is where Rupert fell. He would have been given a field burial here by the Germans and then later reinterred in the cemetery in Oosterbeek. You might like to keep the map. Who knows, perhaps you'll visit Rupert's grave one day. You might even recognize the landscape. Now, wouldn't that be something.'

On the way home in the car Max thought about Robyn. He wanted more than anything to call her, to hear her voice. He wondered whether she had children already. Whether she was happy. She'd been on his mind a lot recently.

When he got home he called Daphne to fill her in. Then he dialled Robyn's number. It rang a few times. He could barely hear the ring tone over the thumping of his heart. He was on the point of hanging up when Daniel answered. 'Hello?' Max took a breath. He was about to speak, but then decided against it. He did not want to talk to Daniel. He quickly put down the phone. Instead, he took his journal into the garden and wrote down an account of the letters from Charlie Shaw and Oliver Giles, and his meeting with Charlie and Willa.

Didn't Olga say that the right people would come into his life at the right time to help him along his path? So far, the coincidental meetings had been extraordinary, but he still did not know the answer to the biggest question: Why had he been allowed to remember his past life? If past lives were meant to be forgotten in order that people focus on the lives they are living now, why was he able to recall his? For what purpose? He knew Robyn would have an answer, but he still shied away from calling her. He missed her friend-ship terribly.

He decided to write to Aubrey again. He didn't reveal the true reason why he wanted to visit Pedrevan, instead he said that he was researching the family history for his grandfather. Once again, he got no reply.

Then Bertha Clairmont called him. 'I thought you might be interested in a cousin of mine who telephoned me the other day with regards to my book. She's been very helpful.'

'I'm interested,' said Max, wondering who she was talking about.

'Cynthia Dash. Aubrey and Rupert's sister.'

Max hadn't considered her. 'I'd love to talk to her,' he enthused.

'Thought so. She was a great friend of Florence's, so I'm sure she'll know what happened to her, and she's a talker. I had her on the phone for an hour. Couldn't get her off. Her husband left her for a younger woman so she's moved back down to Cornwall. I think she's starved of company.'

'Where does she live?'

'Gulliver's Bay.' Robyn immediately surfaced in Max's mind.

He hesitated as the words sank in. Did that mean that the various times he'd been down there, Rupert's sister had been there too? 'Whereabouts?' he asked.

'In a cottage at Pedrevan. That grumpy brother of hers must have lent her a house.'

'Do you think she'll be happy to talk to me?'

'Good Lord, Max, she'll be delighted. If I were you, I'd give her a call and go down and see her. She'll tell you everything you want to know about Rupert and you can have a look around that beautiful house. In fact, if you're going, I'll come too. One in the eye for Aubrey.' She laughed. 'Silly bugger will wish he'd been a little more cordial; after all, blood is thicker than water, one would think. Here's her number.'

Max didn't waste time in telephoning Cynthia. Dizzy with excitement he dialled the number. A few rings and her voice came onto the line. 'Hello?'

'Hello, my name is Max Shelbourne. My grandfather, Hartley Shelbourne, is a cousin of yours ...'

'Hartley?' Her voice lifted. 'Is he still alive?'

'Yes, very much so.'

'How wonderful. He was such fun! Such an eccentric, and you're his grandson, are you?'

'I'm researching his family's history, specifically Rupert Dash.'

There was a pause. 'Ah, Rupert. Poor, darling Rupert.'

'Bertha Clairmont gave me your number.'

'Bertha, yes, I had a lovely chat with her the other day.

Couldn't get her off the phone. I think she's rather deprived of company.'

Max smiled at that. 'I was wondering whether I could come down to Cornwall and see you? I've been to Gulliver's Bay a few times . . .'

'What a capital idea. I'd love to meet you. Do bring Hartley with you. I'd love to see him again.' Max did not think that was a good idea. He didn't really want to bring Bertha, either, and hoped Cynthia wouldn't mention it. 'Why don't you bring Bertha?' Cynthia added to Max's dismay. 'She was telling me how rude Aubrey was.'

'I tried to contact Aubrey too.'

Cynthia sighed. 'He's rather reclusive, I'm afraid.'

'Might you know what happened to Rupert's widow, Florence?'

'Of course. Why don't you come to Pedrevan and I'll fill you in on anything you need to know. It would be lovely to meet you. And bring Bertha. It would be good for her to get out. I think she's been stuck in that flat for so long she's become a piece of furniture!'

Max laughed. 'I'll call her,' he said.

CHAPTER TWENTY-ONE

Gulliver's Bay, 1946

Florence held the poem against her chest and closed her eyes. *Wait for me — I will come back.* It was a message from Rupert; there was no doubt in her mind. Rupert had wanted her to find the book and he had directed her to the flower stall in order for that to happen. There was no such thing as coincidence. Hadn't he said that evening on the beach in Gulliver's Bay: '*Soulmates have more than a physical attraction, they have a deep, spiritual connection that comes from having known each other through many incarnations*'? Rupert was going to come back; all Florence had to do was wait.

There was only one person she could talk to about this and that was Reverend Millar. Her mother and Winifred would question her sanity and her grandparents would worry that grief was causing her to put her hope in impossible dreams. Uncle Raymond would listen with a sympathetic ear, but tell her, sensibly, that dead people don't reappear, and Cynthia would encourage her to let Rupert go and find another man to look after her and Mary-Alice. But Rupert was telling her to wait: *I will come back.*

Reverend Millar lived in the rectory next to the church.

It was a harmoniously proportioned Georgian house set back from the street and covered in pale pink roses. Florence had never been inside it, although she had walked past it on many occasions and admired the flowers. Reverend Millar had a way with flora and fauna.

Florence had telephoned and made an appointment. At this time of year there were lots of weddings and christenings and the vicar was inordinately busy. It would have been rude to have just shown up on his doorstep without prior warning. Florence cycled from Pedrevan with the book and the poem tucked into the basket along with a bunch of sweet peas picked from her own garden. She savoured the smell of brine in the wind that blew in off the sea, but even the wind swept in memories of Rupert to temper her pleasure with wistfulness. Memories were everywhere; in the sound of rustling trees and birdsong, in the sun that warmed her face and in the shadows that lingered both bitter and sweet in every corner of Gulliver's Bay. Her love lay scattered in all the places she and Rupert had frequented – lost, incomplete and full of longing.

She arrived at the rectory and leaned her bicycle against the porch. Then she rang the bell. A moment later a diminutive old woman appeared. It was Mrs Marley, Reverend Millar's housekeeper, who looked after him. As if to emphasize her elevated position she wore a large crucifix around her neck and a pious expression on her wrinkled face. A face most often screwed up in ardent prayer and adulation, for she worshipped both God and her employer with equal enthusiasm. 'Mrs Dash, the vicar is expecting you. Please come in.' Mrs Marley opened the door into the dark interior of the house. The sunshine had been so bright that it took a while for Florence's eyes to adjust and distinguish the heavy wooden furniture and panelled walls. She was immediately assaulted by the smell of steamed cabbage and broccoli wafting out from the kitchen and was glad she wasn't staying for lunch.

The vicar was in his garden in a panama hat and open-neck blue shirt. Florence had never seen him out of his robes before and was surprised. He was in the border tossing nettles and elder into a wheelbarrow. When he saw Florence he took off his gardening gloves and walked across the grass to meet her. 'Hello, Florence my dear. Isn't it a glorious day?' His smile was wide and infectious.

'It's lovely,' Florence replied. 'I cycled from Pedrevan.'

'You must need a glass of something cool, then. Mrs Marley will bring us some tea, I suspect. Would you rather a glass of water?'

'No, tea would be nice. Thank you.' She held out the flowers. 'These are for you.'

'Oh, how kind of you. Delightful.' He pressed them to his nose. 'They smell good too. I'll give them to Mrs Marley to put in a vase. They'll go in my bedroom. Sweet of you to pick them. Come and sit down.'

Mrs Marley took the flowers into the house and Reverend Millar and Florence sat together on a wooden bench beneath an arch of jasmine which was thick and scented and alive with the buzzing of bees. 'How are you doing, Florence?' he asked and Florence understood from his tone of voice that he was no longer making conversation, but getting straight to the heart of her visit.

'It's getting easier to bear,' she told him. 'At first I thought I wouldn't get through it. If it hadn't been for Mary-Alice I might not have. But she's Rupert's little girl and every day she looks more like him.'

'That's nice,' said the vicar with a smile. 'There is nothing like the innocence of a child to heal the heart.'

'Visiting Rupert's grave at Arnhem was difficult, but it did help me to accept that he has gone. You see, without actually seeing the body, it's hard to believe he won't come back.'

'There's a very good reason why we have funerals for our dead. It's not for them. They are at peace. It's for us, so that we can say goodbye and move on with our lives.'

'Do you think we come back?' Florence asked.

The vicar frowned. 'You mean in spirit, as ghosts?'

Florence hadn't considered that possibility. 'Do we?'

Mrs Marley emerged from the house, carrying a tray of teacups, a jug of milk and a teapot. She put them down on the fold-out wooden table beside the bench.

'Thank you, Mrs Marley,' he said, watching her pour the tea. 'The important thing,' he continued after she'd gone back inside, 'is to recognize that our bodies belong to this material world and that when we die, we leave them behind, as one might leave an old, unwanted coat that no longer serves us. Our soul returns to God. Imagine it like a light, Florence, a light that never dies but is eternal. That light returns home from where it came. Now, there are many religious people who would disagree with me, but I do believe that those we love come back to be close to us. Most of us can't see them, of course, but there are many who can and do. I'm sure that Rupert is with you in spirit, Florence. Love binds us to one another and it is that love that enables him to return.'

Florence sipped her tea. 'Do you believe in reincarnation?' she asked.

Reverend Millar paused for a second, musing on her question. Then he answered slowly and with care. 'Christian belief does not subscribe to that idea, Florence. It is heresy. But the idea of reincarnation is as old as time. The Buddhists, Jewish Kabbalists and Hindus believe the soul incarnates time and again on its way towards enlightenment. The Essenes and Pharisees also believed that the soul is reborn time and again. In fact, in Jesus's time the concept of reincarnation was widely accepted.' He paused a moment and looked down at his hands. 'It is a foolish man who thinks he knows everything.'

Florence put down her teacup and showed him the book by Rupert Clinch. She slipped out the poem which she kept as she had found it, tucked within the pages. 'When I stood by Rupert's grave I asked him for a sign to reassure me that he lived on. Then he led me to this, which I found in a basket of second-hand books at the flower market in Wadebridge.'

Reverend Millar unfolded the paper and read it. Florence let her gaze wander around the garden. She imagined the vicar had placed this bench here on purpose so that when he talked to his parishioners, they could look out over the shrubs and flowers and not at him, thus helping them more easily unburden their consciences.

When he finished, he handed the piece of paper back to her. 'It's a beautiful poem,' he said.

'The book was written by a man called Rupert, which is why I noticed it, and the lighthouse called to me somehow. I thought it an extraordinary coincidence to find that message in the poem. *I will come back.*'

Reverend Millar frowned. 'Florence, sometimes when we lose someone we love, our wanting is so strong that it leads us to find meaning in everything. Sometimes, those things can be comforting. But other times, they can mislead. I'm not saying that this isn't a message from Rupert. Knowing Rupert as I did, it wouldn't be at all out of character for him to contact you in this way, with a poem. But by hanging onto hope, when you're young and your life spreads out in front of you with such potential for happiness, you're denying yourself the chance to move on.' He took her hand in his warm one and squeezed it. 'Rupert is with you in spirit. Of that, I am sure. Jesus revealed himself to Mary Magdalene and the disciples in order to show the world that there is no death. There is only death of the mortal body, but the soul, the *real* you, is eternal and doesn't die. Take comfort from that. Rupert will always be with you. But he would want you to live your life and not to hold onto false hope. There is nothing to be gained from waiting. You are here to live. That's what God has given you, a precious, valuable life. Rupert would want you to live it.'

Florence smiled and looked at him steadily. 'Now tell me what *you*, Tobias Millar, think about reincarnation.'

Reverend Millar chuckled. 'You always were a clever girl, Florence Dash.' He inhaled deeply. 'I would not rule it out. We are only given a tiny part of the big picture. Who am I to presume to know the mind of God?'

'Thank you. It's been very helpful talking to you,' she said, slipping the poem into the book.

'It's always a pleasure talking to you. You're strong, Florence. You'll rise like a phoenix out of the ashes. Life is long and you have great potential. God is with you every step of the way. Don't forget that.'

That summer Gulliver's Bay was once again filled with people in search of fun. Pedrevan was teeming with Dash and Clairmont cousins and the church services on Sundays were packed. Reverend Millar's sermons were as exuberant as ever, and afterwards there was much to discuss on the grass outside the church beneath the watchful gaze of seagulls perched on the roof. However, an undercurrent of wistfulness lingered beneath the gaiety. A sense of nostalgia for the past, before the war, when families were complete and without care; a longing for those bright, sunny days, full of parties, scavenger hunts, tennis and croquet. For those innocent kisses behind bushes and flirtations on the beach. Life had become more serious, the tones that defined it more pronounced: dark was now a little darker and light was brighter. Against the backdrop of war and loss, the people of Gulliver's Bay lived with a different attitude. One of gratitude for what they had and appreciation for the small things.

William Dash was determined that the tennis tournament should resume. It had been suspended during the war, but now the fighting was over he saw no reason why it should not be resurrected. He set about putting together pairs with his usual enthusiasm. Then he displayed them on a board beside the pavilion as was tradition. Florence discovered she was to partner Aubrey. What she would have given to have partnered him that summer of '37, she thought when she saw the order of play. Then she thought of Rupert at the netting, scolding John Clairmont for being ungallant and her heart ached for him. It would be hard to throw herself into the tournament with her characteristic aplomb when memories of Rupert haunted that court.

Cynthia was engaged to a dashing captain. Tarquin Smith-Teddington was a family friend and a natural match for Cynthia. Florence thought him rather too pleased with himself. He was handsome in an obvious way, with a big white smile and heavy brown eyes, like a matinee idol. He knew the right thing to say to everyone, especially grandmothers, and all were charmed by him, except for Florence who found him shallow. Even Aubrey, who had the same attractive manner and good-looks, had depth to him. Tarquin was very rich and seemed only interested in other rich people. He dressed immaculately, drove the latest Alvis, and made sure he was at all the most fashionable parties. Florence wondered whether Cynthia was not just another beautiful accessory. But her friend was in love. Florence knew what that felt like and she wasn't about to dampen her joy.

Florence's mother Margaret came down to spend the summer at The Mariners with Winifred and her husband Gerald. Uncle Raymond invited a friend from London to stay for a couple of weeks. His nickname was Monty and Florence never discovered what he was really called. The two men spent a lot of time playing backgammon, smoking on the terrace with Henry and making up a bridge four with Winifred and Joan. Monty was a photographer, which might have been interesting if the object of his art hadn't been exclusively Uncle Raymond. Florence, who was happy in her cottage at Pedrevan, occasionally cycled over to spend time with them.

'You know Mother has a beau,' Winifred told her one evening when they were walking up the beach, just the two of them.

'Does she?' said Florence, surprised. 'I thought she said no one could compare to Daddy.'

'She's changed her mind. Which is a good thing. It's time she moved on.'

Florence felt Winifred's remark was pointed at her. Florence was certainly nowhere near ready to move on. Rupert had not been gone two years.

'Who is he?' she asked.

'A widower, much older than her.'

'When you say "much", what do you mean?'

'Well, he must be in his mid- to late sixties.'

'Is he nice?'

Winifred sat on a dune and lit a cigarette. 'He'll do.'

'You don't sound very enthusiastic,' said Florence, joining her on the sand.

Winifred sighed. 'He'll never be Daddy. I need to accept that. He's kind, that's the main thing.'

'Is she in love with him?'

'I think she's very fond of him.' Winifred exhaled a puff of smoke which was swept away by a gust of wind. 'You know, not everyone is lucky enough to have a passion like you had with Rupert, Flo. In fact, I'd say that's rare. Most people have a deep affection for the person they marry. I'm fond of Gerald but I'm not madly in love with him. Mama is fond of Oliver and I think he's fond of her, but I wouldn't use the word "love". Not in the way *you'd* use it. Life is more complicated than it is in fairy tales.'

Florence smiled tenderly. 'I had a fairy tale. That kind of thing comes only once in a lifetime. I'll probably spend the rest of my life on my own.'

'I doubt that. You're young. Mama thought she'd spend her life on her own, too, but look at her. She's happy. Have you noticed? She's glowing. She's being spoiled rotten and she's enjoying every minute of it.'

'Do you think they'll get married?'

'Yes, I do. In time. I don't think she'll rush into anything. But I think she's tired of being on her own now. There's more to a marriage than passion between the sheets.' Winifred laughed cynically and dropped her gaze onto the sand. 'I can't say I've ever had that.' She took another drag, her face serious suddenly. 'I suppose it was like that with Rupert, was it?'

'Are you asking me whether he was a good lover?' Florence asked with a smile.

'I'm just curious. You don't have to answer. It's a personal question and none of my business, really.'

'He was wonderful, Winifred.' Florence hugged her knees and sighed loudly. 'I miss being held by him so much. It's a strange thing but I crave the solid feeling of him. If I think about it too much, it hurts. I don't just miss him with my heart, I miss him with my body too.'

'I can't imagine what that's like, Flo. I'd rather not be held by Gerald. He tastes of cigars.'

'But you're happy, aren't you?'

'Yes, we have a good friendship. We're a good partnership. A good team. That's the secret of a happy marriage – being a good team. We like the same things. I endure the bedroom part.'

Florence looked at her sister with sympathy. 'Oh, Winifred. It shouldn't be like that. It shouldn't be endured. It should be a beautiful experience.'

Winifred frowned. 'Beautiful? Can it really be that?'

'Yes.'

'Well, we can't have everything in life, can we. Not everyone lives the fairy tale. It must be terrible having to live without Rupert, but at least you've known what a deep and passionate love is like. I will probably never know. I'll only say that to you, Flo. I'm sorry Rupert died, but what a wonderful thing to have loved and been loved so deeply.'

'When you put it like that, I suppose I am lucky. We packed a lifetime of love into six years. To tell you the truth, a lifetime wouldn't have been long enough. But we'll meet again. I believe that. We'll find each other again one day. In the life after, or in another incarnation down here. I just have to wait.' She turned to her sister to see that she was staring at her in puzzlement. Florence chuckled. 'Give me a drag, will you?' she said, reaching for Winifred's cigarette. 'Rupert and I used to sit here and share cigarettes.' She sighed. 'Another summer without him. There will be many. I just have to learn to live in a different way.'

'Time is a great healer,' said Winifred, gazing out to sea. 'And this place is a real tonic.'

Florence's gaze met Winifred's on the distant horizon. 'It is,' she muttered softly.

Florence hadn't wanted to join in the tennis tournament. She really didn't feel like playing tennis. But Aubrey was so enthusiastic that she thought it wouldn't be fair to let him down. Cynthia had been paired with John Clairmont who had partnered Florence that summer of '37, and Bertha Clairmont, John's sister, partnered Tarquin. Tarquin turned out to be extremely good. He was serious competition for both Aubrey and John, much to Cynthia's delight. Florence hadn't played since before the war and was rusty. In spite of hiding at the net and leaving Aubrey to hit most of the balls for her, they still managed to lose in the second round to Tarquin and Cynthia, who went on to beat John and Bertha in the final. When they held up the trophy, Florence leaned over and whispered in Aubrey's ear, 'I think that's what he's going to look like when Reverend Millar proclaims them man and wife.'

Aubrey laughed. 'I think you're right, Flo. Cynthia will be his greatest trophy.'

Aubrey had started calling Florence by the name used by her closest friends. Rupert had called her Flossie, which she had come to cherish, because it had been his special name for her. She didn't notice when Aubrey stopped calling her Florence. In any case, it felt natural that he should and she liked it. She and Aubrey were becoming the best of friends. Ever since their trip to Holland they had grown close. Aubrey had remained in the army and was now stationed in Tidworth in Wiltshire. He took the train to Gulliver's Bay whenever possible to spend time with her and little Mary-Alice and they enjoyed long walks together and quiet evenings, playing cards with William and Celia.

* * *

Cynthia was married in the spring of the following year. Unlike Florence's marriage to Rupert the church was full, with guests having to stand at the back and squeeze into pews in order to witness the ceremony. Afterwards there was a dance at Pedrevan, just like the old days, with the ballroom illuminated by magnificent crystal chandeliers and hundreds of candles. Florence danced with Aubrey. This time Rupert was not present to cut in and steal her for himself. But as Aubrey led her around the dance floor in a waltz, Rupert was in the space between them all the same.

As much as Florence felt comfortable living at Pedrevan, she found the memories of Rupert overwhelming. Not that she couldn't enjoy meeting up at the pub with her friends, or take pleasure from her work, but the happiness she felt was a fragile veneer over the unhappiness beneath. Her smile rarely reached her eyes and her heart only ever felt that wonderful expansion when she gazed upon her daughter. Mary-Alice, who was now two and a half, gave her joy, in its purest form. But even that joy was moderated by the knowledge that Mary-Alice would never know her father. She'd never feel his protective arms around her, his lips pressed against her temple, his hands ruffling her hair. She'd never know a father's love. The child was not starved of affection. She was treasured by everyone in both Rupert and Florence's families, who all stepped up to compensate, but the loving arms of uncles, grandfathers and even great-grandfathers could not make up for the loss of her father.

Sometimes Florence felt as if she were drowning. Then her mother threw her a lifeline.

CHAPTER TWENTY-TWO

The summer of 1947 enjoyed a heatwave. After a cold and snowy February and flooding in March, May saw temperatures soar, climaxing in a sweltering and beautiful June. Margaret invited Oliver to Gulliver's Bay. In spite of a year-long courtship he had yet to go down to Cornwall to meet Henry and Joan. Florence had met Oliver in Kent, when she'd been to stay with her mother with Mary-Alice the previous autumn, and she had liked him very much. He was the cultural correspondent for *The Times*, creative and deep-thinking with a dry sense of humour and patience, which was essential because Margaret was highly strung and anxious. Florence thought them a perfect balance, each one bringing out the best in the other. Margaret was less frightened by life and Oliver was delighted to have a woman to spoil. Two people who had for so long been on their own relished being a couple.

Winifred came down with Gerald in the middle of June and the usual summer programme resumed; picnics on the beach, drinks on the terrace, golf, bridge, backgammon and endless meals. Idle days with nothing to do but seek entertainment. As much as Florence enjoyed the usual routine, the sparkle had gone out of it. She couldn't help but feel a little weary of being jolly all the time, when her heart wasn't in it. When everyone was part of a couple except for her.

Then one evening before dinner, while the family was enjoying a glass of wine in the garden, Oliver, a little tipsy, tapped a knife against his glass and made an impromptu announcement. 'I would like to announce our happy news.'

'Oh, darling. Are we going to do this now?' Margaret asked, startled.

'No better time. I can't hold it in a moment longer.' He looked at her with fondness. Margaret glanced anxiously at her daughters before giving him her hand. 'Margaret has agreed to marry me,' he said.

There were whoops of delight and glasses were raised in toasts as they congratulated the couple. Joan dabbed her eyes with relief that her daughter had at last found someone with whom to share her life. Uncle Raymond caught Monty's eye and something subliminal and secret passed between them. Henry patted Oliver's back so hard that he nearly spat out his wine, and Gerald lit a cigar and extolled the virtues of marriage in a long and boring soliloquy that induced Winifred to flee to the other end of the garden with Mary-Alice, under the pretence of chasing a butterfly. Champagne was brought up from the cellar and flutes were carried out from the pantry. Henry opened the first bottle and the cork flew into the air with a spray of champagne. Then he went into the sitting room and played Jack Buchanan loudly on the gramophone.

Another tap on his glass and Oliver had one more thing to say. 'I know this might come as something of a shock, but Margaret and I are going to live in Australia.' The laughter died in everyone's throats. 'We're marrying here and then moving to Melbourne.' No one raised their glasses to that.

Stunned silence fell over the party. Only Jack Buchanan

sang cheerfully on, *'We're birds of a feather, we ought to get together'*. Joan stared at her daughter in horror. Henry went red and Winifred hurried across the lawn, dragging Mary-Alice by the hand. 'What did you say?' she asked her mother in panic. 'You're going to Australia?'

Margaret looked anxious for the first time in months. 'We're starting afresh in Melbourne. Oliver's sister lives there. We thought it would be nice to try something different. We're not going to be there forever, are we, Oliver? I mean, we're going to try it and see what it's like. Oliver thinks I'll like it. It'll be an extended honeymoon. Think of it like that. Not a goodbye, but a farewell.' She laughed nervously. Oliver put his arm around her waist and chuckled awkwardly.

Florence watched her mother. The announcement did not surprise her as much as it seemed to surprise everyone else. After all, Margaret had lived in Egypt and India with her first husband, why not live in Australia with her second? Besides her family, Margaret had never had much of a life in England. Perhaps those warm, friendly Antipodeans would make her feel more at home.

Then Florence was struck with an idea. It was like a bolt out of the blue and so astonishing that she almost reeled. What if *she* went with them? She and Mary-Alice? Perhaps the only way to move on in her life was to take herself out of Gulliver's Bay and start again in a new country, far away from the shadows that reminded her, at every turn, of Rupert's death.

It was an outlandish idea and one she hadn't thought of before. Leaving England simply hadn't ever crossed her mind. Since Rupert's death Florence had envisaged herself growing old in Pedrevan, alone. It had never occurred to her that she could leave. She wouldn't be running from Rupert. She would simply be running from his death.

It wasn't until after dinner that she was able to get her mother on her own.

Margaret was sitting at her dressing table, taking off her make-up with cold cream. When she saw her daughter in the doorway she smiled through the mirror. 'Come in, darling. I hope you're not upset by our decision to leave England. I would have told you and Winnie before, but I didn't realize Oliver was going to make the announcement today. I think we set the cat among the pigeons. Mama and Papa are putting on a brave face, but I know how they're feeling. I do feel rotten about that. But we won't be gone forever. Just for a while. It's a long way away, but we'll be back.' Her eyes scrutinized Florence's face for her reaction.

Florence sat on the end of the bed and crossed her legs. 'I'd like to come with you,' she said.

Margaret swung round on her stool. 'You want to leave Pedrevan?'

'I want to leave England.'

Margaret looked uncertain. 'Oh, Flo.'

Florence's eyes filled with tears. 'I need to start afresh, somewhere far away from everything that reminds me of Rupert. I think that's the only way I'll ever be able to find a life for myself. I'm tired of missing him.'

'Oh, darling.' Margaret wiped the cream off her face with a tissue, then she got up and went to sit beside her daughter, putting a maternal arm around her and drawing her close. 'I know what grief feels like,' she said softly. 'My heart goes out to you.'

'You're the only person who understands what it's like to be a widow.'

'It never goes away, that pain, but it does become less intense. It becomes a dull ache in the background of your life. I promise you, it gets better.'

'I now understand why you didn't want to marry again.'

'It took me a long time, Florence. But I've found a different kind of love with Oliver. A mutual respect, companionship, affection. It's not the same as what I had with your father. It's different. But it's not less. One day you may find someone who fills the hole that Rupert left. He won't replace Rupert, of course, and you may not love him as much as you loved Rupert. But you'll find a friend to laugh with, and laughter is so important. I didn't realize how much I'd missed it until Oliver made me laugh.'

'Oh, Mama, I'm so happy for you. Oliver's a really nice man. I like him immensely. He's good for you and I can tell from the way he looks at you that he's deeply fond of you too.' Florence lifted her head off her mother's shoulder. 'I want to come with you. Me and Mary-Alice. I know Grandma and Grandpa will be sad, and Winifred and Uncle Raymond too, but we can't live our lives for other people. We need to find happiness where we can. And it won't be forever. I'll come back.'

'You don't want to try and settle in another part of England?'

'No, Mama. I want to go with you to Australia. It'll be an adventure.' She smiled at the thought of it. 'I need an adventure.'

Margaret sighed. 'I'll happily take you both with me, but William and Celia will be disappointed, and those children. Well, they're not children anymore. They'll miss you and Mary-Alice terribly.'

'They'll accept it if I tell them it's not forever.'

'It isn't forever,' Margaret agreed firmly. 'I'm sure we'll come back at some stage. I can't leave my parents and Uncle Raymond and Winnie for too long, can I?'

Florence felt her excitement grow. 'So, we can go too?'

'I'll have to ask Oliver, of course, but I don't think he'll mind. In fact, I think he'll be delighted. He knows how hard it's going to be for me to leave my family behind. If you and Mary-Alice come too, I'll be leaving only some of it behind.' Margaret laughed. Florence hadn't ever seen her laugh like that, without the skin pinching between her eyebrows.

Florence's decision was hard for William and Celia to understand. Mary-Alice was the only part of Rupert left that they could hold onto. The thought of Florence taking her to the other end of the world was incomprehensible. At first they tried to persuade her to stay. But when they saw how determined she was, they advised her to give it a year. If she didn't settle, then she could come back. The cottage would be there for her, 'The fire lit, the bed made and a baked potato in the oven,' Celia said crisply, hiding her emotion behind a veneer of stoic English humour.

Cynthia was devastated. She was now pregnant with her first child and overemotional with it. She threw her arms around her friend and sobbed onto her shoulder. 'I'm sorry,' she said. 'I just can't accept my best friend – and sister-in-law, because you are still my sister-in-law – going to live on the edge of the world. What if you never come back? What if I don't ever see you again? Mary-Alice will grow up and she won't know Pedrevan, or her uncles and aunts and grandparents. She won't know her little cousin.' She touched her belly. 'Imagine that. She won't know her cousin!'

Florence reassured her. They would come back. 'I want Mary-Alice to know her cousin. They're going to be the best of friends like their mothers. It'll only be for a year or so, until I find my feet again. It's just been so hard living here without Rupert.'

Cynthia couldn't begin to understand what it was like to lose a beloved husband, but she knew what it was to lose a brother. She missed Rupert too. 'But I find comfort from my memories, Flo. I see Rupert all over Pedrevan and that makes me feel close to him.'

'I feel close to him wherever I am,' said Florence. 'When I land in Australia he'll be *here*.' She pressed a hand against her heart. 'But while I stay here at Pedrevan I am only reminded of my loss.'

When Aubrey heard the news, he drove straight to Florence's cottage. When he discovered that she wasn't there, he drove to The Mariners. Florence was in the garden with Uncle Raymond and Monty, playing boules. At the sight of Aubrey's stricken face, she left the game and hurried over to find out what had happened. She assumed the worst. 'We need to talk,' said Aubrey, looking at her with feverish eyes. From the urgent way he was staring at her she knew that nothing bad had happened to William or Celia. The reason for Aubrey's distress was *her*. 'Will you walk with me on the beach?' he asked.

Florence accompanied him down the path. Neither spoke. It wasn't until they reached the sand that Aubrey took her hand. 'You're going to Australia?' he said, and Florence's heart stalled because he barely got the words out before his voice thinned with emotion.

'Yes,' she replied. 'In the autumn.'

'Why didn't you tell me?'

'I was going to tell you, when I next saw you.'

He turned his eyes to the sea then back again. His jaw stiffened. 'You can't go,' he said resolutely.

'Oh, Aubrey . . .'

'Don't you see? I love you. I should have told you months

ago, but it would have been wrong not to have allowed you time to grieve for my brother.'

'I don't understand. I thought—'

'We were friends?' Aubrey cut in. 'We *are* friends. The *best* of friends.' He took both her hands and gazed upon her with longing. 'But I feel more than friendship, Flo. I love you.'

Florence didn't know what to say.

'This shouldn't come as a shock to you.' He smiled through his anguish. 'Why do you think I spent so much time with you?'

'Because you liked me. Because you felt sorry for me.'

'Yes, I liked you and I felt sorry for you, because your heart was broken. But I thought if we spent enough time together, that I'd make you forget about Rupert. That you'd feel tenderness for me.' His smile turned sheepish. 'You did love me once.'

'I did, Aubrey. I adored you for years. Every summer I longed for you to notice me. One look from you and I turned to jelly. One smile and I blushed. How I longed to partner you in tennis and how I hurt when you had eyes only for Elise. I *did* love you. At least, I thought I did. But then Rupert appeared at Pedrevan, that summer of '37, and . . .'

'If only I could turn the clock back, Florence,' he groaned.

'But you can't. I wish I could too. Then Rupert would still be alive.' She squeezed his hands. 'I wish I loved you in the way you want me to. Then I could forget about your brother and I could be happy at Pedrevan. Mary-Alice could grow up in the home that was at one point her destiny. And you and I could grow old together, like Rupert and I dreamed we would, surrounded by children and grandchildren, around the drawing room fire. But even if I did love you, I wouldn't allow myself that luxury. I couldn't betray Rupert.'

'Rupert is not alive to be betrayed,' said Aubrey tightly.

'I wouldn't want to betray his memory, Aubrey. I think he would accept my falling in love with anyone in the world except *you*.' She shook her head sadly. 'I'm sorry.'

Aubrey's mouth twisted, as if he was trying hard to control his emotions and failing. 'Is there nothing I can do to persuade you to stay?'

'Nothing,' she replied.

'I can't bear to lose you.' He rubbed the bridge of his nose. 'I just can't bear it.'

'Oh, Aubrey.' Florence wrapped her arms around him. She wished more than anything that she could alleviate his suffering, but she couldn't. The one thing he wanted was the only thing she couldn't give him. 'I'm so fond of you. I truly am. You took me to Oosterbeek and comforted me when I cried. You were patient and kind and generous too. I owe you so much. But I can't be the woman you want me to be. I'm your brother's wife and I always will be.'

'He's not coming back, Flo,' Aubrey said, not unkindly. 'You have to let him go.'

Florence did not reply. She rested her head against his chest, closed her eyes and thought of Rupert. Wait for me – I will come back.

We shall know, we two;
Simply this: you waited as
No one else could do.

In the days before Florence's departure, Aubrey came to visit as much as he could. He did not mention their conversation on the beach, but she knew he hoped that by being present she would grow to depend on him. That she would realize how much she needed him and change her mind.

She did not pack much. She took only the things she most needed and items of Rupert's that she kept for sentimental reasons, like his ID tags, his Leica, his books, letters and cufflinks, and photographs, in particular those of their wedding and the one of her that he had taken on the gate that summer when they had first become friends. The rest she packed into boxes to be kept in the cellar at Pedrevan to pick up on her return. At that point, she never imagined that she wouldn't come back.

Aubrey made one final attempt the day before she left. 'Marry me,' he said. 'I don't mind if you don't love me like you loved Rupert. I just want to be with you. I'll look after you and Mary-Alice and love you both.'

But Florence could not be persuaded.

She took one last look around the cottage where she had, for a time, found a certain degree of peace, then closed the door behind her.

CHAPTER TWENTY-THREE

Gulliver's Bay, 1993

'Isn't this a treat!' gushed Bertha, settling into the front passenger seat of Max's car and strapping herself in. She was wearing a floral dress and cardigan that reeked of a sickly combination of cigarette smoke and lilac perfume. She put her handbag on her lap, a tapestry bag embellished with silver sequins, and rummaged about for her packet of Marlboro. Max loaded her carpet bag into the boot and took his last breath of fresh air before spending the next six hours enveloped in smoke.

As he climbed into the driving seat, Toby barked from his basket behind him. 'He likes you,' said Bertha, turning around to smile at the dog. 'You good boy,' she said, then blew a cloud of smoke into the air between them. Max had driven to London specially to chauffeur Bertha down to Cornwall. He'd taken the opportunity to stay with his sister and meet a couple of old friends at the pub the night before, which had been fun. But he was not unhappy to leave London behind him.

Bertha talked all the way down. A soliloquy punctuated by swigs from a leather and pewter flask which she claimed to be water but which Max knew was something infinitely stronger. He rolled down the window, grateful that it was a warm August day and not raining, for Bertha might have complained of the cold and asked him to shut it. Even with the window open, her constant smoking dried his throat, so that when he swallowed it felt like sandpaper. 'We have a lot of interesting characters in our family,' she said as they left London and headed down the motorway. Max listened with half an ear as she told him about people in his ancestry who were of no interest to anyone but herself. The only people *he* was interested in were Rupert and Florence Dash. He would have preferred to put on the radio or listen to a tape, but Bertha was not going to miss the chance to talk. She spent far too much time on her own and was starved of company. Having Max to herself for six hours, unable to escape except for the odd stop at a petrol station, was an irresistible opportunity for a woman who usually only talked to her dog. Toby had fallen asleep the second the car had moved away from the kerb and Max had envied him as Bertha had started, her eyes gleaming with intent, 'I'm going to start right from the beginning, with Herbert Clarence Vincent Clairmont in 1845.' And she had, quite literally, made her way through every name on the family tree.

By the time Max drove into Gulliver's Bay he was beginning to feel not only weary, but irritated too. Bertha had barely drawn breath and they had only got up to the early part of the twentieth century. 'Isn't it lucky that we have the whole journey back to London to finish going through the family tree,' she said as they motored through the gates into Pedrevan Park. 'Now, you don't drive up to the house but take a left when the drive forks.'

Max was now alert. Every sense was quivering with attention and excitement. He had longed to enter the property and recalled peering at it through the bushes with Robyn. He wondered whether he should call Robyn and let her know that he was here. The thought of seeing her lifted his spirits for a second before they deflated at the humiliating memory of declaring his love to her. No, it was probably better to leave her alone. If she'd wanted to contact him she could have done so at any point during the last four years.

Cynthia lived in a cottage on the Pedrevan estate. It was a white house with a thatched roof, surrounded by a big garden and a high beech hedge. It was mid-afternoon when they arrived. Toby jumped out of the back and cocked his leg on the wheel. Max got out and inhaled the fresh sea air and the scent of pine and freshly cut grass that lingered in the warmth. Toby yapped and the front door opened. An elderly woman with shoulder-length white hair and bright blue eyes stepped out to greet them. 'It's lovely to meet you,' Cynthia said, shaking Max's hand. 'You're incredibly sweet to bring Bertha all the way down from London. It's such a long way.' She spoke with the same clipped enunciation as Bertha, emphasizing the odd word here and there which gave her a certain grandeur, like a queen. 'Bertha, how long has it been?' The two women kissed.

'You haven't changed a bit,' said Bertha, looking her cousin up and down admiringly.

'I'm fatter than I was, that's for certain.'

'Oh, don't talk to me about fat. I gave up caring half a century ago,' said Bertha with a wheezy chuckle.

'Come on in,' said Cynthia. 'I'm sure you're both hungry. What shall I do about the dog?'

'Leave him to roam. It's a novelty for him to have so much space.'

'He won't run off?'

'Absolutely not. He's much too nervous to stray too far from me. He's well aware who feeds him.'

'Very well.' Cynthia closed the door.

Max put Bertha's carpet bag and his holdall in the hall and followed Cynthia into the garden where a table was laid for a late lunch beneath a trellis of purple wisteria. There were big bowls of pasta and salad, and a jug of water. In the centre of the table was a vase of roses. Cynthia offered them wine, which Bertha readily accepted. Max was happy with water. It was hot and he was thirsty. After the usual pleasantries, Cynthia and Bertha began to reminisce. 'It's all coming back to me because of my book,' Bertha told her cousin. 'And I'm curious to know what happened to everyone. I've lost touch with so many relations.'

'It's sad, really,' said Cynthia. 'We were very close once. Pedrevan was heaving with uncles and aunts and cousins. Now it's empty. Aubrey rattles around in there on his own. His children come down to visit him from time to time and bring the grandchildren, but it's not the place of fun that it used to be.'

Max listened as he tucked into the pasta. He hadn't realized how hungry he was.

'How very selfish of him,' said Bertha. 'The least he could do is make it amusing for the grandchildren.'

'How many children does he have?' Max asked.

'Three children with Ellen and one with Minnie,' said Cynthia.

'What happened to Minnie?' Max asked.

'She died of cancer about five years ago. A strange, quiet woman. I never understood why he married her. I think he was just lonely. They were very ill suited. She was more like a housekeeper than a wife.' Cynthia sighed. 'The children have their own lives now and none of them live locally. In our day, we had such fun down here playing tennis and croquet and all those silly games. Do you remember the scavenger hunts, Bertha?'

'Oh yes, I couldn't forget those.'

'I remember Rupert driving us around the countryside. We had to find the oddest items. A duck's feather, well, that wasn't too hard. A cob of corn. Sheep's wool. That was hilarious, Flo and I running around the field chasing sheep and wielding a pair of scissors while Rupert and Elise watched from the car. Elise was much too serious to make a fool of herself like Flo and I did. That was the year Rupert fell in love with Florence. Not that any of us guessed it at the time.'

'Will you tell me about Rupert and Florence?' said Max. 'It's Rupert I'm particularly interested in.'

'You have to understand that my brother Rupert wasn't like the rest of us. He hated sports and was terrible at tennis,' said Cynthia. 'When we were growing up we had a tennis teacher every summer and he simply refused to have lessons. He'd stand in his tennis whites with his arms crossed and a furious look on his face, and there was nothing our father could do to persuade him to try. Rupert knew he was bad and couldn't be bothered to make an effort. Aubrey was a natural, which annoyed Rupert, because Aubrey was his younger brother. But Rupert was very clever, not that he tried at school, either. He just hated authority. He hated being told what to do. But he had the most wonderful sense of humour. He was witty, you see, and sharp. He had an eye for the absurd and no one could tell an anecdote like Rupert. His timing was perfection. He should have been an actor, or a writer. He would have done something very interesting with his life had he lived. Sadly, he was killed at Arnhem. Florence was devastated. They had a daughter, you see, a little girl called Mary-Alice, who never knew her father. It was just awful.'

'You've digressed, Cynthia,' said Bertha, slugging her wine. 'You were going to tell Max about Rupert and Florence falling in love.'

Cynthia smiled. 'Flo was my closest friend but she told me nothing about Rupert. We all presumed she had a thing for Aubrey.' She rolled her eyes. 'Everyone had a thing for Aubrey. He was so handsome in those days and not at all pleased with himself. He was just heavenly. Flo, dear old thing, blushed every time he talked to her. It was a bit of a joke in the family. I used to read her letters out loud. She wrote to me from her boarding school. I don't think her family knew what to do with her. She was terrifically naughty. Not by today's standards. We were all quite innocent in those days. But for her time, she was what you'd call a rebel. Anyway, I'd read out her letters and Rupert and Aubrey thought her terribly funny. Aubrey wasn't at all interested in her. She was my naughty friend. I'm sure he knew she had a crush on him, though. Not that he ever said anything and he certainly wouldn't have let her down by making fun of it. He was a gentleman.

'Then that summer of '37, a couple of years before the war, Rupert came down for the summer and stayed. He didn't usually stay. He'd hop off to the Riviera, to Biarritz or Antibes, and swan around doing the things he loved, like sitting in cafés smoking and reading the papers, or lying in the shade reading a book. He wasn't sociable, really. He was a deep-thinker. But in spite of not really liking people on the whole, people were drawn to him. He was mysterious, a bit of an enigma, and people found that intriguing. Rupert didn't give much away.'

'You're about to digress again, Cynthia,' said Bertha, giving her cousin a stern look.

'Am I? Oh dear. That must be age.' Cynthia smiled apologetically. 'The thing is, that year Rupert stayed, Flo had caught his eye. They spent a lot of time together. Later, when they went public with their romance, it all fitted into place. I remember looking back and spotting the signs, which, had I been more alert, I might have noticed at the time. But I was too busy with the social whirl to pick up the chemistry between them. And what chemistry it was too. They had a wonderful repartee. It was quick-witted and sharp. No one else had that kind of chat with Rupert. He was so aloof. Florence and he had a meeting of the minds. They were both naughty, which I'm sure had something to do with the attraction. But they were kindred spirits too. I'll never forget the moment the penny dropped. We were at a dance in Eastbourne. Rupert and Aubrey were our dates. It was the end of year party given by the headmistress of our finishing school. I assumed that Florence had a thing for Aubrey. The two of them were dancing. Then Rupert strode onto the dance floor and stole her off his brother. As he swept her around the room, the way they looked at each other took my breath away. The intensity of it was something I'd never seen before, or since. It was then that I realized I'd been wrong all along. Flo wasn't in love with Aubrey. She only had eyes for Rupert.'

'How romantic!' Bertha exclaimed, reaching for the bottle of wine and refilling her glass. 'He was jolly handsome.'

'I think Aubrey was a little put out. He was used to everyone fancying him. He just took it for granted that he could have any girl he wanted. Then the girl he'd barely noticed fell in love with his brother and he suddenly decided he wanted her for himself. Rupert and Florence married at the beginning of the war. So sad, they really had very little time together.'

'What happened to Florence after Rupert was killed?' Max asked.

'She didn't cope very well. In spite of Rupert's body being found and buried, she still held on to the hope that he would suddenly appear, that there had been a mistake. Poor thing, she couldn't accept that he was gone. Then Aubrey suggested he take her to Holland to visit Rupert's grave. I think it helped enormously. My parents went later, as did I and my twin brother Julian. It was important for Florence to go. Aubrey accompanied her, which was sweet. He was good like that. But he had a soft spot for her, for certain. I could tell by the way he looked at her and in the way he spoke about her. There was a tenderness. It was sad, really, because she never got over Rupert. Anyway, when she came back she moved in here.' Cynthia swept her eyes over the house. 'It was the perfect place for her. She could be close to Rupert's family as well as her own grandparents who lived at The Mariners. It's now a hotel, you know.'

'Yes, I've stayed there,' said Max.

'Did you know there was a connection between that place and Rupert?'

'Not until Bertha told me.'

Cynthia looked at Bertha. 'I can't wait to read your book,' she said.

'I can't wait to finish writing it. It's been a slog.' Bertha was now slurring her words. She coughed and took a slurp of wine.

Cynthia continued. 'Then Flo announced one day that she was going to live in Australia. It was a terrible blow. She took Mary-Alice with her and that was that. Gone. She never came back.'

Max frowned. 'Do you think it was just too hard living without Rupert?'

Cynthia sighed. 'I remember her telling me that everywhere she looked she was reminded of his death.'

'Did you keep in touch with her?'

'At the beginning, I did. Then we drifted. Her mother came back with her husband, what was he called?'

'Oliver,' said Bertha importantly. 'They were only in Australia for a few years.'

'And Florence stayed?' Max asked.

'She married again, you see. She wrote to me, sending me a photograph of her and her new husband. He was Australian, so she made her life there. It was sad for us because we never knew Rupert's daughter. We exchanged Christmas cards, of course, and when my parents died, we got back in touch for a while. She sent me her change of address whenever she moved. I believe she lives with her daughter and son-in-law now. Florence's second husband died, God knows how long ago. But she never came back and I never went over there. It's too far away. I hate flying.'

'Me too,' said Bertha. 'I think I might go and lie down. I'm feeling a little sleepy.'

'I'll show you to your room,' said Cynthia, getting up. 'Where's that dog?'

'Toby? Did I bring him?'

'Yes, you did.'

'I'll find him,' said Max. He began to wander around the garden, whistling.

'Don't look him in the eye,' said Bertha as she weaved her way across the grass and disappeared into the house.

Toby was nowhere to be found in the garden. Max continued whistling, but the dog had clearly decided to investigate the property on his own. Max decided to wander around the estate to see if he could find him, before driving into Gulliver's Bay in the hope of bumping into Robyn. It was pointless pretending there was any other reason why he'd want to go there. If luck was on his side, there was a good chance they'd find each other in the pub.

Max set off down the drive. When he came to the fork, he chose the route that led to the house. If Aubrey found him trespassing on his property, he would simply explain that he was staying with Cynthia and was looking for Toby.

As he wandered up the track, he thought of Florence. It was astonishing to think that Rupert's wife was still alive. Not that she was particularly old, simply that she might have been his wife in another life. It was extraordinary to think that he had perhaps loved her once and yet had no recollection of it. He knew what Robyn would say, or Olga or Daphne, that he wasn't *meant* to remember, because he was here now to focus on his *present* life, not to get distracted by past ones. But on some deep, subconscious level, his soul loved Florence. Perhaps they had been together in other lifetimes and would be again in the future. How many other people were out there in the world who had once, in another incarnation, meant something to Max? Cynthia for a start would have been his sister and yet he felt no sense of déjà vu. If he had truly been Rupert, wouldn't he feel *something*?

Max walked on, forgetting to whistle for Toby. When the house came into view he stopped and looked at it in wonder. This *did* feel familiar, he thought with rising excitement. But then he wasn't certain that his sense of recognition wasn't because he *wanted* to recognize it. Of course he had already seen it, but only from the side and not up close. The house was like other Elizabethan houses he'd come across. The style itself was, indeed, familiar, and yet, he had the strange sensation of having seen it before – but he couldn't quite hold onto the feeling long enough to explore it. It was intangible and unexplainable. A whiff, no more, of a memory buried deep. A scent sniffed then lost on the wind.

Max didn't feel comfortable wandering around someone else's property. He remembered Toby and whistled, but Toby did not come bounding out of a bush. The garden was quiet but for birdsong, resounding lazily from the trees. Max hoped the dog hadn't got lost. He walked back to the cottage.

Bearing in mind that Daphne was writing a book about reincarnation which would include Max's story, he decided to share his experiences with Cynthia. He grabbed the opportunity while Bertha was asleep upstairs. Cynthia made them both cups of coffee, then they sat outside and drank it as the sun began to sink behind the trees. She listened with interest. When Max finished, she shook her head in disbelief. 'That's a remarkable story, Max. I don't know what to say. I don't believe in reincarnation, but the vicar said something curious to me after Florence left. He said it was probably good for her to leave Pedrevan and start afresh in a new place. You see, she'd gone to see him after finding a poem in a book in the flower market. I'm not sure quite how she came across it, but she seemed to think it was a sign from Rupert. It was called "Wait for Me". I think it went something like, *"Wait for me – I will come back"*. Florence believed Rupert would come back. I'm not sure if she believed he'd come back in spirit or in person. Reverend Millar thought it must be in spirit, because at that point she had accepted that Rupert was dead. But now you mention reincarnation, I have a feeling she may have meant *that*.'

Her blue eyes shone with kindness. 'I'd like your story to be true, Max, because I'd like to think that Rupert lives on. But it's hard to get one's head around, isn't it? I mean, the idea of returning in another body is peculiar. I know it's not a new idea, but it's not one I'm very familiar with.' She smiled gently. 'I'm not a devout Christian, so it's not that it goes against my beliefs. It's more that it feels strange and, well, unbelievable. Like science fiction. I'm glad you've explained it to me, though. It makes sense now why you wanted to hear about Rupert, specifically. You do resemble him, I admit, but we are related, aren't we, so that's not so strange. I don't think Aubrey would buy it. I wouldn't mention it to him if you meet him. He certainly won't want to talk about Florence, or the past for that matter. He was hit very hard by her leaving. They were close friends, you see.'

She narrowed her eyes, thinking for a moment. 'I'll see if I can get Aubrey to allow me to show you Pedrevan tomorrow. He won't want to see Bertha. He won't want to be cross-examined about the family. So he might make himself scarce. But there's no reason why I can't show you around the house myself. Now that you've come all this way, it would be a shame to go home without having seen it.'

'I'd love that, Cynthia,' said Max.

'I'll see what I can do. Now we need to find that bloody dog.' She laughed as she got up. 'I'll show you where you're sleeping.'

'Then I might nip down to the pub. There's an old friend here I'd like to bump into.'

'That's a good idea. Dinner will be at eight. Nothing special.'

'You're very kind to invite us,' he said, following her into the house and up the narrow stair.

'You've done me a favour, actually. It's lonely on one's own. I'm a widow, you see. It hasn't been long, only five years. I'm still getting accustomed to it. It's nice to have some company and you are family, after all.'

Max's room was cosy with a big double bed. Cynthia had put some sweet peas in a vase on the dresser. He placed his bag on the bed. As he did so, Toby scurried out from beneath it. 'Oh, what a relief!' Cynthia exclaimed. 'I visualized us having to trail about the estate, searching for him.'

'Don't look him in the eye,' Max warned. No sooner had those words escaped his lips than the dog jumped up and started humping her leg. 'Too late!' he said and they both laughed.

Max headed into town in his car and parked outside the pub. It was dusk. A warm, copper light had fallen over the town. The mellow light of late summer. He went into the pub. He hoped he'd see Robyn. He knew it was a long shot, but so far serendipity had come into play at every turn, so why not now?

He went to the bar to order a drink. That's when he saw Daniel getting up from a table of men. Excited by his luck, he approached him. 'Hey, Daniel.'

Daniel looked at him in surprise. 'Max, what are you doing here?'

'Visiting an elderly relative,' he said. Daniel didn't look quite as happy to see Max as Max was to see him. 'How's Robyn?' he asked.

'Great. Robyn's great. It's been a long time.'

'Four years,' said Max. 'Since your wedding.'

'Of course.'

'Silly that we lost touch.'

'How long are you staying?'

'Just the weekend. I'll be off the day after tomorrow.'

Daniel nodded. 'I'll let Robyn know you're here.'

'Let me give you my number.' Max went to the bar and asked the bartender for a pen and paper. He wrote down the telephone number of Cynthia's cottage. 'I'm staying with my relative. I'd love to see you both. Perhaps we can come here for supper tomorrow evening?'

'Yeah, that would be great. I'll get her to call you and make a plan.'

Max smiled. 'Good. I'll see you tomorrow then.' He watched Daniel leave and then slid onto a stool at the bar. 'A beer, please,' he said. He sighed with happiness. He was going to see Robyn.

CHAPTER TWENTY-FOUR

Max expected Robyn to call that evening, but the phone didn't ring. Dinner came and went and at ten-thirty he went upstairs to bed, disappointed. Robyn wasn't going to call at that hour. Perhaps she'd call in the morning.

He had a fitful night. The bed was big and comfortable, the rustling of leaves and the odd screech of an owl drifting in through the open window soothing, yet he felt an anxiety in his stomach. A feeling that something wasn't right. Why hadn't Robyn called? He hadn't seen her in four years, so surely on discovering from Daniel that he was here in Gulliver's Bay, she would have immediately picked up the telephone and called him. Why hadn't she?

Dawn crept in through the gaps in the curtains with the tentative sound of birdsong. Max looked at his watch. It was five-thirty. He must have slept, but he felt alert and the nervous fluttering in his stomach had only intensified. He hoped Robyn would call at breakfast.

There was no point trying to go back to sleep, so he dressed, grabbed his camera and tip-toed downstairs, careful not to wake the sleeping dog in case he barked and woke Cynthia. He didn't imagine anything would disturb Bertha's sleep after the amount of wine she had drunk at dinner. It was peaceful in the garden. A sense of pause before the hustle of the day began. He took a few shots of the cottage then wandered around the borders, trying to take pleasure from the flowers and shrubs stirring beneath the veil of dawn. Yet his pleasure was marred. Perhaps Robyn didn't want to see him. After all, she hadn't been in contact for four years. Maybe he really had lost her.

With a stab of nostalgia, he remembered kissing her in the cave; a memory that never dimmed or lost its lustre. He could still feel her against him, her hand on his face, her lips against his. He could still taste her. It had felt so natural. The cliché was true; it was as if they had been made for each other. He wandered restlessly around the garden contemplating how much he loved her. It wasn't simply a physical thing, though: of course, his attraction to her was undeniable, but it was a spiritual thing too. He hadn't felt a connection like this with anyone else, male or female, ever. Robyn was the first person he had met who he could really talk to. The first person who listened and understood him. When he was with her he no longer felt that unquenchable, indefinable longing, that feeling of being alone, of drifting; he felt complete. It no longer mattered that she was married to Daniel. He just wanted her in his life, in whatever form that took. He wanted to be able to pick up the phone from time to time and hear her voice. To know that he had a friend in her. It wasn't like her to turn her back. The fact that she hadn't called last night must have been deliberate. If she didn't call today, he had to accept that she no longer wanted him in *her* life.

Cynthia came down at eight for breakfast to find Max already at the kitchen table, flicking through a book of Cornish beaches he'd found in the sitting room. His Leica was on the table beside him. 'Rupert had a camera like that,' she said, picking it up and giving it a good look. 'He loved taking photographs. I think, if he'd survived the war, he'd have made a very good photographer. You see, he was really very creative. Sadly, he never lived long enough to explore that side of himself.'

This revelation meant more to Max than Cynthia could imagine. 'Really?' he exclaimed in astonishment.

Cynthia was surprised by his reaction. She smiled and put the camera down. 'Yes, he was very proud of his Leica. It went everywhere with him. Now, what do you fancy for breakfast?'

Cynthia made Max coffee and toast and they sat together, chatting, while Bertha slept on upstairs. 'Speaking of cameras, I thought of something in the middle of the night,' she said, getting up from her chair. 'I have a photograph you might be interested in seeing.' She disappeared for a moment, then returned with a silver frame. 'This is Rupert and Florence on their wedding day. It's the only photo I have of the two of them together. I thought you might like to see it.' She handed it to Max.

Max searched within himself for a sense of déjà vu, but felt nothing but curiosity and an intense fascination. Rupert and Florence were smiling. Happiness radiated out of the picture like sunshine. Rupert had indeed been dashing. With his dark hair brushed off his forehead, revealing a widow's peak worthy of a movie star, and dark, deep-set eyes, he looked handsome. He was tall and elegant, Florence a foot smaller than him at least, slim and feminine in her bias-cut dress – they made a glamorous couple. Reincarnation aside, the fact that these two people, so clearly in love, had only a few more years together before they were separated by death made Max feel incredibly sad. He gazed into Rupert's face, trying to reconcile the man he was now with the man he had once been, and felt his sadness deepen, because he couldn't share this photograph with Robyn.

Bertha came down for breakfast at nine with Toby, who rushed into the garden and cocked his leg at the first opportunity. An hour later Cynthia suggested they visit the house. She had tried to call Aubrey that morning, but he hadn't answered. 'I think we just turn up and try our luck.' The telephone hadn't rung. Max still harboured a sliver of hope that Robyn might call, but as they left the cottage that hope died. He had to accept that she wasn't going to.

The three of them cut through the gardens to reach the main house. It was quicker than the route Max had taken the day before, even at their unhurried pace. Toby trotted along, sniffing the ground excitedly. Bertha had smoked two cigarettes at breakfast but managed to hold off during their walk. The air smelt of pine and mown grass and the fresh scent of brine which the wind had picked up as it had travelled over the sea. 'Freddie Laycock kissed me under that tree,' said Bertha, pointing a gnarled and yellowed finger at a majestic cedar that dominated the lawn.

Cynthia laughed. 'You let Freddie Laycock kiss you?' she said.

'It was a dare. John set him up to it. I must have been about fifteen. Poor Freddie was killed in Normandy.'

'Yes, that was very sad,' Cynthia agreed. 'So many of those boys never came home. When I look around this place, I remember them all. They were happy times, before the war, weren't they? It was all so innocent. We never believed there would be another war, not after the previous one. The grown-ups were wiser and knew how foolish people can be, but we went about our lives in blissful ignorance. Until it happened. Then life got serious. It's been serious ever since.'

The house came into view and they stopped a moment to look at it. Max put his camera to his eye and took some photographs. 'Consider Aubrey, rattling around in there on his own. That's sad. He used to be such fun. I don't know what happened,' Cynthia mused.

'I do,' said Bertha. 'The war happened.'

'Perhaps it's as simple as that. I don't know. He just wasn't the same after Rupert died.'

'Maybe Pedrevan is a burden,' Bertha suggested. 'It was meant to go to Rupert, after all. Perhaps Aubrey didn't really want it. It's quite a responsibility. It has such a history of fun, I imagine he found that impossible to maintain. This is a house that should be full of people, not left to languish in shadow.' She sighed. 'It is beautiful, though, isn't it?'

'Very,' Cynthia agreed.

'It must be expensive to run,' said Max, wondering whether money might have played a part in Aubrey's decline.

'I imagine it's a great big black hole, swallowing money like water. Poor Aubrey. Come on, let's go inside.'

They approached the door and rang the bell. There was a long wait before the bolts shifted noisily and a face appeared, pale and angular, in the crack. 'Mrs Smith-Teddington,' said a deep voice on recognizing Cynthia.

'Hello, Bracks. Is Aubrey home?'

'No, he's out.'

'Good. I'd like to show my cousin here the house. May we come in?' Bracks opened the door wide. He was elderly and stooped and looked as if he had been manning that door for centuries. 'I've been trying to ring him,' said Cynthia, striding over the threshold. 'Does no one answer the phone around here?'

'It's a big house. Sometimes no one hears it.'

'Yes, well, you can tell him he should put in more phones or something. It's very inconvenient not being able to get in touch with him.'

'Would you care for tea or coffee?' Bracks asked, closing the front door and bolting it again.

'No, thank you. We've just had breakfast.'

'Do you mind if I smoke?' asked Bertha.

'You may smoke in the morning room,' Bracks told her.

'Ah,' said Bertha, disappointed. However, her desire for a cigarette overrode her interest in the tour. 'Come on, Toby. We'll go and sit in there. After all, I know the house and, by the looks of things, it hasn't changed in fifty years.'

Cynthia showed Max around. He stopped trying to find his old self in the wood-panelled rooms and began to appreciate it for what it was, a stunning Elizabethan mansion. Among the collection of paintings were portraits of Dash ancestors. Cynthia told him a little about the history, but Max was more interested in tales of her growing up there. Every room had a story and she enjoyed stepping back in time and reliving them. When, at last, they reached the drawing room, Max was immediately struck by a portrait of the four Dash children, Cynthia and Julian, Aubrey and Rupert, hanging from two brass chains on the back wall. It stood out from the others because it was more modern, painted when they were teenagers in bright, almost garish colours. Cynthia and Julian were sitting together on the trunk of a felled tree, looking at a book open on Cynthia's knees, while Aubrey stood to their right, in cream-coloured tennis trousers and matching polo shirt, a tennis racquet in his hand. He was smiling with that carefree nonchalance Max had heard so much about. To the left was Rupert. In slacks and a sleeveless V-neck sweater, he was not smiling. His mouth was a petulant pout and his dark eyes brooding. In his hands he held an open silver cigarette case, as if he was about to lift one out and pop it between those sulky lips. He clearly had not wanted his portrait painted. When

Max commented upon it, Cynthia laughed. 'No, he did not. We didn't pose together. Only for the original composition. Then the artist brought each of us into his studio separately. Rupert complained. He didn't like photographs or portraits of himself. He didn't have the patience. Our father insisted and there was no way he could get out of it. Rupert didn't care for the jollity of Pedrevan. Papa was a consummate socialite. He adored people and wanted to create a playground here for everyone to enjoy. Rupert didn't want to be part of it. Aubrey dominated because he was so genial and good at games. The more he shone, the more Rupert withdrew.'

At that moment three Weimaraner dogs loped into the room, followed by Aubrey. Bracks must have told him about Cynthia and her guests wandering around the house because he didn't look in the least surprised to see them. 'Hello, Cynthia,' he said.

Max took in the old man who had ignored his letter and saw not a grumpy curmudgeon, but a man blighted by sorrow. He was slightly hunched as if apologizing for existing. Max put out his hand and introduced himself as Hartley Shelbourne's grandson. At the mention of Hartley, Aubrey smiled. It wasn't the dashing smile of the young man in the portrait, but there were traces of it. 'How is Hartley? I haven't seen him since before the war.'

'As eccentric as ever,' Max replied.

'He always was a character,' said Aubrey. 'Will you remember me to him?'

'Yes, I will.'

'I'm showing Max around the house,' Cynthia told him. 'He's doing some research on the family. I thought he had to visit Pedrevan.'

'Yes, you wrote to me, didn't you?' said Aubrey, his weary

eyes looking sheepish. 'I'm sorry, I don't think I replied. I'm not very good with correspondence.'

'Don't worry,' said Max. 'It's nice to see it now. It's a magnificent house.'

'Yes, it is,' said Aubrey, but his tone betrayed a certain disillusionment, as if the burden of responsibility weighed heavily upon his shoulders.

Max kept the conversation to the present, asking Aubrey about the gardens. Just when it was beginning to get a little sticky, Bertha walked in with Toby. The three Weimaraners loped over to sniff the little dog and Toby, alarmed by the size of the huge trio, rolled onto his back in submission. 'Hello, Aubrey,' said Bertha. 'Come out of the woodwork, have you?'

Aubrey greeted her coolly. 'Hello, Bertha.'

'Don't worry, I'm not going to interrogate you about the family. I have all the information I need already. Everyone else has been very forthcoming.'

'Good,' he said and Max could tell he was relieved to close the subject.

'Goodness, look at that portrait,' said Bertha. 'Weren't you the dashing Dash,' she said with a husky laugh. 'And look at Rupert. He was dashing too, only in a more saturnine way.'

Max glanced at Aubrey. His body language told him that he did not want to be drawn into the past. After all these years it was obviously still painful for him. But Bertha had the sensitivity of a bull and continued blithely. 'So sad that Rupert died. I wonder what he would have made of Pedrevan. Out of the two of you, I'd have thought you'd have continued the fun and Rupert would have closed the gates on it all. Florence would certainly have kept the party going. She loved a good party more than anyone.'

Cynthia's face lit up. 'Do you remember that party on the

beach? The last party of the summer. Florence had gone to so much trouble. It looked beautiful.' She sighed with nostalgia. 'Ah, the bonfire, the twinkling lights and that magical cave, lit up like a fairy's grotto. She was wonderfully creative, wasn't she?'

Again, Max glanced at Aubrey. His face was impassive, but for a slight twist at one corner of his mouth.

Bertha was on a roll now. 'Strange that she left and never came back. I've always wondered why.' She turned to Aubrey. 'Florence takes Mary-Alice all the way to Australia and never comes back. That's not only sad, but selfish. Mary-Alice has never known her family. Why do you think that was?'

'I thought you said you weren't going to interrogate me about the family,' said Aubrey coldly.

Cynthia frowned. 'Flo did say our children would be the best of friends, just like we were. But I suppose life grows up between people and that's that. I really should get in touch with her. I can't think why I let it go.'

Max wondered why the two women were not picking up the awkward energy building around Aubrey. The more they talked about Florence, the more his hackles seemed to rise. Max assumed that Florence had wanted to leave her sorrow behind in England, but he wasn't going to add his two pence, considering he had never known any of them – at least not in this life.

'Strange to deny your daughter a relationship with her father's family. Think of what she missed out on,' Bertha continued.

'Well, she married again, didn't she? Once she'd done that, she'd fully committed to her new home,' said Cynthia.

Max wondered then, at the twist deepening on Aubrey's lips, whether Aubrey had been in love with Florence. Perhaps that was why he had been dogged by unhappiness. He recognized that pained expression on Aubrey's face because he had seen it often enough in the mirror; the expression of unrequited love.

'Would you like to see the garden?' Aubrey asked Max, and Max sensed that he was reaching out for a lifeline. He didn't imagine that Aubrey was interested in showing him the garden, or in spending time with him, he simply wanted to extricate himself from the conversation without being rude.

'I'd love to,' Max replied.

'Good,' said Aubrey decisively, a flash of gratitude livening up his face. He called the dogs and marched out of the drawing room as fast as he could go, leaving Cynthia and Bertha beneath the portrait discussing Florence and her second husband.

Once outside, Aubrey took some deep breaths, as if relieved to be liberated from his sister and cousin. They set off across the lawn, the dogs bounding enthusiastically into the shrubbery. 'Is this your first time in Gulliver's Bay?' Aubrey asked.

'No, I've been a few times. I stayed at The Mariners. Do you know it?'

Aubrey nodded. 'It used to be a private house. I think Edwina and Gryff have done a good job. They've kept it very much as it was.'

'Yes, it doesn't feel like a hotel at all.'

Then Max heard himself telling Aubrey about Robyn. It just all spilled out, like a pan of boiling water on the stove that can no longer be contained by its lid. He hadn't intended to open his heart; in fact, his sorry story about Robyn was not one he ever wished to discuss with anyone. Yet, there was something about Aubrey that told him he'd have a sympathetic ear. That he'd find a kindred spirit, a man who understood what it was to love someone one couldn't have.

'I feel like an idiot,' Max confessed after he'd disclosed

the whole story. 'I should never have told her how I feel. It's ruined everything.'

Aubrey frowned thoughtfully. 'I disagree,' he said. 'If you hadn't told her how you feel, you'd have spent the rest of your life wondering whether things might have been different if only you had told her. You win some, you lose some.' He shrugged. 'Life is a long time, Max. Give her space and she might come to you.'

'I doubt it. She's married to Daniel now. They'll have loads of children and her life will consume her. If she'd wanted to see me, she'd have called me straight away. I know her. She's enthusiastic and proactive. She doesn't want to see me. I embarrassed her, I think.' He grinned. 'I don't regret the kiss, though.'

'Of course you don't,' said Aubrey, grinning back. 'One never regrets a kiss.'

They walked through the trees to the tennis court. The green wire netting had rusted in places to a brown colour and leaves and twigs were strewn across the grass, which had been left to grow wild. 'Hard to imagine that this was once a pristine tennis court,' said Aubrey, as if noticing it for the first time. 'I really shouldn't have allowed it to rot.'

'Cynthia says you were a very good player.'

'I was, in my day. I haven't picked up a racquet in years.' Aubrey poked his fingers through the netting. It seemed like a long moment before he spoke, and when he did, his voice was quiet and wistful. 'Funny how the memories bubble up when one gets older.' He turned to Max. 'You're not writing a book too, are you?'

'No, I became interested in my family history after I learned that Rupert was killed at Arnhem. I was in the army myself, you see.'

'Don't give up on her, Max,' said Aubrey suddenly, changing the subject. 'Life is short and we only get one. I gave up on someone I loved a long time ago, and I've allowed that bitterness to eat away at me. I hate looking at that portrait because it reminds me of what I've lost. It reminds me of the potential I never fulfilled. If you have to let her go, do so without regret and move on, without allowing the past to sour your present.'

Max looked at Aubrey, astonished at the level of intimacy reached in such a short time. Then he remembered what Robyn had said. That life would be very lonely if we were meeting everyone for the first time. Were he and Aubrey connecting on a soul level, he wondered?

'You remind me a little of Rupert, Max,' Aubrey continued, a small smile replacing the previous twist on his lips. 'You even have the same camera as him. Funny how genes skip generations and randomly pop up down the line. Say, do you want to walk around the farm? I'm in no hurry to return to Bertha. She always was highly tedious.'

Max grinned. 'I've got to drive her all the way back to London,' he said, setting off across what was once a croquet lawn.

'Good Lord. You must have the patience of Job.'

'It's the smoking that gets me the worst.'

'Ah yes, in our day we were told it was good for our health. Can't you put her on a train?'

'Unfortunately, I'm the kind of man who keeps his word.'

'An officer and a gentleman.' Aubrey chuckled. 'Then you just have to grin and bear it.'

'And listen to her rattling on about the family. By the way, I'm not sure she's ever going to finish that book.' Aubrey raised his eyebrows. 'I think it's just an excuse to keep in touch with the family.'

'You're probably right. We all have our ways of fighting loneliness.'

'What's yours, Aubrey?'

'Well, I think I'll start with mowing the tennis court.' He smiled. 'Might polish the old trophy. Would you like to see that too?'

CHAPTER TWENTY-FIVE

Robyn never did phone that weekend. Max felt deeply hurt. But after his conversation with Aubrey, he tried hard to be more accepting. It would, indeed, be foolish to let bitterness sour his present moment, as it had clearly done Aubrey's. He would make an effort to cut his losses and move on. The photograph of Robyn, which he had displayed in a silver frame on the dresser in his bedroom, was taken down and placed in a cupboard where it would cease to remind him of his unrequited love.

The months passed and Max found himself enjoying his job more than ever. His relationship fizzled out and he was single again. That's not to say he didn't indulge in the odd fling. There was no shortage of girls who wanted to sleep with him but no one special enough to hold his attention once she'd won it. He liked living in Somerset and had made a solid group of friends. He'd rented for long enough and thought perhaps he'd look to buying a place of his own and putting down some roots. He thought less about Robyn and Rupert Dash. Perhaps their narrative would have ended there, had Daphne not been in touch reminding him of his purpose and setting him once again on the right course.

She had finished her book and wanted him to read the

section on his story before it went to print. Max waited eagerly for it to arrive, then he sat at the kitchen table and read the manuscript slowly. Daphne's words brought it all back to him in a torrent of excitement: the dreams, the psychic reading from Olga Groot, the regression, the research, Gulliver's Bay, Charlie Shaw, Bertha Clairmont, Cynthia and Aubrey Dash. The wind picked up in his sails, injecting him with enthusiasm and that familiar restlessness which had accompanied him along his journey of self-discovery. He felt himself being propelled forward once again, driven towards an unknown destination, at speed. In her letter, Daphne mentioned a possible television interview and asked whether he'd be happy to talk about it on air. Max wasn't sure. Flashes of Elizabeth's mocking face filled his mind with doubt. Robyn had said the world was not full of Elizabeths, but he still felt it to be a place hostile to his beliefs and wasn't keen to put his head above the parapet. He wasn't ready to be doubted. Yet that wind was unrelenting. If his was a story that needed to be told, television was a perfect medium with which to do it.

Max called Daphne and told her he would think about it. Sensing his reservations she said, 'You have to have the courage of your convictions, Max. Yes, there are people out there who will think you're talking rubbish, but there will also be those who are searching for meaning in their lives and your account might help them understand what they're here for. You've been given this awareness of your past life for a reason. It's a gift and one you should share. Don't listen to the voice of doubt, which is your ego. Listen to your Higher Self and trust it.'

Max discussed it with his parents and grandparents. None of them had any experience of the media and were wary. But if it was what he wanted to do, they wouldn't stand in his way. Max thought about it hard. He decided he wasn't going to let Elizabeth control him. If she represented his fear, then perhaps going on national television and announcing to the world that he believed he'd lived before was a good way of overcoming it. He couldn't help being a little amused at the thought of Elizabeth's reaction were she to see it.

In December Max found himself in a brightly lit, functional green room in a television studio in London, having his face dusted with a powder puff and his hair brushed in front of a big mirror framed by glowing round bulbs. Daphne was excited. Promoting her book on a morning show would certainly shift a lot of copies. Max, however, was tense. He was nervous about what people would think. He knew he shouldn't care. But he did. A part of him was already regretting it. He certainly objected to having his nose powdered with a big, fluffy powder puff.

He looked at his reflection in the mirror as a young woman with a nose piercing and heavy black eye liner rubbed a sweet-smelling pomade into his hair. He thought of Robyn. If he hadn't kissed her in the cave perhaps she'd have accompanied him here today and given him support. She was a friend of Daphne's, after all. He wondered, as he had wondered many times since that unfortunate day, whether, had he not confessed his feelings, they'd still be friends. Maybe her marriage to Daniel would have caused them to drift apart anyway. He cursed Daniel for waking up every morning to the woman *he* loved.

'You all right, Max?' the girl asked, noticing his face tighten with resentment.

Max shook Daniel out of his mind. 'Sure, I'm fine. What's this you're putting in my hair?'

She smiled. 'Just something to make you glow on the telly.'

Once on air Max forgot about the lights and cameras and concentrated on telling the hosts about his experience, as eloquently and briefly as possible. He was aware of having only a little time and a great deal to fit into it. Knowing that Robyn was very likely watching fired him up so that he performed like a professional actor, for *her*.

When it was over and they had left the building, he asked Daphne, 'Did that really happen?'

'It went very quickly, didn't it,' she agreed. 'But it was long enough. We got your story out.' She embraced him. 'Thank you, Max. You were amazing. If the book sells well, it will have a lot to do with you. Your story is compelling.'

Max felt on a high after his experience in front of the camera. His heart was still racing. 'It was a pleasure,' he said, and, in retrospect, it really had been. It felt good to tell his story to a wider audience and, for the first time in his life, his self-doubt seemed very far beneath him.

'You know, you should visit Rupert's grave at Arnhem,' Daphne suggested as she hailed a cab. 'It's the one thing you haven't done yet. I think you need to do it. Just a hunch.'

'Your hunches tend to be right,' Max laughed.

'Let me know. I might come with you.'

'I'd like that,' Max replied. 'I'm not sure I can face seeing my own gravestone all by myself.' At the thought of contemplating his own grave, it was Robyn he wished would come with him.

When Max got home to Somerset that afternoon there were lots of messages on his answer machine. Then the telephone rang. He hoped to hear Robyn's voice. But he was to be disappointed.

'Max, it's Elizabeth.' Max was taken aback. Elizabeth was

the last person he expected, or wanted, to hear from. His heart sank. He wished he hadn't picked up. She continued in an officious tone of voice. 'I saw you on television. I was so surprised I nearly upset my herbal tea.'

'How nice of you to call to congratulate me,' he said dryly. His sarcasm passed her by, unnoticed.

'Well, I wouldn't use the word "congratulate",' she said brusquely.

Max could picture her lips pursing. He sighed loudly. 'I didn't think so.'

'It was, well, very strange. Very strange, indeed.'

'I'm sorry if I disappointed you. I did search for Henry VIII's court in my regression, but got a Second World War battlefield instead.'

There was a long pause. Then Elizabeth continued, her voice now a little shrill. 'God knows what my friends are going to think. I mean, I just can't believe you went on national television and told everyone you believe you've lived before. I mean, it's just mad. Reincarnation. What were you thinking?'

'And you called to tell me *that*?' Max took a mug down from the cupboard and dropped in a teabag.

'Someone has to, Max. Someone who cares. Someone brave enough to save you from yourself. That has to be me. I don't think anyone else out there would dare be so blunt, but I can assure you they're all thinking the same as me. They're appalled. I know we didn't work out, but I am still very fond of you. Peregrine and I, we *both* are.'

'In that case, please send Peregrine my love and thank you for calling, Elizabeth.' A surge of happiness flooded his heart. He realized then the whole point of his ex-fiancée. 'You know, I should thank you for your scepticism, Elizabeth,' he continued. 'You've been the key to my spiritual development, because without you I would never have been pushed into digging for the truth and I would never have learned to believe in myself. You, Bunny, have been crucial. Now, scurry back to your burrow and don't ever call me again.' He hung up. Max was done with being polite.

The messages on his answer machine were full of support. He was halfway through listening to them when the telephone rang again. Furious, he picked it up. 'I thought I told you not to call me.'

There was a long pause. Then a soft voice. 'Max? It's Robyn.'

Max sat down, astonished. 'Robyn. Hi. Sorry, I thought you were Elizabeth.'

She laughed. That old familiar laugh he loved so much. 'I suppose she was the first person to call you?'

'Of course.'

'And she was calling to tell you how good you were on television.'

'She thought I was sensational.'

Robyn laughed again. Four years dissolved like pillars of salt. 'Well, *I* thought you were sensational. Really, Max. You were articulate, intelligent, honest and believable.'

'Thank you.'

'I was proud of you. Both you and Daphne. I'm really pleased you allowed her to include your story in her book. People need to hear this. They need to know that there's more to life than what they experience with their five senses.' There was a long pause which Max didn't feel he needed to fill. Then she said in a wistful tone of voice, 'Whatever happened to *our* book?'

'Life got in the way,' Max replied quickly.

'It did. But we mustn't let it get in the way again. We're old friends.' Max knew that Robyn's understanding of the word 'old' was not the same as everyone else's.

'I know. It's a shame we didn't meet up in Gulliver's Bay last year. I should have made more of an effort to get in touch with you.'

'Sorry, Max?' She sounded puzzled. 'Were you intending to come down?'

Now *he* was puzzled. 'I *did* come down,' he said. 'I saw Daniel in the pub and gave him my number to give to you. I was hoping we could have supper – the three of us, I mean.'

Max could sense her surprise down the line; this was the first she'd heard about it. Max knew then that Daniel had never given her his message. 'Oh, Max,' she sighed, her voice heavy with regret. 'You must have thought the worst of me.'

'Not the worst.' His spirits rose at the realization that he hadn't lost her, after all.

'I would have loved to see you,' she said.

'Me too. Don't worry. I'll come down again.'

'I'm so sorry.'

'Don't apologize.'

'I'm mortified that you thought I didn't want to see you. I suppose that's what Dan wanted you to think.' She sighed again, this time with despondency. 'To be honest with you, things aren't great between us.'

Max didn't want to sound too happy to hear that. He contained his delight and said, 'All the more reason for you to see *me*, so I can cheer you up.'

She laughed softly. 'You're a good friend, Max. Why have we not seen each other for so long? What went wrong?'

'Nothing went wrong, Robyn. You married. That's what happens when people marry. It's hard to maintain a close relationship with a person of the opposite sex. Daniel clearly didn't like it.'

'He wasn't possessive *before* we married.'

'People change.'

'And some don't.' Max knew she was referring to *him*. 'Have you found anyone nice to share your life with?' she asked.

I only ever want to share it with you, was what Max wanted to say. But he'd said it before and four years of silence had ensued. He wasn't going to make that mistake again. 'Oh, the odd girlfriend here and there, but nothing serious,' he replied casually. 'I don't think I'm the committing type.'

'You will be when you find the right person.'

Max wanted to scream that he'd already found her. He drew on every reserve of self-control he possessed to hold his tongue.

'I want to hear what you've discovered in the last four years. Do you have time to fill me in on everything now?' she asked.

'I have nothing to do but talk to you,' said Max. He could have talked to her happily all day and all night. Forever.

'Great. So, why did you come down to Gulliver's Bay?'

'I went to stay with Cynthia Dash—'

'No!' Robyn exclaimed excitedly.

'She lives in a cottage on the estate. And I met Aubrey too . . .'

Max told her all the things he had wanted to share with her but couldn't. Time fell away and it could have been four years ago, before Max had confessed to her how he felt, before she had married, before awkwardness had arisen between them like fog. They were two old friends, planning their book.

Max would have liked to jump in his car right away and drive down to Gulliver's Bay, but there was the problem of Daniel.

Things weren't good between the two of them, Robyn had told him that much, but she hadn't elaborated. How bad was it? Bad enough to lead to divorce? Or just a bad patch? Marriages survived bad patches. It didn't necessarily mean that their marriage was over. Max knew that as long as Daniel was her husband, he wouldn't be able to see her. He didn't think she was the type to sneak around – even though Max would have gladly gone behind Daniel's back. He had to wait for *her* to suggest meeting up. In the meantime, they could only speak on the telephone. Again, Max had to wait for *her* to call *him*. Daniel could not be relied upon to relay messages or pass her the phone.

Robyn was keen to write the book. It would be a novel, she'd explained, that weaved its way around the truth, which was Max's spiritual journey. The core of the book – Max's dreams, psychic reading, regression and research – would be real, while everything else would be invented to make a compelling story. Max knew that Robyn would do it justice. He was excited to be working together, at last. After the deluge of support he had received from friends and family following his television appearance, he knew that there were many people out there who wanted to be given proof that there was life after death. Max was confident his story would give them that.

At the back of his mind was Rupert's grave at Oosterbeek. He was curious to see it, but also a little unsure; how strange it would be to see his own grave and know that his body lay buried beneath it. Max was evidence that the only part of a person laid to rest in the ground was the mortal, material part, but still he wasn't sure how he would react. He pushed the idea to the back of his mind; the New Year came and went and the months slipped seamlessly by.

Then Fate interceded in a way that Max could never have

predicted. He knew then, without a shadow of doubt, that he was *meant* to go and visit Rupert's grave. It was 1994, exactly fifty years after the Battle of Arnhem; the coincidence was too much to ignore. The wind in his sails was an unwavering and unrelenting one; it would not stop blowing until he had completed his journey.

Since leaving the regulars, Max had served in the Royal Wessex Yeomanry, taking part during his free time and on weekends. As an accomplished rider he had been selected for the team to compete against Belgium, France and Holland in the Saumur Cup, which had taken place every year since 1970. This year it was to be hosted by Holland over the May Bank Holiday, in Rotterdam – a short drive from Arnhem. The idea behind the trials was to get the Allies messing together. A fun weekend of cross-country, showjumping and a big dinner on the Saturday night. Max was able to invite a date, but this year he didn't have one. He asked Daphne, but she was going to be on a book tour in Canada. This year he decided he would go by himself.

Max took the ferry across the Channel to Calais and drove through France and Belgium. He planned to drive to Arnhem and Oosterbeek on the Sunday, after the competition. He would rather not have gone alone, but what choice did he have? This was an opportunity he couldn't pass over.

Max was put up in a hotel in Rotterdam where he met the other riders on his team, who, like him, had been selected from the army and navy Reserve Forces. Two of them had been in the team the year before, the fourth was someone new. They stayed up late in the hotel bar with some of the competitors from the other teams, drinking beer and getting to know one another. The atmosphere was festive. They were excited to be there.

The following day the event began. The weather was fine, the spirits high. Max dressed in his uniform and went to meet his horse. He was given only twenty minutes to get to know it, a fine chestnut mare, before the start of the cross-country phase. He relished the rush of adrenalin and was confident of his ability. He'd ridden since he was a boy and was a natural in the saddle. Commanding this horse was not going to be too much of a challenge. With grit and enthusiasm, he threw himself into the competition, determined to do his best for his team, and country. He forgot about Robyn as he raced through the woods and leapt over the jumps, but she returned swiftly to his mind when he worked his way around the dining hall that evening, in his mess kit. It seemed as if everyone but him had a woman by their side. Max was alone.

Being alone had never bothered Max before – but it bothered him now. As much as he tried to accept life without Robyn, he was finding it unacceptable. Was his life to be dogged with regret and longing, as he assumed Aubrey's had been? What was the lesson in that? Was it perhaps part of his purpose to travel this path on his own, and, if so, how would he bear it?

CHAPTER TWENTY-SIX

At the end of dinner, the winning team was announced. The British had come second, beaten only narrowly by the home team. But Max's mind had already moved away from the competition and was turning towards Arnhem and Oosterbeek. He had a strange feeling in his gut, a mixture of excitement and nervousness. A sense of impending completion, as if his life had been leading up to this moment. He knew that this trip to the scene of the battle and to Rupert Dash's grave was going to be deeply significant, but he couldn't tell why. He assumed that he would be given the reason once he got there. After all, how many times in his life had the right person appeared at the right time? How many times had he been directed to a certain place only to find it important? How frequently had he stumbled, seemingly by accident, upon some important discovery, as if the higher power he believed in had just dropped it into his path? It was no coincidence that here in Rotterdam he was only an hour and a half's drive from Arnhem.

The following morning Max drove in silence. He didn't play his tapes or listen to the radio. He wanted to be quiet so he could listen to his thoughts. He arrived in Oosterbeek by late morning and went straight to the Airborne Museum at Hartenstein, which had been the headquarters of the 1st Airborne Division during the Battle of Arnhem. The curators had done an excellent job in bringing the battle to life in the displays. Max searched within himself for a sense of déjà vu, but felt only the same fascination he had felt when he visited Pedrevan. He wandered through the Remembrance Room and looked at the black and white photographs of young men, many only boys, who had been killed in action. British and Polish soldiers gazed solemnly out of frames hung alongside their medals. It was a sobering experience and Max took his time. He wanted to honour their sacrifice by giving the displays his full attention. He willed himself to remember, but he remained as detached as any onlooker, peering into the past.

Eventually he came across the fallen from the 10th Battalion and couldn't help but wonder whether Rupert had known any of these men. Once again, he was struck by the erasing of memory when a soul is incarnated into a new life. The people he had known as Rupert Dash were anonymous to him now. While he concentrated on his life as Max Shelbourne, those he had loved before, like Florence, were forgotten. When he eventually stepped *off* the stage, he knew that he would be reunited with those souls and be aware of their connections, but while he was *on* the stage, those attachments would only distract him from his purpose here were he to be conscious of them. And those souls who had travelled with him from past incarnations into this one, like family members, and Robyn perhaps, were only remembered subconsciously, in the warmth of familiarity and in the bond that is forged easily, as a renewing of an old friendship rather than the creation of a new one.

After visiting the museum, Max was pensive. He strolled around the village which had featured so heavily in the battle, although Rupert had never advanced this far, having spent the last twenty-four hours of his life fighting in the woods and heathland. Never before had he felt so lonely on his own, so lost.

After driving out of Oosterbeek, his first port of call had to be Ginkel Heath. He'd studied the map that Charlie Shaw had given him and worked out that he was going to have to drive back up to the Amsterdamseweg and find somewhere to park. The café on the other side of the road from the heath looked a likely spot and he managed to squeeze the little Alfa into the café's car park. He got out and walked to the place where Rupert had landed on the heath mid-afternoon on 18 September 1944. Max felt once again that strange tingling sensation ripping over his body and the strong sense of having been there before. This place had barely changed in fifty years. It felt as if he were revisiting the site as opposed to seeing it for the first time. He stood alone, absorbing it like the aftershocks of an earthquake, travelling up his feet to the top of his head. He swayed, steadied himself and allowed the visions from his dream, from his regression, from his deep subconscious memory, to surface with the ghosts of those who had died long ago.

He ordered a coffee in the café and returned to the car. Following the map closely, he drove gingerly along the sandy track, heading south-west towards the railway line, leaving Ginkel Heath on his right. Rupert might well have taken this route on foot as he made his way to the wooded high ground north of Arnhem. Max's car was not built for this terrain and he had to contain his impatience if he wanted to keep it in one piece. After a few hundred yards Max came to a wire fence. Beyond it was the Amsterdam to Arnhem railway line. The track swung to the left and so did Max, swearing as the bottom of the car scraped on the sand. He passed the landing zone where the 1st Airlanding Brigade had alighted on 17 September, the first day of the battle. It appeared that little had changed in fifty years. Just woods and heathland. For the last twenty-four hours of Rupert's life, this was all he would have seen. The railway embankment was now becoming a significant feature and when Max spotted the culvert that went under it, he pulled off the track and parked.

The rest of his journey he took on foot, walking north-east across the heath, attempting to retrace the steps that the Tenth would have taken during the disastrous withdrawal. It was not hard to imagine the chaos of the Polish Brigade's gliders landing at the same time as the 10th and 156th Battalions were retreating while the Germans pushed them hard. It was the scene of his dreams and his regression and here he was, right now, in the place where it had all happened five decades ago. Max found the Johannahoeve, the farm where Rupert was heading on that fateful afternoon. It was still there, most likely exactly as it had been in 1944. If only those walls could talk, he thought to himself as he looked through Rupert's eyes, reliving his final moments, trying to see what he had seen; flashes of memory coming and going like wisps of cloud that were hard to hold onto.

It was late afternoon when Max made his way to the Commonwealth War Cemetery on the edge of Oosterbeek. The sun was a blood orange in a watery blue sky, the air suddenly colder, the shadows lengthening, creeping across the grass like spectres. He knew exactly where to find Rupert's grave because Charlie had given him specific instructions. It was four up from Captain Lionel Queripel, who had been awarded the Victoria Cross, the highest and most prestigious award for bravery in the face of the enemy, having sacrificed his life during the withdrawal to cover his men as they were pushed inexorably back from their position, which had become impossible to hold.

The cemetery was beautifully maintained with regimented lines of Portland stone headstones, neatly positioned in the mown grass. It was peaceful there.

Max walked solemnly among the stones until he found what he was looking for. He stopped and stood before it. Moved beyond comprehension, he read the words:

CAPTAIN
R. J. DASH
PARACHUTE REGIMENT
ARMY AIR CORPS
19TH SEPTEMBER 1944 AGE 28

BLESSED
ARE THE PURE IN HEART
FOR THEY SHALL SEE GOD
ST MATTHEW V:VIII

Max stared at the gravestone. He gazed at the earth and tried to get his head around the fact that the mortal remains of his previous incarnation lay beneath his feet. He tried to imagine having been someone else. Assaulted by a wave of emotion, he felt fragile suddenly, like a leaf in the wind, blown from life to life, death to death. But then, just as suddenly, that sense of fragility dispersed like mist in sunshine and he realized why he had come here. He realized what it all meant and the wave of emotion turned into gratitude and a feeling of security and peace. Life and death and rebirth are simply a cycle, repeated again and again. There is only death of the body, one after the other, as the soul travels on its way, through many incarnations, towards the greater light.

How fortunate he was to know who he was before. What a gift it was to know, for sure, that the real 'me' does not disintegrate with the body, but rises above the material world in which it has only temporarily resided. This book he was going to write with Robyn was his purpose in this life, which was why he had been given a window into his past incarnation and why he had been guided every step along the way to this point of knowing. *This* was his purpose, to share his experience with others so that they may know, as he knew, that there is no death, only eternal life.

He looked up then and took a breath. A deep, satisfied breath. He felt the energy of that eternal spirit inside of him and for a moment he almost felt himself floating, at one with everyone and everything. A being beyond the limits of time and space.

A small figure in the distance caught his eye. She was walking purposefully across the grass at the other end of the cemetery. He watched her for a moment without realizing who she was. As she got nearer, he took in her familiar walk, her long blonde hair, the serious, concerned look on her lovely face: Robyn.

He blinked. Could it really be her? It seemed impossible. How could she have known? Then he remembered he'd asked Daphne to come with him. Daphne must have spoken to Robyn and told her.

Robyn quickened her pace when she spotted him. Her expression was full of affection and empathy, her smile warm, familiar, intimate. When she reached him, she said nothing, just took his hand and dropped her gaze onto the gravestone. She read the words and nodded slowly. Max knew what she was thinking. She didn't need to say anything. He squeezed her hand. She squeezed it back. They stood together, knowing that this was only the beginning, for they had an important job to do.

At length Max spoke. 'Daniel?' he asked.

Robyn didn't take her eyes off the gravestone. 'It's over, Max,' she said.

'I see.'

'It didn't work out. I should never have married him.'

'I would agree with that,' said Max.

She turned and put her arms around his waist, resting her head against his chest. 'I'm here now,' she said with a deep, satisfied sigh. 'And I'm not going anywhere.'

Max embraced her and held her close. 'Good, because I won't let you get away a second time.'

She lifted her head and grinned. 'I've been a fool,' she told him. 'But I'm not a fool now.' She put a hand on his cheek and the tender look on her face caused Max's body to ache with longing. 'Do you remember the time you kissed me in the cave?' she asked.

'How could I forget?'

'Will you kiss me like that again?'

Max smiled. He took her face in his hands, looked steadily into her eyes and lowered his lips. This time she did not pull away.

* * *

There was one person to whom Max needed to write: Florence. Over the year and a half since visiting Arnhem he had thought about writing to her long and hard and every time he'd picked up a pen and paper he'd changed his mind.

What would she think? His claim was outrageous. It might also be tactless and insensitive: after all, he was claiming to be the reincarnation of her husband. What if she was like Elizabeth? What if she thought it nonsense? Was it really sensible to upset a woman who would now be in her seventies? Was it necessary?

On the other hand, what if she *wasn't* a person like Elizabeth? What if she would be reassured by it? Max decided to take the plunge. He would write to her daughter, Mary-Alice, and leave the decision to her discretion; after all, Max had no idea what state Florence's health was in. Cynthia had given him their address in Australia. If Mary-Alice decided not to give the letter to her, then so be it. That would be the universe's way of telling him that Florence wasn't meant to read it.

Max got out a piece of paper and a pen and began to write. '*Dear Mrs Leveson, May I introduce myself . . .*'

CHAPTER TWENTY-SEVEN

South Australia, December 1995

Florence put down her wine glass. She got out of the bath, dried herself with a towel and slipped into a dressing gown. Then she went to her bedside table and opened the drawer. Inside was a cardboard box. She sat on the bed, put the box on her knees and lifted the lid. Contained within were the few mementoes she had kept in memory of Rupert. Among other things, there were letters tied up with ribbon, his ID tags from the war, his precious Leica, a silk scarf that still smelt of him, his favourite cufflinks, the dog-eared paperback of F. Scott Fitzgerald's *The Great Gatsby* and a poem. She took out the poem. With a racing heart she read the words she had read a thousand times. The words she had wrapped in a thousand wishes. The words that had *meant* so much.

> *Wait for me — I will come back.*
> *Only wait . . . and wait.*
> *Wait though rainclouds louring black*
> *Make you desolate;*
> *Wait though winter snowstorms whirl,*
> *Wait though summer's hot;*

Wait though no one else will wait
And the past forgot;
Wait though from the distant front
Not one letter comes;
Wait though everyone who waits
Sick of it becomes.

She had waited fifty-one years for this.

* * *

Max was in bed asleep when the telephone rang. It took him a moment to realize that it wasn't a dream, that the telephone was really ringing. He reached over and switched on the light. Squinting in the glare, he fumbled clumsily for the receiver and picked it up. 'Hello?' he mumbled.

There was a long pause. Then the distant sound of a voice he did not recognize, crackling down the line. He was jolted into a state of alertness by the premonition that this caller was important.

'Hello, Max, this is Florence Leveson calling from Australia.'

Max sat up. His heart made a loud thwack against his chest. 'Hello, Mrs Leveson. How nice to hear you,' he said.

'I'm sure it's a bit of a surprise.' She chuckled.

'Yes, yes, it is. It's a big surprise.'

Another pause. Max's heart was beating harder now. Then she said in a gentle voice, 'Will you do something for me, Max?'

'Of course,' he replied. 'Whatever you want.'

'Just talk to me, about anything. I'd really like to hear your voice.'

EPILOGUE

It was a cold January morning. Snow covered the ground in the garden of Max's new house. The one he had completed on just before Christmas. It was an old cottage not far from The Mariners in Gulliver's Bay, with wooden beams in the ceilings and a wonky staircase. It needed a lick of paint and a change of carpet. The place didn't look as if it had been touched since the sixties, but it already felt like home. It had big open fireplaces, chunky bookcases and plenty of charm. Many of Max's photographs hung in frames on the walls, for now he no longer bought houses, he took photographs. Whoever said that photographers didn't make money?

Most importantly, his home had Robyn.

When Max came downstairs for breakfast, she was at the kitchen table in her pyjamas, her tousled hair falling messily over her shoulders, a cup of tea and a piece of marmalade toast in front of her. 'This has just come for you,' she said, holding out a parcel. 'Do you want my scrambled egg and smoked salmon special?'

'Do you really have to ask?' said Max, putting his arms around her from behind and kissing her cheek. He placed a hand on her belly. 'How's Junior?'

Robyn laughed softly. She was only three months pregnant

and her stomach was still flat. 'Growing slowly,' she replied, placing her hand on top of his.

He inhaled her scent with a contented sigh. 'Shall we go back to bed?' he murmured, lifting her hair and nuzzling her neck.

She giggled at the rough feel of his bristles. 'Do you really have to ask?' She put a hand against his cheek. 'But you might like to look at this first.'

Max glanced at the parcel. 'It's from Australia,' he said, sinking onto the chair.

Robyn put down her piece of toast and watched Max use a knife to cut through the brown paper. Inside was a black box. It appeared old, like a relic.

Max barely dared breathe. He knew it was from Florence.

'Go on, open it! The suspense is killing me,' said Robyn.

Max lifted the lid. Inside was a silver flask, tarnished with age. Engraved on the side were the initials R.J.D. Slipped inside the box was a poem.

> *Wait for me – I will come back.*
> *Only wait . . . and wait.*
> *Wait though rainclouds louring black*
> *Make you desolate;*
> *Wait though winter snowstorms whirl,*
> *Wait though summer's hot;*
> *Wait though no one else will wait*
> *And the past forgot;*
> *Wait though from the distant front*
> *Not one letter comes;*
> *Wait though everyone who waits*
> *Sick of it becomes.*

Wait for me – I will come back
Pay no heed to those
Who'll so glibly tell you that
It is vain to wait.
Though my mother and my son
Think that I am gone,
Though my friends abandon hope
And back there at home
Rise and toast my memory,
Wrapped in silence pained,
Wait. And when they drink their toast
Leave your glass undrained.

Wait for me – I will come back
Though from Death's own jaws.
Let the friends who did not wait
Think it chance, no more;
They will never understand
Those who did not wait
How it was YOUR WAITING that
Saved me in the war.
And the reason I've come through
We shall know, we two;
Simply this: you waited as
No one else could do.

KONSTANTIN SIMONOV

AUTHOR'S NOTE

Wait for Me is a novel based on Simon Jacobs' true story. Around this true story I have weaved a work of fiction. We thought our readers might like to know what is real and what isn't.

Simon and I are old family friends. We've known each other since we were children. But it wasn't until the early 1990s that our friendship really grew into an independent one. I was working in a shop in Bond Street, having recently left university. I hadn't seen Simon for about four years when he walked in, out of the blue. It was lovely to see him and we decided to catch up over supper that evening. No sooner had we sat down than we were discussing the esoteric. We'd never talked about our recurring nightmares, seeing spirits and other paranormal experiences before, and it was thrilling. That's what happens when two like minds get together! We were at the table, barely drawing breath, until well after midnight. I think the waiters were relieved when we finally paid the bill and left.

I can't remember exactly when Simon told me about his research into his past life, but I do remember being fascinated by it. However, never at any stage did it occur to me to write it. Simon appeared on *Richard & Judy* to talk about his extraordinary story which Judy had included in her book *Deja Who?: A New Look at Past Lives*, gave various interviews for the press and filmed a documentary about past lives for Channel 5. Meanwhile, I was writing a novel a year. With every book I wrote, I dipped my toe deeper into the paranormal. At first, I steered clear of spirits, fearful that readers might think me mad, but nine years into my career I decided to show my true colours. *The Italian Matchmaker* in 2009 was my first unreservedly spiritual book. Looking back, I feel that the parallel roads that Simon and I were travelling along were slowly coming together.

In the autumn of 2020 I had recently published my twentieth novel. Simon called me and said, 'I've got an idea I want to discuss with you.' I drove to his house where he lives with his wife and children, a strange feeling of destiny in my bones. I receive emails on a weekly basis from people suggesting I write their stories. I always decline because I prefer to write my own. However, when Simon suggested I write his, and showed me the box containing his research – diaries, letters, memoirs, books – I didn't hesitate. It felt right. It also felt, in a spooky way, predestined.

Simon's story is the core of the novel, and it's the truth. His childhood nightmares of being in the middle of a horrific battle; his meeting with the psychic who told him those dreams were, in fact, past life memories and that he would one day write a book about it, because *that* was his purpose in this life; his regression into that battle where he was told that souls are often reincarnated down their family line; and his subsequent research. Those things really happened.

Simon discovered in a book about his family that Myles Henry, a cousin of his paternal grandmother's, was killed at Arnhem in September 1944. Myles Henry was the only name on the family tree that could be linked with Simon's dream and regression. Myles was married to Pamela and they had one child, called Carolyn-Anne. When Simon went to research Myles in the Imperial War Museum, it was in the book *The Tenth: A Record of the 10th Battalion, the Parachute Regiment* by Major R. Brammall where he found the witness account, written by Company Sergeant Major Grainger, that describes in detail the moments leading up to Captain Myles Henry's death. That description matched Simon's dreams and his regression exactly.

When I agreed to write this book, I told Simon that I could only do it if the characters were fictional. I couldn't write about someone I knew. Simon was in complete agreement. The important thing was to keep the integrity of his spiritual journey, because the message had to be clear and honest: we don't die, we simply move on into another dimension, and some of us come back, as Simon did. Therefore, I weaved a story around Simon's experiences, giving my imagination full rein.

Pamela wrote a memoire that helped me bring hers and Myles's love story to life through the characters Rupert Dash and Florence Lightfoot. Pamela's book is fascinating and beautifully written and full of wonderfully colourful stories about life during the war. The poem 'Wait for Me' was included after she learned that Myles had been killed at Arnhem. The tingling down my spine as I read it told me that it had to be the title of this novel! I have stuck closely to Pamela's story, but Florence is made up – as are *all* the characters. There is no Gulliver's Bay, The Mariners and Pedrevan Park. Those sprouted in my imagination and gave me a world in which to set Myles's story.

The idea for the silver flask of brandy came from discussing the story with Simon. Myles did have a flask and it is mentioned in the letter from Harry Dicken (Charlie Shaw in our book), but I made more of it. Pamela did not send it to Simon – nor did she send him the poem. She did, however, telephone him from her home in New Zealand, after receiving his letter, asking him to talk so that she could hear his voice.

It takes me six months to write a book. *Wait for Me* took two. I have never been so inspired. The words were coming so quickly my fingers couldn't keep up. It has been an enlightening experience and a privilege to be entrusted with Simon's story so that I may share it with a wider audience.

Some of you will read it as complete fiction, and in that case, we hope you enjoy it. Others will read it as truth wrapped in fiction, in which case we hope that it will deepen your understanding of the soul's purpose.

Lastly, I cannot express how much fun it has been to write a book with someone else. Simon and I have shared this project from the start. Writing is usually such a solitary occupation, but working together has meant that I have never been alone. Simon has been constantly on the end of the telephone as I bombarded him daily with questions. I can't thank him enough for entrusting me with this incredibly personal story. I hope I have done it justice.

I also want to thank Simon's wife, Lisa, and my husband, Sebag, for their support, enthusiasm and interest.

AFTERWORD

A week after *Wait for Me* came out in Holland and Belgium I received an email from Bas Steman, commenting on the extraordinary similarities between his book *Morgan, Een*

Liefde and mine. Like Simon, upon whom this book is based, Bas discovered, through regression and years of research, that he had been a Welshman called Morgan in a previous life. He, too, had been in the famous 10th Battalion, Parachute Regiment, had fought in the doomed Operation Market Garden and been killed on 19 September 1944 – the same day that Myles Henry was killed. The details are identical. How unbelievable is it that two men shared a past life experience at Arnhem and now have books out about it – Bas's was published in 2018. Bas's email astonished me, as I had never heard of him before. It was an incredible coincidence. After responding, I put him in touch with Simon. They have subsequently become firm friends, recognizing their unique and remarkable situation – I don't know of anyone else who has shared a past life and been reunited in this one. That in itself would make a good book! They recently visited Morgan's and Myles's graves at the military cemetery at Oosterbeek and discovered that the two men were buried very close to each other in that peaceful and beautiful place. I cannot imagine what it must be like to contemplate one's own grave – although, it must be a great comfort to know that there is no death.

Morgan, Een Liefde is a fascinating and compelling read. I hope that, with *Wait for Me*, the two books inspire the reader to ponder on the possibility of reincarnation – but if not, that they entertain and delight. It is a great privilege to have been instrumental in bringing these two men together, and in bringing this wonderful, life-affirming story to my readers.

ACKNOWLEDGMENTS

My novels would never achieve the success they do without the experience, enthusiasm and energy of a wonderful team of dedicated people. Therefore, I would like to thank my brilliant agent Sheila Crowley, at Curtis Brown. She's more than my rock, she's my mountain of strength and wisdom in every sense and I couldn't do without her. I'd also like to thank her colleagues at Curtis Brown who work so hard on my behalf: Luke Speed, Anna Weguelin, Emily Harris, Sabhbh Curran, Katie McGowan, Grace Robinson, Alice Lutyens and Sophia MacAskill.

An editor's job is a very sensitive one. On one hand they have to be mindful of the author's hypersensitivity, yet, on the other hand, brave enough to prune and polish and make suggestions to improve the work. It's a wise author who listens to an editor's advice. My editor at Simon & Schuster, Suzanne Baboneau, is both sensitive and wise and in all the twelve years we have worked together we have never disagreed on anything. It is a relationship that I cherish and I am very grateful for the time and trouble she puts into honing my writing. I would also like to thank the CEO/MD Ian Chapman and his brilliant team: Sara-Jade Virtue, Richard Vlietstra, Gill Richardson, Dominic Brendon, Polly Osborn, Sabah Khan,

Matt Johnson, Sian Wilson, Louise Davies and Francesca Sironi. I would also like to extend my gratitude to Simon & Schuster Canada, who publish me so beautifully: my editor Nita Pronovost, Kevin Hanson, Cali Platek, Mackenzie Croft, Shara Alexa and Jillian Levick.

On behalf of Simon and myself I'd like to thank Susan Dabbs, our dear friend, spiritual healer and psychic medium, who has been a valuable teacher to us both, and Judy Hall, who was such an important part of Simon's story.

I thank Simon Jacobs for sharing his story with me; my mother for giving me her opinion on the first draft; my father who has been my spiritual guide throughout my life; my husband Sebag and our children, Lilochka and Sasha, who give me such joy.

Santa Montefiore

Stories that stay

with you forever

Stay in touch with Santa for monthly updates
on her latest books.

Sign up for Santa's newsletter at
santamontefiore.co.uk

You can also connect with Santa on social media,
or follow her on Amazon for new book alerts.

🐦 SantaMontefiore

📷 SantaMontefioreOfficial

📘 /SantaMontefiorebooks

𝒶 bit.ly/FollowSanta